I0655526

Anonymous

The best reading

Hints on the selection of books

Anonymous

The best reading
Hints on the selection of books

ISBN/EAN: 9783337278212

Printed in Europe, USA, Canada, Australia, Japan

Cover: Foto ©Andreas Hilbeck / pixelio.de

More available books at **www.hansebooks.com**

The Best Reading.

HINTS ON THE SELECTION OF BOOKS; ON THE
FORMATION OF LIBRARIES, PUBLIC AND
PRIVATE; ON COURSES OF
READING, ETC.,

WITH

A CLASSIFIED BIBLIOGRAPHY FOR EASY REFERENCE.

NEW YORK:
G. P. PUTNAM & SONS.
1872.

PREFACE.

ONE of the most obvious conclusions of the intelligent reader who glances over *any* manual of this sort, will be that it is *incomplete*—that it certainly does not exhaust the subject.

This little book claims no exemption from the inevitable imperfections of all attempts of this class. Perhaps one of its merits may be its comparative brevity; and its sins of *omission*—numerous as they may be—will probably be more excusable, in the judgment of most readers, than would be the error of burdening such a manual with an inordinate collection of titles, indiscriminately copied from the enormous mass of publications which crowd the market.

We have aimed at a middle course between a meagre catalogue of a bookseller's collection, and the elaborate comprehensiveness of a general bibliography. Under some four hundred different themes or topics, we have quoted briefly the titles of such books on each subject as are best known, and most surely acceptable either in American or English editions. We have included in these selections only those works which are likely to be consulted by the general reader; and we have OMITTED (excepting a few leading specimens): I. Law Books. II. Theological and Religious Treatises. III. Sunday-School Books. IV. Technical works in Science and Art. V. School Text-Books. VI. Many anonymous and doubtful Novels.

Doubtless there are also accidental omissions of good books under the several departments which we *have* undertaken to fill: but this is inevitable in the present crude state of all sources of information as to recent publications. We have expended many months of patient labor in collating catalogues, both English and American, and we trust that a large proportion, at least, of all the best accessible books, relating to each subject indicated, will be found chronicled in our lists, under their respective heads.

EDITIONS—REPRINTS, ETC. In all cases where English books have been reprinted in the United States, the American editions have been quoted, rather than the original. In some instances, however, the English editions being also supplied in this market, and usually being superior to the Reprint, they are also mentioned.

PRICES QUOTED are, usually, the nominal retail prices of the publisher, for copies bound in cloth. These are frequently changed and modified; and, in most cases, libraries can be furnished at a considerable reduction from the published price, especially when many books are purchased. Many English publications have been largely reduced in price since their first publication; and the reduced price has been quoted in this volume, rather than the original price.* Such European books as can be readily purchased in the American market are priced in American currency; others, imported only occasionally, are priced in sterling. The ordinary cost in cur-

---

* After most of these pages were stereotyped, the prices of Bohn's Libraries, for instance, have been reduced to $2.00 and $1.40 per volume.

rency, at present (January, 1872), when duty and expenses are added, is about 40 cents per shilling sterling, or $8 per pound sterling; but this rate is variable. The present tariff, practically, adds about 40 per cent. to the cost of all European books except those more than twenty years old, which are now admitted free of duty. The exemption from duty can be claimed on all books when they are specially imported for incorporated institutions; but ALL purchasers are now exempted from paying duty on books printed prior to 1851.

In several instances we have mentioned works in their proper places that are now out of print, or that have not been found in booksellers' lists, and these are, therefore, not priced. Most of them may be found in some shape, or may be consulted in the older libraries. The ADDENDA, beginning on page 194, include titles of the latest publications, and also several which were omitted in their proper places. At the end of this list is a select catalogue of BOOKS for YOUNG PERSONS, followed by a list of the leading literary PERIODICALS.

The task of indicating in any adequate manner "the best" books on any one topic is obviously a delicate and difficult one. Any such comparisons are "odious," as well as arbitrary. In some departments we do not attempt it at all. But in others we have endeavored to give some aid in making selections, by marking those books which are presumed to be best, on the whole, for those who are making partial selections, according to their needs and their means. Thus:

a. means simply that the book indicated is probably

the safest, on the whole, for those who want the best of the smaller works on the subject, at *moderate cost.*

b. means the best of the more important, elaborate, and more costly books on the same themes.

c. (used in a few instances) indicates a further choice for those who may require more than one book on the same subject. In many instances works of high character have not been marked at all; the choice will be made by the reader.

Works of Fiction are marked by a double sign, indicating, to some extent, the relative estimation of the best (recent) critics, as to each work, and as to the general position of each author.

In the plan and arrangement of this work, and the selection and classification of titles, we are largely indebted to the valuable aid of Mr. Frederick B. Perkins, whose suggestions in regard to "The Owning of Books," "Book Clubs," and " Courses of Reading," are given at the end of the Bibliographical list.

If, as will surely be the case, the judgment of others should differ from ours, and our suggestions of relative values should be in some instances reversed, we may still presume that our classification will prove to be convenient and useful. The excellent works of Bishop Potter, Pycroft, Prof. Porter, and others, will still be consulted for general counsel on the methods of selecting books, and of reading them to the best advantage; but we believe the present classified list of modern publications is more comprehensive, for its purpose, than any other now in print.

The difficulty, in some cases, of assigning a book to its proper heading, is partly obviated by a repetition of the title in the places where it may be sought, or by cross references.

This tabular record of books now in the market is supplemented by a brief selection from the wise words of good men, on the general subject of books, libraries, and systematic reading—which are better worthy of consideration than any suggestions of our own could be.

The PRICES quoted are, in nearly every instance, those for the books in cloth binding. The additional *net* cost of binding in "half calf extra" (the library style usually preferred) is for duodecimos from 75 cents to $2 per volume; for octavos from $1.50 to $3.50 per volume.

The SIZES of books are usually indicated thus:

"4to" (or Quarto).—The sheet folded in 4 leaves.
"r. 8vo," or "imp. 8vo," (large size Octavo,) } Sheet folded in 8
"8vo," Octavo; "cr. 8vo," Crown Octavo, } or 16 leaves.
"12mo," Duodecimo.—Sheet folded in 12 or 24 leaves.
"18mo," Sheet folded into 18 or 36 leaves.
"24mo," and "32mo," Sheet folded into 24 and 32 leaves.

INDEX TO SUBJECTS.

PART SECOND.

ABBREVIATIONS.

Alb.—Albany.
Bohn.—Bohn's Libraries (pub-
    lished in London).
Bost.—Boston.
Camb.—Cambridge
Chic.—Chicago.
Cin., or Cincin.—Cincinnati.
Ed.—Edited.
Edinb.—Edinburgh.
Glasg.—Glasgow.
Ill., or Illus.—Illustrated.
L., or Lond.—London.

L. & N.—London and New York.
L. & B.—London and Boston.
L. & P.—London and Phila-
    delphia.

[The three preceding lines indicate books usually printed in London, and imported in quantities and issued by publishers in New York, Boston, or Philadelphia, usually with their im print.]

Trans.—Translated.
Vol., or v.—Volume.
Wash.—Washington.

CLASSIFIED LIST

MODERN PUBLICATIONS

ENGLISH AND AMERICAN:

NOW SUPPOSED TO BE IN THE MARKET:

Not including technical works on Law, Medicine, Controversial Theology—and exclusive, also, of most of the School text books—Sunday School Books, Popular Religious Books, anonymous and doubtful Works of Fiction, and merely temporary or occasional publications.

Abyssinia and Ethiopia.—[*See also Africa.*]
- *b.* Baker, S. W. Albert Nyanza,.......... 8vo Phil. $3 00
- *b.* ———— Nile Tributaries of A..... 8vo Phil. 2 75
- Hotten, J. C. Abyssinia and its People,
London,....12mo 7s. 6d.
- Hutchinson. Ten Years among Ethiopians,
London,.... 8vo 14s.
- Lepsius, R. Letters from Ethiopia,......12mo Lond. 2 25
- Markham. Abys'n Exped'n, 1869..Lond. 8vo 14s.
- Parkyns. Life in Abyssinia,............12mo Lond. 3 75
- *a.* Russell. Nubia and Abyssinia,.........18mo N. Y. 75
- *a.* Taylor, Bayard. Central Africa,........12mo N. Y. 1 50

Acoustics.
- Macdonald. Sound and Color......Lond. 8vo 3s. 6d.
- *a.* Rudan. Wonders of Acoustics,........12mo N. Y. 1 50
- *b.* Tyndall. On Sound,.................12mo N. Y. 2 00

Aeronautics.—[*See Ballooning.*]

Æsthetics.—[*See Criticism ; Taste.*]

Affghanistan, BELOOCHISTAN, CABUL.
- Burnes, Sir A. Residence in Cabul, 1842.
London,.... 8vo 18s.
- Elphinstone. Kingdom of Cabul, 2 vols.
1819. London,.... 8vo 28s
- Sale, Lady. Disasters in Aff. 1843. Lon., 8vo 2s. 6d.

Africa.—For Ancient History of, *see History, Ancient.*
[*See also names of each country.*]
- Grant, J. A. Walk across Africa. 1863.
London,.... 8vo 15s.
- Hunting Scenes in the Wilds of Africa,..12mo Phil. 1 75
- Kingston. In the Wilds of Africa (for
Boys)....12mo Lond. 2 50
- Merriam. Home Life in Africa,........

Murray, Hugh. Discovery and Adventures
in Africa. London,....12mo 5s.

Africa—CENTRAL AND EASTERN.

b.	Barth. Travels in N. and C. Africa, 3 vols. 8vo N. Y.	$12 00
a.	—— The same, Abridged,........ ....12mo Phil.	1 75
a.	Burton. Lake Regions of Central Africa, 8vo N. Y.	3 50
b.	Du Chaillu. Explorations in Equat'l Af., 8vo N. Y.	5 00
b.	—————— Journey to Ashango Land,. 8vo N. Y.	5 00
	—————— My Apingi Kingdom.......12mo N. Y.	1 75
a.	—————— Wild Life under the Equat'r,12mo N. Y.	1 75
	Krupf, Dr. Travels in East. Africa. Lond. 8vo	
a.	Park, Mungo. Travels and Life,........18mo N. Y.	75
	Petherick, Mr. & Mrs. Cent'l Africa. Lond. 8vo 16s.	
b.	Speke and Grant. Discovery of Source of the Nile,.... 8vo N. Y.	4 00

Africa—NORTH.—[*See also Egypt, etc.*]

	Barth. [*See Africa, Central.*]...........	
b.	Bartlett. The Nile Boat. Illustrated,... 8vo N. Y.	4 00
	Cooke. Conquest and Civilization in North Africa. Edinburgh,....12mo 5s.	
	Ditson. The Crescent and French Crusades. 1859,....12mo N. Y.	
a.	Naphegyi. Ghardaia; 90 Days in the Desert of Sahara,....12mo N. Y.	1 75
	Richardson. Travels in the Sahara. 1848. 8vo 30s.	
a.	Russell. History of Barbary States, ...18mo N. Y.	75
	St. John. Adventures in Lybian Desert,.12mo N. Y.	
	Tristam. The Great Sahara, 2 vols. Lond. 8vo 15s.	

Africa—SOUTH.

	Alexander. Exp'n into So. Africa, 2 vols. London,.... 8vo 21s.	
	Anderson. Lake Ngami,.............. 8vo N. Y.	1 75
	—————— Okavango River,........... 8vo N. Y.	3 25
	—————— South West Africa,........12mo Phil.	1 75
	Baldwin. South African Hunting,...... 8vo N. Y.	1 50
	Chapman, J. Travels in So. Af....Lond., 8vo Lond.	
	Cumming. Five years of Hunter in S. A. 2 vols.,.... 8vo N. Y.	3 00
b.	Livingstone, Dr. Missionary Travels in South Africa,.... 8vo N. Y.	4 50
b.	—————— Exped'n to Zambesi,.... 8vo N. Y.	5 00
a.	—————— Popular Acc. of Missionary Travels in S. A........8vo Lond. and N. Y.	3 00
a.	—————— So. Africa; Popular Ed.,....12mo Phil.	1 75
	Moffatt. Missionary Adventures in S. A.. London,.....8vo 12s.	
	Pringle, T. South Africa,...London,.... 8vo 3s. 6d.	
	Walmsley. Ruined Cities of Zulu Land. London, 2 vols. 8vo 18s.	

Wilmot & Chase.   Hist. of Cape Colony.
London,.... 8vo 15s.

Africa—WESTERN.

Allen.   Expedition to the Niger, 2 vols.
London,.... 8vo 32s.
Burton, R. F.   Abeskuta and the Camer-
oons, 2 vols. Lond.... 8vo 25s.
Forbes.   Missions to Dahomey, 2 vols.
London,.... 8vo 21s.
a. Lander.   Travels in Africa, 2 vols.......18mo N. Y. $1 50
Poole.   Sierre Leone and the Gambia, 2
vols. London, ... 8vo 21s.
b. Reade, W. W.   Savage Africa........... 8vo N. Y.   4 00
Valdez.   Six Years in Western Africa... 8vo Lond.   5 00
a. Wilson, J. L.   Western Africa.........12mo N. Y.   1 50

Agriculture.—[*See also names of Crops, Animals, etc.*
Also Gardening, Botany, etc.]

a. Allen.   New Amer. Farm Book.........12mo N. Y.   2 50
Bentz.   Elements of Agriculture (Saxton).   N. Y.
Buel.   Farmer's Companion.............12mo N. Y.   1 50
——   Farmer's Instructor, 2 vols.......18mo N. Y.   1 50
Boussingault.   Rural Economy.......... 8vo N. Y.   1 60
Clift.   Tim Bunker Papers.............12mo N. Y.   1 50
b. Copeland, W. T.   Country Life. Illus... 8vo Bost.   5 00
Darlington.   American Weeds and Useful
Plants,....12mo N. Y.   1 75
Emerson, G. B.   Manual of Agriculture..12mo Bost.
Enfield.   On Indian Corn...............12mo N. Y.   1 00
French.   Farm Drainage..............12mo N. Y.
a. Farming for Boys, by author of Ten Acres.12mo Bost.   1 50
Flagg.   European Vineyards..........12mo N. Y.   1 50
Gaylord & Tucker.   Amer. Husbandry, 2
vols....18mo N. Y.   1 50
Grant.   On Beet Root Sugar...........12mo   1 25
Greeley.   What I know about Farming..12mo N. Y.   1 50
a. Henderson.   Gardening for Profit.......12mo N. Y.   1 50
b. Johnson, C. W.   Farmers' and Planters'
Cyclope....R. 8vo Phil.   6 00
b. Johnson, S. W.   How Crops Grow......12mo N. Y.   2 00
b. ———   How Crops Feed......12mo N. Y.   2 00
a. Johnston, J. F. W.   Agricultl. Chemistry.12mo N. Y.   1 75
a. Liebig.   Agricultural Chemistry........12mo N. Y.   1 00
Liebig.   Natl. Laws of Husbandry.......12mo N. Y.   1 50
b. Loudon.   Cyclop. of Agriculture. Lond. 8vo 31s. 6d.
Meade.   Grape Culture and Wine Making. 8vo   3 00
Mitchell, D. G.   My Farm at Edgewood..12mo N. Y.   1 75
a. ———   Rural Studies.........12mo N. Y.   1 75
Morrell.   The American Shepherd.......12mo N. Y.   1 75
a. Norton.   Scientific Agriculture.........12mo N. Y.   75
a. Our Farm of Four Acres...............16mo N. Y.   60

Stephens. Book of the Farm, 2 vols. R. 8vo Lond.
Thaer. Practical Agriculture.......... 8vo N. Y.
Todd. Apple Cultivator ....12mo N. Y. $1 50
—— Amer. Wheat Cultivator........12mo N. Y. 2 00
a. Waring. Elements of Agriculture......12mo N. Y. 1 00
—————— Draining for Health and Profit.12mo N. Y. 1 50
b. ————— Handy Book of Husbandry.... 8vo N. Y. 3 50
Watson. American Home Garden.......12mo N. Y. 2 00
White, J. J. Cranberry Culture.........12mo N. Y.

Alabama.
Pickett. History of Alabama, 2 vols....8vo Charlest. 3 00

Alaska.—(Recently Russian America.).
b. Dall. Alaska and its Resources........R. 8vo Bost. 7 50
a. Whymper. Alaska. Illustrated........ 8vo N. Y. 2 50

Albigenses.
Faber. Ancient Valleness and A. Lond. 8vo 12s.
Sismondi. Crusades against the A. Lond. 8vo 8s.

Alchemy.—[*See Demonology—Magic.*]
Hitchcock, E. A. Alchemy & the Alchemists.
1857....12mo Bost.

Algiers.—[*See Africa.*]
Girard. Lion Hunting in Algeria........12mo N. Y. 1 50
Morell. Algeria—Topo. and His. of. Lond. 8vo 6s.
Naphegyi. Among the Arabs...........12mo Phil. 1 75
Shaler. Sketches of Algiers. *o. p.*...... 8vo Bost.
Walmsley. Algeria during Kabyle War.
London,....12mo 10s. 6d.

Alps.
Ball. Guide to West'n Alps, 1863. Lond.12mo 7s. 6d.
b. Brockedon. Passes of the Alps, 2 vols.
London,.... 4to 150s.
Berlepsch. The Alps. 1861. Lond..... 8vo 10s.
Forbes. Tour of Mt. Blanc and Mt. Rosa.16mo Lond. 1 50
Freshfield. The Grisons, etc. '62. Lond.12mo 10s. 6d.
Gridlestone. High Alps without Guides.
1870. London,.... 8vo 7s. 6d.
a. Jones. The Regular Swiss Round. Lond. 8vo 7s. 6d.
Peaks, Passes and Glaciers, 2 vols. R. 8vo Lond. 15 00
a. ————————— The same, cheap ed.12mo Lond. 2 00
Smith, Albert. Story of Mt. Blanc......12mo N. Y. 1 00
Tyndall, J. Glaciers of the Alps. Lond. 8vo 14s.
—— Mountaineering in the Alps. Lond. 8vo 7s. 6d.
—— Hours of Exercise in the Alps..... 8vo N. Y. 2 00
a. Whymper. Scrambles among the Alps.
London,.... 8vo 21s.

America.—[*See Arctic Regions, South America, and separate Countries, United States, etc.*]

American Biography.—[*See under Biography.*]

———— **Antiquities.**

Squier & Davis. Amer. Antiq. and Discoveries in the
    West. 4to. Smith. Inst.....$10 00

America—DISCOVERY OF.

a. Abbott, J. Discovery of America, 3 vols.16mo N. Y. 2 25
 Cabeca de Vaca. Trans. by Smith...... 8vo Alb'y.
 Da Costa, B. F. Pre-Columb. Discov. of A.12mo Alb'y.
a. Irving. Columbus and his Companions.
        3 vols.....12mo N. Y. 6 75
     3 vols. 18mo, $3 75; abridged, 1 50
b. Irving T. De Soto in Florida...........12mo N. Y. 2 00
 Kohl. Discov. of Amer., 2 vols. Lond... 8vo 16s.
 Smith, J. T. Discovery of America by Northmen.
       London.... 8vo

America.—EARLY AND GENERAL HISTORY.

Grahame, Jas. Hist. of the U. S. North America to
   the Revol., 4 vols. *o. p.*.... 8vo Phila.
a. Helps. Spanish.Conquests in A. 4 vols..12mo N. Y. 6 00
a. Parkman, F. Discovery of the Gr't West, 8vo Bost. 2 50
b. ———— Jesuits in North America...... ... 8vo Bost. 2 50
b. ———— Pion'rs of France in the N. World, 8vo Bost. 2 50
b. Prescott. Conquest of Mexico. 3 vols... 8vo Phil. 7 50
b. ————   ———— Peru. 2 vols..... 8vo Phil. 5 00
 Robertson. History of America.......... 8vo N. Y. 2 25
 Willson. American History. 1 vol...... N. Y. 2 00

America.—REVOLUT'N AND INDEPEND'CE OF U. S. OF N. A.

[*See Biography:*—*Irving's Washington, Gen. Greene, etc.
 See also United States.*]

America—SOUTH.—Generally.

Bishop. 1,000 MilesWalk across S. Amer.12mo Bost. 1 50
Humbolt. Equinoc. Regions of South Amer.
      3 vols.... Bohn. 5 25
Paez. Travels in So. and Cent. Amer.... 8vo N. Y. 3 00

America—CENTRAL.

Froebel, J. Seven Years in Cent. Amer.
      London.... 8vo 18s.
Morelet. Travels in Central America. 1871.
      8vo N. Y. 2 00
Norman. Ruined Cities of Yucatan. 1843. 8vo N. Y.
Patterson, W. Seven Years in Cent. America.
     London.... 8vo 2s. 6d.
b. Squier, E. G. Notes on Central America. 8vo N. Y. 4 00
 ———— —— Nicaraugua.............. 8vo N. Y. 4 00
 ———— —— Honduras................. 8vo N. Y. 2 00
 ———— —— Mrs. Travels in Cent. Amer. 8vo N. Y. 2 00
a. Stephens, J. S. Cent. Amer., etc., 2 vols. 8vo N. Y. 6 00
b. ———— —— Yucatan, 2 vols......... 8vo N. Y. 6 00

Wells. Honduras. Illustrated............ 8vo N. Y. $3 50

Amusements—[*See Games and Amusements.*]

Anatomy.—[*See Physiology and Anatomy.*]

Ancient Biography, AND HISTORY. [*See History: Biography.*]

Anecdotes.

	Anecdotes of Clergy in America.........12mo Phil.	1 50
a.	Arvine. Cyclopedia of Lit. Anecdotes.... 8vo Bost.	4 00
a.	——— Moral and Religious Anecdotes.. 8vo Bost.	5 00
a.	Bigelow. Anecdotes of Bench and Bar...12mo N. Y.	1 50
	Gronow. Celebrities of London and Paris, 2 vols.12mo Lond.	3 00
b.	Hood, E. P. The World of Anecdote ; large 12mo Lond.	4 50
b.	——— World of Moral and Relig. Anec.12mo Lond.	4 50
	Jackson. Curiosities of the Pulpit....... 8vo Lond.	2 00
	Jay, Cyrus. The Law—What I have Seen, &c....12mo Lond.	
	Jeaffreson. Book about Lawyers, 2 vols. London,.... 8vo 24s.	
	——— ——— Doctors, 2 vols. Lond. 8vo 30s.	
	——— ——— Clergy, 2 vols. Lond. 8vo 30s.	
b.	Kirkland. Cyclop. of Commerc. A., 2 vols. 8vo N. Y.	8 00
	Neal, J. Great Mysteries and Little Plagues.......16mo Bost.	1 50
	Nimmo. Anecdote Library, 6 vols. Lond.18mo *ea.*	1 25
a.	Percy Anecdotes, 1 vol. 8vo. N. Y. $2 ; 2 vols.12mo Lond.	3 50
b.	Proctor. Bench and the Bar of N. Y.....12mo N. Y.	5 00
	Spence, Jas. Anecd. of Books and Men.12mo Lond.	3 00

Angling.—[*See Fish, Fishing.*]

a.	Davy, Sir H. Salmonia,................16mo Bost.	1 50
b.	Herbert, H. W. Fish and Fishing in N. Y. 8vo N. Y.	5 00
	Moffatt. Secrets of Angling............12mo Lond.	3 00
a.	Norris, T. American Angler's Book.....12mo Phil.	3 00
b.	Roosevelt, R. B. Game Fish of N. Amer.12mo N. Y.	2 00
	——— Superior Fishing.... .12mo N. Y.	2 00
b.	Scott, G. C. Fish and Fishing in Amer.. 8vo N. Y.	3 50
a.	Walton & Cotton's Angler by Bethune....12mo N. Y.	3 00
	——— ——— ——— Illust. by Major..12mo Bost.	2 50

Anglican Church.—[*See also Church History.*]

	Miall. British Churches and Brit. People. London,.... 8vo 4s.	
	Macdonald, Geo. England's Antiphon...12mo Lond.	2 00
b.	Perry, G. G. Hist. of Ch. of England, 2 vols. 8vo Lond., 42s.....	12 50
	Short, T. V. History of Anglican Church.16mo Lond.	
a.	Southey. Book of the Church...........8vo Lond.	5 00

Anglo-Saxons.—[*See also England ; History.*]

	Anglo-Saxon Derivitives...............12mo	1 50

Anglo-Saxon Root Words...............12mo $1 25
b. Bosworth. Anglo-Saxon Dictionary.. 8vo Lond. & P. 4 50
   Earle, J. Two Saxon Chronicles........ 8vo Oxf'd.
   Kemble, J. M. Saxons in England, 2 vols.
                                    London,.... 8vo 28s.
a. Klipstein. Anglo-Saxon Grammar.......12mo N. Y.   1 50
   ——————— Analecta Anglo-Saxonica, 2 vols.12mo N. Y.   3 50
a. Marsh, F. A. Anglo-Saxon Grammar.... 8vo N. Y.   2 50
a. Miller. History of Anglo-Saxons........12mo Lond.   2 50
· a. Palgrave. Hist. of the Anglo-Saxons. Ill.12mo Lond.   2 50
   Shute. Man'l of Anglo-Saxon for Begin'rs.12mo N. Y.
   Thorpe. Anglo-Saxon Vers. of the Gospel, 8vo
                              London and P....   3 00

Animal Magnetism :—MESMERISM.
   Ashburner. Anim'l Mag. and Spiritualism. 8vo Lond.
   Esdaile. Mesmerism in India. Lond... 8vo 6s. 6d.
   Lee E. Animal Magnetism.............16mo Lond.
   Reichenbach. Physico-Physiol. Research.
                              London,.... 8vo 6s. 6d.
   Townshend. On Mesmerism..... .....12mo   1 25

Animals.—[See *Natural History, Darwinism, etc.*]

Antarctic Regions.—[See *Arctic, etc.*]

Anthropology.—[See *Darwinism, Ethnology.*]

Antiquities.—[See *also under names of Countries; Pompeii, etc.*]
   Brande. Popular Antiquities, 3 vols....12mo Bohn.   7 50
a. Bucke. Ruins of Ancient Cities, 2 vols. 18mo N. Y.   1 50
a. Chambers. Book of Days, 2 vols...... R. 8vo Lond.
                              and Phila....   9 00
   Fosbrooke. Encyclo. of Antiqts, 2 vols.
                 Lond. 1843....R. 8vo 35s.
   King, C. W. Antique Gems. Lond..... 8vo 42s.
   ——— ——— Hand Book of Engraved
                 Gems. London, 3 vols..... 8vo 63s.
   Palisser. Historic Devices, Badges, &c.
                              London.... 8vo 28s.
a. Pompeii and the Pompeiians...........12mo N. Y.   1 50
   Stephens. Monuments of Scandinavian
                 England. 2 vols. fol............Lond. 100s.
   Temples, Tombs and Monuments. Illus.12mo Edinb.   1 50
b. Westropp. Hand Book of Archæology.
                 Egyptian, Greek, Roman, &c..... 8vo Lond.   7 50

Apparitions.—[See *also Demonology and Witchcraft, Spiritualism, Dreams.*]
a. Crowe, Mrs. The Night Side of Nature.12mo N. Y.   1 50
   Hibbert, S. Philosophy of Apparitions.
                 Edinburgh........... 8vo 12s.
   Jung-Stilling. Theory of Pneumatology.12mo N. Y.   75
a. Owen, R. D. Footfalls on the Bounda-
                 ries of another World....12mo Phil.   1 75
   ——————— ——— (New work)..............12mo N.Y.

Aquarium.

 a. Butler.   Family Aquarium............16mo N.Y. $ 75
 Hibberd.   Book of the Aquarium; Marine.
                              London....16mo   2s.
 ——————   ——— ——— —————Freshwater.16mo 2s.
 Edwards.   Life Beneath the Waters......
 Gosse.   The Aquarium. London........ 8vo 17s.
 James, (Prof.).   Aquarium Naturalist....
 Wood, J. G.   Common Objects by Seashore.16mo Lond.   50.

Arabia.

 Blackburn, J.   Artists and Arabs. Lond. 8vo 7s.
 Burckhardt.   Travels in Arabia (1835) 2
                          vols. Lond.... 8vo 24s.
 Burton, Lieut.   Pilgrimage to Mecca, &c.12mo N. Y.   1 50
 a. Crichton, A.   History of Arabia, 2 vols..18mo N. Y.   1 50
 Laborde.   Journ. thro' Arabia, 1836. Lond. 8vo 18s.
 Lowth, G. P.   Wanderer in Arabia, 2 vols. Lond. 21s.
 b. Palgrave.   Journey through Arabia.....12mo N. Y.   4 50

Archæology.—[See *Antiquities*.]

Archery.

 Essays on.   Illustrated................ 8vo Lond. 4 50

Arboriculture.—[See *Trees*.]

Archipelago.—[See *Greece*.]

Architecture—HISTORY OF.

 Architecture of the Victorian Age, ½ mor. 4to Lond.   12 00
 Agincourt, d'.   History of Art (and Arch.)
                    by its Monuments, folio....Lond.
 b. Fergusson.   Hist. of Architecture, 3 vols. 8vo
                          London,.... £4 14s. 6d.
 b. ——————   Modern Styles of Architec...8vo Lon. 3. 6d.
 Gallhibaud.   Hist. d'Architecture, 4 vols. 4to Paris.
 b. Lafevre.   Beauties of Mod. Architec...R. 8vo N. Y.   6 00
 a. Lafevre.   Architec. Instructor, Hist., etc. 4to N. Y. 16 00
 a. Lefebre.   Wonders of Architecture......12mo N. Y.   1 50
 a. Ruskin.   Seven Lamps of Architecture...12mo N. Y.   1 75
 —————— ——— Illus.   ......R. 8vo Lond.
 a. ——————   Lectures on Architecture.......12mo N. Y.   1 50
 b. ——————   Stones of Venice, 3 vols.......12mo N. Y.   7 00
 —————— ——— Illus., 3 vols. R. 8vo Lond.
 Sharpe.   Seven Periods of Christian Arch.
                          London..... 8vo 10s.

Architecture—DICTIONARIES, GLOSSARIES, ETC.

 a. Downing's Wightwick's Hints to Arch...8vo N. Y.   2 00
 Ferguson.   Hand Book. [See *Hist. of A*.]
 b. Gwilt.   Cyclopedia of Architect.   Lond. 8vo 42s.

Hand Books to the Cathedrals of Eng., &c.,
                                4 vols. Lond.
a. Hatfield.   American House Carpenter.... 8vo N. Y. $3 50
   Nicholson.   Principles of Architecture... 8vo Lond.
a. Parker.   Glossary of Terms in Architec..12mo Lond.   3 75
a. ———   Intro. to Study of Gothic Arch. 8vo Lond.   2 50
   Pugin.   Gloss. of Eccles. Ornament. Lond. 4to 147s.
   ———   Examples of Gothic Arch., 3 vols. 4to Lond.
   ———   Pointed or Christ. Arch. Lond. 4to 15s.

—— DESIGNS FOR CHURCHES, RESIDENCES, ETC.

b. Cleveland & Backus. Cottage & Farm Arch. 8vo N. Y.   4 00
a. Downing.   Arch. of Country Houses..... 8vo N. Y.   6 00
a. ———   Rural Arch. & Lands. Garden. 8vo N. Y.   6 00
   Field.   City Architecture.............R. 8vo N. Y.   2 00
   Grammar of House Planning............12mo Lond.   2 50
b. Hibberd.   Rustic Adornments for Homes
                            of Taste.... 8vo Lond.   9 00
   Holly.   Designs for Country Seats...... 8vo N. Y.   5 00
b. Lafever.   Architectural Instructor...... 4to N. Y.   16 00
b. Loudon.   Ency. of Cottage, Farm, and
                  Villa Architecture. Lond. 8vo 25s.
   Nicholson.   Carpenters' & Builders' Guide. 4to Phila.   4 50
   Riddell.   Designs for Model Country Res., folio. Phila.
b. Sloane.   Constructive Architecture...... 4to Phila.   9 00
b. ———   City and Suburban Architecture. 4to Phila.   15 00
b. ———   Homestead Architecture........ 8vo Phila.   4 50
a. Todd, S. E.   Country Homes...........12mo N. Y.   1 50
a. Vaux.   Villas and Cottages............ 8vo N. Y.   3 00
a. Wheeler.   Homes for the People........12mo N. Y.   3 00
   Wheeler.   Rural Homes................12mo N. Y.   3 00
   Weidenmann.   Beautifying Country Homes.
                            Illustrated.... 4to N. Y.   15 00
   Woodward.   National Architect........ 4to N. Y.   12 00
a. ——— Suburban and Country Homes,
                  3 works, each....12mo N. Y.   1 50

Arctic and Antarctic Regions.

a. Barrow.   Voyages in Arctic Regions.....18mo N. Y.   1 00
   Back.   Journey to Polar Sea. 1836. Lond. 8vo 30s.
   Franklin.   Voyages to Polar Sea, 4 vols.
                        London... 18mo 20s.
   Hall, C. F.   Explorations and Adventures
                  in Arctic Seas... 8vo N. Y.   5 00
b. Hartwig.   Polar World.   Illustrated..... 8vo N. Y.   3 75
a. Hayes, J. J.   Open Polar Sea........... 8vo N. Y.   3 75
a. ——— ———   Arctic Boat Journey.......12mo Bost.   2 50
a. Kane.   Expd. in Pursuit of Franklin.... 8vo N. Y.   3 00
a. ———   Second Arctic Expedition, 2 vols. 8vo Phila.   5 00
a. Leslie, Sir J.   Discovery and Adventures
                  in Polar Regions..18mo N. Y.   75

McClintock.   Fate of Sir J. Franklin
                    London.... 8vo 16s.
————————   Discovery of N. W. Passage.
Morrell, B.   Voyages. 1845............. 8vo N. Y. $1 50
Osborne.   Discovery of N. W. Passage by
                    McClure....12mo Lond.
a. Parry.   Voyages to Polar Seas, 2 vols....18mo N. Y.   1 50
a. Richardson.   Arctic Expedition..........12mo N. Y.   1 50
————————   The Polar Regions, 2 vols. 8vo Lond.   4 00
Ross.   Voy. to Baffin's Bay. 1818. 2 vols. 8vo Lond.
———   Second Voyage. 1829............ 4to Lond.
———   Antarctic Voyage. 1839. 2 vols. 8vo Lond.
Scoresby.   The Franklin Exped. 1850.
                    London,.... 8vo 6s.
Thirty Years in Arctic Regions..........12mo Phila.   1 75
Weddell.   Voyage to South Pole. 1825. 8vo Lond.
Wilkes.   U. S. Exploring Expedition round the World.
                    5 vols. 4to ; 5 vols. R. 8vo Phila.
————— ———   The same, condensed in 1 vol. 8vo
a. Mangell.   Expedn. to Polar Sea. 1820.18mo N. Y.   75

[NOTE.—The larger works of Back, Franklin, Parry, Mackenzie, Ross
Wilkes, &c., published in quarto, are now out of print and scarce.]

Argentine Republic.

King, J. D.   Twenty-Four Years in Ar-
                    gentine Republic....12mo N. Y.   1 00
Page.   La Plata and Argentine Confedn. 8vo N. Y.   5 00
a   Sarmiento.   Life in Argentine Repub. 1848. 8vo N. Y.   2 50

Arizona.

Maury, S.   Arizona. 1871 ....12mo N. Y.   1 50

Arkansas.

Armenia.

a. Curzon, R.   Armenia and Erzeroom.....12mo N. Y.   1 25
Dwight, H. G. O.   Reformation in Armenia.
                    London. 1854..... 8vo 5s.
Southgate.   Tour through Armenia and
                    Kurdistan, 2 vols. London.... 8vo 15s.

Arms—Armor.

Hewitt.   Anct. Armor & Weapons, 3 vols.
                    Oxford.... 8vo 50s.
Jervis.   Engines of War. London...... 8vo 6s.
a. Lacombe.   Arms and Armor...........12mo N. Y.   1 50
Meyrick   Ancient Armor, (expensive.)
                    London. 3 vols....folio.

Art, Arts.—[See *Fine Arts, Mechanics; also names of sepa-rate Arts.*]

Bigelow.   The Useful Arts, 2 vols.......12mo N. Y.   3 00
Burty.   Chefs d'œuvre of Indus. Arts. Ill. 8vo Lond.   5 00
Five Black Arts: Printing, Gas, Glass, etc.12mo N. Y.   2 25

Lacroix.   The Arts in the Middle Ages.
Illus......R. 8vo Lond. $12 00

Artillery.—[*See Ordnance.*]

Asia.—[*See also East ; also names of Countries.*]
Heeren.   Asiatic Nations, 2 vols.   Lond.. 8vo 24s.
Huc.   Travels in Tartary and Thibet..
Knox, T. W.   Overland through Asia.... 8vo N. Y.
Malcolm.   Mission. Travels in S. E. Asia.
1835. 2 vols.....12mo
a. Marco Polo.   Voyages and Travels......18mo N. Y.   75
a. Pumpelly.   Across America and Asia.... 8vo N. Y.   2 50
a. Taylor, Bayard.   India, China and Japan.12mo N. Y.   1 50
b. Vambery.   Travels in Central Asia..... 8vo N. Y.   4 50

Asia Minor.
Fellowes.   Excursion in Asia Minor.   Lond.12mo 9s.
Hamilton.   Researches in Asia Minor, 2
vols. 1842.   London,.... 8vo 38s.
Leake.   Travels in Asia Minor. 1824. Lond. 8vo 18s.
Van Lennep, H. J.   Travels in Asia Minor.
2 vols. 1870. London,.... 8vo 24s.

Assassins.
Hammer-Purgstall.   Hist. of the Assassins.
1835. London,....12mo 7s. 6d.
Walpole, F.   Ausayrii and Assassins, 3
vols. 1852. London,.... 8vo 42s.

Assaying.—[*See Dictionaries of Arts, Manufact., Mines, etc.*]
Bodeman.   Treatise on Assaying.........12mo N. Y.   2 50

Astrology.—
Astrology as it is.   1856...............12mo Lond.
a. Lilly.   Introduction to Astrology........12mo Lond.   2 25
Zadkiel.   Grammar of Astrology.   2 vols.
London,....12mo 7s.
———— Hand Book of Astrology, 1 vol.   3s. 6d.

Astronomy.—[*See also Cosmology.*]
Airy, G. B.   Lectures on Astronomy.....16mo Lond.   1 50
Arago, F.   Astronomy, 2 vols.   London.. 8vo 45s.
b. Bouvier.   Manual of Astronomy. .. .... 8vo Phila.   3 00
Brewster, Sir D.   More Worlds than One.16mo N. Y.   1 00
a. Burritt.   Geography of the Heavens, and
Atlas, 2 vols....   N. Y.   2 50
a. Dick, Thos.   Celestial Scenery ; Sidereal
Heavens ; *ea*... 12mo N. Y.   75
a. Dick.   Practical Astronomer...........12mo N. Y.   1 00
b. Dunkin.   The Midnight Sky. R. 8vo, Lond. & N. Y.   3 75
a. Denison.   Astronomy without Mathematics.12mo N. Y.   1 75
Ennis.   Origin of the Stars.............12mo N. Y.   2 00

a. Guillemin. The Heavens. Illustrated... 8vo N. Y. $4 50
a. Fay, T. S. System of Astronomy (in press).
a. Flammarion. Wonders of the Heavens..12mo N. Y. 1 50
   Herschel, J. F. W. Outlines of Astron...12mo N. Y. 2 50
   Hind. Solar System..................12mo N. Y. 50
   ——— On Comets........... Lond.... 8vo 5s. 6d.
a. Lockyer. Astronomy....................12mo N. Y. 1 75
a. Mitchell, O. M. Popular Astronomy.....12mo N. Y. 1 75
b. ——— Planetary and Stellar Worlds.12mo N. Y. 1 75
b. ——— Astronomy of the Bible......12mo N. Y. 1 75
   Nichol, J. P. Architecture of the Heavens. 8vo 16s.
   ——— Stellar Universe. Lond.... 8vo 5s. 6d.
   ——— Solar System. Lond....... 8vo 10s. 6d.
   ——— System of the World. Lond. 8vo 10s. 6d.
b. Norton. Treatise on Astronomy......... 8vo N. Y. 3 50
b. Olmsted, Prof. Introduc. to Astronomy.. 8vo N. Y. 3 00
   Plurality of Worlds..................12mo Bost. 1 50
b. Proctor, R. A. Saturn and his System... 8vo Lond. 6 00
   ——— The Sun............... ... 8vo Lond. 5 50
b. ——— Other Worlds than Ours....12mo N. Y. 2 50
   ——— Hand Book of the Stars....12mo Lond. 2 00
   ——— Half H'rs with the Telescope.16mo Phila. 1 25
   ——— Stars..... 4to Lond. 2 50
   Watson, I. C. Theoretical Astronomy..R. 8vo Phila. 10 00
   Whewell. Astronomy and Physics......12mo Lond. 1 50
   Whitall. Planisphere of Heavens, 2 parts, each, 3 00

Atheism.—[*See Infidelity.*]

Athens.—[*See also in works on Greece.*]

   Boeck. Pub. Econ. of Athens. London. 8vo 18s.
b. Leake. Topog. of Athens, 2 vols. Lond. 8vo 30s.
a. Stuart & Revett. Antiquities of Athens.12mo Lond. 2 50

Athletic Sports.—[*See also Gymnastics—Physical Training.*]

a. Depping. Wonders of Bodily Strength.12mo N. Y. 1 50
   Maclaren. Training, in Theory & Practice.
   ——— Physical Education..........
   Peverell. American Pastimes..........
a. Walker. Manly Exercises......... ..12mo Lond. 2 25
   ——— Defensive Exercises........12mo Lond. 2 00
   Wilkinson. Modern Athletics. London.. 6s.
   Wood, W. Manual of Physical Exercise.12mo N. Y.

Atlases.—[*Geographical, not including School Atlases.*]

a. Black. Atlas of the World............folio Lond. 25 00
a. Chambers. Cyclopedia Atlas........R. 8vo Lond. 5 00
b. Colton. General Atlas.................folio N. Y. 20 00
a. Fay. "Great Outline" Atlas .... 4to N. Y. 2 00
a. Globe Atlas of Europe, half bound......:12mo Lond. 4 50
   Johnston. School Classical Atlas........ Lond.
   ——— Royal Atlas of Mod. Geog..folio Lond. 50 00

Lowry.   Universal Atlas................ 4to   N. Y. $6 00
a. Macmillan.   Globe Atlas of the World..12mo Lond.   3 00
b. Mitchell.   New General Atlas......... 4to Phila. 20 00
———   ———   ———   ——— (smaller). 4to Phila. 10 00

Atlases.—PHYSICAL GEOGRAPHY.

b. Berghaus.   Physical Atlas..............folio Leips. 40 00
Collins.   Physical Atlas. 1870.   Lond... 4to 5s.
Johnston, A. Keith.   Atlas of Physical
            Geography.   Edinburgh ..... 8vo 7s 6d.
———   ———   ——— Larger work....Folio.   85 00

Atlases.—HISTORICAL.

a. Gage.   Modern Historical Atlas........ 8vo   N. Y.   3 50
b. Koeppen.   Atlas of the Middle Ages..... 4to   N. Y.   4 50
Sprüner.   Atlas Antiquus..............   Leips. 11 00
———   ——— to Hist. Europe.........   Leips. 26 00
———   ———   ——— Asia, Africa,
            America & Australia....   Leips. 10 00

Australia & Tasmania.

Kennedy.   Four Years in Queensland
                   London,....16mo 5s. 6d.
Stuart, J. M.   Explorations in Australia.
                   1858-62.... 8vo Lond.   3 75

Austria.

Abbott, J. S. C.   Empire of Austria...... 8vo N. Y.
b. Coxe.   Hist. of House of Austria, 3 vols..   Lond.   5 25
Dignomitry. Bohemia under Aus. Despot.12mo N. Y.
Hosier.   Seven Weeks' War. 1867. 2
                   vols. London.... 8vo 28s.
Kohl.   Travels in Austria. Lond........ 8vo 3s. 6d.
Michiels.   Secret Hist. of Austrian Gov't.
                   London.... 8vo 10s. 6d.
Newman, F. W.   Crimes of the House of
                   Austria. London,.... 8vo 1s.
Vehse.   Memoirs of Court of Austria. 2
                   vols.....r. 8vo Lond.
Ward, A. W.   House of Austria........12mo Lond.   1 00

Autobiography.—[*See Biography.*]

Autographic—FAC-SIMILES.

Autographic Album—470 Fac-Similes.... 4to Lond.   6 00
Autographic Mirror, 2 vols. Folio.......   Lond. 21 00
Smith's Literary and Historical Curiosities. 4to Lond. 14 00

Babylon.—[*See Nineveh.*]

Ballads.—[*See also Poetry.*]

Aytoun.   Bon Gaultier's Ballads........   N. Y.   1 50
———   Lays of Scottish Cavaliers.....12mo N. Y.   1 50
Bab Ballads (Comic). Illustrated........ 4to Phila.   2 00

Book of Roxburgh Ballads, ed. by Collier. 4to Lond.
Book of Brave Old Ballads. Lond.......12mo 5s.
Bennett. Ballad Hist. of England. Lond.12mo 5s.
a. Child, Prof. English and Scottish Ballads,
                   Collection of, 8 vols....18mo Bost. $10 00
b. Hall, S. C. Book of British Ballads. Illus.
                  mor. ....*r.* 8vo Lond. 13 50
Hayes. Ballads of Ireland.............12mo N. Y. 1 00
a. Macaulay. Lays of Ancient Rome....... 12mo Bost. 1 00
Moore. F. Songs of American Revolution.12mo N. Y. 1 75
a. —— —— Personal and Political Ballads.32mo N. Y. 1 00
a. —— —— Lyrics of Loyalty.......... 32mo N. Y. 1 00
—— —— Songs of the Soldiers........32mo N. Y. 1 00
—— —— Rebel Rhymes and Rhapsodies.32mo N. Y. 1 00
a. Palgrave. Golden Treas. of Songs and B.16mo Camb. 1 55
b. Percy. Reliques of Old Eng. Poetry. 1 vol. 8vo Phila. 3 00
—— —— —— —— 3 vols.....18mo Lond.
Roberts, J. S. Legendary Ballads. Lond. 8vo 7s. 6s.
Rimbault. Book of Songs and B. Lond.12mo 5s.
Scott. Minstrelsy of the Scottish Border.12mo Edinb.
Wilkins. Political Ballads............. 8vo Lond. 5 00

Ballooning.

Glaisher. Travels in the Air.......... *r.* 8vo Phila. 10 00
a. Marion. Wonderful Balloon Ascents....12mo N. Y. 1 50
Verne. Five Weeks in a Bal. (imaginary).12mo N. Y. 1 25

Banks.—BANKING.

Francis. History of Bank of England.... 8vo N. Y. 3 00
Gibbons, J. S. Banks of New York, &c...12mo N. Y. 1 50
Gilbart. History of Banking. London... 8vo 9s.
Gilbart. Treatise on Banking, 2 v. Lond. 8vo 16s.
Hankey. Principles of Banking........ 8vo Lond.
a. —— —— —— 1 vol.... 8vo Phila.
——Logic of Banking. London........12mo 12s. 6d.
Lawson. Hist. of Banks in Gt. Brit. Lond. 8vo 7s. 6d.
Martin. Stories of Banks and Bankers.
                   London....16mo 7s. 6d.
McCulloch. Money and Banks. Lond. 4to 5s.

Battles.

Battles of America, by Sea and Land. Ill. 4to N. Y. 13 50
a. Creasy. Fifteen Decisive Battles of World.12mo N. Y. 1 50
Jomini. Campaign of Waterloo........12mo N. Y.
Persse. Battle Record........ .... 8vo N. Y.

Belgium.—[*See Holland and B.*]

Belles-Letters.—[*See Literature.*]

Bees.

Bee Keeping. By ".the Times'" Bee Master.
                  London....12mo 2s. 6d.

a. Huber. Nat. Hist. of Honey Bee. Lond.12mo 6s.
a. Langstroth. The Honey Bee...........12mo Phila. $2 00
   Pettigrew. Handy Book of Bees. Lond.12mo 2s. 6d.
   Richardson. Hive & Honey Bees(Saxton).12mo N. Y.
   Weeks. Management of Bees (Saxton)..12mo N. Y.

Bible (The).—Its History.—[*See also Church History, etc.*]
   Anderson. Annals of the English Bible, 2
                vols. London,.... 8vo 15s.
a. ———— The same, abridged by Prime. 8vo N. Y.   2 50
   Baker. Manual of Bible History. Lond.12mo 2s. 6d.
   Blunt. Plain Account of the Eng. Bible.12mo N. Y.   1 50
a. Gleig. History of the Bible, 2 vols......18mo N. Y.   1 50
   Kitto. History of Palestine............12mo Bost.   1 75
b. Kitto. Biblical Encyclopedia, 3 vols..R. 8vo Lond.   24 00
a. ——— Popular Cyclopedia of Bible Lit.. 8vo Bost.   4 00
a. Rawlinson. Historical Evidences of Truth
                 of Bible....12mo Bost.   1 75
a. Ramsard, Mrs. The Book and its Story.12mo N. Y.   1 50
b. Smith, W. History of the Old and New
              Testament, each.... 8vo N. Y.   2 50
b. ———— Dictionary of the Bible. [*See Dictionaries.*]
   Stuart, Moses. Hist. of Old Test. Canon. 8vo Andov.   1 75
   Tischendorf. Discovery of Sinaitic Mss..
   Westcott. History of English Bible.....
   Walden. Hist. of English Bible and its seven Ances-
              tors. 12mo Lond.   1 25

Bible.—AIDS TO THE STUDY OF THE.—[*See Holy Land.*]
   Abbott, Lyman. Old Testa. Shadows of New Testa.
              Truths....12mo N. Y.   3 50
   Alford. How to Study the New Testam't,
             3 vols. London,....18mo 10s. 6d.
b. ——— New Test. Commentary, 4 vols.. 8vo Lond.   16 00
b. Alexander, J. A. The Psalms; 2 vols., $5; Isaiah,
        2 vols., $4; Matthew and Mark, each.12mo N. Y.   2 00
   Angus. Bible Hand Book. Lond.......12mo 10s.
   Ayre, J. Treasury of Bible Knowledge.
             Lond. and N. Y...18mo   4 00
   Bengel. Gnomen of the New Testament,
             2 vols.....R. 8vo N. Y.   9 00
a. Barnes. Notes on Isaiah, 2 vols........   N. Y.   3 00
a. ——— ———— Psalms, 3 vols........   N. Y.   4 50
a. ——— ———— On New Test., 11 vols.   N. Y.   16 50
b. Bible Comment ("The Speaker's"). Ed. by
        Canon Cook. per vol.......r. 8vo N. Y.   5 00
a. Blunt, J. J. Key to the Knowledge and
             Use of Bible....12mo Phila.   1 00
   Boardman, H. A. The Bible in the Family.12mo Phila.   1 00
   ——————— ——— Bible in Count'g House.12mo   1 00
a. Bush. Notes on Genesis, Exodus, Leviticus, Deut.
          Joshua, 4 vols....12mo N. Y. *ea.* 1 25
   Clarke. Bible Atlas.................. 4to Lond.   15 00

b. Conybeare & Howison. Life and Epistles
           of St. Paul, 2 vols. in one.... 8vo N. Y. $3 00
      Critical and Expl. Pocket Bible, with comt.12mo Bost. 6 50
a. Cruden. Concordance to the Bible.....*r.* 8vo Lond. 2 75
b. Crosby, Howard. New Test. with Notes.12mo N. Y. 1 50
b. Dunn. The Study of the Bible..........12mo N. Y. 1 50
b. Eadie. Analytical Concordance to Bible. 8vo Bost. 4 00
      Hackett, Prof. H. B. Comment. on the
                              Acts.... 8vo Bost. 3 00
      ——— —— Illustrations of Scripture.12mo Bost. 1 50
      Hunt, E. M.   Bible Notes for Daily
                         Readers, 2 vols..... *r.* 8vo N. Y. 7 00
b. Horne. Introduc. to the Bible, 2 vols.. *r.* 8vo N. Y. 5 00
      ——— —— New edition, 4 vols...... 8vo Lond. 20 00
      Inglis. The Bible Text Cyclopedia...... 8vo Phila. 3 00
b. Kitto. Daily Bible Illustrations. 8 vols.12mo N. Y. 14 00
b. Kip, Bp. The Unnoticed Things of Scrip-
                              ture....12mo N. Y. 1 50
b. Lange. Biblical Commentary, 13 vols... 8vo N. Y. ea. 5 00
b. McClintock & Strong. Bibli. and Theol.
                   Cyclopedia, 4 vols ....*r.* 8vo N. Y. 20 00
a. Malcom. Bible Dictionary.............18mo Bost. 1 25
b. Maunder. Treasury of Bible Knowledge.18mo N. Y. 4 00
      Olshausen. Comment. on New Testament,
                         6 vols... 8vo N. Y. 18 00
      Owen, Prof. J. J. Commentary on Mark,
                   Luke and John, each....12mo N. Y. 1 75
      Portable Comment. on Old and New Test.
                   By Jamieson, etc., 2 vols.... 8vo Bost. 6 00
      Ripley, Prof. Notes on Gospels; Acts,
                   Rom. and Heb., 4 vols....12mo Bost. 5 75
      Ritter. Geogr. of Palestine, for Biblical Students.
                   Trans. by Gage, 4 vols.... 8vo N. Y. 14 00
      Robinson. Calmet's Dic. of the Bible... *r.* 8vo Bost. 6 00
      ——— & Smith. Biblical Researches
                   in Palestine, 4 vols.... 8vo Bost. 10 00
b. ——— Physical Geogr. of Palestine. 8vo Bost. 3 50
b. Smith, W. Dictionary of the Bible. Ed. by Prof.
                   Hackett, etc., 4 vols. 8vo N. Y. 26 00
      ——— ——— Abridged in 1 vol..... N. Y. 5 00
      ——— ——— London edition, 3 vols. 8vo 18 00
a. ——— ——— Concise Dict. Lond. & N. Y. 8vo 4 00
      ——— ——— Smaller Dic. ——— 8vo Lond. 3 00
      ——— ——— Another ed. Appleton. 8vo N. Y. 5 00
      " Speaker's ", (The) Commentary on the Bible. Pub-
                   lishing in large 8vo. vols., each. N. Y. 5 00
      Tholuck. Comment. on Gospel of St. John. 8vo N. Y. 3 00
      Trench, R. C. Studies on the Gospels...12mo N. Y. 1 25
      Tyng, S. H. Light in the Dwelling : Com-
                   mentary on Gospels.... 8vo N. Y. 2 50
      Wood, J. G. Bible Animals............ 8vo N. Y. 5 00

Bible.—GENERAL ASPECTS OF.

Halsey. The Literary Attractions of the
                    Bible....12mo N. Y. $1 75
Liber Librorum : Its Structure, Limita·
             tion and Purpose....18mo N. Y.   1 50
Matthews, J. M.   The Bible, and Men of
                 Culture.... 8vo N. Y.   3 00
Spring, Gardiner.   The Obligations of the
           World to the Bible.... 8vo N. Y.   2 00

Bibliography.

b. Allibone.   Dictionary of Authors in English
           Language. 3 vols.....r. 8vo   22 50
b. Brunet.   Manuel de Libraire, — vols..... 8vo Paris.
Collier.   Bibl. Act. of Rare Books in Eng.
          Literature, 4 vols..... 8vo N. Y. 12 00
Darling.   Cyclo. of Biblical and General
          Literature, 3 vols......r. 8vo Lond.
a. Lowndes.   Bibliographer s Manual, 6 vols.12mo Lond. 13 50
c. Malcom, H.   Index to Religious Litera. 8vo Phila.   4 00

Bible and Science.—[*See Science and Religion.*]

Billiards.

Crawley.   The Billiard Book........... 8vo Lond.   7 50
Phelan.   Hand Book of Billiards.........16mo N. Y.   1 50

Biography.—DICTIONARIES.

Allen.   American Biog. Dict. (o. p.)...... 8vo Bost.
Beeton.   Dict. of Universal Biography. 8vo L. & N. 3 50
a. Godwin.   Cyclo. of Biog. By Shepard...12mo N. Y.   3 50
b. Haydn.   Index of Biography........... 8vo Lond.   7 50
Hawks.   Biographical Dictionary........ 8vo N. Y.   5 00
Hole & Wheeler.   Brief Biog. Dictionary.12mo N. Y.   1 50
Imperial Dict. of Biography, 3 vols... .r. 8vo Lond. 18 00
a. Men of the Time (contemporary biog.).... 8vo Lond.   6 00
Maunder.   Biographical Treasury.......18mo N. Y.   4 00
b. Smith.   Dict. of Greek and Rom. B.,3 vols. 8vo Lond. 22 50
a. —— —— —— —— —— abridg.12mo N. Y.   2 50
b. Thomas.   Cyclo. of Biography (Lippin-
           cott), 2 vols....r. 8vo Phila. 22 00
Valpereau.   Dict. des Contemporaines... 8vo Paris. 12 50

Biography.—COLLECTED WORKS ; AMERICAN.

Barrett.   The Old Merchants of New York,
           4 vols....12mo N. Y.   7 00
Belknap.   American Biography, 3 vols...18mo N. Y.   2 25
Cooper, J. F.   Dist. Naval Officers, 2 vols.12mo Phila.
b. Ellett, Mrs.   Women of the Revolution,
           3 vols....12mo N. Y.   5 25
Eminent Individuals in Amer. Hist., 3 vols.12mo N. Y.   4 50

Flanders.	Lives of Chief Justices of Sup. Court of U. S., 2 vols.... 8vo N. Y.		$5 00
Hamersly.	Living Officers of U. S. Navy. 8vo Phila.		5 00
Headley.	Washington and his Generals, 2 vols....12mo N. Y.		3 50
Lanman.	Dict. of Congress............. 8vo Hartf'd		4 00
b. Lossing.	Eminent Americans........... 8vo N. Y.		
	Pioneer Biography: Ohio.............. 8vo Cincin.		3 50
Parker, Theo.	Historic Americans...... 8vo Bost.		1 50
Sabine.	Loyalists of Amer. Revol., 2 vols. Bost.		7 00
b. Sparks.	American Biogr. Library of. 1st Series, 10 vols.............12mo N. Y.		12 50
b.	2d Series, 15 vols.............12mo Bost.		15 00
Sprague.	Annals of American Pulpit, 9 v. 8vo N. Y.		36 00
Thatcher.	Indian Biography, 2 vols.....18mo N. Y.		1 50
Raymond.	Women of the South, 2 vols. Phila.		6 00

Biography.—COLLECTED WORKS; WOMEN.

Adams.	Cyclopedia of Female Biography.12mo		1 75
Balfour, C. L.	Working-Women of Last Century. London.... 8vo 3s. 6d.		
a. Child, Mrs.	Celebrated Women.... ....12mo N. Y.		75
——— ———	Good Wives.............12mo Bost.		1 50
——— ———	Mad. de Stael & Roland ...12mo N. Y.		75
——— ———	Noble Deeds of Am. Women.12mo Bost.		1 50
a. Crossland (Mrs.)	Memorable Women....18mo N. Y.		1 50
Ellett, Mrs.	Pioneer Women of the West.12mo N. Y.		1 50
——— ———	Queens of Society.........12mo N. Y.		3 00
——— ———	Women Artists............12mo N. Y.		1 50
b. Hale, Mrs.	Woman's Record.........r. 8vo N. Y.		5 00
a. Jameson, Mrs.	Female Sovereigns, 1 vol.12mo Phila.		1 50
	2 vols.18mo N. Y.		1 50
Kavanagh.	English Women of Letters, 2 vols. London.... 8vo 21s.		
———	Exemplary Women of Christ'y. 8vo Lond.		
———	French Women of Letters, 2 vols. London... 8vo 21s.		
a. St. Beuve.	Portraits of Celebr'd Women.16mo Bost.		2 00
b. Strickland, Agnes.	Queens of England, 6 vols.... Lond.		13 50
——— ——— ———	Abridged, 1 vol. N. Y.		2 50
——— ———	Queens of Scotland, 8 vols.12mo N. Y.		12 00
Trollope, T. A.	Decade of Ital. Women, 2 vols. London.... 8vo 22s.		
Warton;	The Queens of Society.........12mo L. & N.		2 50
Women of History.	By eminent Writers.18mo Lond.		2 00

Biography.—COLLECTED; SCIENTIFIC.

Arago.	Distingu. Scientific Men. Lond. 8vo 18s.		
a. Brewster, Sir D.	Martyrs of Science....18mo N. Y.		75
Dirchs.	Inventors and Inventions. Lond. 8vo 4s.		
Milzia.	Celebrated Architects........ 8vo Lond.		4 50

Smiles. Lives of the Engineers, 3 vols...   Lond.
—— —— —— Stephensons.......12mo N. Y. $1 50
a. ——   —— —— Industrial Biog.....12mo Bost.   1 50

Biography.—COLLECTED ; LITERARY.

Brougham. Men of Letters and Science.
　　　　Time of George III. London.... 8vo 5s.
Curwen. Successful Booksellers. 1871.. 8vo Lond.
a. De Quincey. Biographical Essays.......12mo Bost.   1 50
Fenelon. Ancient Philosophers..........18mo N. Y.   75
French Authors at Home, 2 vols........   Lond.   2 00
Hall, S. C. Book of Memories of Great
　　　　Men and Women of the Age..... 8vo Lond. 10 00
b. Homes of American Authors............ 8vo N. Y.   5 00
b. Howitt, W. Homes and Haunts of British
　　　　　　Authors, 2 vols..... 8vo N. Y.   3 50
Jeaffreson. Lives of British Novelists.
　　　　　　London, 2 vols....   21s.
a. Johnson, Dr. Lives of the Poets, 2 vols.12mo Phila.   3 00
Montgomery. Authors of Italy, Spain and
　　　　Portugal (E. C. L.), 3 vols.....   Lond.
Morley. English Writers, 3 vols........ 8vo   15 00
Russell. Book of Authors.... ....12mo Lond.   1 75
Scott, Sir W. Lives of Eminent Novelists
　　　　(In his Prose Works)....
Shelley, Mrs. Authors of France (Ed.Cab.
　　　　　　Lib.) 2 vols.....12mo Edinb.
Stebbins. Lives of Italian Poets........12mo Lond.   1 75

Biography.—COLLECTED ; ARTISTS.

Bryan. Dictionary of Painters (chiefly
　　　　included in Spooner).....r. 8vo Lond.
b. —— Supplement to do. Liv. Artists. .r. 8vo Lond.   4 50
Cunningham. Lives of Brit. Paint. and
　　　　Sculpt. 6 vols. 18mo. Lond.; or 5 vols.18mo N. Y.   3 75
a. Jameson, Mrs. Lives of Italian Painters.16mo Bost.   2 00
b. Lanzi. History of Painting, &c., 5 vols.   Bohn.   8 75
Perkins, Ch. C. Tuscan Sculptors ; their
　　　　Lives and Works, 2 vols.... 4to Bost. 22 50
—————— Italian Sculptors ; their Lives
　　　　and Works. Imp.... 8vo Bost. 16 00
b. Spooner. Dict. of Painters, Sculptors, etc.
　　　　2 vols.....r. 8vo   10 00
a. Tuckerman, H. T. Book of the Artists ;
　　　　American Artist Life.... 8vo N. Y.   5 00
—————— —— —— Illust. Ed..-r. 8vo N. Y. 30 00
Urbino, Mrs. The Princes of Art, Painters,
　　　　etc....12mo Bost.   2 00
b. Vasari. Lives of the Painters, 5 vols....12mo Bohn.   8 75

Biography.—COLLECTED ; POLITICAL, LEGAL, MILITARY,
　　　　MEDICAL.

Barrow. Naval Worthies of Reign of Qu'n
　　　　Elizabeth. (1845.) London.... 8vo 14s.

Brougham. Statesmen of Time of Geo.
　　　　　　III., 3 vols. Lond.... 8vo 31s. 6d.
——————— & Lyndhurst, Lives of. By
　　　　　　　　Campbell.... 8vo Lond.   6 00
b. Campbell. Lives of the Lord Chancellors.
　　　　　　　　10 vols.... 8vo Lond. 20 00
—————— —————— —— Chief Justices. 3
　　　　　　vols. London.... 8vo 42s.
Cust, Sir E. Lives of the Warriors......12mo Lond.
b. Foster, John, Statesmen of Common-
　　　　　　　wealth.... 8vo N. Y.   2 25
Foss. Biog. Dict. of Judges of England. 8vo L. & B. 6 50
Gleig. Lives of Brit. Commanders, 3 vols.16mo Lond.
James. Foreign Statesmen. (1837.) 5 v. Lond.17s. 6d.
———— Great Commanders. Lond......12mo 5s.
Kaye. Lives of Indian Officers, 3 vols....   Lond.   7 50
Lives of Drake, Cavendish and Dampier..18mo N. Y.   75
Mitchell, Gen. Eminent Soldiers of last
　　　　　　four Centuries.....
Proctor. The Bench and Bar of New York. 8vo N. Y.   5 00
Pettigrew. Biogr. Mem's of Physicians...*r.* 8vo Lond.   6 00
Shiel. Sketches of the Irish Bar, 2 vols.
　　　　　　London ... 12mo 21s.
a. Smith, Goldwin. Three Eng. Statesmen.12mo N.Y.   1 50

Biography.—COLLECTED; SELF-TAUGHT MEN.

a. Craik. Pursuit of Knowledge under Diffi-
　　　　　　culties, 2 vols...18mo N. Y.   1 50
Davenport. Lives of Self Made Men.
　　　　　　London....18mo 3s. 6d.
Seymour. Self-Made Men..............12mo N. Y.   1 75
a. Smiles. Self-Help...................12mo Bost.   1 50

Biography.—COLLECTED; MISCELLANEOUS.

a. Abbott, J. Biog. of Illustrious Men and
　　　　　　Women, 29 vols................16mo N. Y. *ea.*1 20
Bourne. Famous London Merchants.....16mo N. Y.   1 00
a. Book of Golden Deeds (Golden Treasury).16mo Lond.   1 25
Bulwer, H. L. Histor. Characters. Lond. 8vo 6s.
Chambers, W. Lives Eminent Scotsmen,
　　　　　　4 vols. Edinburgh.   60s.
Cornelius, Nepos. Roman Biographies...12mo N. Y.   1 50
Coleridge, S. T. Notes on Eng. Divines.
　　　　　　2 vols....12mo Lond.
a. Edgar. Boyhood of Great Men..........16mo N. Y.   1 20
———— Sea Kings and Naval Heroes..16mo N. Y.   1 20
Farrar. Seekers after God: Seneca, &c..12mo Phila.   1 75
Fuller. Worthies of England, etc., 3 vols.
　　　　　　London.... 8vo 18s.
b. Grote. Plato and the Companions of Soc-
　　　　　　rates, 3 vols....ʼ   Lond. 16 50
Houssaye. Men and Women of 18th Cen-
　　　　　　tury, 2 vols.....   N. Y.   3 00

Houssaye.   Philosophers and Actresses, 2 vols.   N. Y. $3 00
James, G. P. R.   Lives of De Retz, Col-
                bert, etc.... 8vo Lond.
b. Jesse.   Lives of the Pretenders.........12mo Lond.   2 50
    Jones, J. W.   Boyhood of Great Men.....12mo N. Y.   1 00
b. Lodge.   Portraits of Illustrious Persons.
                   8 vols ...12mo Lond. 18 00
    Martin.   Contemporary Biography........
    Macaulay.   Biographies, from Ency. Brit.12mo 3s. 6d.
b. Martineau, Harriet.   Biographl. Sketches. 8vo N. Y.   2 50
    Middleton.   Evangel. Biography, 4 vols.. 8vo Lond.
    Montalembert.   Monks of the West..... 8vo Edinb.
a. Plutarch.   Lives of Famous Men.   Edited
            by A. H. Clough, 5 vols.... 8vo Bost. 15 00
   ————   ———— (or) by Langhorn. 4 vols.12mo N. Y.   5 00
   ————   ————   1 vol. 8vo N. Y.   2 00
    Russell.   Eccentric Persons.............12mo N. Y.
    Redding.   Remarkable Misers, 2 vols.
                London.... 8vo 21s.
a. Smiles.   Brief Biographies.............12mo N. Y.   1 50
    Stebbings.   Lives of the Italian Poets...12mo Lond.   1 25
    St. John.   Celebrated Travels, 3 vols.....18mo N. Y.   2 25
    Taylor.   Modern British Plutarch.......12mo N. Y.   1 50
    Thatcher.   Indian Biography, 2 vols.....18mo N. Y.   1 50
   ———— American Medical Biog..*o. p.* 8vo
a. Thackeray.   The Four Georges.........12mo N. Y.   1 25
    Timbs.   School Days of Eminent Men.
   ———— English Eccentricities...........
                London....12mo 5s.
    Ware.   American Unitarian Biog. 2 vols.12mo Bost.   3 00
b. Walton.   Lives of Hooker, Donne, etc...12mo N. Y.   2 25
    Wharton.   The Queens of Society.......12mo N. Y.   1 75
   ———— Wits and Beaux of Society...12mo N. Y.   1 75
    Wilson.   Wonderful Characters........12mo Lond.

Biography—INDIVIDUAL.—(Alphabeted by names of sub-
           jects, not authors.)

    Abernethy.   By MacIlwain..............12mo N. Y.   1 50
    Abrantes, Duchess d'.   Memoirs, 8 vols.
                London.... 8vo 112s.
    Adams, Saml., Life.   By Wells, 3 vols... 8vo Bost.   12 00
b. ———— John.   By J. Q. Adams & Ch. F. A. 8vo Phila.   3 00
   ———— John Quincy.   By Ch. Fr. Adams.12mo Phila.
    Addison.   By Lucy Aikin. 1834. 2 vols.   Lond.
    Agrippa, Cornelius. By Henry Morley....12mo Lond.
    Albert, Prince, Early Years. By Grey...12mo N. Y.   2 00
    Allibone, Susan.   By Rev. A. Lee........ 8vo Phila.   2 25
b. Alexander, Rev. Dr.   By H. C. Alexander,
               2 vols....12mo N. Y.   5 00
    Alfieri, Count, Autobiography, 2 v. Lond. 8vo 18s.
a. Alfred the Great. By Thos. Hughes.....18mo Bost.   · 1 50
a. Alexander the Great. By J. Abbott.....16mo N. Y.   1 20

	Ames, Fisher. By Kirkland............				
a.	Andersen, Hans. Story of my Life......12mo N. Y.	$1 75
b.	Andre, Major. By Winthrop Sargent.... 8vo N. Y.	2 50
	Angelo, Michel. By Grimm, 2 vols.. ... 8vo Lond.	5 00
	——— ——— By Harford, 2 vols....... 8vo Lond.	6 00
	——— ——— & Raphael. By Duppa....12mo Lond.	2 25
	Anne of Austria. By Freer, 2 vols....... 8vo Lond.	7 50
	Aquinas, Thos., Life of. By Hampden...16mo Lond.	
	Arminius. By Bangs..................18mo N. Y.	75
b.	Arnold, Dr. By Dean Stanley, 2 vols. in 1.12mo Bost.	2 00
	Arnold, Thos. By Worbaise............ 8vo Lond.	1 50
	Ars, Curé of. By Grimm..............12mo Balt.	2 00
a.	Audubon, J. J., Life and Journals. By his	
	widow....12mo N. Y.	2 50
a.	Augustine, St., Life. By Schoff.........	
	Austen, Jane. By Austen-Leigh. Lond..12mo 12s.	
	Bacon, Lord. By W. H. Dixon.......*o. p.*12mo Phila.	1 50
	——— ——— By Macaulay (in his works).	
	Balboa, Cortes and Pizzaro..............18mo N. Y.	75
	Barante. By Guizot. Translated by	
	M. Craik..... 8vo Lond.	2 00
	Barham, Rev. R. H. By R. D. Bach, 2 vols.	
	London.... 8vo 21s.	
	Barnum, P. T. Struggles and Triumphs.12mo N. Y.	1 50
	Barrington, Sir J. Sketches of his Own	
	Times, 2 vols..... 8vo Lond.	6 00
	Bayard, Chevalier. By W. G. Simms....12mo N. Y.	1 50
	——— ——— By Walford..... ...16mo Lond.	1 25
	Beaumarchais and his Times. By Lomeire.	
	4 vols. London.... 8vo 42s.	
	Becket, Thos. à. By Millman..........	
	Beecher, Lyman. Autobiography. Ed. by	
	Chas. B. 2 vols.....12mo N. Y.	5 00
b.	Beethoven. By Moscheles.............16mo Bost.	2 00
	——— ——— By Schindler.	
	Belisarius. By Lord Mahon...........12mo N. Y.	1 50
	Bentham. By Bowring (in his Works)..	
	Béranger. Autobiography, 2 vols. Lond. 8vo 14s.	
	Bethune, Mrs. By her Son.............12mo N. Y.	1 50
	Bismarck. By Hesekiel. By 8vo N. Y.	3 00
	Blake, Admiral. By W. H. Dixon.......12mo Lond.	
	Blake, Wm. (Painter). By Gilchrist, 2 v. 8vo Lond.	8 00
	Blessington, Lady. By Madden, 2 vols...12mo N. Y.	3 00
	Boardman, G. D. (Missionary). By Dr.	
	Williams....12mo Bost.	1 25
	Boone, Daniel. By Bogart.............12mo Bost.	1 50
	Borgia, Lucrezia. By Gilbert, 2 vols. Lond.12mo 21s.	
	Bourbon Prince (Louis XVII.). By Tomes.18mo N. Y.	75
	Brainerd, Rev. T. By M. Brainerd.......12mo Phila.	2 50
	Brant (Indian Chief). W. L. Stone, 2 vols. 8vo Albany.	5 00
b.	Bremer, Fredrika and Post.Wks. By Stone.12mo N. Y.	1 75
	Bright, John. By McGilchrist...........16mo N. Y.	50

a. Brontë, Charlotte. By Mrs. Gaskell.... 16mo L. & P. $1 25
Brougham, Lord. By Lord Campbell. Lon. 8vo 16s.
b. —————— —— By himself, 2 vols.....12mo N. Y. 4 00
Brown John. By Redpath.............12mo Bost. 1 00
Brunel, Sir I. By I. K. Brunel..........
Bruce (Traveller). By Sir F. B. Head.....18mo N. Y. 75
Buckingham, Duke of. By Mrs. Thompson.
      London. 3 vols....12mo 30s.
b. Bunsen, Baron. By his Widow, 2 vols...12mo Lon&P. 7 50
b. Burke, Edmund. By Prior, 2 vols.......12mo Bost. 3 00
———— ———— By John Morley....... 8vo Lond. 2 50
Burns, Robt. By Carlyle...............18mo N. Y. 1 00
b. ———— —— By Chambers, 4 vols......12mo N. Y. 6 00
a. ———— —— By Lockhart.............18mo N. Y. 75
Burr, Aaron. By M. L. Davis. 2 vols.... 8vo N. Y. 4 00
a. —— ———— By Jas. Parton, 2 vols...... 8vo Bost. 6 00
Buxton, Sir Fowell. By C. Buxton. Lond.12mo 2s. 6.
b. Byron, Lord. By Moore, 2 vols.......... 8vo N. Y. 4 00
———— —— By Guiccioli.............12mo N. Y. 1 75
Cabot, Sebastian. By Biddle. 1831....... 8vo Phila.
b. Cæsar, Julius. By Napoleon III., 2 vols. 8vo N. Y. 7 00
Canning, Geo. By Bell.................12mo N. Y. 1 00
Calderon. By French..........Lond....12mo 7s. 6d.
Calhoun, J. C., Life and Writings, 6 vols... 8vo N. Y. 15 00
Carson, Kit. By Burdett....... ....12mo Phila. 1 75
Cartwright, Inventor of power loom......12mo Lond. 2 50
Calvin, John. By Dyer.......8vo, Lond.; 12mo N. Y. 1 50
Campbell, Thos. By Beattie, 3 vols. 8vo,
      London ; 2 vols.12mo N. Y. 3 00
———— Alex. By Richardson, 2 vols.. 8vo 3 50
Carlyle, Dr. A. Memoirs........Lond... 8vo 14s.
Catherine II. of Russia. By herself.... 8vo N. Y. 1 25
Cavour, Count. By Botta.............. 8vo N. Y. 1 25
———— ———— By Dicey.............. 8vo Lond.
———— ———— By De la Rive.......... 8vo Lond. 2 50
a. Cellini, Benvenuto. By herself.........12mo Lond. 1 75
Cervantes. By Roscoe................12mo Lond. 1 75
b. Chalmers, Dr. Thos. By Hanna, 4 vols...12mo N. Y. 6 00
———— ———— By Dr. Wayland........12mo Bost. 1 00
———— ———— By J. Dodds...........12mo N. Y. 1 25
b. Channing, Rev. Dr. W. E. By W. H.
      Channing, 1 vol, $1 ; 3 vols..12mo Bost. 2 50
a. Charlemagne. By G. P. R. James......18mo N. Y. 75
Charles V. Cloister Life. By Stirling. Lon. 8vo 8s.
———— Autobiography. Trans. by Clay-
      ton. London.... 8vo 6s. 6d.
b. ———— By Robertson. Ed. by Prescott,
      3 vols. 8vo Phila. 7 50
a. Charles I. and II. By J. Abbott, each....16mo N. Y. 1 20
b. Charles XII., Sweden. By Voltaire......12mo N. Y. 2 25
Chatterton. By Dix. 1845.............12mo Bost.
———— —— By Prof. Wilson..........12mo Lond. 2 00

b.	Choate, Rufus. By Brown..............	8vo	Bost.	**$2 50**
	Chopin (Musician). By Liszt............16mo		N. Y.	1 50
b.	Cicero. By Forsyth, 2 vols.............	8vo	N. Y.	2 50
	Clay, Henry. By Colton, 2 vols.........	8vo	N. Y.	4 50
	—— —— By Smucker..............12mo		Phila.	1 75
	Clinton, Dewitt. By Campbell. 1849....	8vo	N. Y.	
	Clive, Lord. By Gleig. [*See also Macaulay.*]			
	London....12mo 6s.			
	Cobden, Richard. By McGilchrist........16mo		N. Y.	50
	Cochrane, Lord. By himself and his son,			
	3 vols.... 8vo		Lond.	
	Coligny. By D. D. Scott........ ....16mo		Edinb.	
a.	Columbus. By Irving, 3 vols. 3 75. 3 v.12mo		N. Y.	6 75
b.	—— By Arthur Helps...........12mo		Lon&P.	2 00
b.	Coleridge. Biographia Literaria. Lon. 1 75.			
	2 vols....12mo		N. Y.	8 00
	—— —— By Gillman................			
	Colonna Vittoria. By Mrs. Roscoe.......12mo		Lond.	
	Conde ("the Great"). By Lord Mahon...12mo		N. Y.	
	Confucius. By Jas. Legge, D. D.........	8vo	Phila.	4 00
	Constable (the Painter). By C. R. Leslie.	4to	Lond.	6 00
a.	Cortes, Hernando. By Arthur Helps....12mo		N. Y.	2 00
	Corneille and his Times. By Guizot.....12mo		N. Y.	1 50
	Cowper. By Hayley. London.........	8vo	12s.	
	—— (with his Works). By Southey.			
	Cranmer, Archbishop. By Le Bas, 2 vols.18mo		N. Y.	1 50
a.	Cromwell. By Carlyle, 2 vols............12mo		N. Y.	8 50
	4 vols....16mo			8 60
	—— By Guizot, 2 vols..........*o.p.*	8vo	Phila.	
	—— By Headley.................12mo		N. Y.	1 50
	—— By Southey.................18mo		N. Y.	1 00
	Cumberland (Dramatist). By himself. '56.	8vo	Phila.	
	Curwen (American Loyalist) Journal and			
	Letters....*o.p.* 8vo		N. Y.	
	Curran (Irish Orator). By Phillips. Lond.	8vo	7s. 6d.	
	Cuvier (Naturalist). By Mrs. Lee........12mo		N. Y.	75
	Dante; Life and Times. By Balbo, '52, 2 v.			
	London....12mo 21s.			
	—— By Prof. Botta..................12mo		N. Y.	2 50
	Davis, Jefferson. By Pollard............	8vo	Phila	8 00
	Davy, Sir H. By Dr. J. Davy. 1835. 2 v.	Lon.	28s.	
	De Foe. By Chadwick. London........	8vo	10s. 6d.	
	De Genlis, Madame. Memoirs, Illust. of			
	18th and 19th Cent., 2 vols. Lon.. 8vo 18s.			
a.	De Quincey. Autobiographical Sketches.12mo		Bost.	1 50
a.	— —— Literary Reminiscences, 2 v.12mo		Bost.	8 00
	De Soto (Discov.). By F. A. Willmott. '58.	8vo	Phila.	
	Dickens, Chas. By F. B. Perkins.......12mo		N. Y.	1 00
	—— —— By R. S. Mackenzie....12mo		Phila.	2 00
	—— —— Story of his Life (Hotten).12mo		Lond.	
a.	—— —— By John Forster. 1871–2.		L. & P.	
	D'Israeli, Benj. By McGilchrist.........16mo		N. Y.	50

Douglas, Stephen A. By H. M. Flint....12mo Phila. $1 75
a. Drake, Admiral. By Barron...........18mo N. Y. 75
Dryden. By Scott (in his Works).......
Dürer, Albert. By Mrs. Heaton. Illust...8vo Lond. 12 00
———— By W. B. Scott. London. 8vo 16s.
Eldon, Lord Chancellor. By Twiss, 2 vols.
                    London.... 8vo 21s.
Eliot, John (Missionary). By N. Adams..12mo Bost.
Eliot, Sir John. By Forster, 2 v. Lond. 8vo 30s.
Edward III., of England. By W. Longman
        2 vols. London.... 8vo 28s.
a. Evelyn, John. (Diary and Corres.) By Bray.12mo N. Y. 2 50
Fairfax, Lord. By Markham. 1871.... 8vo Lond. 5 00
Faraday (Chemist). By Bence Jones, 2 v. 8vo Phila. 10 00
a. ———— as Discoverer. By Tyndall....12mo N. Y. 1 00
Farragut, Admiral. By Headley.........12mo N. Y. 1 50
Fechter, J. G. By W. Smith. 1865. Lon.12mo 4s.
Fitch, John (Inventor). By Westcott.....12mo Phila. 1 25
Foster, John ; Life and Correspondence.
        By Ryland..........12mo Bost. 2 00
Fox, Chas. J. By Lord John Russell, 2 v. Lond. 6 00
Francis of Assisi. By Mrs. Olyphant....12mo Lond. 1 75
Francis, Sir Philip ; Memoirs of, 2 v. Lon. 8vo 30s.
Fourier, Chas. By E. Pellarin. Lond.12mo 2s.
a. Franklin, Benj. Autobiog. Ed. by Bigelow. 8vo Phila. 2 50
b. ———— —— Life. By Parton, 2 vols. 8vo Bost. 6 00
———— —— —— Illust. By Chapman. 8vo N. Y. 4 00
a. ———— —— (for Boys). By Mayhew.18mo N. Y. 1 50
a. ———— —— Life and Writings, 2 vols.18mo N. Y. 1 50
b. ———— —— By Sparks............. 8vo Phila. 3 00
b. Frederick the Great. By Carlyle, 6 vols.12mo N. Y. 12 00
———— —— — new ed. 10 vs.16mo Lond. 9 00
b. ———— —— —— By J. S. C. Abbott. Il. 8vo N. Y. 5 00
———— —— —— By Lord Dover, 2 v.18mo Lond. 1 50
———— —— —— By Macaulay.......18mo N. Y. 1 00
Fry, Mrs. (Philanthropist). By Mrs. Cres-
        well. London.... 8vo 8s. 6d.
Fuller, Margaret. (See Ossoli.)
Fulton, Robt. By Colden. 1817......... 8vo N. Y.
Fuseli (Artist). By Knowles, 3 vols. Lond. 8vo 21s.
a. Galileo (Astronomer) ; Private Life of....12mo Bost. 1 50
———— ——————— Life of. L. & N. Y..12mo
Garibaldi. By T. Dwight...............12mo N. Y.
———— By himself ....12mo Lond.
Garrick. By Fitzgerald, 2 vols.........8vo Lond. 15 00
George IV. of England. By Croly.......18mo N. Y. 75
Gibbon ; Autobiography and Correspond.12mo Lond. 1 75
———— Life. By Lord Sheffield. '37. Lon. 8vo 14s.
Gifford, W. (Critic) ; Autobiog. Lond...18mo 3s. 6d.
Gladstone. W. E. By McGilchrist........16mo N. Y. 50
Goethe ; Characteristics of. By Mrs. Aus-
        ten, 3 vols.....12mo Lond.

b.	—— Life. By G. H. Lewes.........	8vo	Lond.	$8 00
	—— Autobiography. Translated by			
	Godwin, etc., 2 vols....12mo	N. Y.		
	—— —— Trans. by Oxenford, 2 v.		Lond.	3 50
b.	Goldsmith. By John Forster. Illus. 2 v. 8vo		Lond.	5 00
a.	—————— By Irving. 16mo, $1.25 & $1.75.12mo	N. Y.		2 25
	—————— By Prior, 2 vols. 1837. Lond. 8vo 21s.			
	Goodrich, S. G. (Peter Parley) Recollec-			
	tions, 2 vols....12mo	N. Y.		3 50
	Gough, J. B. (Autobiography)...........	8vo	Lond.	3 25
	Grammont, Count. By Hamilton........12mo		Lond.	1 75
b.	Grant, U. S., Prest. By Gen. Badeau, 1 v. 8vo		N. Y.	4 00
	—— —— —— By Richardson......	8vo	N. Y.	
	Grattan, Henry (Irish Orator). By his son.			
	5 vols. London....	8vo	70s.	
	Greeley, Horace. Recollec. of Busy Life. 8vo		N. Y.	4 00
b.	—— —— Life. By Parton.........	8vo	Bost.	3 00
b.	Greene, Gen. Nath'l. By G. W. Greene,			
	3 vols....	8vo	N. Y.	12 00
	—— By Johnson and by Caldwell, o. p.			
	Greenough, Horatio. By Tuckerman, 1853.12mo	N. Y.		
	Gresham, Sir Thos. By McFarland. Lon.12mo 1s. 6d.			
	Gustavus Adolphus. By Chapman. Lon. 8vo 5s.			
	—— —— By Harte. 1767. 2 vols. 8vo		Lond.	
	Guyon, Madame. By Upham. 2 vols...12mo	N. Y.		3 00
	Guizot. Memoirs of a Minister of State.			
	London....	8vo	14s.	
b.	Hall, Rev. Robt. By Dr. Gregory........12mo	Lond.		1 75
	Hamilton, Alex. By J. C. Hamilton. 1840.			
	2 vols....	8vo	N. Y.	
	—— —— By Renwick.............18mo	N. Y.		75
	—————— Rev. J. By Arnot........s.....12mo	N. Y.		2 50
	—————— Sir Wm. By Veitch.........	8vo	Edinb.	
	—— —— Life and Remains, 2 vols.			
	London....12mo	10s.		
b.	Hampden and his Times. By Lord Nugent.12mo	Lond.		2 25
	Handel (musician). By Schoelcher..·.....12mo	N. Y.		2 50
a.	Hannibal. By Arnold (?) By J. Abbott...16mo	N. Y.		1 20
	Harrison, Prest., W. H. 1840...........18mo	N. Y.		
	Hastings, Warren. By Gleig. 3 vols. Lon. 8vo 30s.			
	—— By Macaulay. [See his Essays.]			
	Hatton, Sir Christ. By H. Nicolas. Lond. 8vo 15s.			
a.	Havelock, Gen. By Brock.........·. ...18mo	N. Y.		75
	—— —— By Headley............12mo	N. Y.		1 50
	Haydon, R. B. (artist.) Autobiography.			
	1853. 2 vols....	8vo	N. Y.	3 00
	Hazlitt, Wm. (Essayist.) By his son. 2 vols. 8vo		Lond.	6 00
	—— —— Literary Remains, 2 vols. Lon. 8vo 13s. 6d.			
	Heber, Bishop. By his widow. 1830. 2 vols. 4to		Lond.	
a.	Henry, Patrick. By Wirt..............·...	8vo	Phila.	1 50
	Henry V. of England. By Towle........	8vo	N. Y.	2 50
b.	Henry IV. of France. By James. 2 vols.12mo	N. Y.		3 00

b. Henry IV. Memoirs. By Sully, 4 vols..12mo Lond. $7 00
    Hill, Rowland. By Jones......Lond....12mo 4s.
b. Hood, Thos. Memorials. By his son, 2 vols.12mo Bost.   3 00
    Hook, Theo. By Barham, 2 vols. Lond. 8vo 21s.
    Howard, J. (Philanthropist.) By W. H.
                  Dixon. Lond....16mo 2s. 6d.
    Holbein, Hans (Painter). By Wornum.
                  Illus. R. 8vo Lond.   9 00
    Hughes, Archb. of N. Y. By Hassard.... 8vo N. Y.   3 00
    Hugo, Victor. By his son...............12mo N. Y.   1 75
b. Humboldt, Baron Alex. By Stoddard ...12mo N. Y.   1 50
    ———— A. & W. By Klincke & Schlesier.12mo N. Y.   1 50
    Hume, David. Autobiography. Lond...18mo 3s. 6d.
b. Hunt, Leigh. Autobiography, 2 vols.....12mo N. Y.   3 00
    ———— 16mo Phila.   1 25
    Huntington, Lady. Life and Times, 2 vols.
                  Lond.... 8vo 14s.
b. Hutchinson, Col. By his wife..........12mo Lond.   1 75
    Huss, John. By E. H. Gillett, 2 vols.... 8vo Bost.   7 00
    Inchbald, Mrs. (Dramatist.) Mem. & Corr.,
                2 vols. Lond.... 8vo 28s.
    Irving, Washington. By his nephew, 4 vols.12mo N. Y.   9 00
a. ———— Condensed, 3 vols., $3.75 ; 3 vols.12mo   6 75
b. Irving, Edward, Rev. By Mrs. Olyphant,
                2 vols....12mo N. Y.   3 50
    Jackson, Andrew. By Cobbett..........18mo N. Y.   75
    ———— ———— By Walker..........12mo Phila.   1 75
b. ———— ———— By Parton, 3 vols..... 8vo N. Y.   9 00
    Jackson, "Stonewall." By J. E. Cooke... 8vo N. Y.
    ———— ———— By Dabney........ 8vo N. Y.
    Jay, John (Ch'f Justice). By W. Jay, 2 vols. 8vo N. Y.
    ———— —— By Hamilton and Renwick.....18mo N. Y.   75
    Jefferson, Thos. Autobiog. 1830. 4 vols. 8vo Bost.
    ———— —— Life. By Randall, 3 vols. 8vo Phila.   10 00
    ———— —— By Tucker. 1853. 2 vols. 8vo Phila.
a. ———— —— By Randolph .... 8vo N. Y.   2 50
    ———— —— Domestic Life. Illus..... 8vo N. Y.   2 50
    ———— —— Character of. By Dwight. 8vo N. Y.   2 50
    ———— —— Observations on. By Lee. 1833.
    Jeffrey, Lord (Critic). By Cockburn. 1853.
              2 vols. 8vo Phila. ; 2 vols., Lond., 25s.
    Jerdan, W. Autobiography. 4 vols. Lond.12mo 20s.
    Jerrold, Douglas. By W. B. Jerrold..... 8vo Lond.   12 00
    Jewell, Bishop. By Le Bas. Lond......12mo 6s.
    Joan of Arc. By Michelet... ....18mo N. Y.   1 00
    Johnson, Dr. By Boswell. 2 vols....... 8vo N. Y.   4 00
b. ———— —— — ———— 4 vols......12mo Lond.   5 00
a. ———— —— —— ———— Globe ed. 1 vol.12mo Lond.   1 75
    Jones, John Paul. By Mackenzie. 2 vols.12mo N. Y.   2 00
    Jones, Sir Wm. By Lord Teignmouth,
              2 vols. Lond.... 10s. 6d.
a. Josephine (Empress). By Abbott........16mo N. Y.   1 20

	Josephine, Empress. By Headley......12mo N. Y.	$1 25
	———————— ———— By Le Normand...12mo Phila.	1 75
b.	Judson, Dr. A. By Dr. Wayland.......12mo N. Y.	2 25
	———— The Three Mrs. Judsons. By Hartley....12mo Phila.	1 75
	Jung-Stilling. Autobiography.......... 8vo N. Y.	75
	Keats, the Poet. By Milnes.............12mo N. Y.	
b.	Kane, E. K. By Dr. Elder............. 8vo Phila.	1 50
	———— ———— By Smucker.............12mo Phila.	1 75
	Keble, J. By Sir J. T. Coleridge, 2 vols..12mo N. Y.	4 00
	Knox, John. By McCrie...............	
	Kossuth.................................12mo Bohn.	1 75
	La Fayette. Mem. and Corresp. 3 v. Lon. 8vo 42s.	
	Lamb, Chas. By " Barry Cornwall."....16mo Bost.	1 75
a.	———— ———— Life and Works. By Talfourd, 2 vols.... N. Y.	3 00
b.	Landor, W. Savage. By Forster........ 8vo Bost.	3 50
	Larochejacquelin. Memoirs.............18mo Lond.	
	Latimer, Hugh ....Relig. Tract Soc.	
	Laud, Archb. By Le Bas..... Lond.*o. p.*12mo 6s.	
	Law, John. By Thiers (?)..............	
b.	Lawrence, Amos. Diary and Correspon..12mo Bost.	1 75
	Las Casas, Apostle to Indies. By Helps..12mo Lond.	2 75
	Ledyard (the Traveller). By Sparks.....12mo (In American Biography.)	
	Lee, Gen. Chas; Memoirs.	
	Leibnitz. By Mackie..................18mo Bost.	
a.	Leo X. (Pope). By Roscoe, 2 v. 12mo $3.50. 8vo Lond.	6 00
b.	Leslie, Chas. R. (Artist). By his sister...12mo Bost.	2 00
	Lessing, G. E.; Life and Works. By E. P. Evans, 2 vols.... 8vo Bost.	5 00
	Lincoln, Abm. By Raymond............ 8vo N. Y.	1 50
b.	———— ———— By Arnold.............. 8vo Chicag.	3 00
	———— Six Months at White House. By Carpenter....18mo N. Y.	1 50
	Livingston, Edw. By C. H. Hunt .... 8vo N. Y.	4 00
	Livingston, Wm. By Sedgwick.....*o. p.* 8vo N. Y.	
	Locke, John. By Lord King..........12mo Lond.	1 75
	Longueville, Mad. de. By Cousin.......16mo N. Y.	1 25
b.	Louis XIV. By James.................12mo Lond.	1 75
	———— ———— By Miss Pardoe, 2 vols.....12mo N. Y.	4 00
	———— XVII. By Beauchesne, 2 vols.....12mo N. Y.	4 00
	Loyola and Jesuitism. By J. Taylor. Lon.12mo 5s.	
	Luther. By Bunsen...................18mo N. Y.	1 00
	———— By Mrs. Lee. 1839.............16mo Bost.	
b.	———— By Michelet....................12mo Lond.	1 75
	———— By Worsley, 2 vols............. 8vo Lond.	6 00
	Lyndhurst, Lord, & Brougham. By Campbell.... 8vo Lond.	
	McClellan, Gen. By Geo. S. Hillard.....12mo Phila.	1 25
	Madison, Jas. By W. C. Rives, 3 vols.... 8vo Bost.	10 50
b.	Mann, Horace. By Mrs. Mann.......... 8vo Bost.	3 00

a. Marie Antoinette. By Abbott...........16mo N. Y. $1 20
—— ——— By Madam Campan...12mo Phila. 1 75
Marion, Gen. By W. G. Simms...... ...12mo N. Y. 1 50
—— —— By Hartley...............12mo Phila. 1 75
Marlborough, Duke of. By Alison.......12mo N. Y. 1 75
——————— ——— By Coxe, 3 vols..12mo Lond. 5 25
——————— Duchess of. By Mrs. Thomp-
son, 2 vols..... 8vo Lond.
Mary, Queen of Scots. By Miss Benger, 2 v.12mo Phila.
a. —— ——— —— By Bell. 2 vols.....18mo N. Y, 1 50
—— ——— —— By Meline........ 8vo Lond. 1 75
—— ——— —— By Mignet, 2 vols..
London.... 8vo 6s.
—— ——— —— By
Mary de Medici. "By Miss Pardoe.
Mathew, Father. By McGuire ....12mo N. Y.
Matthias, the Impostor. By W. L. Stone. '34.18mo N. Y.
Mathews, Charles (Actor). By Mrs.
Mathews, 4 vols....12mo Phila.
——————— ——— By Yates...........12mo Lond. 1 25
a. Medici, Lorenzo de. By Roscoe..........12mo Lond. 1 75
—— ——— — fine ed............ 8vo Lond. 3 50
—— Marie de. By Miss Pardoe, 3 vols. 8vo Lond.
Mendelssohn (Composer). By Lampading.12mo Lond. 1 75
——————— —— By Devrient. London. 8vo 10s. 6d.
——————— —— By Polko...........12mo N. Y. 1 75
Michel Angelo & Raphael. By Duppa, &c.12mo Lond. 2 50
—— ——— (see Angelo).
Millburn, Rev. W. H.; Ten Years of
Preacher's Life....12mo N. Y.
Milton, John. By Ivimey. London..... 8vo 10s.
—— —— By Keightley. London.. 8vo 10s. 6d.
b. —— —— By Masson, 1 vol. ...... 8vo Bost. 3 50
—— —— By Todd................ 8vo Lond. 3 00
Mirabeau. By Dumont. London........ 8vo 10s. 6d.
—— Memoirs. 1838, 4 vols.... .. 8vo Lond.
b. Mitford, Mary; Recollections of Lit. Life.12mo N. Y. 1 50
—— —— Memoirs. By L'Estrange, 2v.12mo N. Y. 3 50
a. Miller, Hugh; My Schools and School Mast.12mo Bost. 1 75
—— —— Life. By
Mohammed. By Geo. Bush..... ....18mo N. Y. 75
a. —— By Irving, 2 v. 16mo $2.50, 2 v.12mo N. Y. 4 50
—— By Muir, 4 vols. London.... 8vo 42s.
Monk, Gen. By Guizot................12mo Lond. 1 75
Montrose, Marquis of. By Napier, 2 vols.
London.... 8vo 36s.
Montaigne. By St. John, 2 vols. London.12mo 21s.
More, Sir Thomas. By Roper........... 8vo Lond.
More, Hannah. By Knight............18mo Lond.
b. —— —— Life and Corresp. 2 vols. ..12mo N. Y. 3 50
Moore, Thomas (Poet). By Russell, 1 vol. 8vo Lond.
Montgomery, James. By Holland, etc. 2 v. Lond.

Montgomery, James. By Mrs. Knight....12mo Bost. $1 50
Mowatt, Anna Cora ; Autobiography......12mo Bost.
Mozart, Anna. By Rau................12mo N. Y. 1 75
—— By Holmes...................12mo N. Y. 1 00
Munden (Actor) ; Memoirs.............. 8vo Lond. 2 75
Napier, Sir C. J. By his son, 4 vols. Lond.   48s.
b. Napoleon I. By J. S. C. Abbott, 2 vols... 8vo N. Y. 10 00
—— at St. Helena. By Abbott. Illus. 8vo N. Y 5 00
—— By Duchess d'Abrantes, 2 vols. 8vo N. Y. 5 00
a. —— By Lockhart, 2 vols..........18mo N. Y. 1 50
—— By Antomarchi, 2 vols.. Lond. 8vo 16s.
—— By Bourrienne, 4 vols. Edinb.16mo 14s.
—— By Hazlitt, 4 vols., Lond ; 3 v.12mo Phila. 3 75
—— By Jomini (Military), 4 vols.... 8vo N. Y. 25 00
b. —— By Sir Walter Scott, 5 v. Lond. 8vo 20s.
b. —— at St. Helena. By Las Casas. 4 v.12mo N. Y. 6 00
—— Voice from St. Helena. By
                  O'Meara, 2 vols....12mo N. Y. 4 00
—— Life. By Laurent del 'Ardeche. 8vo N. Y. 3 00
Napoleon III. By J. S. C. Abbott........ 8vo Hartf. 5 00
Neal, Jno.   Autobiography............12mo N. Y. 2 00
a. Nelson, Lord. By Southey.............18mo N. Y.   75
a. Newton, Sir Isaac. By Brewster ....18mo N. Y.   75
Niebuhr (Historian). By Chev. Bunsen.12mo N. Y. 1 50
Nollekens (Sculptor). By Smith..o. p. 2 v. 8vo Lond.
Northcote (Painter). By Hazlitt..   do. 8vo Lond.
O'Connell, Daniel. By Daunt.....2 vols. 8vo Lond.
Oglethorpe, Gen. By Rob. Wright......12mo Lond. 3 50
Ossoli, Margaret Fuller, March. d', By
                  Emerson, 2 vols....12mo Bost.
Otis, James. By Tudor. 1823........ 8vo Bost.
Opie, Amelia. By Brightwell. Lond....12mo 2s. 6d.
Palissy, B. ("The Potter.") By Morley...12mo Lond. 2 25
Palmerston, Lord. By Bulwer, 2 vols... 8vo L. & P. 5 00
———— By McGilchrist......18mo N. Y.   50
Paine, Thos. By G. Vail .... 8vo N. Y.
Parker, Theo. By Weiss, 2 vols......... 8vo N. Y. 6 00
Paulding, J. K. By his son. ....12mo N. Y. 2 50
Paul, St. By Renan.... ....12mo N. Y. 1 50
b. —— By Conybeare & Howison...... 8vo N. Y. 3 00
Pascal, Blaise. Convent Life at Port Royal.12mo N. Y.
b. Pellico, Silvio. Imprisonments. By Sar-
                  gent....12mo Bost. 1 75
Penn, Wm. By W. H. Dixon..........12mo Phila.
—— —— By Macaulay (in his works).
—— —— By Janney............... 8vo Phila.
a. Pepys, Sam'l. Diary and Correspondence.12mo L. & N. 2 50
Peel, Sir Robt. Life and Times. By Tay-
                  lor, 4 vols. Lond.   42s.
Perceval, J. G. (Poet.) By Ward, 2 vols. .12mo Bost. 3 00
Perry, Commodore. By Mackenzie, 2 vols.18mo N. Y. 1 50
Perthes, Fred'k. By C. F. Perthes. Edinb.12mo 6s.

a.	Peter the Great. By Barrow...........18mo N. Y.	**$** 75
	—— —— By Voltaire. Lond....12mo 6s.	
	Petrarch. By Thos. Campbell. Lond.... 8vo 16s.	
	Petigru, J. L., Life of. By W. J. Grayson.12mo N. Y.	1 50
	Pfeiffer, Ida. Autobiography and Travels.12mo N. Y.	1 50
	Phillidor (Chess Player). By Allen...... 8vo Phila.	
	Philip II. (of Spain.) By Chas. Gayarré. 8vo N. Y.	3 00
b.	Philip II. (of Spain). By Prescott, 3 vols. 8vo Phila.	7 50
	—— III. —— By Watson. Lond. 8vo 8s.	
	Pickering, Timothy. By...........1 vol. 8vo Bost.	3 50
	Pierce, F. (Prest.). By Hawthorne.......12mo Bost.	75
	Pinckney, Wm. By Wheaton (Sparks, American Biography)....	
	Pitt, Wm. By Macaulay...............18mo N. Y.	1 00
	—— —— By Earl Stanhope, 4 v. Lond. 8vo 42s.	
	Pizarro. By Arthur Helps.............. 8vo L. & P.	2 75
	Pocahontas. By Rev. E. D. Neill........12mo Alb.	1 00
	Porson, Rich'd. By Watson............ 8vo Lond.	3 75
	Prentiss, S. S. By G. L. Prentiss, 2 vols..12mo N. Y.	3 50
b.	Prescott, Wm. H.(Historian). By Ticknor.12mo Bost.	2 00
	Pugin, A. W. & A. M.; Recollections. By Ferry. London.... 8vo 7s. 6d.	
	Pulzsky, Theresa. By herself, 2 vols. Lond.12mo 12s.	
	Potter, A.(Bp. of Pa.). By Rev. Dr. Howe. 8vo Phila.	3 00
b.	Quincy, Josiah. By Edmund Quincey.... 8vo Bost.	3 00
	Quitman, Gen. By Claiborne, 2 vols.....12mo N. Y.	3 50
	Raikes, T.; Journal, 2 vols. London..... 8vo 12s.	
	Raleigh, Sir Walter. By Edwards, 2 vols. 8vo Lond.	9 00
	—— — —— By Kingsley..... 12mo Bost.	1 75
	—— — —— By St. John, 2 vols. London....16mo 10s. 6d.	
	—— — —— By Mrs. Thompson. London....12mo 2s. 6d.	
	Randolph, John. By Garland, 2 vols.... 8vo N. Y.	3 00
	Raphael & Michel Angelo. By Duppa...12mo Lond.	2 50
	Red Jacket (Indian Chief). By W. L. Stone. 8vo Alb'y.	5 00
b.	Recamier, Madame. By Luyster........12mo Bost.	2 00
	Reed, Joseph, Gen. (Sparks' Amer. Biog.)	
	Rembrandt. By John Burnet. Lond ... 4to 12s.	
	Retz, Cardinal de. Memoirs, 4 vols......12mo Lond.	
	Reynolds, Sir Joshua. By Leslie........ 8vo Lond.	
	—— —— By Northcote, 2 v. Lond. 8vo 21s.	
	Richelieu, Cardinal. By Robson. Lond..12mo 5s.	
	Richter, Jean Paul. By himself. Lond..12mo 7s. 6d.	
	—— —— —— By Lee........... 12mo Bost.	
	Riedesel, Baroness. By W. L. Stone..... 8vo Alb'y.	3 00
	Ritter, Carl. By W. L. Gage............12mo N. Y.	2 00
b.	Robertson, F. W. Life and Letters......12mo Bost.	2 00
	—— —— —— ......12mo N. Y.	1 50
	Robespierre. By Lewes........Lond....12mo 9s.	
b.	Robinson, H. Crabbe. Diary, 2 vols......12mo Bost.	4 00
	Rogers, Samuel (Poet). Recollections....12mo N. Y.	1 50

b. Roland, Madame. By Abbott...........16mo N. Y. $1 20
——— ——— By Mrs. Child........12mo N. Y. 1 50
Romilly, Sir J. Autobiography, 2 v. Lon.12mo 12s.
Rossini (Composer). By Edwards........12mo N. Y. 1 75
Rosseau. Confessions. Abridged. Lond. 12mo 2s. 3d.
Rosseau. Confessions. Illustrated......12mo Lond. 3 00
Rubens, Peter Paul. By Waagen. Lond.12mo 6s.
Russell, Lord Wm. By Earl Russell. Lond.12mo 5s.
Salvator Rosa. By Lady Morgan........ 8vo Lond. 1 25
Savanorola. Life and Times. 1843. Lond.12mo 6s. 6d.
Schæffer, Ary. By Mrs. Grote. Lond... 8vo 8s. 6d.
b. Schiller. By Carlyle. 16mo. Lond., 90cts.12mo Bost.
Schimmelpenick, Mrs. Life and Letters.
London....12mo 10s. 6d.
Schleirmacker. Reminiscences, 2 vols.12mo Edinb. 21s.
Scott, Sir Walter. By Chambers, 2 vols. 8vo 21s.
——— ——— By Gilfillan.........12mo Lond. 1 25
b. ——— ——— By Lockhart, 9 vols..12mo Bost. 11 25
——— ——— By McLeod..........12mo N. Y. 1 25
a. ——— ——— By Mackenzie.... ...12mo Bost. 2 00
Scott, Gen. Winfield. Autobiography, 2 v.12mo N. Y. 4 00
——— ——— ——— By Headley.......12mo N. Y. 1 00
——— ——— ——— By Mansfield.. ...12mo N. Y. 1 75
Schuyler, Gen. Philip. By Lossing.....12mo N. Y. 2 50
Seaton, W. W. By his Daughter........12mo Bost. 2 00
Seward, W. H. By G. E. Baker........12mo N. Y. 1 50
Sedgewick, Miss C. M. By Mary E. Dewey.12mo N. Y. 2 00
Shakespeare. By Chas. Knight.........8vo Lond.
b. ——— By Grant White......... 8vo Bost. 2 50
——— and his times. By Guizot.12mo N. Y. 1 50
Shaftesbury, Earl of. By Martin, 2 v. Lond. 8vo 28s.
Shelley ; Memorials of. London.........12mo 5s.
——— Life and Works. By Rosetti...12mo Lond. 1 75
b. Sheridan, R. Brinsley. By Moore, 2 vols.12mo N. Y. 3 00
Siddons, Mrs. By Thos. Campbell. • 1834.12mo N. Y.
Sidney, Sir Philip ; Life and times......12mo Bost.
——— — ——— H. F. Bourne....... 8vo Lond. 3 50
——— Algernon. By Van Santvoord.....12mo N. Y. 1 00
Silliman, Benj. By Geo. P. Fisher, 2 v.12mo N. Y. 5 00
Smith, Capt. John. By G. S. Hillard. ...12mo N. Y. 1 25
——— — By Simms.........12mo Phila. 1 75
——— Sidney. By Lady Holland, 2 vols.12mo N. Y. 3 00
——— Sol.; Thirty Years' Theatricals... 8vo N. Y.
Sobieski, J. By Palmer.
b. Socrates. By Grote....................18mo N. Y. 1 00
Southey, Robt. ; and Correspondence..... 8vo N. Y. 2 00
Spring, Gardiner ; Personal Reminis., 2 v.12mo N. Y. 4 00
St. Augustine. By Bailey..............16mo N. Y. 1 25
St. Paul ; Continuous History. By Tait..12mo Lond. 3 00
St. Simon, Duke de. Memoirs, 4 v. Lond.12mo 42s.
b. Sterling, John. By Carlyle............16mo Lond. 90
Stephenson George. By Smiles........12mo Bost. 1 50

Story, Judge. By W. W. Story, 2 vols.... 8vo Bost. $5 00
b. Steuben, Baron. By Fredk. Kapp....... 8vo N. Y. 3 00
——— ——— (Sparks' American Biography).
Stirling, Lord. By Duer................ 8vo N. Y.
Swetchine, Madame. By Falloux........12mo Bost. 2 00
Swedenborg, E. By White...... .... 8vo L. & P. 5 00
——— — — ....12mo Phila. 1 50
Swift, Jona. By Scott (see his Works).
Talleyrand. By McHarg. 1857.........12mo N. Y
Tasso. By Millman, 2 vols. London....12mo 12s.
Tappan, Arthur. By L. Tappan.........12mo N. Y. 2 00
Telford, Thos. (Engineer). By Smiles....12mo L. & P. 3 00
Thackeray, Wm. M. By Yates.......... 8vo N. Y.
b. ——— — — By Theo. Taylor...12mo N. Y. 1 00
Titian. By Northcote, 2 vols. London.. 8vo 21s.
Tocqueville, A dé. By Beaumont, 2 vols.12mo Bost. 3 00
Toussaint l'Ouverture. By Redpath. 12mo Bost.
Thorwaldsen. By J. N. Thiele...........12mo N. Y.
Trenck, Baron. London................12mo 6s.
Trumbull, John; Reminiscences......... 8vo N. Y. 3 00
——— — Jona. By Stuart........ 8vo Bost.
Turner, J. W. M. By W. Thornbury, 2 v.
London.... 8vo 30s.
Velasquez. By Sterling. London.......12mo 5s.
Vespuccius, Americus. By Sartorius....16mo Bost.
Vidocq; Memoirs. By himself, 4 vols..16mo Lond.
Vittoria Colonna. By Roscoe......... 12mo Lond. 3 00
Voltaire. By Bungener. Edinburgh....12mo 5s.
Warren, Gen. Jos.; Life and Times. By
Frothingham.... 8vo Bost. 3 50
Walpole, Horace. By Coxe, 2 v. Lond. 8vo 25s.
Ware J. By H. Ware, Jr.
a. Washington, Geo. By Irving, 5 vols.....12mo N. Y. 11 25
——— ——— ——— 5 v. $6.25, 1 v. r.8vo N. Y. 5 00
——— ——— ——— Condensed,1 vol.12mo N. Y. 2 50
——— ——— ——— By Everett.........12mo N. Y. 1 50
——— ——— ——— By Guizot. 1840....16mo Bost.
——— ——— ——— By Marshall, 3 vols.. 8vo Phila.
——— ——— ——— By Paulding,2 vols..18mo N. Y. 1 50
b. ——— ——— ——— and Writings. By
Sparks, 12 vols. 8vo Bost. 24 00
b. Wayland, Dr. F. Life and Labors. By
his sons, 2 vols. N. Y. 4 00
Watt. Jas. By Muirhead.............. 12mo N. Y. 2 00
——— ——— .... 8vo Lond. 3 00
b. Webster, Daniel. By G. T. Curtis, 2 vols. 8vo N. Y. 10 00
——— ——— By his son, 2 vols...... 8vo Bost. 7 50
——— ——— By Lanman...........12mo N. Y. 1 25
——— ——— By C. W. Marsh....12mo N. Y. 1 50
Wedgewood, "the Potter." By Meteyard,
2 vols.... 8vo Lond. 12 00
——————————————— By Jewett... 8vo Lond. 8 00

Wellington, Duke of. By Brialmont &
    Gleig. Lond.... 8vo 15s.
———————— By Maxwell, 3 vols. Lon. 8vo 27s.
———————— By Stocqueler, 2 v. Lon. 8vo 12s.
a. Wesley, Chas. By Southey, 2 vols......12mo N. Y. $2 50
———— ———— By Janes...............12mo N. Y. 1 50
———— ———— By Wakeley...........12mo N. Y. 1 25
———— ———— By Watson............12mo N. Y. 1 25
———— ———— By Jackson............ 8vo N. Y. 2 70
Whately, Archb. By Miss Whately, 2 v.Lon. 15s.
———————— Life and Correspond.. 8vo Lond. 3 75
Whitefield, Rev. Geo. By Gillies. Lon. 8vo 7s.
———————— ———————— By Gledstone.... 8vo Lond.
———————— ———————— By Harsha.......
u. Wiclif. By Le Bas.....................18mo N. Y. 75
Wilberforce, Wm. By his sons, 5 v. Lon. 8vo 21s.
——————— ——————— abridged.18mo N. Y. 75
Wilkie, Sir David. By Cunningham, 3 v. 8vo Lond. 7 50
Williams, Roger. By Prof. Gammell....12mo Bost. 1 25
Wilson, Alex. (Sparks' Amer. Biography.)
b. Wirt, Wm. By John P. Kennedy, 2 vols.12mo N. Y. 4 00
Wordsworth, Wm. By Rev. C. Words-
    worth, 2 vols....12mo N. Y. 2 50
Worcester, Marquis of. By H. Dircks... 8vo Lond. 4 50
Wraxall, Sir Nath. Memoirs of his own
    Times....*o. p.* 8vo Phila.
Xavier, F., ("Apostle to the Indies.") By
    H. Venn. Lond.... 8vo 7s.
Ximenes, Cardinal. By B. Barrett. Lond. 8vo 9s.

Birds.—[*See Cage Birds : Ornithology.*]

Bokhara and the Indus. By A. Burnes. Lon. 8vo 18s.

Book Binding.

a. Art of Book Binding. By J. B. Nicholson.12mo Phila. 2 25
Art of Book Binding. By J. Hannett. Lon.12mo 6s.
Ornamental Book Binding. By Jos. Cun-
    dall. Lond.... 4to 15s.

Book Keeping.

Bryant & Stratton. Counting-house Book
    Keeping.... 8vo N. Y. 3 75
Crittenden, S.W. Induct. & Practical ——— 8vo Phila. 2 75
. Duff, P. Book Keeping .... 8vo N. Y. 3 75
Marsh, C. C. Theory and Practice of Book
    Keeping ... 8vo N. Y. 6 00
Jones. Practical Book Keeping........... 8vo N. Y. 2 50

Borneo.

Brooke. Rajah : Narrative of Events in
    Borneo, 2 vols. Lond.... 32s.
——— Ten Years in Sarawak, 2 vols..12mo Lond.
a. Keppel. Expedition to Borneo. 1846...12mo N. Y. 1 00

Botany.

	Chapman. Flora of Southern U. S. Illus. 8vo	N. Y.	$3 60
b.	Figuier. The Vegetable World. Illus.. 8vo	Lond.	4 50
a.	Gray, Prof. Asa. Botanical Text Book... 8vo	N. Y.	3 50
a.	—— —— First Lessons in Botany.....12mo	N. Y.	1 30
	—— —— Genera of Plants of North America, 2 vols., *o. p.* 8vo	N. Y.	
a.	—— —— How Plants Grow.........12mo	N. Y.	1 12
a.	—— —— Man'l of Botany of N. States. 8vo	N. Y.	2 25
	—— —— —— with Mosses, etc. 8vo	N. Y.	3 75
b.	—— —— Structural and Syst. Botany. 8vo	N. Y.	3 50
	Grindon, L. H. Phenomena of Plant Life.12mo	Bost.	1 00
	Karr, Alph. Tour round my Garden.... 8vo	Lond.	2 50
b.	Lindley, Prof. J. Vegetable Kingdom... 8vo	Lon.	36s.
	—— & Moore. Treasury of Botany, 2 v.18mo	N. Y.	7 00
b.	Loudon. Enclyclo. of Plants. Lond.... 8vo		73s. 6d.
	—— Cyclo. of Shrubs and Trees, thick 8vo	Lond.	15 00
	—— Mrs., Gardening for Ladies......12mo	N. Y.	2 00
b.	Maunder. Treasury of Botany..........18mo	N. Y.	4 00
b.	Michaux & Nuttall. N. Amer. Sylva, 6 v. *r.* 8vo	Phila.	75 00
	Rhind. Hist. of the Vegetable Kingdom. 8vo	Lond.	4 50
a.	Youman, Miss. First Book of Botany...12mo	N. Y.	1 00

Brazil—AND THE AMAZON.

a.	Agassiz, Prof. & Mrs. Journey in Brazil. 8vo	Bost.	5 00
	Bates. 11 Years of a Naturalist on Amaz. 8vo	Lond.	6 00
	Burton, Capt. Explor. of the Highlands of Brazil, 2 vols.... 8vo	Lond.	15 00
	Codman, J. Ten Months in Brazil. Lond.12mo		5s.
b.	Ewbank. Brazil. Illustrated.......... 8vo	N. Y.	3 00
a.	Fletcher & Kidder. Hist. of Brazil...... 8vo	Bost.	4 50
	Gardner. Travels in Interior of Brazil... 8vo	Lond.	3 75
b.	Hartt, C. F. Geology and Phys. Geog. of Brazil.... 8vo	Bost.	5 00
	Herndon & Gibbon. Exploration of the Amazon, 3 vols.... 8vo	Wash.	2 50
	Orton. The Andes and the Amazon..... 8vo	N. Y.	2 00
	Southey. Hist. of Brazil. 1810. 3 v. Lon. 4to		155s.
	Wallace, A. R. The Amazon and Rio Negro. 1870. Lond. 8vo		12s.

British America.—[*See Canada, Nova Scotia, British Columbia.*]

Waddington, A. Overland Route through British America. Lond. 8vo 1s.

British Columbia.

Leonard. Travels in Brit. Columbia. Lon. 8vo	14s.
Macfie. Vancouver's Island and British Columbia. 1865.... 8vo	**Lond.**
Rattray. Vancouver's Island and British Columbia. Lond.... 8vo	62s.

Buccaneers.

Burney, Admiral. Hist. of the Buccaneers. 4to Lond.
Thornbury. Monarchs of the Main. Lon. 8vo 5s.

Buddhism.

Hardy, R. S.; Legends and Theories of
                              Buddhists....16mo Lond.
Modern Buddhist. By a Siamese. Lond.12mo 3s. 6d.
Schlagintweit, Evan. Buddhism in Thibet. 8vo Leips.
Upham. History and Doctrines of Budd-
                              hism. London.... 8vo 21s.

Buenos Ayres.

Hutchenson. Buenos Ayres, etc. 1865... 8vo Lond.
Random Sketches of Buenos Ayres, 1865. 8vo Lond.

Burmah.

Crawford. Embassy to Court of Ava. '34.
                        2 vols. London.... 8vo 32s.
Cox. Residence in Burmah.
Gouger, H. Two Years' Imprisonment in
                        Burmah. London....12mo 12s.
Palmer, J. W. Up and down the Irawaddy.12mo N. Y.
Symes, Maj. Embassy to Ava. 1827. 2 v. 8vo Lond.

Business.—MORALS OF—PRINCIPLES, ETC.

   Chalmers, Thos. Christianity ap. to Com.12mo N. Y.
   Dewey, Orville. Morals of Trade.......12mo N. Y.
a. Freedley. Treatise on Business.........12mo Phila. $1 25
   Hillard, Geo. S. Dangers and Duties of
                        Mercantile Pursuits.......12mo Bost.   25
b. Medberry, J. R. Men and Manners of
                        Wall Street ...12mo Bost.   2 00

Business.—MANUALS OF—COMMERCIAL STATISTICS, ETC.

a. Anderson. Prac. Merc. Letter Writer.12mo N. Y.   1 25
   Colwell, J. Ways and Means of Payment;
                        Credit, etc.... 8vo Phila.   5 00
   Commercial Code of France.
   De Veitelle. Mercantile Dictionary......12mo N. Y.   2 00
   Francis. History of the Stock Exchange. 8vo N. Y.
   ——— History of the Bank of England. 8vo N. Y.   3 00
b. Homans. Cyclo. of Commerce..... .... 8vo N. Y.   7 50
b. McCulloch, J. R. Dicty. of Commerce.
                        New Edition.... 8vo Lond.   25 00
——————— ——— Treatise on Commerce.
                        1838. London.... 8vo 1s. 8d,
   Simmonds. Commercial Dictionary......12mo L. & N.   2 00

Cabul.—[*See Affghanistan.***]**

Cage Birds.

American Bird Fancier (Saxton).........18mo N. Y.

Avis. The Canary........ ....16mo N. Y. $ 50
b. Beckstein. Nat'l History of Cagd Birds.12mo Lond.   2 50
                  (Colored, $3.75.)

California.

Annals of San Francisco. By Soulége.... 8vo N. Y.   5 00
a. Brace, C. L. The New West: California
                          in 1869....12mo N. Y.   1 75
Capron. History of California..........12mo Bost.   1 00
Colton, W. 3 Years in California. 1850.12mo N. Y.   1 50
Farnham, T. J. Early Days of California.12mo Phil.   1 75
Forbes, Alex. History of California. 1839.
                          London.... 8vo 14s.
Greenhow, Robt. History of Oregon and
                   California. 1848.... 8vo Bost.   2 50
a. Hittett. Resources of California. 1867..12mo San F.   1 50
a. Taylor, Bayard. Eldorado: Mexico and
                   California. 1849–59....12mo N. Y.   1 50
Wood, D. B. Gold Diggings of California.12mo N. Y.   1 00
Geology of ; Publicat. of Geol. Survey, 7 vols., r. 8vo Bost.

Calisthenics.—[See Gymnastics.]

Canada.

Chesshyre, Canada in 1864. Lond......12mo 2s. 6d.
Copplestone, Mrs. Canada ; Why we live
                          there. Lond.... 8vo 2s. 6d.
Head, F. B. Forest Scenes in Canada....
——— ——— Emigrant in Canada. Lond. 8vo 2s. 6d.
Hogan. Prize Essay on Canada. Mont.. 8vo 5s.
King. Sportsman and Naturalist in Can. 8vo Lond.
Kohl, J. G. Travels in Canada......... 8vo Lond.   2 50
b. McMullen, J. History of Canada to 1867. 8vo L. & P.   3 50
Moodie, Mrs. Roughing it in the Bush..12mo N. Y.   1 25
——— Life in the Clearings. 1853. Lon.12mo 10s. 6d.
Morris, A. Canada and her Resources.
                          1855.... 8vo Montr.
a. Murray. Hist. Acc't of Brit. America, 2 v.12mo N. Y.   1 50
Patterson, W.J. Home and Foreign Trade
                   of Canada. Montreal.... 8vo 7s.
a. Thoreau./ A Yankee in Canada.........12mo Bost.   2 00
a. Warburton, E. Conquest of Canada, 2 v.12mo N. Y.   3 00

Capital Punishment.

a. Boyce, M. H. Christ and the Gallows..12mo N. Y.
Cheever, Geo. B. Defence of Cap. Punish.12mo N. Y.   50
Lewis, Tayler. Penalty of Death........12mo N. Y.

Cape Colony.—[See Africa—South.]

Carbonari.—-[See Secret Societies.]

Cards, Playing.

Chatto. History of Playing-Cards. Lon. 8vo 21s.
Taylor. History of Playing-Cards.......16mo Lond.

Caricatures.

Gilray. Caricatures, Political. hlf. moroc.folio Lond. $60 00
Leech. Sketches of Life and Character, 3 v.folio Lond. 30 00
Malcolm. History of Caricaturing......
Napoleon III.; Story of, as told by Popular
     Caricatures of 25 years.... 8vo Lond. 3 50
Punch, London. 30 vols..........Lond. 4to 210s.
Tenniel. Cartoons from Punch......... 4to Lond. 10 50
Wright. Caricature Hist. of the Georges.12mo Lond. 3 50

Carthage.

Davis. Carthage and its Remains........ 8vo N. Y. 4 00

Cattle.—[See Domestic Animals.]

Caucasus.—[See Circassia.]

Haxthausen. Trans-Caucasia. 1854. Lond. 8vo 18s.
———— Tribes of the Caucasus. Ln.12mo 5s.
a. Kennan, Geo. Georgia and the Caucasus.12mo N. Y.
Spencer. Travels in Western Caucasus..
    2 vols. London.... 8vo 28s.

Celibacy.

a. Lea, H. C. History of Sacerdotal Celibacy. 8vo Phila. 3 75

Ceylon.

Baker, S. W. Eight years in Ceylon. Lon. 8vo 15s.
Forbes. Eleven years in Ceylon, 2 v. Lon. 8vo 21s.
Hoffmeister. Travels in Ceylon. Edinb.12mo 10s.
Pridham. Hist. of Ceylon. 1849. 2 v. Lon. 8vo 28s.
Rifle and Hound in Ceylon. 1869........12mo Phila.
Tennent, J. E. History of Ceylon, 2 v. Lon. 8vo 50s.

Charities.

Camman and Camp. Charities of N.Y.'68. 8vo N. Y.
a. Church, P. Philoso. of Benevolence....12mo N. Y. 1 25
De Liefde. Charities of Europe. 1865. 2v.12mo Lond.
Howson. Deaconesses.................16mo Lond.
Jameson, Mrs. Sisters of Charity.......12mo Bost.
Jerrold, W. B. Signals of Distress. Lond.12mo 7s. 6d.
Kirkland, Mrs. The Helping Hand.......12mo N. Y.
a. Low. Charities of London. Lond.......16mo 3s. 6d.
Mayhew. Lond. Labor and Lond. Poor, 3 v. 8vo Lond. 7 50
Sieveking. Principles of Charitable Work.
     London....12mo 4s.
Stephens, Miss. Service of the Poor, Sis-
     terhoods, etc....12mo Lond. 2 25
Stollard, J. H. London Pauperism. Lon. 8vo 12s.

Chemistry.—GENERAL WORKS.

Day. Chem. in its Rela. to Physiology, etc. 8vo Lond. 3 75
Elliot & Storer. Manual of Inorganic Ch. 8vo N. Y. 2 75
Fownes. Manual of Chemistry. Lond...12mo 12s. 6d.
Gmelin. Hand Bk. of Chem., 15 v. Lond. 8vo £8 18s. 6d.

Graham. Elements of Chemistry, 2 vols. 8vo Lond. $10 00
Hoffman. Introduction to Chemistry.
Miller. Chemical Physics.............. 8vo N. Y.   4 00
——— Organ. and Inorgan. Chem., 2 vols. 8vo N. Y.   16 00
b. Muspratt, S. Chemistry; Theoretical, Prac-
        tical and Analytical, 2 vols....r. 8vo Lond.   20 00
Normandy. Chem. Atlas and Dic. Lond. 4to 28s.
Pynchon. The Chemical Forces, Heat, etc.12mo N. Y.   8 00
Stockhart. Agricultural Chemistry......12mo Bohn.   2 50
——— Principles of Chemistry.....12mo Bohn.   2 50
Stocquard. Manual of Chemistry........12mo Phila.   2 75
Silliman. Chemistry..................12mo N. Y.   2 00
Topham. Chem. Made Easy, for Farmers. Lond. 12mo, 2s.
b. Watt. Dictionary of Chemistry, 5 vols... 8vo Lond. 65 00
a. Wells. Principles of Chemistry.........12mo N. Y.   1 60
a. Youmans. Class Book of Chemistry.....12mo N. Y.   1 75
——— Chart of Chemistry, on roller.   N. Y.   8 00
——— Correlation of Forces........12mo N. Y.   2 00
₊ *Many School Text Books, not included in this list.*

Chemistry.—ANALYSIS.

Apjohn. Manual of Metalloids..........
Bloxam. Laboratory Teaching. Lond... 8vo 5s. 6d.
Bolley & Paul. Manual of Technical
        Analysis. London....12mo 5s.
a. Fresenius. Qualitative Anal. (by Johnson). 8vo N. Y.   4 50
a. ——— Quantitative ——— ——— 8vo N. Y.   6 00
Noad. Qual. and Quantitative Analysis.. 8vo N. Y.   6 00
Perkins. Qualitative Chemical Analysis.12mo N. Y.   1 00

Chemistry.—APPLIED.

Farraday. Lect. on Forces of Matter. Lon.16mo 3s. 6d.
a. ——— Chemistry of a Candle.......12mo N. Y.   1 00
Hassall. Food and its Adulterations.
        Sanitary Report. 1857. Lon.   28s.
a. Johnston. Chemistry of Common Life, 2 v.12mo N. Y.   3 00
a. Mace. History of a Mouthful of Bread..12mo N. Y.   1 75
Muspratt. Chemistry applied to Manu-
        factures, 2 vols....r. 8vo Lond.   20 00
Shaw. Chemistry of Pottery. 1837....r. 8vo Lond.
a. Youmans. Household Science..........12mo N. Y.   1 75

Chequers. —[*See Draughts.*]

Chess.

a. Agnell. ' Book of Chess ; a complete Guide.12mo N. Y.   2 50
American Chess Player's Hand Book.....
Hazeltine. Brevity & Brilliancy in Chess.12mo N. Y.   1 00
Healy. Collection of Chess Problems....12mo   2 00
Jaenisch, C. F. Chess Preceptor........ 8vo Lond.   3 00
Kenny. Manual of Chess for Beginners.18mo N. Y.   50
Lowenthal. Morphy's Games of Chess..12mo N. Y.   1 50
Morphy. Exploits and Triumphs in Eu-   ·
        rope in Chess....12mo N. Y.   1 25

a. Staunton. Chess Player's Hand Book...12mo Bohn. $2 50
——————— Chess Player's Companion....12mo Bohn.   2 50
——————— Chess Praxis.................12mo Bohn.   3 00
——————— Chess Player's Tournament..12mo Bohn.   2 50

Children's Health.—[*See Maternity.*]

Chili.

Gardiner. Chili Indians. 1841. Lond..12mo 6s.
Hunter, D. J. Chili. 1866.............. 8vo N.Y.
Molini. History of Chili................12mo N.Y.
Strain, J. G. Journey in Chili, etc. 1853.12mo N.Y.   1 00
Smith, E. R. Auracanians: Travels in Chili.12mo N.Y.   1 50

China—HISTORY, ETC.

China and Japan, Treaty Ports, Guide to. 8vo Lond.
b. Confucius and the Chinese Classics. By
                        Rev. A. W. Loomis.12mo N.Y.   2 00
a. Davis, J. F. History of China, 2 vols....18mo N.Y.   1 50
——— China during and after the War, 2 v.12mo N.Y.
b. Doolittle, Rev. J. Social Customs of the
                        Chinese, 2 vols....12mo N.Y.   5 00
Fortune. Tea Countries of China....... 8vo Lond.
Gutzlaff. Chinese History, 2 vols....... 8vo Lond.
——— China Opened, 2 vols....... ...Lond., 24s.
Martin, R. M. China, Political, etc., 2 v. Lon. 8vo 14s.
Medhurst. The Interior of China. Lond. 8vo 5s. 6d.
Olyphant. Mission of Lord Elgin to China.
                    2 vols. Lond.... 8vo 21s.
Thornton. History of China. Lond. ... 8vo 16s.
a. Williams, S. W. The Middle Kingdom;
                    History, etc., 2 vols....12mo   4 00
Williamson, Rev. A. Journeys in North
                    China, 2 vols. Lond.... 8vo 21s.

China—TRAVELS IN.

Conwell. Why the Chinese Emigrate...12mo Bost.   1 50
Downing. Stranger in China, 3 v. Lond. 8vo 21s.
Elgin, Lord. Mission to China & Japan, 2 v. 8vo Lond.
Forbes. Five Years in China. Lond.... 8vo 15s.
a. Huc. Journey through the Chinese Em-
                        pire, 2 vols....12mo N.Y.   4 00
Loch. Personal Narrative.............
Macaulay. Kathay. 1854.............12mo N.Y.   1 00
Nevins. China and the Chinese........12mo N.Y.   1 50
b. Olyphant, Lawrence. China and Japan.. 8vo N.Y.   3 50
Rennie. Pekin and the Pekinses, 2 vols.   Lond.
a. Smith, Rev. G. The Consular Cities of Ch.12mo N.Y.   1 50
Williams, Mrs. Year in China... ......12mo N.Y.   1 50

Chinese Rebellion, etc.

Callery & Yvan. Insurrection in China.'.12mo N.Y.   75
Meadows. · The Chinese and their Rebel-
                        lion. Lond.... 8vo 18s.

b. Tai Ping. The Chinese Rebellion. Illus.
2 vols....т. 8vo Lond. $8 00
Webster, G. J. War with China in 1860. 8vo Lond.

Chivalry.

Addison. History of Knights Templars.. 8vo Lond. 2 50
a. Bulfinch. The Age of Chivalry.........12mo Bost. 3 00
a. James, G. P. R. Chivalry and the Crusades.18mo N. Y. 75
b. Mill. History of Chivalry, scarce, 2 vols. 8vo Lond.
Vance. Romantic Episodes of Chivalric
and Mediæval France....12mo Lond.

Christ.

a. Abbott, Lyman. Life of Christ. Illus... 8vo N. Y. 3 50
Andrews, S. J. Life of our Lord......... 8vo N. Y. 3 00
a. Beecher, H. W. Life of Christ.......... 8vo N. Y. 3 50
Bushnell, Horace. Character of Jesus...12mo N. Y. 1 00
b. Crosby, Howard. Life of Jesus......... 8vo N. Y.
Ecce Deus Homo. The Work and King-
dom of Christ....12mo Phil. 1 50
Ellicott, C. J. Life of our Lord, Historical.12mo Bost. 1 75
Fleetwood, Rev. J. Life of Christ.......12mo Phil. 1 75
Hanna. Our Lord's Life on Earth, 6 v. in 3.12mo N. Y. 4 50
Liddon. The Divinity of our Lord....12mo Lond. 2 50
Neander. Life of Christ............... 8vo N. Y. 2 50
a. Parker, Jos. Ecce Deus: the Life and
Doctrine of Christ....18mo Bost. 1 50
Pressensé. Jesus Christ: His Life and
Work. Lond....12mo 5s.
Renan. Life of Jesus.................12mo N. Y. 1 50
a. Seeley, Prof. Ecce Homo.............18mo Bost. 1 50
Strauss. New Life of Jesus, 2 vols..... 8vo Lond.
Schaff, Ph. The Person of Christ—Reply
to Renan, etc....12mo N. Y. 1 25
Schleiermacher. Lectures on Life of Christ. 8vo
Schenkel. Character of Jesus Portrayed.
Trans. by Furness, 2 vols. 8vo Bost. 4 50
Townsend, Rev. L. T. The Divine Man. Lond.
Ulhorn. Mod. Represent. of Life of Jesus.16mo Bost. 1 00

Christianity.—[See also Church History, Devotion, Evidences of Christianity, Natural Theology, Science and Religion.]

Cocker. Christianity & Greek Philosophy. 8vo Lond. 2 75
Coleman, L. Ancient Christi. Exemplified. 8vo Phila. 2 50
Döllinger, Prof. First Age of Christianity
and the Church.... 8vo Lond. 6 25
Elliot. History of Early Christians..... 8vo Lond. 4 25
Farrar. Crit. History of Free Thought
in reference to Christianity.12mo N. Y. 2 00
Fisher, G. P. Supernatural Origin of
Christianity ... 8vo N. Y. 3 00

Grayson. True Theory of Christianity.16mo N. Y. $1 25
James. Christianity, the Logic of Creation.12mo   1 00
Keith.   Demonstration of Truth of Christ.12mo N. Y. 1 50
McCosh. Lectures on Christianity and
                       Positivism.... 8vo N. Y. 1 75
Marcy, E. E. Christi. and its Conflicts...12mo N.Y. 2 00
Miall. Memorials of Early Christianity.12mo Bost. 1 50
a. Millman. Hist. of Christianity. [See p. 55.] 8vo N. Y. 2 00
a. Pressensé. Early Christi. : Apostolic Era.12mo N. Y. 1 75
  —— —— —— The Apostles and
                        Martyrs....12mo N. Y. 1 75
Thompson, J. P. Theology of Christ....12mo N. Y. 2 00

Chronology.

Blair. Chronological Tables.............12mo Bohn 5 00
Haines, S. Synchronology............. 8vo Bost. 2 50
b. Haydn. Dictionary of Dates with Ameri-
               can Supplement ... 8vo L. & N. 9 00
  —— —————————— Condensed.... 8vo N. Y. 5 00
Nicolas, Sir H. Chronology of History... 16mo Lond.
a. Putnam. The World's Progress, a Dic-
               tionary of Dates....12mo N. Y. 3 50
Tegg. Dictionary of Chronology........12mo Lond. 2 00
Townsend. Manual of Dates........... 8vo Lond. 8 00

Church History.—[*See also Christianity, Missions, Monastic Orders, Reformation, Romanism.*]

a. Aubigne, J. H. Merle d'. History of the Reformation
           in the 16th Century. Illus.... 4to N. Y. 10 00
  —— The same, cheap edition.... 8vo Phila. 6 00
                   5 vols....12mo N. Y. 6 00
Bede. Ecclesiastical History. Trans....12mo Bohn 2 50
Bingham. Antiquities of the Christian
              Church, 2 vols....*r.* 8vo Lond. 11 00
Blunt. The Reformation of the Church
              of England.... 8vo Lond. 5 00
Bungener. Rome and the Council in the
             19th Century. Lond....12mo 5s.
  —— History of Council of Trent...12mo Lond. 8 00
  —— The Priest and Huguenot—Per-
              secutions time Louis XV..12mo Bost. 8 00
b. Burnet, Bp. History of the Reform., 7 v. 8vo 84s.
Butler, C. M. Ecclesiastical History. 1868. 8vo Phila.
Chillingworth. Religion of Protestants..12mo Bohn 1 75
Coleman, L. The Apostolic and Primitive
              Church.... 8vo Phila. 2 00
Dollinger, J. J. Heathenism and Judaism. 8vo Lond.
Dorner. Hist. of Protest. Theology, 2 v. 8vo Lond. 10 00
Elliot. Hist. of the Early Christians, 2 v. 8vo Lond. 4 50
Eusebius. Ecclesiastical History........12mo Bohn 2 50
Felt, J. B. Ecclesiastical History of New
              England, 2 vols.... 8vo Bost.

Giesler.   Ecclesiastical History, 4 vols.. 8vo N. Y. $9 00
Hagenbach.   History of Doctrines, 2 vols. 8vo N. Y.   6 00
————   History of the Church, 2 vols. 8vo N. Y.   6 00
Hardwick.   History of Christ. Church, 2 v. 8vo Lond.   5 00
Hase.   History of Christian Church...... 8vo N. Y.   3 50
Janus.   The Pope and the Council.......18mo Bost.   1 50
Jones.   History of the Church during
                                    Revolution.... 8vo N. Y.   3 50
King, C. W.   The Gnostics............
Krauth.   The Conservative Reformation
                            and its Theol.... 8vo Phil.   5 00
Lea, H. C.   Studies in Church History... 8vo Phil.   3 00
b. Merivale.   Conversion of the Northern
                                    Nations.   1866.... 8vo N. Y.   1 50
b. ————   Conversion of Roman Empire. 8vo N. Y.   1 50
a. Mosheim.   Eccles. History, 2 vols...... 8vo N. Y.   4 00
a. Millman.   History of Christianity, 3 vols. 8vo N. Y.   5 25
a. ————   History of Latin Christ., 8 vols. 8vo N. Y. 14 00
b. Neander.   History of Christ. Church, 6 v. 8vo Bost. 24 00
b. ————   First Planting of Christ. Ch.. 8vo N. Y.   4 00
————   Hist. of Christian Dogmas, 2 v.12mo Bohn.   3 50
b. Pressensé.   The Early years of the Chris-
                                    tian Church, 2 vols....12mo N. Y.   3 50
Prideaux.   Connection of Sacred and Pro-
                                    fane History, 2 vols.... 8vo Lond.   5 00
b. Ranke.   History of the Popes, 3 vols....12mo Bohn.   5 25
Riddell.   History of the Papacy at Period
                                    of Reformation.... 8vo Lond.   4 00
Schaff, Philip.   Hist. of Apostolic Church. 8vo N. Y.   3 75
b. ———— ——— History of Christian Church, 2 v. 8vo N. Y.   7 50
b. Shedd, W. G. T.   Hist. of Christ. Doctrine.
                                    2 vols.... 8vo N. Y.   5 00
Smedley.   Reformed Religion in France.
                                    3 vols....18mo N. Y.   2 25
Smith, Henry B., Prof.   History of Church
                    of Christ in Chron. Tables..folio N. Y.   6 75
Socrates.   Ecclesiastical History.........12mo Bohn.   2 50
Soames.   Anglo-Saxon Church.........12mo Lond.   2 00
Sozomen.   Ecclesiastical History........12mo Bohn.   2 50
b. Stanley Dean.   History of Jewish Church.
                                    2 vols.... 8vo N. Y. *ea.* 2 50
b. ———— ——— History of Eastern Church. 8vo N. Y.   2 50
Stevens   History of Methodism, 3 vols... 8vo N. Y.   5 25
Stoughton, J.   Ecclesiastical History of
                    England, 2 vols.   1870. Lond.. 8vo 25s.
Theodoret & Evagrius.   Eccles. History..12mo Bohn.   2 50

Church of England.—[*See Anglican Church.*]
Stanley, Dean, on Church and State. Lon. 8vo 15s.

Civilization.—[*See Ethnology.*]
b. Buckle.   History of Civilization, 2 vols.. 8vo N. Y.   6 00

b. Guizot. History of Civilization, 4 vols...12mo N. Y. **$6 00**
——— ——— abridged, 1 vol.12mo N. Y.   1 50
Ozanom. Civiliza. in the 5th Century. 2 v.12mo Lond.
Tytler. Early History of Mankind......

Classics—GREEK & LATIN; COLLECTED TRANSLATIONS.

b. Bohn. Classical Library, 90 vols., 12mo, London.
                          Average per vol., about   2 25
    Collins, W. L. Anct. Classics for English
                          Readers, — vols.... L. & P. *ea.* 1 00
a. Harpers. Classical Library, 22 vols......12mo *each*   1 50

Climatology.—[*See also Health.*]

Blodgett. Climatology of the U. States. *r.* 8vo Phila.   5 00

Clocks and Watches.

a. Booth, Mary L. Clock and Watch Makers'
                          Manual....12mo N. Y.   2 00
b. Denison, E. B. Clock and Watch Making.16mo Lond.   1 75
    Reid, T. Clock and Watch Making. 1847. 8vo Glasg.
    Wood. Curiosities of Clocks and Watches
                    from Earliest Times.... 8vo Lond.   5 00

Coal—COAL MINING.

Amer. Coals Applica. to Steam Navi., etc. 8vo N. Y.   6 00
Daddow & Baunan. Coal, Iron and Oil... 8vo Pottsv.   7 50
Lesley, J. P. Coal and its Topog. 1856.12mo Phila.   1 00
Phillips. System of Mining Coal. 1858.12mo Phila.
Smyth, W. W. Coal and Coal Mining. '67.12mo Lond.   4 00
a. Taylor. Statistics of Coal............. 8vo Phila.   5 00

Coins.—[*See Numismatics.*]

Collections of Useful Knowledge.—[*See Addenda.*]

Collections—ENTERTAINING.

a. Chambers. Miscellany of Ent. Tracts, 10 v.12mo E. & P. 12 50
b. ————— Papers for the People, 6 vols.12mo E. & P.   9 00
b. ————— Pocket Miscellany, 12 vols...18mo E. & P.   9 00
b. ————— Book of Days, 2 vols........*r.* 8vo E. & P.   9 00
a. D'Israeli. Curiosities of Literature, 4 vols.12mo N. Y.   7 00
b. ————— Amenities of Literature, 2 vols.12mo N. Y.   3 50
b. ————— Literary Character, 1 vol......12mo N. Y.   1 75
    Dodd, H. P. Epigrammatic Literature. Lon. 8vo 10s. 6d.
b. Doran, Dr. Table Traits....:.......... 8vo N. Y.   1 75
    ————— Habits and Men .... 8vo N. Y.   1 75
    ————— Knights and their Days..... 8vo N. Y.   1 75
b. ————— Monarchs Retired from Busi-
                          ness, 2 vols ... 8vo N. Y.   3 50
a. Holmes, O. W. Autocrat of the Breakfast
                          Table....12mo N. Y.   2 00
a. ————— ——— Professor at Breakfast.:12mo N. Y.   2 00
b. Hone, W. Every Day Book, 4 vols...... 8vo Lond. 18 00
    King. 10,000 Wonderful Things, 2 vols..Lond. 7s. 6d.

Maginn, W. Miscellanies, 5 vols........12mo N. Y. $11 25
a. Thackeray. Miscellanies, 5 vols........12mo Bost.   6 25
b. Wilson, John. Noctes Ambrosiana, 5 v..12mo N. Y.   8 75

Colleges.—[*See also Education.*]

Blake, Sophia Jex. Amer. Cols. & Schools.12mo Lond.   1 75
Bristed. Five Yrs. in an Eng. Univer. *o.p.*12mo N. Y.
   Four Years in Yale. 1871.............12mo N. Y.   2 50
a. Porter, Noah. American Colleges.......12mo N. Hav. 1 50
a. Schaff, Ph. Universities of Germany....12mo Phila.   1 25

Colonization.—[*See Emigration.*]

Colorado.

Taylor, Bayard. Colorado; a Sum'r Trip.12mo N. Y.   1 50

Comedies.—[*See Drama.*]

Comic Prose and Poetry.—[*See Humorous Works.*]

Commerce.—[*See Business.*]

Common Schools.—[*See Education.*]

Complete Works—MISCELLANEOUS.—[*See Addenda.*]

Composition.—[*See also Rhetoric.*]

Bain, A. Composition and Rhetoric.....12mo N. Y.   1 75
Day, H. A. English Composition........12mo N. Y.   1 50
a. Parker. Aids to English Composition...12mo N. Y.   1 25

Communism.—[*See Co-operation.*]

Conchology—MOLLUSCS.

Adams, H. G. Beautiful Shells... .....12mo Lond.   1 60
Agassiz. Seaside Studies............... 8vo Bost.   3 00
Brown, Thos. Elements of Conchol. Lon. 8vo 8s.
Catton. Popular Conchology. Lond.... 8vo 14s.
Crouch. Introduction to Lamarik's Conchology.
Fleming. Moluscous Animals. Lond... 8vo 6s.
Jay, I. C. Catalogue of Shells......... 4to N. Y.
Johnston. Introduc. to Conchology. Lon. 8vo 21s.
Roberts, Mary. Popular Hist. of Mollusca.
             London ...12mo 7s. 6ᵈ
Sowerby. Pop. British Conchology. Lon.12mo 7s. 6d.
———— Conchological Manual (colored,
          30s.) Lond ... 8vo 18s.
———— Conchological Illustrations, 6
          vols. Lond.... 8vo 150s.
Swainson. Exotic Conchology. Lond.... 4to 52s. 6d.

Concordance.

———— To Bible. [*See under Bible*]
———— To Shakespeare. [*See under Shakespeare.*]
———— To Milton. By Cleaveland.
———— To Tennyson. By Brightwell. 8vo Lond.   8 00

Connecticut.

Barber. Historical Collections of Conn.. 8vo N. Hav.
Bacon, L. Historical Discourses......... 8vo N. Hav. $1 50
Blue Laws of Connecticut...............12mo Hartf.
Carpenter. History of Connecticut......18mo Phila.
Hoadley, C. J. N. Haven Colonial Records. 8vo N. Hav.
Trumbull, B. History of Connecticut.... 8vo
Trumbull, J. H. Conn. Historical Records. 8vo

Constitution of the United States.

Bayard. On the Constitution, U. S.......12mo Phila.   75
Bowen, F. Documents on the Constitu...12mo
Conkling. Young Citizens' Manual......18mo Phila.
Curtis, G. T. On the Constitu. U. S., 2 v. 8vo N. Y.   6 00
Cutts, J. M. Constit'l & Party Questions.12mo N. Y.   1 25
Elliot. Debates on the Federal Const., 5 v. 8vo Phila. 20 00
a. Farrar. Manual of the Const. U. S....... 8vo Bost.   3 50
Federalist, The. Edited by Dawson..... 8vo N. Y.   3 00
b. —————— Ed. by J. C. Hamilton... 8vo Phila.   3 50
Hickey. Manual of the Const. U. S......12mo Phila.
a. Prince, L. B. E Pluribus Unum : Articles
                   of Confederation....12mo N. Y.   1 00
b. Story, Jos. Judge. Coment. on the Cons. 2 v. 8vo Bost. 10 00
a. ——— ——— ——— ——— —— abridged.12mo N. Y.   1 50
a. Towle. Hist. and Analysis of Const. U. S. 8vo Bost.   2 00
   Whiting, Wm. Powers of the President. 8vo Bost.   2 50

Constitution of England.

Bagehart. Hist. of English Constitution..16mo Lond. 9s.
Creasy. Rise and Progress of English
                    Constitution. Lond....12mo 9s. 6d.
a. De Lolme. On the Constitution of Eng..12mo Bohn.   1 75
b. Hallam. Constitutional History of Eng.. 8vo N. Y.   2 00
Hallam & May. Consti. Hist. of Eng., 3 v.12mo N. Y.   5 25

Conundrums—PUZZLES, ETC.—[*See also Games, etc.*]

Book of 500 Curious Puzzles............16mo N. Y.   50
Howard. Conundrums and Puzzles......16mo N. Y.   50
One Hundred Double Acrostics. Lond...12mo 2s. 6d.
Puniana........ ....12mo Lond. 6s.

Cookery and Food.—[*See also Chemistry (applied), Health.*]

Beecher, Cath. E. Receipt Book.........12mo N. Y.   1 50
a. Bellows, Dr. F. W. Philosophy of Eating.12mo N. Y.   1 50
a. Beard, G. M. Food and Diet in Health and
                             Disease....12mo N. Y.   75
a. Blot, P. Hand Book of Cookery.........12mo N. Y.   1 50
Breakfast, Dinner and Tea............12mo N. Y.   2 00
Brillat-Savarin. Hand Book of Dining...12mo N. Y.   1 00
—————— Physiology of Taste....16mo Phila.   1 00
a. Cornelius, Mrs. Young H'keeper's Friend.12mo Bost.   1 50
Delamere. Wholesome Fare : the Doctor
                    and the Cook.... 8vo Lond.   4 50

Francatelli, C. E. Modern Cook. Illus... 8vo Phila. $5 00
b. Gouffé. Royal Cookery Book. Illus....r. 8vo Lond. 21 00
a. "Harland, Marion." Common Sense in the
    Household....12mo N. Y.   1 75
Lankester, Dr. On Food...............12mo Lond.   1 50
Leatherby. Lectures on Food..........12mo Lond.
Leslie, Miss. Receipt Book. Cookery..ea.12mo Phila. 1 75
Mann, Mrs. Christianity in the Kitchen.12mo Bost. 1 25
a. Putnam, Mrs. Receipt Book............12mo N. Y. 1 75
Soyer. Culinary Campaign in Crimean
    War. Lond.... 8vo 5s.
——— Cookery ....Lond.... 8vo 15s.
b. Warne. Model Cookery and Housekeeping.12mo Lond. 3 75
a. ——— ——— ——— Cheap edition ...12mo Lond.   75

Co-operation of Labor.

Constitu., etc. of Co-operative Build. Asso.16mo N. Y.   15
Co-operative Stores....................16mo N. Y.   50
Grant, E. P. Co-operation: Attractv. Indus.16mo N. Y. 50
Thurlow. Trades' Unions Abroad. 1870. 8vo Lond.

Copyright.

Carey, H. C. Let. on Internat'l Copyright. 8vo N. Y.   50
Inter. Copyright, Inter. Copyright Asso.,
    Speeches and Letters.... 8vo N. Y.

Corporal Punishment.

Cobb, Lyman. On Corporal Punishment.12mo N. Y. 1 00
Cooper. Hist. of the Rod in all Countries. 8vo Lond. 5 00

Correspondence—COLLECTIONS OF LETTERS, ETC. [See also Biography.]

Ellis. Letters Illustrative of Eng. Hist. 3 series, 11 vols.
——— Letters of Eminent Literary Men.
Hale, Mrs. Library of Standard Letters.
a. Holcombe. Literature in Letters........12mo N. Y. 2 00
b. Knight. Half Hours with the Best Letter
    Writers, 2 vols. 8vo Lond. 6 00
Wallace, Lady. Let. of Disting. Musicians.12mo Lond.
Willmot, R. A. Gems of Correspondence.12mo Lond.
——————— Let. of Emi. Persons. Lon.12mo 4s.

Correspondence—INDIVIDUAL. [For much Correspondence see the Biographies of the Writers —as Byron; Life & Letters, etc.]

Abelard & Heloise Letters..... ....18mo Lond.
Adams, Mrs. Letters of Mr. John Adams,
    2 vols....12mo Bost.
Beethoven, Letters. Translated by Lady
    Wallace, 2 vols....16mo N. Y. 2 00
Cicero, Letters and Life, (3 vols. Lond.
    1854. 16s.) Lond ...r. 8vo 16s.

Goethe. Correspondence with Schiller...12mo N. Y. $1 00
——— ——————— with Leipsic Friends.12mo Lond.
——— ——————— with a Child.........12mo Bost.   1 75
Gray (the Poet), Letters to Mason. 1853. 8vo Lond.
Guerin, Mad. de. Letters..............12mo N. Y.   1 25
Humboldt, A. Von. Letters to Von Ense.12mo N. Y.   1 25
———————— Wm. Letters to Female Friend.16mo N.'Y.   1 25
Hunt, Leigh. Correspondence, 2 vols....12mo Lond.   5 00
a   Junius, Letters of, 2 vols..............12mo Lond..   3 50
Lewis, Sir Geo. C.   Letters to various
                        Friends. Lond.... 8vo 14s.
Mendelssohn. Letters, 2 vols...........16mo N. Y.   3 50
a. Montagu, Lady Mary W. Letters......12mo Bost.   2 00
           (2 vols. 8vo, Lond., 18s.)
b. Mozart. Letters, 2 vols................16mo N. Y.   8 50
Napoleon. Correspond. with Josephine..12mo N. Y.
——————— Confidential Correspondence
                with Josephine, 2 vols....12mo N. Y.   2 00
a. Sevigné, Madame de. Letters.........12mo Bost.   2 00
Southey, Robert. Letters, 4 vols. Lond.12mo 48s.
b. Walpole, Horace. Letters, 9 vols. Lond.. 8vo 81s.
Wellington. Select. from Correspon. Lon. 8vo 18s.

Corsica.

Campbell, F. E. Notes on Corsica. 1868.
                        London....16mo 2s. 6d.

Cosmology—THE CREATION; SYSTEM OF THE EARTH.

[*See also Astronomy, Geology, Phys. Geography.*]
Anderson, J. Course of Creation. Lond.12mo 7s. 6d.
Buchner. Force and Matter. Lond..... 8vo 7s. 6d.
Higgins. The Earth: Popular Phys. Geog.
                        London....18mo 5s.
Humboldt. Aspects of Nature, 2 v. Lon.12mo 7s.
b.   ———— Cosmos. (5 vols. Bohn.), 5 vols.12mo N. Y.   6 25
Jones, H. B. Matter and Force. 1868. Lon.12mo 5s.
McCosh. Typical Forms in Creation..... 8vo N. Y.   2 50
a. Pouchet. The Universe; the Infinitely Great and
                Infinitely Little. Illus. r. 8vo Lond.   12 00
Ramsay, G. M. Cosmology.............12mo Bost.   2 00
a. Reclus. The Earth: Phenomena of the Life of the
                Globe. Illus. 2 vols.... 8vo L. & N.   10 00
Vestiges of the Natural Hist. of Creation.12mo N. Y.   1 50
Warrington. G. The Week of Creation.12mo Lond.   1 50
a. Winchell. D. S. Sketches of Creation....12mo N. Y.   2 00

Costume.

Book of Costume. By a Lady of Rank. Lon. 8vo 21s.
Cooley. The Toilet in Anct. & Mod. Times.12mo Lond.   1 75
Corset and Crinoline; Hist. of. By a Lady.
                        London..... 4to 7s. 6d.
b. Fairholt. History of Costume in England.
                        Illustrated.... 8vo Lond.   6 00

Fosbrooke.   Synopsis of Anct. Cost. Lon. 4to   8s.
Hinton, H.,L.   Historical Costume....... 8vo N. Y.
b. Hope. Costumes of the Ancients, 2 v. Lon. 8vo 45s.
Martin.   Civil Costume of England (col'd).
                              London.... 4to 52s. 6d.
Modes et Cost. Historiques, colored plates. 4to Paris. $20 00
Shaw.   Dresses and Decorations of Middle
                    Ages, 2 vols. London.... 4to 115s. 6d.

Cotton—COTTON MANUFACTURE.

b. Baines.   History of the Cotton Manufac.. 8vo Lond. 15s.
a. Baird.   American Cotton Spinners' Guide.12mo Phila.   1 50
Cassel.   Cotton and its Culture.........r. 8vo Bombay.
Ellison.   Hand Book of the Cotton Trade.
                    1858.   Lond.... 8vo 7s. 6d.
a. Geldart.   Hand Book of Cotton Manufact.12mo N. Y.   2 50
Hyde.   Science of Cotton Spinning. 1867. 8vo Manch. 5 25
Loring & Atkinson.   Cotton Culture at the
                    South. 1869....12mo Bost.   50
Montgomery. On Cotton Spinning. Glasg. 8vo 9s. 6d.
Turner.   Cotton Planters' Manual. 1857.12mo N. Y.   1 00
b. Ure.   Cotton   Manufactures of Great
                    Britain. 2 vols....12mo Lond.   4 50
Watts.   Facts of the Cotton Famine. '66. 8vo Lond.   2 50
Wheeler.   Madras vs. America. 1866....12mo L. & N.   1 00

Crete.

Howe, S. G.   Cretan Refugees and Ameri-
                    can Helpers....12mo Bost.   1 00
Pashley.   Travels in Crete. '37. 2 v. Camb. 8vo 42s.
Skinner.   Roughing it in Crete. '67. Lond.12mo 10s. 6d.
Spratt.   Travels in Crete. 1865. 2 vols. 8vo Lond.

Cricket.—[See also under Games and Sports Generally.]

Pycroft, Jr.   Cricket Field.............16mo L. & B.

Crimea—CRIMEAN WAR.

b. Chambers.   History of the Russian War. r. 8vo Edinb.   6 00
a. Kinglake.   Invasion of the Crimea, vols. 1 & 2.   N. Y.   4 00
Koch, J. G.   Crimea and Odessa. Lond. 8vo 10s. 6d.
Olyphant, L.   Rus. Shores of Black Sea.12mo N. Y.   75
Russell.   Todleben's Def. of Sebastopol.12mo N. Y.   2 00
Slade.   Turkey & the Crimean War. Lon. 8vo 12s.

Crimes and Punishments.—[See also Capital Punishment.]

Beaumont & De Tocqueville. Beccaria. o. p.
Carpenter.   Reformed Schools... ...o. p.
Dix, Miss.   On Prisons.............o. p.
Hill.   On Suppression of Crime. Lond.. 8vo 16s.
——   On Juvenile Delinquents. Lond...8vo 6s.
Mayhew.   Crim. Prisons of Lond. Lond. 8vo 10s. 6d.
Pierce.   Half Centu. with Juven'l Delinq.12mo N. Y.   3 00
Woods, Mrs. C.   Woman in Prison.......16mo N. Y.   1 25

Criticism—LITERARY.—[*For Art Criticism see Fine Arts,
                        Architecture, Painting, etc.—
                        Also Essays—Also Literature.*

a. Arnold, Matthew. Essays in Criticism...12mo Bost. $2 00
      Austin, Alfred. Poetry of the Period. Lon. 8vo 7s. 6d.
b. Coleridge. Biographia Literaria, 2 vols..12mo N. Y.   3 00
      —————— See Shakespeare (Drama).....
b. Dallas, E. J. The Gay Science, 2 v. Lon. 8vo 28s.
b. De Quincey. Hist. & Critical Essays, 2 v.12mo Bost.   3 00
      Fitzgerald, P. Comedy & Dramatic Effect.
                              London.... 8vo 12s.
b. Godwin, Parke. Critical Essays.........12mo N. Y.   2 00
      Hazlitt. Lectures on Eng. Poets, etc., 4 v.12mo Phila.
      Jeaffreson. Novels and Novelists........   Lond.
a. Kaimes. Elements of Criticism.......... 8vo N. Y.
a. Lowell, J. R. Among my Books.........12mo Bost.   2 00
b. ————— —— My Study Windows......12mo Bost.   2 00
      ————— —— Fable for Critics....... 12mo Bost.   75
      Masson. Brit. Novelists and their Styles.12mo Bost.   1 25
      Ossoli (Marg. Fuller). Papers on Lit. & Art.12mo Bost. 1 50
      Poe, E. A. Literati and Marginalia......12mo N. Y.   1 50
b   Schlegel. Dramatic Art and Literature.12mo Bohn.   1 75
      St. Beuve. Celebrated Women..........16mo Bost.   2 00
b. Taine. English Literature, 2 vols....... 8vo N. Y.   10 00
      Wallace, H. B. Literary Criticisms......12mo Phila.   2 00
b. Whipple, E. P. Essays and Reviews, 2 v.12mo Bost.   3 00

Crochet.—[*See Needle-Work.*]

Croquet.

      Fellow, R. Croquet....................12mo N. Y.   50
      Routledge. Game of Croquet..........16mo Lond.

Crusades.—[*See Chivalry.*]

      Edgar. Crusades and Crusaders........18mo Bost.   75
a. Gray. Children's Crusade in 13th Cent...12mo N.·Y.   1 00
      Michaud. History of Crusades (New York
                  Edition, *o. p.*). 3 vols. London....12mo 15s.
b. Mill. Hist. of the Crusades (scarce), 2 v. 8vo Lond.
      Proctor. History of the Crusades. 1854. 8vo Phila.
      Sybel, H. Von. History and Literature of
                  the Crusades. London.... 8vo 10s. 6d.

Cuba.

      Carleton, G. W. Our Artist in Cuba.....12mo N. Y.   1 50
      Cuba and the Cubans (1850)............12mo N. Y.
a. Dana, R. H., Jr. Trip to Cuba..........16mo Bost.   1 25
      Howe, Mrs. S. G. Trip to Cuba.........16mo Bost.   1 25
      Humbolt, A. Von. Island of Cuba. Lond.12mo 7s. 6d.

Currency.—[*See Banks—Money.*]

Cyclopedias.—[*See Encyclopædias.*]

Dancing.

      De Walden. Ball Room Companion......12mo N. Y.   50

a. Ferrero.   Art of Dancing (D. & F.).......12mo N. Y. $1 50
Hillgrove.   Ball Room Companion.......12mo N. Y.   75
a. Wilkinson, W. C.   Dance of Mod. Society.12mo N. Y.   75

Dark Ages.—[*See Middle Ages.*]

Darwinism.—[*See also Natural History.*]
b. Darwin.   Animals and Plants under Do-
                          mestication, 2 vols....12mo N. Y.   6 00
——— Origin of Species..............12mo N. Y.   2 00
a. ——— Descent of Man, 2 vols........12mo N. Y.   4 00
Homo *vs.* Darwin.   A Refutation of Darwin.12mo Phila.   1 00
a. Huxley, Prof.   Man's Place in Nature....12mo N. Y.   1 25
b. Mivart.   Genesis of Species..........12mo N. Y.   1 75
Morris, F. V.   Difficulties of Darwinism.
Muller, F.   Facts and Arguments for Dar-
                          win.   London....12mo 6s.
Stebbing.   Essays on Darwinism.........12mo Lond.
a. Wallace, A. R.   Natural Selection.......12mo Lond.   2 00
——— Review of Descent of Man......

Decorative Art—ILLUMINATING, ETC.
Copley.   Alphabets..............oblong 4to N. Y.   3 00
a. Dunlevy, Alice.   Art of Illuminating.....   4to   N. Y.   3 00
Dresser, C.   Decorative Design.   Lond...   8vo 21s.
b. Eastlake.   Hints on Household Taste, in
                          Furniture and Decoration.   Lond. 8vo 18s.
Gruner.   Fresco Decorations in Italy.   Lon..folio, 168s.
Illuminated Crest Book.   Lond.........   4to 21s.
b. Jones, Owen.   Grammar of Ornament....folio Lond.   40 00
Lillie.   Alphabet of Monograms.   Lond..folio 5s. 6d.
Shaw.   Decorative Arts of the Middle
                          Ages.   Lond....   4to 42s.
——— Encyclo. of Ornament.   Lond....   4to 25s.
——— Hand Book of Illuminating.....*r.* 8vo Lond.   15 00
——— Medieval Alphabets, etc........*r.* 8vo Lond.   7 50
——— Illuminated Ornaments, 6th to
                          17th Century.   Lond....   4to 36s.
Standard Sign Writer................ . 4to   N. Y.
Treasury of Ornamental Art...........*r.* 8vo Lond.
Tymms & Wyatt.   Art of Illuminating...   8vo Lond.   3 50
Whitlock.   Decorative Painter's and Gla-
                          cier's Guide ...   4to Lond.
a. Wornum.   Analysis of Ornament.   Lond.. 8vo 8s.

Democracy.—[*See Government.*]

Demonology and Witchcraft—THE SUPERNATURAL, ETC.
Craik.   Modern Palmistry ; Book of the
                          Hand....12mo N. Y.   1 75
a. Dendy, W. C.   Philosophy of Mystery...12mo N. Y.   1 00
Drake, S. G.   Mather's Wonders of Invisi-
                          ble World, &c., 3 vols....   Bost.
b. Ennemoser.   History of Magic ....12mo Bohn.   2 25

Godwin, W.   Lives of the Necromancers.12mo N. Y. $ 75
Gould, S. B.   Book of Were Wolves.... 12mo Lond.   1 75
Howitt, Wm.   History of the Supernatural, 2 vols....12mo   3 00
Michelet.   La Sorcier (in English). Lon.12mo 7s.
a. Salverté.   Philosophy of Magic, 2 vols...12mo N. Y.   2 00
b. Scott, Sir W.   Letters on Demonology and Witchcraft..........18mo N. Y.   75
b. Upham.   Híst. of Salem Witchcraft, 2 v. 8vo Bost.   7 50
Whittier, J. G.   Supernaturalism of New England....16mo Bost.

Denmark.

Dunham, S. A.   Hist. of Denmark, Sweden, etc., 3 vols. 12mo; 3 vols. 18mo N. Y.   2 25
Gallenga, A.   Invasion of Denmark in 1864. 2 vols. Lond....   21s.
Laing.   Social and Political State of Denmark. Lond.... 8vo 5s.
Syndig.   History of Scandinavia......... 8vo Lond.
Wheaton.   History of the Northmen..*o. p.* 8vo N. Y.

Devotion.—[*See also Poetry ; Religion.*—This list may be largely extended.]

Angel Voices.........................16mo Bost.   1 25
a. Baxter.   Saints' Rest..................12mo N. Y.   1 25
b. Beecher, H. W.   Prayers from Plymouth Pulpit....12mo N. Y.   1 75
———— Morning and Even'g Exercises.12mo N. Y.   2 00
b. Boyd.   Graver Thoughts (of Country Pastor)....12mo Bost.   1 75
a. Bunyan.   Pilgrim's Progress: Golden Treas. Series....16mo Lond.   1 50
——— Various other plain and illustrated editions.
b. Child, G. C.   Benedicite: the Power and Wisdom of God....12mo N. Y.   2 00
Devotional Libraries, several collections, published by Randolph, N. Y.; Lothrop, Bost., etc...
Doddridge.   Rise and Progress of Religion in the Soul....12mo N. Y.   1 25
b. Fuller, Thos.   Good Thoughts in Bad Times....16mo Bost.   2 00
b. ——— ——— Holy and Profane State..16mo Bost.   1 50
Gasparin, Madame.   The Near and Heavenly Horizons ...12mo N. Y.   1 75
a. Goulburn.   Thoughts on Personal Religion.16mo N. Y.   1 00
Greenwell, Dora.   The Patience of Hope.16mo N. Y.   1 25
——— ——— Present Heaven... ..16mo N. Y.   1 25
——— ——— Two Friends.........16mo N. Y.   1 25
Hare, J. C.   The Mission of the Comforter.12mo Bost.   1 75
a. Jay,   Morning and Evening Exercises..'..12mo N. Y.   2 00
a. Keble, J.   The Christian Year..24mo and 18mo N. Y.
a. Kempis, Thos. à   Imitation of Christ....18mo Bost.   1 25

Kempis, Thos. à. Lond ed., 2s. 6d. to 9s...18mo Bost. $1 25
Larcom, Lucy. Breathings of a Better Life. 4to Bost.   2 50
Martineau, Jas. Endeavors after a Chris-
                                    tian Life....12mo Bost. 1 00
b. Pascal, Blaise. Thoughts on Religion...12mo N. Y.   2 25
a. Prentiss, E. Stepping Heavenward.....12mo N. Y.   1 75
b. Prayers of the Ages..................12mo Bost.   2 50
b. Robertson, F. W. Sermons............12mo Bost.   2 00
Scougal. Life of God in the Soul of Man.18mo N. Y.
Swetchine, Mad. de. Writings.........16mo Bost.   1 50
Taylor, Jeremy. The Golden Grove. Lon.18mo 2s. 6d.
a. —————— Holy Living and Dying, 2 vols.12mo Bost.   2 50
Tholuck, A. Hours of Christian Devotion.12mo Bost.   2 00
b. Thompson, Jos. P. Book of Fam.Worship. 4to Bost.
Zschokke. Hours of Meditation, 2 vols.16mo Bost. ea.   1 50
b. —————— Medita. on Death and Eter.12mo Bost.   1 50
—————— —————— on Life and its Duties.
                          (by Rowan)....12mo Bost.   1 50

Diaries.—[*See under Biography.*]

Dictionaries.—[*See also Encyclopedias ; and for Technical
              Dictionaries, as of Biography, Chemistry,
              &c., see names of subjects.*]

Dictionary.—ENGLISH LANGUAGE.

b. Bartlett. Dictionary of Americanisms... 8vo Bost.   2 50
Craik. Universal English Dictionary, 2 v. 8vo L. & N. 15 00
Johnson. English Dict. (by Latham).....
Richardson. English Dictionary, 2 v. Lon. 4to 94s. 6d.
b. Webster. Unabridged Dictionary. Illust. 4to Spring. 12 00
—————— National Pictorial Dictionary. r. 8vo Spring. 5 00
a. —————— Royal Octavo ; Imperial...... 8vo N.Y. ea. 5 00
—————— Count. House & Fam. Dic. Imp.12mo N. Y. 3 50
—————— School & Pocket Dic. (various).
b. Worcester. Dict. of English Language. 4to Bost.   10 00
a. —————— —————— Abridged.............r. 8vo Bost.   5 00
—————— Comprehensive Dictionary.. 8vo Bost.   1 80

Dictionary—LATIN.

b, Andrews. Lat. Eng. and Eng. Lat......r. 8vo N. Y.   7 50
Ainsworth. ————— ———— ———— ...... 8vo Phila.
Anthon. ————— ———— ———— ...... 8vo N. Y.   3 50
Leverett. ————— ———— ———— ...... 8vo Phila.   6 25
a. Riddell & Arnold.— ———— ———— ...... 8vo N. Y. 5 00
White. ————— ———— ———— ...... 8vo Phila.   4 50

Dictionary—GREEK.

a. Drisler. Greek & Eng. and Eng. Greek D. r. 8vo N. Y. 7 00
b. Liddell & Scott ————— ———— ———— r. 8vo N. Y.   7 50
Pickering. ————— ———— ———— r. 8vo Phila.   6 25
—————— Abridged.................. 8vo Oxfo.   4 50

Dictionary—FRENCH.

Mole. Fr. & Eng.—Eng. Fr. Dictionary.. 8vo L. & N. 2 00

b. Spier & Surenne. Fr. Eng. & Eng. Fr...*r.* 8vo N. Y. $6 00
a. —— — —— — — — Students' ed.12mo N. Y. 2 50
Surenne. —— —— —— — 16mo N. Y. 1 25
Weller. French and English Dictionary. 8vo Phila. 4 00

Dictionary—GERMAN.

b. Adler. Ger. Eng. & Eng. Ger..........*r.* 8vo N. Y. 6 00
James —— —— —— —— .... 8vo L. & N. 2 00
a. Oehlschlager —— —— ——·............18mo Phila.

Dictionary—SPANISH.

De Veitelle, Merc. Dict. Eng. Sp. Fr......12mo N. Y. 2 00
Neuman & Barretti. —— —— ......12mo Phila. 1 88
b. Seoane. Sp. Eng. & Eng. Span.........*r.* 8vo N. Y. 6 00
a. —— —— —— — abridged......12mo N. Y. 1 75

Dictionary—ITALIAN.

Graglia. Eng. Ital. & Ital. Eng.........18mo L. & N. 1 50
a. Meadows. —— —— ——...........16mo N. Y. 2 50
b. Millhouse. —— —— —— 2 vols..... 8vo N. Y. 6 00

Diet.—[*See Health.*]

Diplomacy.

Prescott. Diplomacy of the Revolution..12mo N. Y. 1 75

Divorce—[*See Marriage and Divorce.*]

Dogs.

a. Dinks, Mayhew & Hutchinson. On the Dog.12mo N. Y. 3 00
Herbert, H. W. The Dog...............12mo N. Y.
Hutchinson. On Dog Breaking. Lond...12mo 9s.
a. Jesse. Anecdotes of Dogs. Illust.......12mo Lond. 2 25
Richardson. On the Dog....... ....12mo N. Y. 60
Taylor. On the Dog............ ....
Walsh, J. H. (" Stonehenge.") The Dog,
in Health and Dis. Lond.. 8vo 15s.
—— —— The Greyhound. Lond.... 8vo 21s.
a. Youatt. On the Dog.................. 8vo Phila. 1 50

Domestic Animals.—[*See also separate names.*]

Allen. Diseases of Domestic Animals....12mo N. Y. 1 00
Cole. The Veterinarian...............12mo N. Y. 75
Dun. Veterinary .... 8vo Edinb.
Gamgee. Our Domestic Animals, 4 v. Edin.12mo 6s.
McClure. On Diseases of Horses, Cattle and Sheep.
Morton. Manual of Veterinary Pharmacy.
London.... 8vo 10s.
Richardson. On the Hog....... ....12mo N. Y. 60
Youatt. On the Hog.......... ....12mo N. Y. 1 75

Domestic Economy.—[*See also Cookery, Furniture, etc.*]

Beecher, Miss C. E. Domestic Economy..12mo N. Y. 1 50
—— —— —— — Receipt Book..12mo N. Y. 1 50
b. —— —— and Mrs. Stowe. Amer. Woman's
Home. Illus.... 8vo N. Y. 2 50

Beecher. Principles of Domestic Science.12mo N. Y. $2 00
Beeton. Book of Household Management.12mo Lond. 3 75
b. De Voe. The Market Assistant......... 8vo N. Y. 3 00
Draper & Croffut. Helping Hand, for Town
    and Country.... 8vo Cinci. 4 25
Eastlake, C. L. Hints on Household Taste.
    London....12mo 18s.
Ellett, Mrs. Practical Housekeeping. '69. 8vo N. Y.
Haskell. Housekeeper's Cyclopedia..... 8vo N. Y. 1 75
Stowe, Mrs. House and Home Papers...16mo Bost. 1 75
Six Hundred Dollars a Year...........16mo Bost. 75
Warren, Mrs. How to Live on £200 a Year.12mo Bost. 50
————— —— Comfort for Small Incomes.12mo Bost. 50
————— —— How to Furnish a House on
    small means....12mo N. Y. 50
b. Webster. Cyclopedia of Domes. Economy. 8vo N. Y. 5 00
a. Youmans. Household Science...........12mo N. Y. 1 75

Drainage.—[*See under Agriculture.*]

Drama—HISTORY OF THE.—[*For Criticism, see under Criticism.*]

Blake. History of the Providence Stage.12mo Prov. '68.
Brown, T. A. Hist. of the American Stage. 8vo N. Y. 3 00
a. Doran. Annals of the English Stage, 2 v. 8vo N. Y. 3 50
Donaldson. Theatre of the Greeks. Lon. 8vo 14s.
Dunlap. History of American Stage, 2 v. 8vo N. Y.
Ireland. Record of the N. Y. Stage, 2 v. 8vo N. Y.
Wemyss. Chronology of Amer. Stage.'52.12mo N. Y.
Wilson, H. H. Theatre of the Hindus, 2 v. 8vo Lon. 21s.

Drama—SHAKESPEARE; editions edited by

b. Clarke, Mr. & Mrs. Cowden, 4 vols....... 8vo Lond. 12 00
————— ——— —— ——— 1 vol........r. 8vo Lond. 8 00
b. Dyce (large type), 9 vols................. 8vo Lond. 24 00
Furness. Variorum ed. I. Romeo & Juliet.'71. 8vo Phila. 7 50
a. Globe edition, 1 vol....................12mo Phila. 1 50
a. Handy Volume ed., 12 vols.............32mo Lond. 10 00
a. Hudson, Rev. W. N., 11 vols ....12mo Bost. 16 50
Keightley, Thos., 6 vols.................18mo Bost. 12 00
b. Knight, Chas. Pictorial ed., 8 vols......r. 8vo Lond. 40 00
————— —— Stratford ed., 6 vols......12mo Lond. 10 00
a. White, Richard Grant, with Life, 12 vols.12mo Bost. 18 00
b. ————— ————— ——— fine ed., 12 vols.... Bost. 36 00
Also some 20 editions in 1 vol..........from 50 cts. to 15 00

Drama—COMMENTARIES, ETC. ON SHAKESPEARE.

Abbott, E. A. Shakespearian Grammar.... Lond.
Bible Truths with Shakespeare Parallel's.12mo Lond. 2 00
b. Clarke, Mrs. Concordance to Shakesp....r. 8vo Bost. 10 00
Coleridge. Lectures on Shakesp. Lond. 8vo 3s. 6d.
Craik, G. L. The English of Shakespeare.12mo Lond. 5s.
Gervinus. Commentaries on Shakespeare.
    2 vols. London.... 8vo 24s.

Giles. C. Human Life in Shakespeare....12mo Bost.　$2 00
Guizot. Shakespeare and his Times....12mo N. Y.　1 50
Halliwell, J. O. List of Works Illust.
　　　　　　Shakespeare...............16mo Lond.
Hazlitt, W. C. Characters of Shakes....12mo Lond.　1 75
Hudson, H. N. Lectures on Shakesp., 2 v.12mo N. Y.　3 00
Holmes, N. Authorship of Shakespeare.12mo N. Y.　2 25
Jameson, Mrs. Female Characters of Sh. 8vo N. Y.
Jervis. Dict. of the Language of S. Lon. 4to 12s.
Keightley. Shakespeare Expositor. Lon.12mo 7s. 6d.
Rolfe. Some of the Plays of Shakespeare,
　　　　　　　　with Notes....16mo N. Y. *ca.*　90
Ruggles. Shakespeare's Method as an
　　　　　　　　Artist....12mo N. Y.　1 75
a. Stearns, C. W. Shakespeare's Treasury of
　　　　　　　　Wisdom, etc....12mo N. Y.　2 00
b. White, R. G. Shakespeare's Scholar.... 8vo N. Y.　2 50
Wordsworth, B. Shakespeare's Know-
　　　　　ledge of Bible. Lond....12mo 6s.

Drama—COLLECTIONS OF PLAYS.

Bell. British Theatre...............⎫
Cumberland's　do.　43 vols. 18mo...⎬ *Out of print,*
Dodsley's Old Plays................⎪ *and scarce.*
Inchbald's British Theatre..........⎭
French. Standard and Minor Drama....　N. Y. *ea.*　15
De Witt. Acting Plays (100)...........　N. Y. *ea.*　15
Lacy. Acting Plays ....　N. Y. *ea.*　25
Sargent (Epes). Acting Plays..........
Lamb, Chas. Specimens of Dramatic Poets.12mo N. Y.
Kettle. Works of Brit. Dramatists. Edinb. 8vo 5s.

Drama—PARLOR DRAMAS.

a. Baker, G. M. The Social Stage..........16mo Bost.　1 50
———— ———— 　Amateur Drama..........16mo Bost.　1 50
———— ———— 　Mimic Stage..............16mo Bost.　1 50
Fowle. Parlor Dramas................12mo Bost.　1 25
Gill. Parlor Tableaux.................12mo Bost.　1 50
Hudson & Howard. Private Theatricals.16mo N. Y.　1 50
Steele, J. S. Drawing-Room Plays .....
Spirit of '76. By Mrs. Curtis...........12mo Bost.　1 00

Drama—DRAMATIC WORKS.

a. Æschylus. Literal Trans. N. Y., $1.50..12mo Bohn.　1 75
———— By Potter. 18mo, 75c. N. Y. By
　　　　　　Coppleston....12mo　1 00
Aristophanes. Translated, 2 vols........　Bohn.　5 00
Baillie, Joanna. Lond.................. 8vo 21s.
b. Beaumont & Fletcher, 2 vols........... 8vo Lond.　10 00
———— Selections by Leigh Hunt.12mo Bohn.　1 75
Boker, Geo. H. (with Poems), 2 vols......12mo Bost.
Bulwer, Lytton, (with Poems)...........16mo Bost.　1 25

Calderon (Spanish). 1853. Lond........12mo 4s. 6d.
Cibber, 5 vols.; Colman, 4 vols.; (both scarce.)
Congreve (with Farquhar, etc.).......... 8vo Lond. **$5 00**
Corneille.   Translated (?)................
Dryden. (In his works.) 2 vols......... 8vo N. Y.   4 00
———— 5 vols........................18mo Bost.   6 25
b. Euripides. Trans. 2 v., Bohn., $5; 3 v.18mo N. Y.   2 25
Farquhar (with Congreve, etc).......... 8vo Lond.   5 00
Fielding. (In his works).............. 8vo Lond.   5 00
Ford. (With Massinger).............. 8vo Lond.   5 00
b. Goethe.......................(Bohn)....12mo Lond.   1 75
Goldsmith. (In his Works)...........12mo Lond.   2 00
Guarini...................Lond....12mo 7s. 6d.
Hertz. (King Rene)... ....16mo N. Y.   1 25
b. Jonson, Ben. Complete Works......... 8vo Lond.   5 00
Knowles, Sheridan, 2 vols. Lond........12mo 12s.
Lessing. Nathan the Wise.............16mo N. Y.   1 50
Lytton, Bulwer...............Lond....12mo 12s.
Marlowe.............................. 8vo Lond.   4 50
b. Massinger. (With Ford, $5)...........12mo Lond.   3 50
Metastasio. Trans. by Hoole, 3 vols. ... 8vo Lond.
Millman. (With Poems.) 3 vols. Lond.18mo 18s.
Otway. Rowe. Both scarce............
Plautus. Trans. by..................2 v.12mo Bohn.   5 00
Racine (in French)................12mo Paris.   1 25
———— The Suitors, Trans. by Browne...12mo N. Y.   ·1 00
b. Schiller. Trans. by various hands, 3 vols.12mo. Bohn.   5 25
b. Sheridan. Dramatic Works.............12mo Lond.   1 75
a. Sophocles. Trans. by..................
12mo N. Y. $1.00.12mo Lond.   1 75
Talfourd........................Lond.12mo 6s.
Taylor, Henry. Edward the Fair, Ph. Van
Artevelde, 2 vols. Lond. *etc*. 5s.
Terence & Phædrus. Trans . ...12mo Bohn.   2 50
Vega, Lopez de. By Wiffen. Lond......12mo 12s.
Vanburgh (with Congreve, etc.).......⎫
Wycherley —— —— —— ......⎭ 8vo L.&N.   5 00

Draughts—GAME OF.
Scattergood. Game of Draughts.........18mo N. Y.   50
a. Spayth. Game of Draughts......... ...12mo N. Y.   1 50
———— Amer. Draught Players.........12mo N. Y.   3 00
———— Draughts for Beginners.........12mo N. Y.   75
Sturges. Guide to Draughts.............12mo Phila.

Drawing Books—PERSPECTIVE, ETC.
b. Appleton. Cyclo. of Drawing (Mechan.) *r.* 8vo N. Y.   10 00
Burn. Illust. Drawing Book..............   L. & N.   1 50
———— Illust. Arch. & Engin. & Mech. D. Bk.   L. & N.   1 50
———— Ornamental & Architectural D. Bk.   L. & N.   1 50
———— Figure & Perspective Drawing Bk.   L. & N.   6 00
a. Cavé. New Method of Learning to Draw.12mo N. Y.   1 00
Metz. Drawing Book of Human Figure.12mo N. Y.   7 50

Minifee, W. Geometrical Drawing...... 8vo N. Y. $4 00
Chapman. Amer. Drawing Book........ 4to N. Y. 6 00

Dreams.

Dendy. Phenomena of Dreams. Lond...12mo 4s.
Seafield. Lit. and Curios. of Dreams, 2 v.12mo Lond. 5 00

Duelling.

Millengen. History of Duelling, 2 v. Lond. 8vo 9s.
a. Sabine. History of Duelling............ 8vo Bost. 1 75
b. Steinmetz. History of Duelling, 2 vols.. 8vo Lond. 8 00

Dutch Republic.—[*See Holland.*]

Earth.—[*See Astronomy, Cosmology, Physical Geography, Geology.*]

Earthquakes.—[*See Volcanoes.*]

East (The)—GENERALLY.—[*See also Asia, Asia Minor.*]

Addison, C. G. Journey from Malta to
Palmyra, etc., 2 v....Lond. 32s.
Bartlett. Forty Days in the Desert. Lon. 8vo 7s. 6d.
Burder. Oriental Customs. Illus. Script. 8vo Lond. 9s.
Browne, J. Ross. Yusef: A Crusade in
East....12mo N. Y. 1 75
a. Bryant, W. Cullen. Letters from the East.12mo N. Y. 1 50
Chateaubriand. Travels................} *o. p. and*
Clarke, E. D. Travels ....} *scarce.*
Dicey, E. The Morning Land, 2 vols....12mo Lond. 5 00
Heeren. Carthage, Egypt, Ethiopia, etc.. 8vo Lond. 8s.
Keppel—Travels. Kinnear—Journey. Both *o. p.*
a. Kinglake, Eothen. Traces of Travel in East.12mo N. Y. 1 25
b. Kitto. Scripture Lands (col'd Maps)..... Lond. 3 75
Lamartine. Travels in the East, 2 vols..Lond. 5s.
Lenormant & Chevalier. Travels, 2 vols. Lond.
Lenormant, F. Students' Manual of Orien-
tal History, 2 vols.... 8vo Lond. 5 50
Lindsay, Lord. Egypt, Edom and Holy
Land, 2 vols.... Lond. 6s.
Madden. Travels.—Morier. Journey. Both *o. p.*
Maundeville. Travels from Aleppo to
Jerusalem. Lond ... 8vo 8s.
Marco Polo, Book of. By Col. H. Yule, 2
vols. Lond.... 8vo 42s.
Olin, Stephen. Egypt, Arabia, &c., 2 vols.12mo N. Y. 3 00
Prime, S. I. Europe and the East, 2 vols.12mo N. Y. 3 00
Richardson, Fredrika. The Iliad of the
East. Lond.... 7s. 6d.
Smith, Ph. Students' Ancient History of
the East....12mo N. Y. 2 00
a. Stephens, J. L. Egypt, Arabia and Holy
Land, 2 vols.... N. Y. 3 00
a. Warburton. The Crescent and the Cross. 2 v. 8vo, Lon.
(12mo N. Y., *o. p.*)

East Indies—AND ISLANDS.

  a. Bickmore, A. S. East Indian Archipelago. 8vo N. Y. $3 50
     Earl. Voyages to Eastern Seas. Lond.. 8vo 12s.
     —— Native Races of Indian Archipel.. 8vo Lond.   3 00
     Lukes. Voyage in Eastern Archipelago.
                      2 vols. Lond.... 8vo 36s.
     Marryatt. Borneo.—Marsden. Sumatra. Both *o. p.*
     Munday. Borneo.—Newbold. Malacca. Both *o. p.*
     Raffles. History of Java. 1830. Lond.. 8vo 18s.
     St. John. Indian Archipelago. 1853. 2 v.12mo Lond.
  b. Wallace, A. R. Eastern Archipelago.... 8vo N. Y.   3 50

Eating.—[*See Cookery, Health.*]

Ecclesiastical History.—[*See Church History.*]

Education and Instruction.—[*See also names of Studies,
   etc.; Colleges, Corporeal Punishment, School Architecture, Object Teaching.*]

     Bryce. Native Education in India. Lond. 8vo 9s. 6d.
     Burton, W. The Dist. School as it was...12mo N. Y.
     Farrar. Essays on Liberal Education.... 8vo Lond.   2 50
     Kay. J. S. Social Condition of Ed. in Eng.12mo N. Y.   1 50
     Lowell, A. C. J. Theory of Teaching.
  a. Mann, Horace. Lectures on Educa., 2 v. 8vo Bost.   6 00
  a. Page, D. P. Theory & Pract. of Teaching.12mo N. Y.   1 50
  b. Randall, S. S. Com. School System of N. Y. 8vo N. Y.   5 00
     Richter, Jean Paul. Levana...........12mo Bost.   2 00
     Rogers, J. C. T. Educa. at Oxford. Lond.16mo 6s.
  a. Schermerhorn. Library of Education, 6v.18mo paper. *ea.* 25
     viz.: Locke. On Education.............
        Locke. On Study and Reading........
        Milton. On Education..............
        Mann. On Physiology in Schools......
        Scottish Univer. Addresses. By Mill, &c.
        Bible in Public Schools...............
  a. Spencer, Herbert. On Education........12mo N. Y.   1 25
     Staunton. The Great Schools of Eng. Lon.16mo 7s. 6d.
     Taylor, Orville. The District School.....12mo N. Y.
     Wyse, Thos. Education Reform. Lond. 8vo 15s.
  a. Youmans. Cult. Demand. by Modern Life.12mo N. Y.   2 00

Egypt—THE NILE; PYRAMIDS.—[*See also Abyssinia;
   East; Mediterranean; Levant.*]

     Adams, W. H. D. The Land of the Nile,
                  Past and Present....18mo Lond.   1 50
     Baker, S. W. See Abyssinia...........
  b. Bartlett. The Nile Boat Illust.......... 8vo Lond.   4 00
     Belzoni. Travels in Egypt and Nubia, 2 v.
                 London.... 8vo 28s.
     Bruce. Travels to Discover the Source of
             the Nile. London....18mo 3s. 6d.
  b. Bunsen, Chev. Egypt's Place in Univer-
            sal History, 5 vols. London.... 8vo 171s.

a. Curtis, G. W. Nile Notes................12mo N. Y. $1 50
a. Dall, Mrs. C. H. Egypt's Place in History.12mo Lond. 1 50
  Day, St. J. Great Pyramid..........folio, Edinb. 28s.
  Eden, Fr. The Nile without a Dragoman.
        London....12mo 7s. 6d.
  Farr. Hist. of Egypt, Assyria, &c., 4 vols.12mo Lond.
  Hawks, F. L. Monuments of Egypt; or,
    Egypt a Witness for the Bible....12mo N. Y.
  Kenrick, J. Ancient Egypt. 1852. 2 vols. 8vo Lon. 30s.
b Lane, E. W. Modern Egyptians, 2 vols. 8vo Lon. 18s.
  Lanoye, F. de. Egypt 3,000 Years Ago...12mo N. Y. 1 50
  Lepsius. Egypt.......................12mo Bohn 2 50
  Lindsay, Lord. Letters from Egypt......12mo Bohn. 2 50
  Palmer, W. Egyptian Chronicles, 2 vols. 8vo Lond. 7 50
a. Prime, W. C. Boat Life in Egypt.......12mo N. Y. 2 00
a. Russell, M. History of Egypt..........18mo N. Y. 75
- Sharpe. History of Egypt to the Conquest
   by the Arabs, 2 vols. London.... 8vo 18s.
  Smyth, C. Piazzi. Life and Work at
   Great Pyramid, 3 vols. Edinburgh.... 8vo 56s.
  Smyth, C. Piazzi. Our Inheritance in
      the Great Pyramid.... 8vo Lond. 5 00
b. Speke. Discov. of the Source of the Nile. 8vo N. Y. 4 00
  Wilkinson, J. G. Ancient Egyptians, 5 v. 8vo Lon. 84s.
a. —————— —— Egyptians of Time of
      Pharaoh, 2 vols....12mo N. Y. 3 50

Electricity.

b. Bakewell, F. C. Manual of Electricity...12mo Lond. 2 50
b. Farraday, M. Researches in Electricity.
     3 vols. London.... 8vo 45s.
b. Ferguson, R. M. Electricity. Illus....16mo Lond. 1 75
a. Fonvielle. Thunder and Lightning......12mo N. Y. 1 50
a. Harris, W. Snow. Elect. Magnet. & Galvan.12mo Lond. 75
 —————— —— Frictional Electricity.... 8vo Lond. 7 00
 Miller. Electricity and Magnetism...... 8vo N. Y. 2 50
 Noad. Text Book of Electricity......... 8vo Lon. 24s.
 —————— Introduction to Electricity......16mo Lond. 1 50

Elocution.—[*See also Oratory.*]

  Bantain. Art of Extempore Speaking...12mo N. Y. 1 50
  Day, H. N. Elocution.................12mo Cincin. 1 50
  Frobisher. The Force of Action.........12mo N. Y. 1 50
  McIlvaine, J. H. Elocution.............12mo N. Y. 1 75
  Monroe, L. P. Physical & Vocal Training.12mo Phila. 1 00
  Murdock & Russell. Vocal Culture......12mo Bost.
  Randall. Elocution....................12mo N. Y. 1 50
b. Rush, Jas. Philoso. of the Human Voice. 8vo Phila. 3 75
a. Reeves. Students' Own Speaker and
     Guide to Oratory:...12mo N. Y. 75
a. Vandenhoff, G. Elocution..............12mo N. Y.

Eloquence.—[*See Oratory.*]

Emblems.

Bunyan. Emblems....................16mo Lond. $1 50
Green. Shakespeare & Emblem Writers.
　　　　　　　　　　　　London.... 8vo 31s. 6d.
a. Quarles. Emblems. 16mo Lond. 4s.....18mo N. Y.　　75
b. Whitney. Choice of Emblems.......... 4to Lond. 12 50

Emigration—COLONIZATION.

Bromwell. Immigration into U. S. '19-'55. 8vo N. Y.
Brougham, Lord. Colonial Policy, 2 vols. *o. p.*
Bury, Lord. Exodus of West. Nations, 2 v. 8vo Lon. 32s.
Chickering. On Emigration. 1848....... 8vo Bost.
Dufferin, Lord. Irish Emigration and Ten-
　　　　　　　　　　　ure of Land.... 8vo 10s. 6d.
Goddard. Where to Emigrate and Why. 8vo N. Y.　3 00
Union Colony of Colorado, with Map......12mo N. Y.　　75

Encyclopedias.—[*See also under names of Subjects, as Agriculture, Bible, Chemistry, Mechanics, etc.*]

b. Appleton. American Encyclopedia, 16 v. *r.* 8vo N. Y.　80 00
　　───── Annual Cyclo., 9 vols. pub. *r.* 8vo N. Y.　45 00
　Brande. Cyclo. of Lit. Science & Art, 3 v. 8vo Lon. 60s.
a. Chambers. Cyclopedia, new ed., 10 v. *r.* 8vo Edinb.　45 00
b. Encyclopedia Britannica, with Steel Plates.
　　　　　　　　8th edition, 21 volumes.... 4to Edinb. 125 00
　English Cyclopedia, 22 vols ....*r.* 8vo Lon. £12
b. Iconographic Cyclopedia. Illus., 6 vols. 8vo & 4to, N. Y.　50 00
　Imperial Jour. of Lit. Arts & Sciences, 2 v. 4to Lond.　35 00
c. Maunder. Treasury of Knowledge; His-
　　　　　　tory, Bible, Botany, &c., 8 vols. 18mo Lond.　32 00
　National Cyclopedia. 13 vols............. 8vo Lond.　60 00
c. Zell. Popular Encyclopedia, 2 vols...... 4to Phila.

For Kitto's Bible Encyclopedia, Smith's Dict., Dic. of Engineering, etc., see those subjects.

England.—[*See also Anglo-Saxons, Ireland, Scotland. Also Biography, such as Cromwell, etc.*]

─────────GENERAL HISTORIES.

c. Cassell. Pictorial History of England, 8
　　　　　　　　　　vols. Imp.... 8vo Lond. 24 00
　Creasy. History of England, 5 vols. Lon. 8vo 52s. 6d.
　Half Hours of English History, 2 vols.... 8vo Lond.　6 00
a. Hume. History of England to....3 vols. 12mo N. Y.　7 50
or b. ───── ───── The same, 6 v. 12mo, $9; 6 v. 8vo Bost. 15 00
　───── Smollett & Miller. ....4 vols. 8vo Phila. 16 00
　───── ───── ─────........8 vols. 8vo Lon. 63s.
　───── Smollett & Hughes, to Vict., 21 v. 12mo Lond. 26 00
　Knight. Pictorial Hist. of England, 8 v. *r.* 8vo Lond.
b. ───── Popular History of England, 8. v. 8vo Lond. 25 00

Lingard. Hist. of England (R. Cath), 13 v.12mo Lon. **54s.**
Mackintosh, 3 vols...................16mo N. Y.   3 00
    (*See England : partial Histories.*)

England—CONDENSED AND ABRIDGED GENERAL HISTORIES.

a. Dickens. Child's History of England, 2 v.16mo N. Y. **$2 00**
  ————— The same, 1 vol..............12mo Bost.   1 50
  Freeman. Early Hist. of Eng., for Child.16mo N. Y.   1 50
  Goldsmith. Hist. of England by Pinnock.12mo Phila.   1 75
  Goodrich, S. G. Pict. Hist. of England,...12mo Phila.   1 75
b. Hume. Smith's "Student's" ed. of Hume.12mo N. Y.   2 00
b. Keightley. History of England, 5 vols...12mo N. Y.   3 75
a. Lossing. History of England, with maps.12mo N. Y.   2 50
  Lingard. History of England, abridged..12mo N. Y.   1 50
  Markham. History of England.........12mo N. Y.   1 50
  Smith, Wm. Smaller Hist. of England..12mo N. Y.   1 00
  Yonge, Chr. Parallel Hist. of England and
               France. Lond... 12mo 7s. 6d.

England—PARTIAL HISTORIES—SPECIAL PERIODS.

a. Aikin, Lucy. Court & Times of Elizabeth.12mo N. Y.   2 00
  ————— — James I., 2 v. Charles, 2 v. *Scarce.*
  Brodie. Constitutional Hist. from Charles
             I., 3 vols.... 8vo Lond. 12 00
c. Burnet, Bp. Hist. of his own Time. Lon. *r.* 8vo 10s. 6d.
  Carlyle. Cromwell's Life and Letters, 2 v.12mo N. Y.   3 50
b. Clarendon. History of the Rebellion, 7 v.12mo Lon. 25s.
  Court and Society. Elizabeth to Anne, 2
             vols. Lond.... 8vo 30s.
  Croly. Life of George IV..............18mo N. Y.   75
  Ellis. Original Letters, Illustrative of
            English History, 11 vols. Lond.
  Freeman. Hist. of Norman Conquest, 3 v. 8vo Oxf. 54s.
a. Froude. History of England from Henry
        VIII. to Eliz., inclusive, 12 vols.12mo N. Y.   15 00
c. Forster, Jno. Statesmen of the Common-
            wealth.... 8vo N. Y.   2 25
c. Guizot. Revolution of 1640............12mo Bohn.   1 75
  ———— Life of Gen. Monk.............12mo Lond.   1 75
  ———— Revolution of 1688.............
 • Halliwell. Letters of the Kings of Eng.. 8vo Lond. 12s.
  Halsted, Caroline. Reign of Rich. III. 2 v. 8vo Lon. 30s.
  James. Naval History of England, 6 vols.12mo Lon. 36s.
c. Jesse. Lives of the Pretenders.........12mo Bohn.   2·25
c. —— Court of Eng. under Stuarts, 3 vols.12mo Bohn.   6 75
  —— Memoirs of Reign of Geo. III., 3 v. Lond. 42s.
a. Macaulay. Hist. of England, Jas. II. to
        Wm. III., inclusive, 8 volumes....12mo N. Y.   18 00
           Cheap Ed. 4 vols. $8 00. 5 v. 8vo Phila.   7 50
  Mackintosh, Sir. J. Revolution of 1688...
  ————————— History of England to
        Geo. III., 2 v. 8vo $6.00. 3 v....12mo N. Y.   3 00
  Mahon, Lord. England, under........2 v. 8vo N. Y.   5 00

Massey. Hist. Eng. 1745-1801. 4 vols.... 8vo Lon. 48s.
b. Martineau, Harriet.   History of England
                        during the Peace, 4 vols.... 8vo Bost. $10 00
Martin. Hist. British Colonies, 6 v. Lond. 8vo 84s.
Olyphant, Mrs. Reign of George III., 2 v. 8vo Lon. 21s.
Pearson. Hist. of Eng. Early & Mid. Ages. 8vo Lon. 12s.
Roberts, Emma. Houses of York and Lan-
                        caster, 2 volumes.... 8vo 26s.
Stanhope, Earl. History of England from
                        Anne to Peace of Utrecht.... 8vo Lond.   8 00
b. Strickland. Queens of Eng., 1 v. $2.25. 8 v.12mo Bohn. 18 00
Towle, G. M. Hist. of Henry V......... 8vo N. Y.   5 00
b. Thierry. Hist. of the Norman Conq't., 2 v.12mo Bohn.   3 50
c. Thackeray. The Four Georges...... ...12mo N. Y.   1 00
Walpole. Reign of George II. and III., 5 v. 8vo Lon. 78s.
Yonge. Hist. of the British Navy, 2 vols. 8vo 42s.

England—ILLUSTRATIVE WORKS ON ENGLISH HISTORY.

Blanc, Louis. Letters on Eng., 2 v. Lond.   16s.
Dixon, W. H. Her Majesty's Tower ; Hist.
                        Study, 2 volumes....12mo Phila.   3 00
Donne, W. B. Correspondence of George
                        III. and Lord North, 2 v.   1867.   Lon. 32s.
a. Evelyn. Diary of Times of Charles II., etc.12mo N. Y.   2 50
a. "Mary Powell." Maiden & Married Life.16mo N. Y.   1 75
Pauli. Alfred the Great..............12mo Bohn.   2 50
a. Pepys. Diary of Charles II. and James II.12mo N. Y.   2 50

England—TRAVELS IN ; RESIDENCE THERE.

Burritt, Elihu. Walks in the Black Coun-
                        try. London....12mo 6s.
——— From Land's End to Johnny Groat's.12mo Lon. 6s.
Coxe, A. C. Bishop. Impressions of Engl.12mo Phila.   1 25
a. Emerson. English Traits.............12mo Bost.   2 00
Felton, C. C. Letters from Europe......12mo Bost.   1 50
a. Hawthorne. Our Old Home...........12mo Bost.   2 00
a. ———   English Note Books, 2 vols.12mo Bost.   4 00
b. Hoppin, J. M. Old England...........12mo N. Y.   1 75
Howitt. Rural Life in England. Lond.. 8vo 12s.
——— Visits to Remarkable Places.
                        2 volumes. London.... 8vo 12s. 6d.
b. ——— Homes & Haunts of Brit. Poets, 2 v. 8vo N. Y.   3 50
b. Miller, Hugh. First Impressions of Engl.12mo Bost.   1 75
Murray. Hand Books of England, 6 vols. Lond. 47s. 6d.
Olmsted, F. L. Walks & Talks of Ameri-
                        can Farmer. 1854....12mo N. Y.   1 25
Sen, Keshub Chunder. English Visit....
        ⁎ The earlier Travels of Carter, Colton, Humphrey, Lester,
            Kohl, and many others, are now out of print.

English Language.—[*See also Composition, Dictionaries,
                        Grammar, Literature, Philology.*]

Abbott, F. & J. R. Seeley. English Lessons
                        for English People....16mo Bost.   1 50

Alford, Dean. The Queen's English......16mo Lond. $1 25
a. Bartlett, J. R. Dictionary of Americanisms. 8vo Bost. 2 50
Chambers. History of English Language.16mo Edinb. 1 25
Clark. Outlines of English Language....12mo N. Y. 1 25
b. Crabbe. English Synonymes........... 8vo N. Y. 2 50
b. Craik. Hist. Eng. Language and Lit., 2 v. 8vo N. Y. 7 50
a. De Vere. Studies in English...........12mo N. Y. 2 50
——— Americanisms...............12mo N. Y. 2 00
Donald. Etymologl. Dict. of Eng. Lang.12mo Phila. 2 50
Ehener & Greenway. Words and Deriv. 8vo Phila.
Fowler. English Language: Elements,&c. 8vo N. Y. 2 50
Gould, E. S. Good English.............12mo N. Y. 1 50
Johnson. Meaning of Words...........12mo . 1 25
Latham. Hand Book of English Language. 8vo Lon. 7s.6d.
b. Marsh. Lectures on English Language.. 8vo N. Y. 3 00
b. ——— Origin and Hist. Eng. Language. 8vo N. Y. 3 00
Moon. The Dean's English............12mo Lond. 1 75
——— Bad English. London..........12mo 3s. 6.
Smith. English Synonymes Explained... 8vo Lond. 6 50
Soule, R. Dict. of English Synonymes... 8vo Bost. 2 00
Strattman. Dict. of Old Eng. Language
12th and 15th Centuries.... 8vo Lond.
Taine. Hist. English Literature, 2 vols.. 8vo N. Y. 10 00
Trench. English Past and Present......12mo Lond. 4s.
a. ——— Study of Words..............12mo N. Y. 1 25
——— Deficiencies in Eng. Dictionaries.12mo Lond. 3s.
Underwood, F. U. Hand Book Eng Lit.12mo Bost. 2 50
c. Wedgewood. Eng. Etymology, new ed. 2 v. 8vo Lond.
b. White R. Grant. Words and their Uses.12mo N. Y. 2 00

English Literature.—[*See Literature.*]

Engraving.

a. Duplessis. Wonders of Engraving.......18mo N. Y. 1 50
Hamerton. Etchers and Etching. Lond. r. 8vo 31s. 6d.
b. Jackson. Treatise on Wood Engraving. r. 8vo Lond. 21 00
Sharpe. On Etching. Edinburgh....... 4to 63s

Epigrams.

Martial. Epigrams. Trans.............12mo Bohn. 3 75

Essays—LITERARY; COLLECTIONS OF.—[*See also Natural Science.*]

a. British Essayists. Viz.: Tatler, 4 v.; Spectator, 8 v.; Guardian, 3 v.; Idler, 1 v.; Rambler, 3 v.; Observer, 3 v.; Adventurer, 3 v.; World, 3 v.; Looker On, 3 v.; Mirror, 2 v.; Connoisseur. 2 v.; Lounger, 2 v. 38 volumes....................16mo Bost. *ea.* 1 25
⁎ Either work may be had separately.
a. Modern British Essayists. Viz.; Macaulay, 1 v.; Carlyle, 1 v.; Alison, 1 v.; Jeffrey, 1 v.; Sydney Smith, 1 v.; Macintosh,

     1 v.; Wilson, 1 v.; Talfourd & Stephen.
     1 v. ....8 volumes... 8vo N.Y. *ea.* $2 00
       ⁎ Either Work may be had separately.

a. Addison. Works, including part of " Spec-
              tator," 6 volumes....12mo Phila. 9 00
    Alford, H. Essays and Addresses. 1869. 8vo Lond.
    Alger, W. R. Solitude of Nature and Man.
                   1867....12mo Bost.
b. Alison, Arch. Essays and Reviews, 1 vol. 8vo N. Y. 2 00
    Arnold, M. Culture and Anarchy. 1869. 8vo L.10s.6d.
    Ascham, R. Works .. ..16mo Lond.
    Bacon, Lord. Advancement of Learning.12mo Lon. 5s.
a. Bacon. Essays; Golden Treasury Series.16mo Lond. 1 25
or b. —— —— Annotated (by Heard)... 8vo Bost. 3 50
c. Beecher, H. W. Star Papers, 2 series....12mo N. Y. 3 00
c. Boyd, A. K. H. "Country Parson" Books, viz.:
    Autumn Holidays....................16mo Bost. 1 75
    Counsel & Comfort..................16mo Bost. 1 75
    Every Day Philosopher..............16mo Bost. 1 75
    Leisure Hours in Town..............16mo Bost. 1 75
    c. Recreations, 2 volumes................16mo Bost. 3 50
a. Brown, John, M. D. Spare Hours, 2 series.16mo Bost. 4 00
b. Browne, Sir Thos. Religio Medici, etc., 3 v.16mo Bost. 7 50
    Buckle, H. T. Essays.................12mo N. Y. 1 00
b. Burke, Edmund. Works, 12 volumes....12mo Bost. 18 00
b. Burnand. Happy Thoughts, 2 vols......16mo Bost. 2 00
a. Carlyle, Thos. Essays, Criti. and Misc., 4 v.12mo N. Y. 9 00
    —— —— ——————8 v.16mo Lond. 7 20
    —— —— —— —— ——1 v. 8vo N. Y. 2 00
a. —— —— Sartor Resartus,12mo N.Y.16mo Lond. 90
c. Channing, W. E. Essays and Works,
          1 vol. $1.00. 3 vols....12mo Bost. 3 00
    Congdon, C. G. "Tribune Essays."......12mo N. Y. 2 00
c. Chesterfield, Lord. Essays, Maxims, etc.16mo Lond. 1 25
    Cobbe, Frances P. Hours of Work & Play.12mo Phila. 1 50
    —— —— Essays on Ethical and Soc. Subj. 8vo Lond.
    Cowley. Essays.....................16mo Bost. 1 25
    Crit. and Social Essays from " The Nation".16mo N. Y. 1 50
a. Curtis, G. W. Potiphar Papers........12mo N. Y. 1 50
    —— —— Prue & I................12mo N. Y. 1 50
    Davy, Sir. Consolations in Travel.......16mo Bost. 1 50
b. De Quincey. Works, 22 vols...........12mo Bost. 33 00
       ⁎ Any work separate.
b. D'Israeli, I. " Amenities" and Curiosities.
                   [*See Literature.*]
c Dodge, Miss. "Gail Hamilton." Works, viz.:
    Country Living.....................16mo Bost. 2 00
    Gala Days.........................16mo Bost. 2 00
    New Atmosphere ....16mo Bost. 2 00
    Skirmishes and Sketches... ....16mo Bost. 2 00
    Stumbling Blocks ....16mo Bost. 2 00
a Emerson, R. W. Works in prose, 2 vols..12mo Bost. 5 00

Emerson's separate Works, viz.:

	Representative Men.............		$2 00
	Conduct of Life.....................		2 00
	Society and Solitude.................		2 00
b.	Epictetus. Works ed. by Higginson..... 8vo Bost.		2 50
	Essays from London " Times"...........16mo N. Y.		50
	Fichte, J. G. Works, 2 vols............12mo Lon. 20s.		
b.	Freeman, E. A. Hist'l Essays. 1871. Lon. 8vo 10s. 6d.		
b.	Foster, John. Decision of Character.....12mo N. Y.		1 25
	—— —— Popular Ignorance, etc....12mo N. Y.		1 25
c.	Franklin, Benj. Essays and Letters, 2 v.18mo N. Y.		1 50
c.	Friswell, J. H. The Gentle Life........12mo Lond.		3 00
	—— —— Other Essays, 6 vols.....12mo Lond. ea. 3 00		
a.	Froude. Short Essays on Great Subjects,2 series.N. Y. ea. 1 50		
	Giles, Henry. Lectures and Essays, 2 vols.12mo Bost.		3 00
a.	Godwin, Parke. Out of the Past, Crit.		
	and Misc. Essays....12mo N. Y.		2 00
a.	Goldsmith, Oliver. Miscellaneous Works.		
	" The Bee," etc., 4 vols... 12mo Phila.		6 00
c.	Hall, Rev. John. Papers for Home Read'g. 8vo N. Y.		1 75
c.	Hare, J. & C. Guesses at Truth.........12mo Bost.		2 00
	Hamilton, Gail. [See Dodge.]		
a.	Hawthorne. American Note Books, 2 vs. Bost.		4 00
b.	Hazlitt, W. Essays and other Works, 6 v.12mo Phila.		9 0.)
	—— —— The same, 5 vols...........12mo Bohn.		9 50
a.	—— —— Round Table..............16mo Lond.		1 25
c.	Helps. Friends in Council, 2 vols.......12mo N. Y.		4 00
	—— Essays. Organization in War...16mo Bost.		1 50
c.	—— —— in Intervals of Business..16mo Bost.		1 50
	—— Short Essays and Aphorisms.....16mo Bost.		1 50
b.	Higginson, T. W. Out of Door Papers...12mo Bost.		1 50
	Holmes, O. W. Sound'gs from the Atlantic.12mo Bost.		1 75
a.	—— " Autocrat " and "Professor".....12mo Bost. ea. 1 75		
a.	Holland, J. G. " Timothy Titcomb"....16mo N. Y.		1 50
c.	—— Gold Foil, $1.75; Plain Talk..16mo N. Y.		1 75
	—— Lessons in Life..............16mo N. Y.		1 75
	—— Letters to Jones..............16mo N. Y.		1 75
b.	Hunt, Leigh. Works (Miscell.) 4 vols....12mo Phila.		6 00
b.	—— —— A Day by the Fire ......16mo Bost.		1 50
b.	—— —— The Seer, 2 vols..........16mo Bost.		3 00
a.	Irving, W. Sketch Book and other Essays.		
	4 vols. 16mo, ea. $1.25 ; 12mo N. Y.		2 25
c.	Jameson, Mrs. Essays on Litera. & Art, 10 v.16mo Lond.		20 00
	[See Fine Arts for separate Works.]		
c.	Jeffrey, F. Essays and Reviews......... 8vo N. Y.		2 00
c.	Jerrold, Douglas. Complete Works, 4 v..12mo Lond.		11 00
a.	Lamb, Chas. Complete Works, 5 vols...12mo N. Y.		9 00
a.	—— —— Elia, separate............12mo N. Y.		2 25
c.	Landor, W. Savage. Complete Works, 2 v.r.8vo Lond.		9 00
a.	—— —— ' Selections from, by Hillard.16mo Bost.		1 25
b.	—— —— Pericles and Aspasia.......16mo Bost.		1 50
	—— —— Imaginary Conversations...12mo Lond. 5s.		

a.	Lowell, J. R. Among my Books.........12mo Bost.	$2 00
a.	——— ——— My Study Windows ......12mo Bost.	2 00
b.	Maistre, Xavier de. Journey Round my Room....12mo N. Y.	1 50
a.	Macaulay, Lord. Essays; best ed., 6 vols.12mo N. Y.	13 50
	——— Cheaper ed., 5 v., $6.25 ; 1 v. ed.. 8vo N. Y.	2 00
c.	Mackintosh. Essays and Miscellanies.... 8vo N. Y.	2 00
	Martineau, Jas. Essays, 2 vols..........12mo Bost.	5 00
c.	Maginn. Reliques of Father Prout......12mo Lond.	3 00
	Millman, H. H. Savanarola and other Essays. Lond.... 8vo 15s.	
b.	Mill, John Stuart. Dissertations and Discussions, 4 vols.... 8vo Bost.	9 00
b.	Mitchell, D. G. Dream Life and other Works, 4 vols.... N. Y.	7 00
c.	More, Hannah. Works (2 v. 8vo, $4;) 7 v. 8vo N. Y.	8 75
c.	Montaigne. Essays; best ed., 4 vols.... 8vo N. Y.	9 00
	——— ———1 vol. 8vo ; Gentle Life ed.12mo Lond.	3 00
	Morte d'Arthur ....12mo Lond.	2 00
	Newman,J.Henry. Essays. Hist.&Crit.,2 v. 8vo Lon. 12s.	
b.	Salmagundi. By Wm. Irving, Washington Irving and Paulding. 16mo $1.25 & $1.75.12mo N. Y.	2 25
c.	Seeley, Prof. Roman Imperialism, etc...12mo Bost.	1 50
	Senior, N. W. Hist. & Philos. Essays, 2 v. 8vo Lond.	
	Shaftesbury, Lord. Characteristics, 3 vs. London.... 8vo $5.00 to 10 00	
	——— ——— ——— New Ed. (by Hatch). 1 vol. London..... 8vo 14s.	
	Small Books on Great Subjects, 22 vols. London....16mo ea. 3s. 6d.	
c.	Smith, Sydney. Essays, etc., from Edinburgh Review....12mo Lond.	4 00
	1 vol. 8vo, N. Y. $2.00. 4 vols. Lond. 8vo 30s.	
	Southey. Common Place Book, 4 v. Lond. 8vo 30s,	
c.	——— ——— ——— 2 vols.... 8vo N. Y.	3 00
	——— The Doctor, a part..........12mo N. Y.	1 25
	——— ——— London.... 8vo 12s. 6d.	
	——— Essays, 2 vols. London. ..... 12s.	
a.	Spectator, The. 8 v. 18mo Bost. $10. 6 v. 8vo N. Y	16 00
	——— ——— complete in 1 volume...... 8vo N. Y.	2 00
c.	Stephen, Sir J. & Talfourd. Essays,etc. 1 v. 8vo N. Y.	2 00
c.	Swift, Dean. Works; carefully selected. 8vo Lond.	2 50
c.	Stowe, Mrs. The Chimney Corner.......12mo Bost.	1 75
	Tattler ; Observer ; Idler, etc. See British Essayists.	
a.	Thackeray. Miscellanies and Essays, 5 v.12mo Bost.	6 25
	——— Early and Late Papers.....12mo Bost.	2 00
a.	Thoreau. Walden, or Life in the Woods.12mo Bost.	2 00
	——— Week on the Concord, etc.....12mo Bost.	2 00
c.	Warner. My Summer in a Garden......12mo Bost.	1 00
b.	Whipple, E. P. Essays and Reviews, 2 v.12mo Bost.	3 00
	——— Success and its Conditions.....12mo Bost.	1 50
	——— Literature and Life.........12mo Bost.	1 50

Whipple. Charac. and Characteristic Men.12mo Bost. $1 75
c. ———— Works complete, 6 vols.......12mo Bost. 8 00
a. Wilson, Prof. John. Essays, 1 vol..... 8vo N. Y. 2 00
c. ———— Noctes Ambrosiana, 6 vols... 8vo N. Y. 10 50
———— Recreations of Christ. North, 2 v. Lon. 12s.
Willis, N. P. Rural Essays & other Works,
12 vols....12mo N. Y. *ea.*1 75

Etching.—[*See Engraving.*]

Ethics.—[*See Moral Science.*]

Ethnology.—[*See also Darwinism, Geography, Natural History.*]

b. Argyll, Duke of. Primæval Man........12mo Lond. 1 50
Baldwin, J. D. Pre-historic Nations.....12mo N. Y. 1 75
b. Brace, C. L. The Races of Men......... 8vo N. Y. 2 50
Cobbell, Prof. J. L. The Unity of Mankind. 8vo N. Y. 1 25
Denison, W. The Antiquity of Man..... 8vo Lond.
Earle. Races of Indian Archipelago. Lon. 8vo 10s. 6d.
a. Figuier. Primitive Man. Illustrated... 8vo N. Y. 4 00
b. Guyot. Earth and Man............ ...12mo Bost. 1 75
b. Huxley, Prof. Man's place in Nature.... 8vo N. Y. 1 50
———— Origin of Species........ 8vo N. Y. 1 25
Knox. The Races of Men.............. 8vo Lond. 4 00
Latham. Native Races of Russian Empire. 8vo Lond. 3 00
———— Natural Hist. of Varieties of Man. 8vo Lon. 21s.
c. Lesley, J. P. Man's Origin & Destiny.... 8vo Phila. 4 00
a. Marsh, G. P. Man and Nature......... 8vo N. Y. 3 00
c. Moore, G. D. The First Man and his place
in Creation. 1866.... 8vo Lond.
Nott & Gliddon. Indigenous Races......*r.* 8vo Phila. 5 00
c. —— ———— Types of Mankind....*r.* 8vo Phila. 5 00
Page, W. Man: Where, Whence, Whither?
Edinburgh....12mo 3s. 6d.
Pickering. The Races of Man... ......12mo Bohn. 2 50
———— —— ———— —— Colored....12mo Bohn. 3 75
b. Prichard. Natural History of Man. Illus.
2 volumes....*r.* 8vo Lond. 11 50
———— Six Ethnographical Maps......folio Lond. 6 00
———— Physical History of Mankind.
5 vols. London.... 8vo 82s.
Thoms, W. J. The Longevity of Man... 8vo Lond.
a. Tylor, E. B. Early Hist. of Mankind. Lon. 8vo 12s.
b. ———— Primitive Culture, 2 vols..... 8vo Lond. 12 00
Wilson, Dr. D. Pre-historic Man........ 8vo Lond. 5 00
Wood, J. G. Uncivilized Races......... 8vo Lond.
b. —— Natural Hist. of Man, 2 vols. *r.* 8vo Lond. 14 00

Etiquette—SOCIAL LIFE AND CUSTOMS.
Art of Conversation.................,....12mo N. Y. 1 50
a. Bazaar. Book of Decorum..........16mo N. Y. 1 00
Calvert, Geo. H. The Gentleman... ...16mo Bost. 1 25
b. Chesterfield. Letters to his Son, etc.....12mo Phila. 1 50

Etiquette for Gentlemen, 75c. ; for Ladies.18mo N. Y. $ 75
a. Habits of Good Society..................12mo N. Y.   1 50
Hartley, Flor. Ladies' Book of Etiquette.
Hand Book of Etiquette.................18mo N. Y.   75
Hervey.   Principles of Courtesy.........12mo N. Y.   1 50
——— Rhetoric of Conversation.......12mo N. Y.   1 50
b. Lieber, Dr. The Character of the Gentle-
man....12mo Phila.   75

Etruria.
Dennis, Geo.   Cities and Cemeteries of
Etruria, 2 vols..... 8vo Lon. 42s.
Gray, Mrs. History of Etruria, 2 vols.....12mo Lon. 24s.
——— Tour to the Sepulchres of Etruria.12mo Lon. 21s.

Evidences of Christianity.
b. Barnes, Rev. Albert. Evidences of Christi.12mo N. Y.   1 75
a. Butler, Bp. Analogy of Religion........12mo N. Y.   1 50
b. Chalmers, Thos. Evidences of Christ'y, 2 v.12mo N. Y.   2 50
Dodge, E.   Evidences of Christianity.....12mo Bost.   1 50
Gregory, Olinthus. Evidences of Christ'y.12mo Bohn.   1 75
a. Keith.   Evidences of Christianity........12mo N. Y.   1 50
Lardner. Credibility of the Gospel Hist., 2 v.12mo Lon. 7s.
Lord, Rev. C. E. Evidences of Natural and
Revealed Religion.... 8vo Phila.   3 50
Paley.   Evidences of Christianity.......18mo N. Y.   75
b. Potter, Bp. A. Evidences of Christianity. 8vo Phila.   2 50
b. Rawlinson. Historic Truth of the Sacred
Records....12mo Bost.   1 75
Watson. Apology for the Bible........18mo N. Y.   60
Whately, Archb. Evidences of Christ'y..12mo N. Y.

**Europe—GENERALLY—ITS HISTORY.—[*See also Chivalry,
Crusades. Middle Ages : names of Countries,
as England, France, etc.*]**
b. Alison. Hist. of Europe. 1789–1815. 20 v.12mo Lond.   30 00
a. ——— The same, 4 vols.. ....:...... 8vo N. Y.   8 00
——— Hist. of Europe. 1815–1852. 8 v.   Lon. 27s.
——— The same, 4 vols..... .... 8vo N. Y.   8 00
——— History to 1815, abridged........ 8vo N. Y.   2 50
a. Arnold, T.   Lectures on Modern History. 8vo N. Y.   1 75
Bury, Viscount. Exodus of the Western
Nations, 2 vols.... 8vo Lon. 32s.
b. Draper, J. W.   Intellectual Development
of Europe.... 8vo N. Y.   5 00
b. Dyer. History of Modern Europe, 4 vols. 8vo Lon. 42s.
——— ——— The same, condensed.....12mo N. Y.
a. Greene.   History of Middle Ages ....12mo N. Y.   1 75
Heeren.   Political System of Europe. Lon. 8vo 14s.
Michelet.   Element. Mod. Hist. of Europe.18mo N. Y.   75
Raumer, F. Von. History of 16th and 17th
Centuries, 2 vols. London.... 8vo 21s.
a. Russell. History of Modern Europe, 3 vs. 8vo N. Y.   6 00
——— ——— ——— ——— 4 vs. 8vo Lond.   10 00

b. Schlegel. Lectures on Modern History...12mo Bohn. $1 75
Sewell & Yonge. European Hist., v. 1 & 2.12mo Lon. *ea.* 1 75
b. Smyth. Lectures on Modern Hist., 2 vols.   Bohn. 3 50
Steinmetz. Hist. Mod. Europe, for Schools.12mo Lon. 5s.
b. Taylor, W. C. Manual of Mod. History. 8vo N. Y. 2 25

Europe—TRAVELS IN.—[*See also England, France, etc.*]
a. Bellows, H. W. The Old World in a New
                              Face, 2 vols....12mo N. Y. 3 50
Colman, H. European Life and Manners.
                        1850. 2 vols..... 8vo Bost.
b. Darley, F. O. C. Sketches Abroad....... 8vo N. Y. 3 50
Durbin, J. P' Observations in Europe.
                        1844. 2 vols....12mo N. Y. 3 00
b. Guild, Curtis. Over the Sea. Tour in Eu. 8vo Bost. 2 50
c. Harper. Hand Book for Europe and East.12mo N. Y. 5 00
a. Longfellow. Outre Mer....... ....12mo Bost. 1 50
c. MacGregor. 1000 Miles in Rob Roy Canoe.16mo Bost. 1 25
Latrobe. Hints for Six Months in Europe.12mo Phil. 1 50
.   Murray. Hand Books for Travellers, viz.:
      The Continent; Northern Europe, 2 v.,
      20s. 6d.; Holland and Belgium; North-
      ern Italy, 12s.; Central Italy, 10s.;
      Southern Italy, 10s.; France, 12s.; Sicily,
      12s.; Switzerland, 10s.; Turkey, 10s.;
      Greece, 15s.; Spain, 2 v., 24s.; Portugal, 9s.12mo Lond.
a. Stephens, J. L. Greece, Turkey, Russia,
                        etc., 2 volumes....12mo N. Y. 3 00
a. Taylor, Bayard. Views Afoot.........12mo N. Y. 1 50
b. ——— ——— Greece and Russia....12mo N. Y. 1 50
b. ——— ——— Northern Europe......12mo N. Y. 1 50
a. ——— ——— By-Ways of Europe...12mo N. Y. 1 50
Wallace, H. B. Art and Scenery in Europe.12mo Phila. 2 00
Ware, Wm. European Capitals. 1851..12mo Bost. 1 00
      ⁎ Many other books of Travel, now *o. p.*

Exercises.—[*See Athletic Sports, Gymnastics, etc.*]

Extravagancies and Superstitions.—[*See Superstitions,
                              Demonology, etc.*]

Extracts.—[*See Quotations.*]

Fables.
Æsop. Fables. Illustrated, 8vo, $2 ; do.   N. Y. 3 00
——— ——— Illustrated by Griset.... 4to   5 00
a. Bewick. Fables, with his own wood-cuts. 8vo L. & N. 3 00
Bidpai, Fables of. By Knatchbull....... 8vo Lond. 3 50
Gay, John. Fables. Illustrated. Lond.16mo 4s. 6d.
Krilof and his Fables....... .... 8vo L. & N. 2 50
a. La Fontaine. Fables. Trans. by Wright. 8vo N. Y. 3 00
b. ——— ——— Illustrated by Doré....'.... 4to Lond. 15 00
Northcote. Artists' Book of Fables. Lon.12mo 6s.
a. Pilpay. Fables. Illustrated............12mo N. Y. 1 50

Facetiæ.—[*See Humorous Works.*]

Fairy Tales and Legends.—[*See also Juveniles.*]

a.	Andersen, Hans C. Fairy Story B'ks, 4 v. (Miller) *ca.*	**$1 25**
a.	——— ——— Wonder Stories.....12mo N. Y.	2 25
	Croker. Fairy Legends of South Ireland.12mo Lon. 5s.	
	Frere. Old Deccan Days (Hindoo Fairy L.)12mo Phil.	1 50
b.	Grimm, Bros. German Popular Stories..12mo N. Y.	3 00
	——— ——— Household Stories... ....12mo N. Y.	2 75
	Hamilton, Count. Fairy Tales..........12mo Bohn.	1 75
a.	Hawthorne N. The Wonder Book.......16mo Bost.	1 50
b.	Keightley. Fairy Mythology........... 12mo Lond.	2 25
	Kingsley. Greek Fairy Tales...........12mo Lond.	1 50
a.	Kingsley. The Water Babies..........12mo Bost.	1 75
b.	Laboulaye. Fairy Tales of all Nations...12mo N. Y. ·	2 00

Family.—[*See Marriage.*]

Farming.—[*See Agriculture.*]

Female Education.—[*See Education.*]

Fiction.—[*See also Fables, Fairy Tales, Juvenile Legends.*]

——— **History of Fiction.**

a.	Dunlop, J. History of Fiction........... 8vo Lond.	3 50
	Forsyth. Novels and Novelists of 18th Cent. L. 10s. 6d. N.	1 50
	Jeaffreson. Novels & Novelists, 2 v. Lon.12mo 21s.	
b.	Masson. British Novelists............ . 8vo Lond.	2 00

Fiction—NOVELS.—[Author's names arranged alphabetically.]

[This classification of Fiction is naturally made on a somewhat different basis from that of the remainder of the list.   Any classification is necessarily arbitrary and incomplete, and we submit this as merely suggestive, and without any claims to finality or infallibility.   No standard can be adopted which, however true for the larger portion of the works classified, will not be open to criticism for its arrangement of many books, concerning which opinions are divided, or whose position in the scale is naturally doubtful.   We have endeavored in our distribution to follow the opinions of the best critics, and the judgment of the better class of readers.   The number of works of fiction is so enormous, and is increasing so rapidly from year to year, that it would be hardly possible to compile any catalogue without omissions and deficiencies.   We trust, however, that in our list, these may not be found numerous or important.

In our classification we have divided works of Fiction into three classes.   The first class contains those which, from their acknowledged literary merit, or from their value in representing some important historical period, social movement, or phase of thought, have come to be regarded as belonging to standard literature.

The second contains the books that come under the designation of good novels, and which can be recommended to the readers of fiction ; and in the third we have inserted those that we consider less desirable, but which may, in most cases, be added without detriment to an extended collection of fiction. It is by no means certain, however, that all of these are even worth reading ; possibly some may be positively mischievous.

The names of the authors, the majority of whose works belong to the first class, are marked *a*. The authors of the second class *b*; and those of the third, *c*. As in many cases, however, the works of one author are of varying merit and value, and would naturally come under different classes, we have used a further designation for the books themselves. Those in the first class are marked with two "stars ;" those in the second with one, and those in the third have been inserted without " star."

When it is considered that the English press alone turns out some three hundred novels every year ; and on our side, including the " yellow-covered," we manufacture nearly as many more, it is obvious that even the long list which we give here is merely a selection from the vast mass of " fiction" now afloat, and indicates only those books which have been most generally recognized as (more or less) worth reading. But even this list comprises a great deal more than any library, private or public (less than the British Museum), is likely to want. Those who select the books indicated by ** in this list will be reasonably secure of having the best works of fiction now in the market.]

    b. About. (French.)
        The Fellah. Translated.... ....12mo Lond. 9s.
      * King of the Mountains...............16mo Lond. 1s.
        Man with Broken Ear................16mo N. Y. $1 25
      * Tolla..............................12mo Edinb. 2s.
        Germaine ; Nose of a Notary........
    b. Aguilar, Grace.
        Days of Bruce, 2 vols..............12mo N. Y.   2 00
      * Home Influence......................12mo N. Y.   1 00
        Home Scenes and Heart Studies......12mo N. Y.   1 00
      * Mother's Recompense...............12mo N. Y.   1 00
        Vale of Cedars.....................12mo N. Y.   1 00
      * Woman's Friendship...............12mo N. Y.   1 00
        Women of Israel, 2 vols...........'..12mo N. Y.   2 00
    c. Aimard, G. ("Sensational" Novels.)
        Gold Seekers, Indian Chief & 6 others..12mo Phila. *ea.* 75

c. Ainsworth, W. H.   (Sensational ?)
    Flitch of Bacon, Jack Shephard, *Jas. ⎫
      II., Lancashire Witches, Merwyn ⎬ 16mo Lon. *ea.* $ 50
    Clithero, * Rookwod, Spendthrift, ⎮
      * The Tower ; 8 vols............. ⎭
    His Novels, 16 vols, bound in 8 vols...16mo Lond. 12 00

a. Alcott, Louisa M.
    * Hospital Sketches..................12mo Bost.   1 50
    * Little Men, $1.50. ** Little Women, 2 v.16mo Bost. 3 00
    * Moods .....:................12mo Bost.   1 50
    * Old Fashioned Girl...............12mo Bost.   1 50
    * Three Proverb Stories..............16mo Bost.   75
    * Morning Glories................ ....16mo N. Y. 1 50
    Allston, Washington.
    Monaldi.............................12mo Bost.   1 50

b. Ames, Mary Clemmer.
    * Eirene ; A Story of New England..... 8vo N. Y. 1 25

a. Andersen, H. C.
    ** Improvisatore.....................12mo N. Y. 1 75
    * Only a Fiddler....................12mo N. Y. 1 75
    * O. F.............................12mo N. Y. 1 75
    * Two Baronesses...................12mo N. Y. 1 75
    Appleton's Library of Romance, 17 vols.. 8vo N. Y. *ea.* 1 50
    Library of Choice Novels, 23 v., paper.   *ea.*   60
    ** Arabian Nights Entertainments, Lane's
             Translation, 2 vols... 12mo N. Y. 3 50

c. Arthur, T. S.   Forty-two Works........   Phila.

a. Auerbach, Berthold.
    * Barefooted Maiden..................12mo Lond. 6s.
    ** Black Forest Stories...............12mo N. Y. 1 50
    * German Tales.....................16mo Bost. 1 00
    ** On the Heights...................16mo Bost. 2 00
    * Professor's Wife...........Lond....12mo 2s. 6d.
    * Villa on the Rhine, 2 vols.........12mo N. Y. 2 00
    * Villa Eden (same as above)..........16mo Bost. 2 00
    * Edelweiss........................16mo Bost. 1 00

a. Austen, Jane.
    ** Emma ; ** Mansfield Park......... ⎫
    ** Pride and Prejudice.............. ⎬ 12mo Bost. *ea.* 1 75
    ** Sense and Sensibility, 4 vols........ ⎭

c. Austen, Mrs. J. G.
    Cipher, 8vo, N. Y., $1.50 ; Moloch Mount. 8vo N. Y. 1 50
    Azeglio, M. d'Ettore. Fieramosca........16mo Bost.

b. Baker, W. M. * The New Timothy.....12mo N. Y. 1 50
a. Balzac, H. De.
    ** Alchemist, The.....................
    * Cæsar Birotteau.....................
    * Petty Annoyances of Married Life....
              (And others.)

c. Banim, J. Works. (Sadlier). 12 vols...12mo N. Y. *ea.* 1 50
b. Baring-Gould. * In Exitu Israel.......12mo L. & N. 1 50
a. Beckford, W. Vathek, an Oriental Tale..16mo N. Y. 1 25

b. Beecher, H. W.   * Norwood............12mo N. Y. $1 50
c. Bird, R. M.   (*Out of print.*)
     Calavar, 12mo, $2; Nick of Woods....12mo Phila.   2 00
     Hawk Hollow, Peter Pilgrim, Infidel..12mo Phila.
a. Bjornsen, B.   (Swedish Novelist).
     **Arne, 12mo, $1.00.   Fisher Maiden....16mo N. Y.   1 25
     * Happy Boy.......................12mo N. Y.   1 00
     * Love and Life in Norway...........16mo N. Y.   1 25
b. Black, W.
     * In Silk Attire, * Kilmeny, * Love and ⎫
        Marriage, *Mincing Lane, *Daugh- ⎬ 8vo N. Y. *ea.*   50
        ter of Heth, paper.............. ⎭
c. Blessington, Lady. 5 Novels (now *passé*).
     **Blindpits.   A Story of Scottish Life...12mo N. Y.   1 75
a. Boccacio.   **The Decameron. 10 days Ent.12mo Bohn.   1 75
b. Bolté, Amely (German).   Mad. De Stael..12mo N. Y.   1 50
b. Borrow, Geo.
     * Lavengro, * Romany Rye........... 8vo N. Y. *ea.*   50
     Bound to John Company, paper......... 8vo N. Y.   75
c. Braddon, Miss.   (Sensational ?)
     * Aurora Floyd, Black Band, Birds of Prey, ⎫
        Markham, Diavolo, Doctor's Wife, Elea- ⎪
        nor, H. Dunbar, Marchmont, * Lady ⎪   *each*
        Audley's Secret, Lady Lisle, Only a Clod, ⎬ 8vo N. Y.   75
        Rupert Godwin, Sir Jasper, Lovells of ⎪   (paper.)
        Arden (1871), and some others not re- ⎪
        printed .... ⎭
b. Bradley ("Cuthbert Bede").
     * Adventures of Verdant Green.......12mo N. Y.   1 50
a. Bremer, Fredrika.
     * Fathers and Daughters, * Four Sis- ⎫
        ters, ** Home, ** The Neighbors. ⎬ 12mo Phil. *ea.* 1 50
     The same, 4 vols...................12mo Bohn.   7 00
     —— —— 4 vols., paper............. 8vo N. Y.   2 00
     * President's Daughter, Every Day Life, ⎫
     * Parsonage of Mora, Midnight Sun.. ⎬ 8vo N. Y. *ea.*   25
     * H. Family, 50c.; Nina, 50c........... 8vo N. Y.
c. Brewster, Anne M. H. (Phila.)
     Compensation ....12mo Phila.   1 75
     St. Martin's Summer................
a. Bronté, Charlotte ("Currer Bell ').
     **Jane Eyre, ** Professor, ** Shirley, ⎫
     **Villette .... ⎬ 12mo N. Y. *ea.* 1 50
b. Bronté, Anne.   Tenant of Wildfell Hall...12mo N. Y.   1 50
b. Bronté, Emily.
     Agnes Grey and Wuthering Heights..12mo N. Y.   1 50
c. Brooke, H.   (An old writer.)
     Fool of Quality, 2 vols..............12mo Lon. 21s.
b. Brooks, Shirley.
     * Aspen Court, paper, 50c.; *Silver Cord. 8vo N. Y.   2 00
     * Gordian Knot, 50c.; * Sooner or Later. 8vo N. Y.   2 00

c. Broughton, Rhoda.
    Red as a Rose is She..........paper. 8vo N. Y. **$** 60
    * Cometh up as a Flower......paper. 8vo N. Y.   60
c. Brown, Chas. Brockedon. (Early American writer.)
    Arthur Mervyn, Edgar Huntley,⎫ 12mo Phila. 6 00
    Jane Talbot, Ormond, Wieland, 6 v.⎭
a. Brown, John, M. D. ** Marjorie Fleming..16mo Bost.   25
    Brunton, Mary. (Early English Writer.)
    Discipline, Self Control...........ea.12mo *o. p.*
    Bulwer.—[*See Lytton.*]
a. Burney, Miss. ** Evelina.............12mo N. Y. 1 50
    * Cecilia, * The Wanderer, *o. p*..... ...
b. Carlen, Emilie (Swedish).
    * Brothers, 25c.; Home in Valley, 50c. ;⎫
    * Ivar, 50c.; John, 25c.; Lovers' ⎪ 8vo N. Y.
    Stratagem, 50c.; Woman's Life, ⎬
    75c.; Seven more *o. p.*, paper.....⎭
b. Carleton, Wm.
    * Traits & Stories of Irish Peasantry, 2 v. 8vo L. & N. 6 00
a. Carlyle, T.
    **Specim's of German Romance. Trans.12mo N. Y. 1 25
b. Cary, Alice.
    * Clovernook, * Married Not Mated..*ea.* 12mo N. Y.
    The Bishop's Son..................12mo N. Y. 1 75
a. Cervantes.
    **Don Quixote, 1 vol. $1.50. 4 vols.....12mo Bost. 5 00
    —— —— Illustrated. Various editions. 4to Lond. 3 75
c. Chamier, Capt. Ben Brace. Life of Sailor.   Lon. *ea.* 80
a. Chamisso, A. Von. ** Peter Schlemihl.
b. Charles, Mrs.
    **Chronicles of Schonberg Cotta Family..12mo N. Y. 1 50
    * Diary of Kitty Trevelyan...........12mo N. Y. 1 50
    * Davenants and Draytons............12mo N. Y. 1 75
    * Early Dawn......................12mo N. Y. 1 50
    * Both Sides of the Sea..............12mo N. Y. 1 75
    * Winfred Bertram.................12mo N. Y. 1 75
    Victory of the Vanquished...........12mo N. Y. 1 75
    Cripple of Antioch.................16mo N. Y. 1 25
    Martyrs of Spain..................16mo N. Y. 1 25
    Sketches of Christianity............16mo N. Y. 1 25
    Two Vacations....................16mo N. Y. 1 25
c. Charlotte, Elizabeth. Works, 12 vols...   N. Y.
a. Chateaubriand.
    * Atala, * Aben Hamet, * The Martyrs..   Lond.
b. Chesebro, Caroline.
    * Foe in the Household..............12mo Bost.
    * Beautiful Gate, Dreamland, Isa, Philly ⎫
    and Kit, Victoria, Amy Carr ....⎬
    Peter Carradine...................12mo N. Y. 1 75
b. Chubbock, Emily (Fanny Forrester).
    Alderbrook, 2 vols.................

c. Church, Mrs. Ross (Florence Marryatt).
    * For Ever and Ever, Girls of Feversham, ⎫   *each*
      Love's Conflict, Too Good for Him, ⎬ 8vo Bost.   75
      Woman *agst*. Woman, Veronique.. ⎭   paper.
    * Prey of the Gods, Poison of Asps..*ea*. 8vo N.Y.&P. 30
    Her Lord and Master, Gerald Estcourt, ⎫
    Petronel, Temper................. ⎬ Lond.
b. Clarke, C.
    * Mademoiselle Mori....... ....12mo Bost. 1 50
    * On the Edge of the Storm............12mo N. Y. 1 50
b. Clarke, Mary Cowden.
    * The Iron Cousin..............Lond.12mo 80c. and 1 50
    Clemens, J.
    The Rivals, Bernard Lile, and others, 4 v.12mo Phila. 5 50
c. Cockton, Henry. Valentine Vox..Lon. 80c. 8vo Phila. 2 00
               (And six others.)
b. Collins, Mortimer.
    * Marquis and Merchant; Vivian...... 8vo N. Y. *ea.* 50
a. Collins, Wilkie.
    * After Dark, 8vo, $1 ; *Armadale, 8vo, $2 ; *Antonina,
      8vo, 50c.; * Basil, 16mo, 60c.; ** Dead Secret,
      12mo, $1.75; * Hide and Seek, 8vo, $1 ; * Man
      and Wife, 8vo, $1.50; * Moonstone, 8vo, $2 ; ** No
      Name, 8vo, $2 ; * Queen of Hearts, 8vo, $1.50 ;
      * Sister Rose, 8vo, 25c.; * Stolen Mask, 8vo, 25c.;
      ** Woman in White, 8vo, $2; * Yellow Mask,
      8vo, 25c. N. Y.
    * Constance Aylmer, a Tale of 17th Century.12mo N. Y. 1 50
b. Conscience, Hendrick. (Flemish Novelist).
    * Tales of Flemish Life (and 8 others)..16mo Bost. 75
c. Cooke, J. Esten (of Va.).
    Henry St. John and other Novels, 4 vs.12mo N.Y. *ea.* 1 50
a. Cooper, Fenimore.
    Novels, complete, 32 vols., fine ed., $72.12mo N. Y. 40 00
    Each Work separate (fine ed., $2.25)..12mo N. Y. 1 25
      Viz.: ** Spy, Crater, Pilot, Red Rover, Precaution,
      Lincoln, Mohicans, Pathfinder, Deerslayer, Mer-
      cedes, Admirals, Wing and Wing, Wyandotte,
      Afloat and Ashore, Prairie, Pioneers, Wishton-
      wish, Homeward Bound, Home as Found, Water-
      witch, Bravo, Heidenmauer, Headsman, Monikins,
      Wallingford, Chainbearer, Satanstoe, Red-skins, -
      Jack Tier, Sea Lions, Oak-Openings, Ways of
      the Hour.................. ....
    **The Sea Tales (separately) 10 vols. (fine ed., $22.50.) 12 50
    **Leather Stocking Tales, 5 vols. (fine ed., $11.25.) 6 25
b. Cottin. * Elizabeth, or Exiles of Siberia..32mo N. Y. 50
a. Craik, Mrs. (Dinah Muloch.)
    * Agatha's Husband, paper, 50c.; ** A Brave ⎫
    Lady, $1.50; * Christian's Mistake, $1.50; ⎬
    * Head of Family, 75c.; ** John Halifax, ⎬ N. Y.
    $1.50; * Life for Life, $1.50............ ⎭

a. Craik, Mrs. (Dinah Muloch.)
  * Mistress and Maid,50c.; **Noble Life,$1.50;⎫
  ** Ogilvies, 50c.; * Olive, 50c.; * Two⎪
  Marriages,$1.50; * Unkind Word, $1.50;⎪
  ** Woman's Kingdom, $1; * Faith Un-⎬ N. Y.
  win, 60c.; * Leslie Tyrrell, 60c.; * Lost⎪
  and Won, 60c.; *Mildred, 50c.; * Ester⎪
  Hill; Hannah (1871), 8vo.............⎭

b. Craven, Mrs. A.
  * Anne Severin, $1.25; ** Sister's Story...12mo N. Y. $2 50
a. Croly, Rev. Geo.   * Salathiel, 3 vols.....12mo Lond.
c. Crouch, Julia.   * Three Successful Girls..12mo N. Y.   1 50
b. Cummings, Miss M. S.
  * El Fureidis, $1.75; * Haunted Hearts,⎫
    * Lamp Lighter,$1.75;Mabel Vaughan.⎬ 12mo Bost.
b. Curtis, G. W. [*See Essays.*]   * Trumps..12mo N. Y.   2 00
c. Dasent, G. W.
  * Gislè, the Outlaw.................... 8vo L. & P.   3 50
  * Popular Tales from the Norse.... ...12mo L. & P.   1 50
b. Davis, L. C. (Phila.) * The Stranded Ship..16mo N. Y.   75
b. Davis, Mrs. R. H. (Phila.)
  * Dallas Galbraith........ .... 8vo Phila.   2 00
  **Margaret Howth.....................12mo Bost.   1 25
  * Waiting for the Verdict.............. 8vo N. Y.   2 00
a. De Foe. ** Robinson Crusoe (16mo, $1.50).12mo N. Y.   2 50
b. De Forest, J. W.   Seacliff..............12mo Bost.
  * Miss Ravenel's Conversion............12mo N. Y.   1 50
  Kate Beaumont: Southern Society....12mo Bost.
De la Rame, Julia. The "Ouida" Novels. (Sensational.)
  Beatrice Boville,$1.75; Rand. Gordon.12mo Phila.   1 75
  Granville de Vigne, Puck, Strath-⎫
    more, Tricotrin, Under Two Flags.⎬ 12mo Phil.*ea.* 2 00
c. De Mille, J.
  Cryptogram........................ 8vo N. Y.   2 00
  Cord and Cheese.................... 8vo N. Y.   75
  * Lady of the Ice..................... 8vo N. Y.   1 25
c. De Leon, T. C.   Askaros Kassis, the Copt.12mo Phila.   1 50
a. De Stael, Madame.
  **Corinne, 12mo N. Y., $1.75; **Delphine.12mo N. Y.
b. De Witt, Madame.
  * French Country Family.   *Motherless.12mo N. Y.*ea.*1 50
c. De Vere.   The Great Empress, a portrait..12mo Phila.   1 75
a. Dickens.
  **Complete Works, Globe edition, 15 vols.12mo N. Y.   22 00
  ————— ——— Household ed., 55 vs.12mo N. Y.   54 00
  ————— ——— Riverside, ed., 28 vs.12mo N. Y.   54 00
  ————— ——— Chas. Dickens ed.,15 v.12mo Bost.   22 00
  ————— ——— Diamond ed., 15 vols.16mo Bost.   22 00
  ————— ——— Plum Pudding ed., 6 v.12mo N. Y.   10 50
  Separate Works, in cloth.............   *ea.* 1 50
  ————— —— in paper...... ....   *ea. abt.*   30
  Viz.: Nickleby, Old Curiosity and Part 1 Sketches,

a. Dickens. Separate works, in paper......   *ea. abt.* $ 30
Barnaby Rudge, Sketches, Chuzzlewit, Dombey,
Oliver Twist & Great Expectations, Copperfield,
Two Cities and Hard Times, Bleak-House, Little
Dorrit, Christmas Stories, American Notes and
Italy, Mutual Friend, Pickwick, Uncommercial
and Humphrey's Clock, Nickleby, Edwin Drood.
c. Dickinson, Anna E. What Answer?......12mo Bost.   1 50
b. Dinglestedt. ** The Amazon. Trans...12mo N. Y.   1 00
a. D'Israeli. Novels Complete, 6 vols......12mo Lond.   15 00
**Coningsby,*Cont. Fleming,Henrietta ⎫
  Temple, * Sybil, ** Tancred, * Ve-   ⎬   or
  netia,*Vivian Grey,*Alroy, Young   ⎪ *r.*8vo N. Y.*ea.*   50
  Duke........................ ⎭
  * Lothair............................ 8vo N. Y.   2 00
**Dorothy Fox. (By Mrs. Parr.)........12mo N. Y.
c. Douglas, Amanda.
  * With Fate against Him.............12mo N. Y.   1 50
                (Four others.)
a. Droz, Gustave.
  **Around a Spring .... 8vo N. Y.   75
c. Drury, Ann H. Eastbury..............12mo N. Y.   1 50
  Misrepresentation................... 8vo N. Y.   1 00
b. Dumas, Alex. Count of Monte Cristo, 2 v.12mo Lond.   1 50
  Three Musketeers; 20 Years After...12mo Lond.*ea.*1 00
  Margaret de Valois............. .....12mo Lond.   1 00
  Brageloue, 2 vols...................   Lond.   2 50
        (48 stories in all—chiefly in 8vo, paper, Phila.)
b. Ebers. The Daughter of an Egyptian
                King. Trans. by Reed....12mo Phila.   1 75
b. Eden, Emily. * Semi-Detached House..
  * Semi-Attached Couple..............12mo Bost.   1 25
a. Edgeworth, Maria
  **Tales and Novels, 20 vols. in 10......12mo N. Y.   15 00
  The same, 10 vols...................12mo L.& B.   15 00
b. Edwards, Amelia B. * Barbara's Hist. ⎫
  * Debenham's Vow, 75c.; *Half a Mil- ⎪
    lion, 75c.; *Hand and Glove, 50c.; ⎬
    * Ladders of Life, 50c.; * Miss   ⎪ 8vo N. Y.
    Carew, 50c.; * My Brother's Wife,   ⎪
    50c.; * The Sylvestres.......... ⎭
b. Edwards, Mrs. Annie.
  **Archie Lovell (Lond. 12mo, $1)....... 8vo N. Y.   1 75
  * Stephen Lawrence, ** Susan Fielding. 8vo N. Y.*ea.*2 00
  * Ought We to Visit Her.............. 8vo N. Y.   2 00
b. Edwards, Miss M. Betham.
  * Doctor Jacobs, 16mo, $1; Kitty. .... 8vo N. Y.   50
  * The Outcasts. Illustrated.......... 8vo Phila.
  Eiloart, Mrs. Cris. Faülie's Boyhood..
  Curate's Discipline,50c; From Thistles. 8vo N. Y.   50
  Eliot, Geo. [See *Lewes, Mrs.*]
  Elliott, C. W. Wind and Whirlwind....12mo N. Y.   1 50

c. Ellis, Mrs.
Hearts and Homes...................12mo N. Y. $1 50
Home or Iron Rule ....12mo N. Y.   1 50
Look at the End....... ....paper. 8vo N. Y.   50
    (8 other Works, not reprinted.)
  * Episodes in an Obscure Life...paper.. 8vo Phila.   75
a. Erckmann—Chatrian. (French authors, trans.)
  **Blockade, ** Conscript, * Madame ⎫
    Therese,** Waterloo, * Plebiscite, ⎬ 16mo N. Y. *ea.*   90
    Invasion of France .... ⎭
Evans, Augusta J. [*See Wilson, Mrs.*]
  Fair Harvard; a story of College Life.....12mo N. Y.   1 50
a. Farjeon, B. L.
  **Grif, 30c.; * Joshua Marvel, paper.... 8vo N. Y.   40
c. Fay, Theo. S. * Norman Leslie.........12mo N. Y.   1 75
  Countess Ida; Hoboken, *o. p.*
a. Fenelon. *'Telemachus.................12mo N. Y.   2 00
c. Ferrier, Miss. Marriage, 80c. Inheritance.12mo Lond.   60
b. Feuillet, A.
  * Romance of a Poor Young Man.......12mo N. Y.   1 50
a. Fielding. Whole works 1 v.8vo,$5; or 10 v. 8vo Lond. 40 00
  **Amelia, 12mo $1.50. * Tom Jones, 2v.12mo N. Y.   2 75
  * Joseph Andrews....................16mo Lond.   80
Fouqué.
  Wild Love, 12mo; ** Aslauga's ⎫
    Knight, 5s. 6d.; * Minstrel Love, ⎪
    4s.; *Magic Ring, 4s.: *Sir Elidve, ⎬ Lond.
    7s.................................. ⎭
  * Theodolph, $1.50; **Undine & Sintram.12mo N. Y.   1 25
c. Fraser, J. B. Kuzzilbash (and two others).*o.p.* Lond.
c. "Foxton, E." Agnes Wentworth.........12mo Phila.   1 50
a. Freytag.
  **Debit & Credit, $1.50; Lost MSS., *pa.*8vo N. Y.   75
  * Friends and Acquaintances. By Author ·
    of Episodes of Obscure Life......... 8vo Phila.
b. Fullerton, Lady Georgiana.
  Constance Sherwood, 2 vols.; * Ellen ⎫
    Middleton; * Lady Bird, 2 v., paper, ⎬ 16mo Leip.*ea.v.* 60
  * Mrs. Gerald's Niece, paper........... 8vo N. Y.   60
  * Stormy Life, 8vo $1.50; Too Strange. 8vo N. Y.   1 50
b. Galt, John (Scotch Novelist).
  * Annals of the Parish, * Provost, The ⎫ Lond. *ea.* 2s. 6d.
    Entail, Sir A. Wylie............. ⎭
  Laurie Todd.....................12mo Lond. 3s. 6d.
c. Garibaldi (Italian Patriot).
  The Rule of the Monk, paper........ 8vo N. Y.   50
a. Garrett, Edward.
  **The Crust of the Cake..............12mo Lond.   1 75
  **Occupations of a Retired Life. ....12mo Lond.   1 75
b. Garrett, Edw. & Ruth.
  * White as Snow...................12mo N. Y.   1 50
  * Quiet Miss Godolphin...............16mo Phila.   75

a. Gaskell, Mrs.
> **Cranford, 1.25 ; * Dark Night, paper, 50c. ; ** Mary Barton, paper, 50c. ; *Lady Ludlow, 25c. ; **North and South, 50c. ; *Right at Last, $1.50 ; **Ruth, 2 v.(Tauch.), $1.20 ; **Sylvia and Lovers, 75c. ; ** Wives and Daughters, Illust., $2 00......... } 8vo N. Y.

b. Gautier, T. Romance of the Mummy... 8vo N. Y.
b. Gerstaecker, F. (German.)
> Feathered Arrow, 2s. 6d. ; Two Convicts.12mo Lond. 2s.
> * Frank Wildmew ....18mo Bost.
> * How a Bride was Won.............. 8vo N. Y. $1 50

c. Gilbert, W. De Profundis, 2 v., 12s. Dr.⎫
> Austin, 6s. ; Goldsworthy Family, 2 ⎬   Lond.
> v., 21s. ; The Wizard, 21s......... ⎭
> * King George's Middy............12mo Bost.   2 50
> Monomaniac ....12mo N. Y.   1 75
> * Struggle in Ferrara.............. 8vo Phila.   1 50

b. Girardin, Madame (French).
> * Marguerite ; Stories of Old Maid.....
b. Godwin, Wm. * Caleb Williams........16mo N. Y.   37
c. Gleig, Rev. L.
> * The Subaltern ; The Hussar (2 others).12mo Lond.   80
a. Goethe. * Elective Affinities.........⎱ 12mo Lond.   1 75
> * Sorrows of Werter................⎰
> **Wilhelm Meister, 2 vols.............12mo Bost.   3 50
a. Goldsmith. The Vicar of Wakefield....12mo Phila.   1 00
c. Gore, Mrs. Abednego, the Money Lender. 8vo Phil.   50
> (28 more novels, 8vo, paper, Phila.)
c. Grant, Jas. Scottish Cavalier (15 more)..12mo Lond. *ea.*   80
c. Grattan, T. C. Heiress of Bruges (and 3 more), *o. p.*
b. Greek Romances of Heliodorus, Longus,
> * Achilles Tatius, 1 vol..............12mo Bohn.   2 50
c. Grey, Mrs. The Gambler's Wife (17 more),
>   paper.... 8vo N. & P.
b. Griffin, Gerald. Works, 10 vols........12mo N. Y.   12 00
a. Grimm (German). Household Stories....12mo Bost.   2 50
b. Guerazzi, F. D. * Beatrice Cenci.......12mo N. Y.   1 75
> * Isabella ....12mo N. Y.
b. Gutzkow, Karl (Russian).
> * Through Night to Light.............12mo Lond. 3s. 6d.
b. Hacklander. * Clara..................12mo N. Y.   1 50
> * Enchanting and Enchanted.........12mo Phila.   1 25
a. Hale, E. E.
> * If, Yes, and Perhaps, **Sybaris, *Ten ⎱ 12mo Bost. *ea.* 1 50
> Times One, ** Ingham Papers. . ...⎰
> Halifax, Jno., Author of. [*See Craik.*]
a. Haliburton, T. C.
> **The Clockmaker, or Sam Slick...·....12mo N. Y.   1 25
> * Old Judge, paper.................. 8vo N. Y.   75
> * Nature and Human Nature.........

b. Hall, Mrs. S. C.
  Tales of Woman's Trials, paper...... 8vo N. Y. $ 75
  Midsummer's Eve, Whiteboy, paper.. 8vo N. Y. *ea.* 50
  * Sketches of Irish Character.........*r.* 8vo Lond. 8s.
  * Stories of Irish Peasantry............12mo Lond. 2s. 6d.
  Uncle Horace, 8s. ; Marian...........12mo Lond. 2s.
  Can Wrong be Right? 2 vols.........12mo Lond. 21s.
  Groves of Blarney, Harry O'Reardon.. Lond.
c. Hannay, D. Ned Allen, paper........... 8vo N. Y. 50
c. Hamilton, Capt. Cyril Thornton...*ro. p.*..12mo N. Y.
b. Hamley, E. B.
  **Lady Lee's Widowhood, paper....... 8vo N. Y. 50
b. Hardy, Lady. * Daisy Nichol, paper..... 8vo N. Y. 50
 "Harland, Marion." [*See Terhune, Mrs.*]
b. Harrington, F.
  * Inside ; a Chronicle of Secession......12mo N. Y. 1 75
b. Harris, Miriam, Mrs.
  "Rutledge" Novels, viz. : * Rutledge, }
  *St. Philip, *Sutherlands, *Frank }
  Warrington,*Roundhearts, Louie's } 12mo N. Y. *ea.* 1 75
  Last Term, * Vandermarcke...... }
  Hartman. Last Days of a King........12mo Phila. 1 25
b. Harte, Bret. * Condensed Novels........12mo Bost. 1 50
  **Luck of Roaring Camp....... ......12mo Bost. 1 50
c. Hatton, Jos. * Christopher Kenrick.....12mo N. Y. 1 50
a. Hawthorne. ** Blithedale Romance.....12mo Bost. 1 50
  **House of Seven Gables...............12mo Bost. 2 00
  **Marble Fawn ; Mosses............ ...12mo Bost. *ea.* 2 00
  **Scarlet Letter and Blithedale, 2 v. in 1.12mo Bost. 2 00
  **Twice Told Tales. 2 vols. in 1........12mo Bost. 2 00
  (Posthumous work) ....12mo Bost.
b. Helps, Arthur. **Realmah......... ...16mo Bost. 2 00
c. Hentz, Caroline Lee.
  Planter's Northern Bride.............12mo Phila. 1 75
   (Twelve others, each $1.75.)
c. Herbert, H. W. Roman Traitor........12mo Phila. 1 75
  ("Brothers" and six others *o. p.*)
b. Heyse, P. **Arabiata, etc., paper.......16mo Leips. 60
b. Higginson, T. W. Malbone.............12mo Bost. 1 50
b. Hillern, W. *Only a Girl..............12mo Phila. 2 00
b. Hoefer, E. * The Old Countess.........12mo 1 00
b. Hoffman, C. F. * Greyslaer, 1849,(*o. p.*) 2 v.12mo N. Y.
b. Hofland, Mrs. (Author of *Juveniles* also.)
  * Czarina, *Dan'l Denison, Unloved One. 8vo N. Y. *pa.* 50
b. Hogg, James ("The Ettrick Shepherd").
  * Brownie of Bodsbeck, paper.......... 8vo N. Y.
  (Six other novels, Edinb. and Lond.)
c. Holmes, Maria J.
  * Lena Rivers, Millbank, * Ethelyn's }
  Mistake, Dora Deane, Darkness and } 12mo N. Y. 1 50
  Daylight, Tempest and Sunshine.. }
   (And 8 others, same price.)

b. Holmes, Oliver Wendell.
    * Elsie Venner, * Guardian Angel.. ...12mo Bost.*ea.* $2 00
b. Hood, Thos., * Tylney Hall.............12mo Bost. 2 00
c. Holland, J. G., * The Bay Path.........12mo N. Y. 2 00
b. Hook, Theo.
    Gilbert Gurney, Gurney Married,   Lond. *ea.* 2s.
      * Sayings and Doings, Maxwell...
    All in Wrong, Widow and Marquis...   Lon. *ea.* 1 00
c. Hope, Thos. Anastasius................12mo N. Y. 1 50
c. Howard, Edward. Old Commodore...... 8vo N. Y.
    Jack Ashore, Outward Bound, * Ratt-   N. Y.
      lin the Reefer, Sir H. Morgan....
b. Howitt, Mary.
    * Author's Daughter, paper........... 8vo N. Y. 25
    * Heir of West Wayland.............. N. Y. 1 50
    * Peasant and Landlord............... N. Y. 1 50
    [*See also Juveniles.*]
b. Howitt, Wm.
    * Jack of the Mill, paper.............. 8vo N. Y. 25
    Hall & Hamlet; Woodburn Grange...   Lond.
a. Hughes, Thos.
    * Scouring of the White Horse........16mo Lond. 1 25
    **Tom Brown at Oxford & Rugby, 3 vols.12mo Bost. 4 25
    ——— ——— ——————— *pa.* 2 vols. 8vo N. Y. 1 25
a. Hugo Victor.
    Claude Gueux.....................12mo N. Y. 1 50
    **Hunchback of Notre Dame, paper.... 8vo N. Y. 75
    Man who Laughs................... 8vo N. Y. 1 50
    **Les Miserables .. .. 8vo N. Y. 2 50
    * Toilers of the Sea. Illust........... 8vo N. Y. 1 50
b. Inchbald, Mrs. * Simple Story, paper... 8vo N. Y. 50
c. Ingraham, J. H. La Fitte, Monterama, etc., 4 vols., *o. p.*
    * Prince of House of David...........12mo Bost. 2 00
    * Throne of David...................12mo Bost. 2 00
    * Pillar of Fire.....................12mo Bost. 2 00
a. Irving, Washington.
    **The Alhambra, ** Bracebridge Hall,   16mo, $1.25, or 1 75
      **Knickerbocker, **Tales of a Trav-   12mo, $2.25, or 2 50
      eller, * Wolfert's Roost...........
b. James, G. P. R.
    Attila, Agnes Sorrel, Agincourt, Anah
      Neil, A Whim, Arabella Stuart,   12mo bds. Lon. 50
      Beauchamp, Convict, Forest Days,   or 8vo pa. N. Y. 50
      Russell, Margaret Graham. ...*ea.*
      (25 other novels, 8vo., pa., N. Y., *ea.* 50c.)
    Club Book, De Lorme, Old School,
      * Gypsey, * Henry of Guise, * H.
      Masterton, Man at Arms, Chs.
      Tyrell, Jacquerie, Morley Ernstein,   12mo N. Y. *ea.* 1 50
      One in a Thousand, * Phil. Augus-
      tus, Cœur de Lion, Ancient Re-
      gime, Robber, * Richelieu........

b. James, G. P. R.
 * Huguenot, King's Highway, String of ⎫
  Pearls, Mary Burgundy, * Darnley, ⎬12mo N. Y.*ea.*$1 50
  * Marst. Hall, Desultory Man..... ⎭
 These can be had also in 16mo Leip., or 12mo bds. Lon. *ea.* 50
c. Jeaffreson, I. C.
 * Olive Blake's Good Work, paper..... N. Y. 75
 Isabel, 12mo., N.Y., $1.50; Live it Down. 8vo N. Y. 1 00
 Not Dead Yet .... 8vo N. Y. 1 75
b. Jenkin, Mrs. C. * Madame de Beaupré..16mo N. Y. 1 00
 * Two Fr. Marriages ;* Who Breaks Pays.16mo N. Y. 1 00
 * Within an Ace...................16mo N. Y. 1 00
b. Jerrold, Douglas. Works, 4 vols........12mo Lond. 11 00
c. Jewsbury, Miss.
 Constance Herbert; Zoe, paper....... 8vo N. Y. *ea.* 50
 Half Sisters, Adopted Child.........16mo N. Y. *ea.*1 00
a. Johnson, Dr., * Rasselas.............32mo N. Y. 37
b. Judd, S. * Margaret.................16mo Bost. 1 50
b. Kavanagh, Julia.
 Adele, Beatrice, *Daisy Burns, *Dora, ⎫
  * Grace Lee................... ⎬ 12mo N. Y. *ea.*1 50
 Madeleine, $1 ; Nathalie, Queen Mab.12mo N. Y. *ea.*1 00
 Rachael Gray, $1; *Seven Years, *Sybil.12mo N. Y. *ea.*1 50
a. Kennedy, John P.
 **Horse Shoe Robinson..............12mo N Y. 2 00
 * Rob of Bowl, $2.00. * Swallow Barn.12mo N. Y. 2 00
 Quodlibet ....12mo N. Y. 2 00
b. Kimball, R. B.
 * St. Leger, To-Day, * Undercurrents, ⎱
  Was he Successful, * Student Life. ⎰12mo N. Y. *ea.* 1 75
a. Kingsley, Charles. ** Alton Locke.....12mo N. Y. 1 50
 * Hereward, ** Hypatia, ** Two Years ⎱ 12mo Bost. *ea.* 1 75
  Ago, * Amyas Leigh............ ⎰
 **Yeast ....12mo N. Y. 1 50
b. Kingsley, Henry. Austin Elliot........12mo Bost. 1 75
 * Hetty, paper......................... 8vo N. Y. 25
 **Hillyars & Burtons, *Leighton Court, ⎱ 12mo Bost. 1 75
  * Ravenshoe, * Geoff. Hamlyn...... ⎰
 * Silcotes, paper, 8vo., 75c. Stretton, *pa.* 8vo N. Y. 40
 The Harveys, 12mo Lon.; The Lost Child. 4to Lond. 1 50
b. Laboulaye, E. * Abdallah.............16mo Lond. 1 25
b. Lamartine, A. * Genevieve, paper....... 8vo N. Y. 25
 * My Youth, paper, 25c. Raphael......12mo N. Y. 1 25
 * Stone Mason of St. Point............12mo N. Y. 1 25
c. Landon, Miss ("L. E. L.")
 Ethel Churchill (and 4 others.)........ Lond.
c. Lawrence, Geo. A. Anteros, 1 50. paper, 8vo N. Y. 50
 Brakspeare, paper .... 8vo N. Y. 50
 Breaking a Butterfly................. 8vo Phila. 35
 Guy Livingstone, 12mo., Lond., $1...12mo N. Y. 1 50
 Maurice Dering, 50c. Sans Merci, *pa.* N. Y. 50
 Sword & Gown, paper............... N. Y. 25

Lee, Holme. [See *Parr, Harriet.*]
a. Lee, Sophia & Harriet.
   **Canterbury Tales, 3 vols............12mo N. Y $6 75
b. Le Fanu, S.
   All in the Dark, Guy Deverell, Lost ⎱ 8vo N. Y. 50
     Name,* Tenants of Mallory, paper. ⎰
   * Uncle Silas, paper..................8vo N. Y. 75
a. Le Sage. ** Gil Blas.................12mo N. Y. 1 50
   ——————— Best Edition, 3 vols.16mo Bost. 3 75
b. Lever, Chas. Arthur O'Leary...........12mo Lond 1 00
   **Charles O'Malley, 2 v.; * Con Cregan.12mo Lond. 1 00
   Barrington; *H. Lorrequer..........12mo Lond. 1 00
   Daltons, 2 v. $2.00. or 1 vol.........12mo Lond. 1 50
   Dodd Family, $1.25; *Jack Hinton...12mo Lond. 1 00
   Knight of Gwynne.................12mo Lond. 2 00
   * Maurice Tierney...................12mo Lond. 1 00
   * That Boy of Norcott's, paper.......8vo N. Y. 25
   (And several others.)
Lever. Works complete. Illus. 21 vols.12mo L. & N. 50 00
a. Lewes, Mrs. G. H. (George Elliot.)
   ** Adam Bede, ** Felix Holt, **Mill on ⎱ 12mo N. Y. *ea.* 75
     Floss, ** Romola, ** Silas Marner. ⎰
   Works, including above, 5 vols.......12mo Bost. 5 00
c. Lippard, Geo. Quaker City (and several
             others).... Phila.
b. Lockhart, J. G. Matthew Wald, etc.....12mo Lond. 4s.
   Reginald Dalton, * Valerius.......*ea.* 12mo Lond. 4s.
a. Longfellow, H. W. ** Hyperion.... ...12mo Bost. 1 50
   **Kavanagh ....12mo Bost. 1 25
b. Lover, Samuel.
   * Handy Andy, 2 v., $2; * Rory O'Moore.12mo Lond. 1 00
   Treasure Trove....................
b. Lowell, R. T. S.
   * New Priest-of Conception Bay, 2 vols.12mo Bost. 1 75
a. Lytton, Lord (Bulwer). Novels complete
           in 22 vols....12mo Phila. 33 00
   Or separately, viz. :
   **Caxtons ....12mo., N. Y., $1.00.12mo Phila. 1 50
   **My Novel, 2 vols...12mo., N. Y., $3.50.12mo Phila. 3 00
   * What will he do with it? N. Y., $2.00.2 v. Phila. 3 00
   * Devereux, ** Pompeii, Leila, etc., ⎫
     * Rienzi, * The Barons, * Harold,   ⎪
     * Eugene Aram, * Zanoni, ** Pel- ⎬12mo Lon. *ea.* 1 50
     ham, Disowned, Paul Clifford, Mal- ⎪ 8vo N. Y. pa. 50
     travers, Godolphin, *Alice, *Night ⎪
     and M.; *Lucretia, *Strange Story. ⎭
b. McCarthy, Justin.
   * My Enemy's Daughter.............8vo N. Y. 50
   * Lady Judith (and 3 others)..........8vo N. Y. *ea.* 75
a. Macdonald Geo. Adela Cathcart........12mo Bost. 1 75
   **Alec Forbes... :..................12mo Bost. 1 75
   **Annals of a Quiet Neighborhood.....12mo N. Y. 1 75

**David Elginbrod, $1.75 ; Guild Court..   N. Y.*ea.*$ 50
**Phantastes, $1.50 ; ** Portent.... ...   1 75
**Bannerman's Boyhood, $1.50 ; Robert
  Falconer, $1.75 ; Seaboard Parish...   1 75
b. Mackenzie, H. * Man of Feeling, etc....12mo N. Y.   1 50
b. Mackenzie, Shelton.
  * Tressillian and Friends.............   Phila.
b. Mackinstosh. Miss M. J.
  Charms and Counter Charms........12mo N. Y.   1 25
  Lofty & Lowly, 2 v. $2.50. Two Lives..12mo N. Y.   1 25
    (And also Juveniles.)
b. Malory, Sir T. * Morte d'Arthur........12mo Lond.   2 00
b. Manning. Miss Anne. ** Mary Powell...16mo N. Y.   1 75
  * Cherry & Violet, $1. ; Sir Thos. Moore.16mo N. Y.   1 00
  * Fair Gospeller, $1. ; Jacques Bonneval.16mo N. Y.   1 00
    (And other works ; Essays. etc.)
b. Manzoni (Italian). * The Betrothed. Lon.12mo 3s. 6d.
a. " Marlitt, E."
  **Countess Gisela. $1.75 ; ** Gold Elsie.12mo Phila.   1 75
  **Old Mam'selle's Secret.............12mo Phila.   1 50
  * Over Yonder, *pa.*, 35c. ; * Magdalena, *pa.* 8vo Phila.   30
Marryatt, Miss. [*See Church, Mrs.*]
b. Marryatt, Capt. Works complete, 12 v...12mo N. Y.   12 00
  Or Cheap ed. separately, paper........12mo N. Y. *ea.* 50
  Viz : * Jacob Faithful, Japhet, * Peter
  Simple, ** Midshipman Easy, Pacha,
  Snarleyow, etc.
c. Mrs. Marsh. Adelaide Lindsay, paper.... 8vo N. Y.   50
  Angelo, 12mo., $1.50 ; Aubrey, *pa.* ⎫
  75c. ; Castle Avon, 50c. ; E.Wynd- |
  ham, 75c. ; E. Marston, 50c. ; Father ⎬ 8vo N. Y. *pa.*
  Darcy, 75c. ; (and 9 others) each |
  50c........................... ⎭
b. Martineau, Harriet. Deerbrook. Lond..12mo 1s. 6d.
  * Hour and the Man. Lond.........12mo 1s. 6d.
    (Also Juveniles.)
b. Maxwell, W. H. Brian O'Linn.........12mo Lond.   75
  Hector O'Halloran, 12mo., 80c. ; * Sto- ⎫
  ries of Waterloo, 12mo., 75c. ; Capt. ⎬ 12mo Lond.
  Blake, 2s. ; Bivouac, 2s. ; Captain |
  O'Sullivan, 1s. 6d............... ⎭
c. Mayhew, H. Mr. & Mrs. Sandboy. .....12mo Lond. 6s.
  Greatest Plague of Life.............12mo Lond. 2s.
b. Mayo, W. S. ** Kaloolah..............12mo N. Y.   2 00
  * The Berber......................12mo N. Y.
  —— —— (New Work)............
b. Meinhold, Dr. The Amber Witch.......12mo Lond. 2s.
  Sidonia the Sorceress.............12mo N. Y.   1 00
b. Melville, G. Whyte. * Cerise.........12mo Phila.   1 50
  **Interpreter, 8vo ; M or N............. 8vo N. Y. *ea.* 75
  * White Rose, $1.50 ; The Gladiator...12mo N. Y.   1 00

b. Melville, Herman. ** Typee............12mo N. Y. $1 50
  * Mardi, 2 vols, $3 ; ** Moby Dick......12mo N. Y.   1 75
  * Pierre, 2v., $1.50 ; * Omoo..........12mo N. Y.   1 50
  * Redburn, 2 vols., $1.50 ; * White Jacket.12mo N. Y.   1 50
  **Israel Potter.....................12mo N. Y.
** Member for Paris, The, paper........... 8vo N. Y.   75
c. Meredith, Geo. Evan Harrington........12mo N. Y.   1 50
  Ordeal (and 3 others) ...., Lond.
* Miss Van Kortlandt.................... 8vo N. Y.   1 00
b. Mitchell, D. G. ** Dream Life.........12mo N. Y.   1 75
  * Doctor Johns, 2 vols., $3 ; ** Bachelor.12mo N. Y.   1 75
b. Mitford, Mary Russel. ** Our Village, 2 v.12mo N. Y.   2 25
  * Belford Regis............. Lond....12mo 3s. 6s.
b. Moore, Dr. John. ** Zelucco............ Lond.
b. Moore, Thomas. ** The Epicurean......12mo   1 50
b. More, Hannah. **Cœlebs in Search of Wife.12mo Phila.   1 50
c. Morford, Henry. Shoulder Straps (2 oth's).12mo Phil. ea. 1 50
c. Morgan, Lady. Florence Macarthy......12mo N. Y.   1 50
  Wild Irish Girl................12mo Lond. 2s.
b. Morier, J. Ayesha, 2s. ; * Haji Baba..Lon.12mo 1s. 6d.
  Zohrab, the Hostage.................12mo Lond. 2s.
  Mügge, Theo. Afraja............Lond.12mo 10s. 6d.
c. "Muhlbach," Louisa. Novels, 17 vols... 8vo N. Y. ea. 1 50
  A. Hofer, Old Fritz, Napoleon, Josephine,
  Life Paths, Q. of Prussia, Prince Eugene,
  Daughter of Empress, Marie Antoinette,
  Joseph II., Henry VIII., Frederick the
  Great, Frederick and Family, Berlin and
  Sans Souci, Merchant of Berlin, Louisa
  of Prussia.............................
  Muloch, Miss. [See Craik, Mrs.]
  Murray, Chas. A. The Prairie Bird..... 8vo N. Y.   1 00
  * My Daughter Elinor................ 8vo N. Y.   1 75
c. Newby, Mrs. C. J.
  Margaret Hamilton, pa.; Right and Left. 8vo N. Y. ea.   50
  (3 others, not reprinted.)
  Nichols, Mrs. [See Brontë, Charlotte.]
  Norton, Hon. Mrs. Lost and Saved......12mo Phila.   1 25
  Old Sir Douglas...................12mo Phila.   1 50
b. Oliphant, Mrs.
  * Agnes, *Atheling, * Brownlows...... 8vo N. Y. ea.   75
  **Carlingford, (paper, $1.25)............ 8vo N. Y.   1 75
  * Days of Life, * House on Moor........12mo N.Y. ea. 1 50
  **John, 8vo, 50c. ; * Katie Stewart...... 8vo N. Y.   75
  * Laird of Norlaw, * Last of Mortimers..12mo   ea. 1 50
  * Lost Love, $1.75 ; *Lucy Crofton, ea. 12mo N. Y.   1 50
  * Madonna Mary.................... 8vo N. Y.   50
  **Margaret Maitland.................12mo N. Y.   1 00
  * Minister's Wife.................... 8vo N. Y.   75
  * Miss Majoribanks................ 8vo N. Y.   50
  **Perpetual Curate, * Son of the Soil..ea. 8vo N. Y.   1 50
  * Lilliesleaf, * Three Brothers, **Zaidee.

b. Opie, Mrs. Tales; eight in 1 vol........ 8vo
"Ouida." [*See de la Rame.*]
b. Owen, Robt. Dale. * Beyond the Breakers. 8vo Phila. $2 00
c. Pardoe, Julia.
   Adopted Heir, $1.75; Pretty Woman.. 8vo Phila. 1 75
   Jealous Wife, 8vo, 50c. ; Life Struggle.12mo Phila. 1 75
   Rival Beauties, paper........ .... 8vo Phila. 75
   * Wife's Trials....... ....12mo Phil. *ea.* 1 75
   .Reginald Lyle, Romance of Harem... 8vo Phil. *ea.* 1 75
   Speculation, Earl's Secret..........12mo Phila. 1 75
b. Parr, Miss Harriet "Holme Lee."
   * Against Wind and Tide, paper........ 8vo N. Y. 75
   * Annie Wardleigh, paper............. 8vo N. Y. 75
   * Mrs. Wynyaw, 50c. ; ** Sylvan Holt... 8vo pa. N. Y.
b. Parr, Louisa. ** Dorothy Fox, paper.... 8vo N. Y. 75
b. Paulding, J. K. Works and Life, 5 vols...12mo N. Y. 12 50
   Dutchman's Fireside, $2.50 ; Bulls and
                     Jonathans.... 2 50
b. Peacock, T. L.
   **Headlong Hall, $1 ; * Melincourt.....12mo Lond 2s.
a. Phelps, E. S. ** Gates Ajar...........12mo Bost. 1 50
   * Hedged In, $1.50; * Silent Partner....12mo Bost. 1 50
c. Pickering, Ellen. Sixteen novels, paper.. 8vo N. & P.
   (Nine published by Peterson, Phil., 8vo, paper.)
c. Ploennies, Louise Von. Princess Ilse....16mo Bost. 1 25
a. Poe, E. A. ** Tales, 2 vols.............16mo N. Y. 3 50
b. Poole, John. * Little Pedlington....... 12mo
a. Porter, Jane. ** Thaddeus of Warsaw...12mo Phila. 1 25
   **Scottish Chiefs.....................12mo N. Y. 1 25
   * Pastor's Fireside...................12mo Lond. 80
"Powell, Mary," author of. [*See Manning.*]
a. Prentiss, E. ** Stepping Heavenward...12mo N. Y. 2 00
   * Aunt Jane's Hero..................12mo N. Y. 1 50
   (Also Juveniles.)
b. Preston, Louisa. * Aspendale..........16mo Bost. 1 50
   Prescott, Harriet E. [*See Spofford.*]
 * Quiet Heart.......................... 8vo N. Y. 25
a. Rabelais. Works, 2 vols...............12mo Bohn. 3 50
b. Radcliffe, Mrs. ** Mysteries of Udolpho.12mo Phila. 1 25
   Romance of the Forest...............12mo Phila. 1 25
a. Reade, Chas. Novels. 10 vols........12mo Bost. *ea.* 1 00
       Or separate, viz. :
   **Cloister and Hearth; *Course of True Love; * Foul ⎫
    Play ; *Good Fight, etc.; * Griffith Gaunt; Terri- ⎪
    ble Temptation ; ** Christie Johnson, etc., 1 vol.; ⎬
    ** Never too Late ; ** Love me Little ; * Put ⎪
    Yourself ; * Hard Cash ; * White Lies........ ⎭
c. Reid, Mayne. Novels, 16 vols.. ....12mo N. Y. *ea.*1 50
         [*See Juveniles.*]
   Regester, S. [*See Victor, Mrs.*]
c. Reynolds, G. W. M.
   "Sensational" novels, 40 vols. (!)...... 8vo Phila.

b. Richardson, Saml. ** Clarissa Harlowe..12mo Lond. $1 25
   * Pamela, ** Sir Chas. Grandison.......
a. Richter, Jean Paul.
   * Hesperus, 2 vols; *Titan, 2 vols......12mo Bost. *ea.* 4 00
   * Walt and Vult, 2 vols................12mo Bost.
   **Fruit, Flower and Thorn Pieces, 2 vols.12mo Bost.
b. Reuter. ** In the Year '13...............16mo N. Y. 1 00
c. Riddell, Mrs. J. H. * Race for Wealth... 8vo N. Y. 75
   * Far above Rubies; Rich Husband.....
   Life's Assize ; Phemie Keller, each pa. 8vo N. Y.' 50
b. Robertson, Margaret M. * Christie......
   **Janet's Love and Service.............12mo N. Y. 1 75
c. Robinson, Mrs. Edw.
   Heloise ; Life's Discipline............12mo N. Y.
b. Robinson, F. W. * Anne Judge, paper... 8vo N. Y. 75
   * Stern Necessity, Sweet Nineteen,⎱ 8vo N. Y. *ea.* 50
     True to Herself, Poor Humanity.⎰
   For Her Sake, Carry's Confession,⎱ 8vo N. Y. *ea.* 75
     Mattie, No Man's Friend.........⎰
b. Roche, Anna M. Children of the Abbey.12mo N. Y. 1 50
c. Roe, A. S. Cloud on the Heart. Long⎫
   Look Ahead, To Love and be Loved, ⎪
   Time and Tide, I've been Thinking, ⎬ 12mo N. Y. *ea.* 1 50
   Star and Cloud, True to the Last, ⎪
   (and six others)...........⎭
b. Rosetti, C. G. ** Common Places and
            other stories....12mo Bost. 1 50
b. Ruffini. ** Doctor Antonio, * Lavinia,⎱ 12mo N. Y. *ea.* 1 75
   * Vincenzo ....⎰
   * Carlino, 8vo, paper, 35c. ; ** Lorenzo⎱ N. Y.
    Benoni ; * Paragreens ; *Quiet Nook.⎰
"Rutledge," Author of (Miss Coles). [*See Harris.*]
c, Rydberg, V. Last Athenian...........12mo Phila. 2 00
a. St. Pierre. ** Paul & Virginia.......16mo N. Y. 1 25
a. Saintine, X. B. ** Picciola, best ed......16mo N. Y. 1 25
a. "Sand, Geo." (Madame Dudevant).
   * Antonia, 16mo ; **Consuelo (P.), 12mo;⎫
   * Countess Rudolf (P.); **Fadette; ⎪ Bost. ⎫
   * Indiana (P.) ; * Jealousy (P.) ; ⎬ and ⎬ *ea.* 1 50
   **Mauprat; *Miller; *M. Sylvestre; ⎪ Phila. ⎭
   **Snow Man...............⎭
   * Handsome Lawrence.............. 1 00
     ✱ Those marked (P.) pub. by Peterson, Phila., with 15
      more, in paper, Others by Roberts, Boston.
      (Several others not reprinted.)
b. Sartoris, Mrs. A. Kemble.
   **Week in a French Country House.... 8vo Bost.
c. Saunders, J. Abel Drake's Wife, paper.. 8vo N. Y. 75
   Bound to Wheel, 75c. ; *Hirell, paper. 8vo N. Y. 50
   Martin Pole...................... 50
b. Savage, M. * Bachelor of the Albany....12mo N. Y. 1 50
   Falcon Family. 12mo, London, $1.00. 8vo N. Y. *pa.* 75

b. Savage, M.
  * Woman of Business, paper........... 8vo N. Y. $ 75
    Reuben Medlicott, paper............ 8vo N. Y. 1 00
b. Schmid, Hr. * The Habermeister.......16mo N. Y. 1 00
b. Scott, Michæl. Cruise of the Midge.....12mo Lond. 4s.
  * Tom Cringle's Log................. 8vo N. Y. 6s.
b. Schwartz, Marie S. * Birth and Education. 8vo Bost. 1 50
  * Gold and Name; * The Right One.... 8vo Bost. *ea.* 1 50
  * Guilt and Innocence; * Two Family..
a. Scott, Sir Walter. Novels, 27 vols.......12mo Phila. 33 50
  —— — ——— ——25 vols ....12mo Bost. 37 50
  —— — ——— ——centen. ed. 25 vols.12mo Lond. 43 75
  —— — ——— ——6 vols ....12mo N. Y. 10 50
  —— Separate Novels, paper.....8vo or 12mo E. & N. *ea.* 25
b. Sedgwick, Cath. M. ** Hope Leslie, 2 v.12mo N. Y. 3 00
  * Linwoods, 2 v., $3.00; * Redwood, 1 v. N. Y. 1 50
  * Clarence, 1 v.,; * N. Eng. Tale, 1 v..... N. Y. *ea.* 1 50
            [*See Juveniles.*]
b. Seemüller, Mrs. A. M. C. * Emily Chester.12mo Bost. 2 00
  * Opportunity, 12mo; * Reginald Archer.12mo Bost. *ea.* 2 00
b. Sewell, Miss E. M. Amy Herbert.......12mo N. Y. 1 00
  * Cleve Hall, $1.00; Earl's Daughter...12mo N. Y. 1 00
  * Experience of Life, $1.00; Gertrude..12mo N. Y. 1 00
  * Glimpse of World, $1.00; * Hawkstone.12mo N. Y. 1 00
    Ivors. 2 v., $2.00; * Kate Ashton, 2 v.12mo N. Y. 2 00
  * Laneton Parsonage, $2.00; * Margaret
                Percival, 2 vols....12mo N. Y. 2 00
    Ursula, 2 v., $2.00; Walter Lorimer, 1 v.12mo N. Y. 1 00
  * Home Life, 1 vol....... ....12mo N. Y. 1 00
b. Shelley, Mrs. * Frankenstein..........12mo N. Y. 1 00
  * Perkin Warbeck. ....12mo Lond. 80
b. Sheppard, Elizabeth. * Chas. Auchester.. 8vo N. Y. 75
  **Counterparts, 8vo, 1.25; * Rumour.... 8vo N. Y. 1 25
c. Simms, W. G. Works (paper 75c.) 17 vols.12mo N. Y. 30 00
    The best separately, viz.: Beau-⎫
      champe, Guy Rivers, Martin Faber. ⎬ 12mo N. Y. *ea.* 1 75
    Mellichampe, Partizan, Yemasee. ⎭
c. Sinclair, Catherine. Modern Flirtations..12mo Phila. 1 75
    Beatrice, Jane Bouverie, Lord and Lady ⎫
    Harcourt, Sir E. Graham. Modern Ac- ⎬ 12mo Lond.
    complishments .... ⎭
c. Sisters of Orleans....................12mo N. Y. 1 50
c. Smart, H. * Breezie Langton, paper..... 8vo N. Y. 75
    Race for a Wife.................... 8vo N. Y. 50
b. Smedley, Frank E. *Frank Fairleigh...12mo Lond. 1 25
    Harry Coverdale, $1.25; Lew. Arundel. Lond. 1 50
b. Smith, Albert.* Mr. Ledbury (3 others)..12mo N. Y. *ea.* 80
b. Smith, Alex. Alfred Hagart's Household.12mo N. Y. 1 00
    Dreamthorpe.......................16mo N. Y. 1 50
b. Smith, Horace. Brambletye House......12mo Lond.
        (And others not reprinted.)

a. Smollett, Tobias. Novels, 3 vols........16mo Lond. $3 75
     * Count Fathom, **Humphrey Clinker,   } 12mo Lon. *ea.* 1 50
      Peregrine Pickle, *Rod'rk Random. }
     Cheaper editions of above............12mo Lon. *ea.*   80
c. Southworth, Mrs. E. D. E. N. 37 Novels.12mo Phila.*ea.*1 75
a. Souvestre, E. **Attic Philosopher.......12mo N. Y.   1 00
     * Lake Shore, *Family Journal.........12mo N. Y.   1 50
     * Legends of Brittany.................
c. Spindler. The Jew....................
b. Spielhagen, F. **Problemat'l Characters.12mo N. Y.   2 00
     * Hammer & Anvil, $2.00; *Hohenstein's.12mo N. Y.   2 00
     * Through Night to Light.....12mo N. Y.   2 .00
b. Spofford, Mrs. Harriet Prescott. .
     **Amber Gods, $1.75; *Azarian....... 12mo Bost.   1 50
     * Sir Rohan's Ghost..................12mo Bost.
a. Stael, Madame de. **Corinne...........12mo N. Y.   1 50
     * Delphine ....
c. Stephens, Mrs. A. 14 Novels...........12mo Phil.*ea.* 1 75
     * Fashion and Famine......... .. ....12mo Phila.   1 75
c. Sterling, John. Onyx Ring.............16mo Bost.
a. Sterne, Laurence. **Tristam Shandy....12mo N. Y.   1 50
a. Stowe, Mrs. **Uncle Tom's Cabin, *Ag-}
     nes of Sorrento, * May Flower, |
     **Minister's Wooing, **Old Town }12mo Bost.   2 C0
     Folk, *Nina Godwin, *Pink and |
     White Tyranny.................}
     * My Wife and I.....................12mo N. Y.   1 75
b. Sue, Eugene. * Mysteries of Paris......12mo N. Y.   1 25
  ————— Wandering Jew ....12mo N. Y.   1 25
  ———— Martin, the Foundling....   Phila.   2 00
b. Swift, Jona. ** Gulliver's Travels......12mo Phila.   1 00
  Tales from Blackwood. 12 vols in 6.....18mo Edin.   15 00
  Tales from the German. By Oxenford,&c. 8vo Lond.
a. Tautphœus, Baroness. ** At Odds......12mo Phila.   1 75
     **Initials, $1.75; ** Quits.............12mo Phila.   1 75
     * Cyrilla, paper..................... 8vo Phila.   75
a. Taylor, Bayard.
     * Hannah Thurston, * John Godfrey,} 12mo N. Y. *ca.* 1 50
     **Story of Kennett, * Joseph & Friend. }
b. Terhune, Mrs. V. (" Marion Harland ").
     * Alone, * Hidden Path, Moss Side,}
     Nemesis, Miriam, At Last, He- |
     len Gardener, Sunnybank, Hus- }12mo N. Y. *ea.* 1 50
     band and Home, Ruby's Husband, |
     Phemie's Temptation, Empty Heart}
a. Thackeray, W. M. Novels, complete, 6 v.12mo Bost.   7 50
  ———— ———— ———— 3 v. 8vo N. Y.   6 50
  ———— Works, complete, best ed., 22 v. 8vo Lond.   66 00
  ———— ———— now publishing in 11 v. 8vo Lond.   33 00
     Separate, viz: ** Vanity Fair, ** Pen-}
     dennis, **The Newcomes, **Philip, } 12mo Bost. *ea.* 1 25
     **Esmond & Lovel, **Virginians. }

a. Thackeray, W. M.
   Novels......Complete in paper.. 8vo N. Y. **$4 00**
  * Miscellanies, Short Tales, &c., 5 v.....12mo Bost. 6 25
a. Thackeray, Miss, ** Tales, &c., 2 vols....12mo Bost. 2 00
c. Thomas, Annie.
  Called to Account, Only Herself, paper 8vo N. Y. *ea.* 50
  Dennis Donne, Played Out, paper..... 8vo N. Y. *ea.* 50
  Dower House, 50c.; High Stakes...*pa.* 8vo N. Y. 25
  False Colors, Theo. Leigh, paper...... 8vo N. Y. *ea.* 50
  On Guard, Walter Goring, paper...... 8vo N. Y. *ea.* 50
b. Townsend, Virginia F. * The Hollands..12mo N. Y. 1 50
  Max Meredith......................12mo N. Y.
  Janet Strong, * Mills of Tuxbury.....12mo
b. Trollope, Anthony.
  **Barchester Towers, paper, 75c.; * Lottie ⎫
  Schmidt, 2 v., $2.50; * Belton Estate, |
  pa., 50c.; *Miss Mackenzie, *pa.*, 50c.; |
  *Bertrams, 12mo, $1.50; *Oiley Farm, |
  cloth, $2.00; *Castle Richmond, 12mo, |
  $1.50; *Phineas Finn, *cloth*, $1.75; |
  *Can you Forgive Her, 8vo, $2.00, 12mo, |
  $1.00; *Rachel Ray, *pa.*, 50c.; *Claver- |
  ings, 8vo, $1.00; *Ralph the Heir, *cloth*, |
  $1.75; **Doctor Thorne, 12mo, $1.50; ⎬ N. Y.
  *Sir H. Hotspur, *pa.*, 50c.; *Framley |
  Parsonage, 12mo, $1.75; *Small House, |
  cloth, $2.00; *He Knew he was Right, |
  12mo, $1.50; *Struggles of Brown, etc., |
  pa., 50c.; *Kellys & O'Kellys, 12mo, |
  $1.25; *Three Clerks, 12mo, *cloth*, |
  $1.50; *Chronicle of Barset, 8vo, $2.00; |
  *Vicar of Bulhampton, *cloth*, $1.75; |
  *Warden (with Barchester Towers). ⎭
b. Trollope, T. A.
  * Beppo the Conscript, Dream Num- ⎫
  bers, *Garstang Grange, Gemma, ⎬12mo Phila.*ea.*1 75
  Leonora .... ⎭
   Lindisfarn, 8vo, N. Y., $2. A Siren. 8vo *pa.* 50
  Tucker, B. Geo. Balcombe; Partisan Leader (*o. p.*)
b. Turgeneff (Russian). *Fathers & Sons..16mo N. Y. 1 25
  Liza............................
c. Tupper, M. F.
  Crock of Gold; Hearts and Twins. *ea.*12mo N. Y.
a. Tytler, Sarah. **Citoyenne Jacqueline.. 8vo N. Y. 2 00
  * Days of Yore; *Diamond Rose........ 8vo N. Y. 2 00
  **Huguenot Family.................... 8vo 2 50
c. Verne. Five Weeks in a Balloon........18mo N. Y. 1 25
  Centre of the Earth; The North Pole.12mo Lond.
  Vigny, Alfred de. Cinq Mars, paper.....12mo Bost. 50
c. Victor, Mrs. M.
  Dead Letter, 12mo, $1.50; Too True..12mo N. Y. 1 25
  Figure Eight; Who Was He?.....*ea.*12mo N. Y.

b. Walpole, Horace.   The Castle of Otranto..12mo Phila.
　　Warburton, Eliot.   Darien ....
　　　　Reginald Hastings.................
c. Walworth, M. T.   Hotspur; Lulu;⎫
　　　　Storm Cliff, Warwick............⎬ 12mo N. Y.*ea.*$1 75
　　Ward, R.   Tremaine (and 5 others) *o. p.*...
a. Ware, Wm.
　　**Aurelian; **Zenobia; *Julian, 2 vols..　　N. Y.*ca.*2 00
　　Warfield, Mrs. C.
　　　　Romance of Beausaincourt..........
b. Warner, Misses Anna and Susan.   (" S. Wetherell.")
　　**Wide World, **Queechy..........*ea.* 12mo Phila.   1 75
　　 * Daisy, $1.75; * Say and Seal, 2 vols...12mo N. Y.   3 00
　　 * Dollars and Cents...................12mo Phila.   1 75
　　 * Hills of the Shatemuck.............12mo N. Y.   1 75
　　 * Old Helmet.......................12mo N. Y.   2 25
　　 * Melbourne House..................12mo N. Y.   2 00
　　 * What she Could, * Opportunities..*ea.* 12mo N. Y.   1 25
　　　　House in Town....................12mo N. Y.   1 25

[See also Juveniles.]

a. Warren, Saml. **Diary of a Physician, 3 v.18mo N. Y.   2 25
　　 * Ten Thousand a Year...............12mo Phila.   2 00
　　　　Now and Then ; Merchant's Clerk....
　　　　Works, fine edition, 5 vols...........12mo Lond.   12 00
　　Webber, C. W.   Old Hicks, the Guide... 8vo
　　　　Tales of Southern Border...........8vo Phila.   2 00
　　What the World Made Them..........12mo N. Y.   1 25
a. Whitney, Mrs. A. D. T.   **Faith Gartney.16mo Bost.   1 50
　　**Gayworthys, $1.75; **Hitherto.......12mo Bost.   2 00
　　**Leslie Goldthwaite................12mo Bost.   1 75
　　 * Patience Strong ; ** We Girls.......12mo Bost. *ea.* 1 50
　　 * Zerub Throop....................12mo Bost.   1 75
b. Whittier, J. G.   * Marg't Smith's Journal.12mo Bost.   1 50
b. Wilson, Prof. Jno.   *Margaret Lindsay..12mo Edin.
　　　　Tales of Borders. (3 others.)
c. Wilson, Mrs. (Augusta J. Evans.)
　　 * Beulah, Inez, Macaria..............12mo N. Y.*en.* 1 75
　　　　St. Elmo, Vashti....................12mo N. Y.*ea.* 2 00
　　Wise, Henry A.   Captain Brand........ 8vo N. Y.   2 00
c. Wood, Mrs. Henry.
　　　　Novels, 13 vols....................12mo Phila.*ea.* 1 75
　　　　Novels, (add'n'l to above,) 10 vols. paper. 8vo Phila.*ea.*　 50
　　　　The Channings ; Roland Yorke.....*ea.* 8vo Phila.   1 50
b. Wormeley, Miss.   Annabel..........*o. p.*12mo N. Y.
b. Yates, Edmund.   * Black Sheep, paper... 8vo N. Y.   50
　　 * Broken to Harness.................12mo Bost.   2 00
　　 * Forlorn Hope, *Running Gauntlet,⎫
　　 * Nobody's Fortune................⎬ 12mo Lond. *ea.* 1 00
　　 * Kissing the Rod, * Wrecked in Port,⎫　　paper,
　　 * Land at Last.....................⎬ 8vo N. Y. *ca.*　 50
　　Yelverton, Mrs.   Zanita...............12mo N. Y.   1 50

b. Yonge, Miss C. M. ** Daisy Chain, 2 vols .12mo N. Y. $2 00
    * Dynevor Terrace, 2 vols.............12mo N. Y. 2 00
    * Beechcroft........................12mo N. Y. 1 50
    * Clever Woman, 2 vols..............12mo N. Y. 2 00
    **Heir of Redcliffe, 2 vols.............12mo N. Y. 2 00
    * Heartsease, 2 vols.................12mo N. Y. 2 00
    * Hopes and Fears, 2 vols.... ....12mo N. Y. 3 00
    * Kenneth, $1.50; * Linwood.........12mo N. Y. 1 25
    * Young Stepmother, 2 vols...........12mo N. Y. 3 00
b. Zschokke, H. * The Dead Guest, paper.. 8vo N. Y. 50
    **Goldsmith's Village.................
    * Labor on Golden Feet.............12mo N. Y. 1 25
    * Select Tales, * Social Life Tales......12mo N. Y.
    * Veronica..................paper.... 8vo N. Y. 50

Field Sports.—[*See also Angling ; Hunting.*]
    Carlton, J. W. Sporting Sketch Book...12mo Lon. 16s.
    Greenwood, J. Wild Sports of the World. 8vo L. 7s. 6d.
    Herbert, H. W. Field Sports, 2 vols.... 8vo N. Y.
    Trollope, A. British Field Sports.......12mo Lond.
    Walsh, J. H. (Stonehenge.) Cyclopedia of
              Rural Sports.... 8vo Lon. 15s.

Fiji Islands.
    Smyth, Mrs. Ten Months in Fiji Islands. 8vo Oxf. 10s.
    Williams, T., & Calvert, J. Fiji and the
              Fijians. 1859.... 8vo N. Y.

Finance.—[*See Banking, Money, Political Economy, Taxation.*]

Fine Arts.—[*See also Architecture, Decorative Art, Drawing,*
              Music, Painting, Sculpture.]

——(1.) HISTORY, THEORY, PRACTICE.
    Allston, W. Lectures on Fine Arts......
    Art of Illuminating (col'd ed., $14)......r. 8vo Lond. 3 50
    Art Union Journal, 31 annual vols.....ea. 4to Lon. 30s.
b. Art, Pictorial and Industrial (monthly),
              annual vols....folio L. & N. 16 00
    Art Workmanship, Choice Examples of.r. 8vo Lon. 25s.
    Barnard. On Landscape Painting.......r. 8vo Lond.
b. Bell. Anatomy of Expression..........r. 8vo Lond. 6 00
    Blanc, Ch. Hist. of Painters of all Nations.folio Lond. 6 00
b. Burnet. Treat. on Color, Perspective, etc. 4to Lond. 22 00
    Bryan. Dictionary of Painters........r 8vo Lon. 42s.
a. ——— Supplement to Dictionary of Liv-
              ing Artists....r. 8vo Lond. 4 75
b. Chaffer's Hist. of Pottery & Porcelain. Ill. 8vo Lond. 9 25
    Chevreul. Laws of Contrasts in Color... 8vo Lond, 2 00
a. Clement, C. C. Legendary Art. Illus...12mo N. Y. 3 25
    Cleghorn. Ancient & Modern Art, 2 vols.16mo Edn. 12s.
    Cunningham. Lives of Painters & Sculp-
              tors, 6 v., 16mo, Lond. 21s. ; or 3 v...18mo N. Y. 2 25
    Cummings. Hist. of Nat. Acad. of Design. 8vo N. Y. 2 00

D'Agincourt. Hist. of Art by its Monum'ts. folio Lon. 105s.
Delamotte. Art of Sketching from Nature.folio Lon. 63s.
Dwight, M. A.   Introd'n to Study of Art..12mo N. Y. $1 25
Dunlap, W.   History of Arts of Design in
        United States, 2 vols....o. p. 8vo N. Y.
Eastlake, C. L.   Lit. of Fine Arts, 2 vols. 8vo Lon. 24s.
Falkner, E.   Ancient Art..............r. 8vo Lon. 42s.
Fairholt. Dictionary of Terms in Art.... 8vo L. 10s. 6d.
c. ——— History of Costume in England. 8vo L. 31s. 6d.
General View of Fine Arts. By a Lady.
        Introduction by Huntington....12mo N. Y.   1 75
a. Hamerton. Thoughts about Art.........16mo Bost.   1 50
     ——— Contem. French Painters, Ill. 4to Lond. 10 00
a. Hand Books on Art, (Windsor & Newton's)
    viz.: on Figures, Oil, Water Colors, etc.
    Illustrated, 27 vols................ea. 12mo Lon. 44s.
b. Harding, J. D. Lessons on Art.........folio Lon. 15s.
c. ——— Guide and Companion to above.r. 8vo Lond.   4 50
c. ——— Principles and Practice of Art...folio Lon. 63s.
Harris, G. Theory of the Arts, 2 vols.... 8vo Lond. 10 50
Hazlitt, W. C, Essays on Fine Arts.....12mo Edin. 5s.
c. Hobbes' Picture Collector's Manual, 2 v.. 8vo Lon.32s. 4 50
Howard, R. On Color as a Means of Art.. 8vo Lon. 8s.
Howitt, Miss. Art Student in Munich, 2 v. 12mo Lon. 14s.
b. Jackson. History of Wood Engraving..r. 8vo Lond. 21 00
a. Jarves, J. J. The Art Idea.............12mo N. Y.   1 75
a. ——— Art Thoughts................12mo N. Y.   2 50
b. Jameson, Mrs. Legends of the Madonna ⎤ 6 vols. Illus.
  ——— ——— ——— Monastic Orders... ⎬ large
  ——— ——— ——— of our Lord....... ⎬ 8vo Lond. 40 00
  ——— ——— Sacred and Legend. Art. ⎦
a. ——— ——— Writings on Art,&c., 6 v..18mo Bost. 12 00
  ——— ——— ————— blue & gold.32mo Bost.   9 00
Jones, Owen. Grammar of Ornament, Ill. folio Lond. 50 00
Keramic Gallery. History and Examples of
        Porcelain, 2 vols.... 8vo Lond. 28 00
b. Küghler. Hand Books of Painting: Italian
        School, 2 v ... 8vo Lon. 30s.
b. ——— ——— Flem. & Dutch Schools, 2 v. 8vo Lon. 24s.
b. Lacroix. Arts of the Middle Ages, Illus. r. 8vo Lond. 12 00
Long, S. P. Art; Its Laws, and Reasons
        for them....12mo Bost.   3 00
Lubke. Hist. of Art, Illus., 2 vols......r. 8vo L. & P. 18 00
  ——— Hist. of Sculpture, Illus., 2 vols.r. 8vo Lond.
Muller, C. O. Ancient Art & its Remains. 8vo Lond.   5 00
Palgrave, F. T. Essays on Art..........16mo Lond.   1 50
Reynolds, Sir J. Works on Art, 2 vols...12mo Bohn.   3 50
Rochette. Lectures on Ancient Art...... 8vo Lond. 5s.
Rosetti, W. M. Fine Art, chiefly Contemp.12mo L. 10s. 6d.
a. Ruskin. Lectures on Art...............12mo N. Y.   1 50
b. ——— Modern Painters, 5 vols........12mo N. Y. 18 00

Ruskin. Miscellaneous Works on Art and
     kindred themes, 6 vols.12mo N. Y. $15 00
———— Stones of Venice. Ill.,3 v., Lon.*r.* 8vo £5 15s. 6d.
———— Modern Painters. Ill.,5 v., Lon.*r.* 8vo £8 3s.
———— Lectures on Sculpture. Illust.. 8vo Lond.
Samson, G. W. Elements of Art Criticism.12mo Phila.   3 50
———— ——— Same, abridged.........12mo Phila.   1 75
Simmons. Sculptor's Manual..........
Stanley. Dutch and Flemish Painters...12mo Bohn.   2 50
b. Spooner. Dictionary of Fine Arts, 2 v., *r.* 8vo N. Y.   10 00
   *** With the Supplement to Bryan ($4.75), this work is the best.
Shaw. Decorative Arts of Middle Ages.. 4to Lon. 42s.
——— Dresses and Decorations of Mid-
     dle Ages....4to Lon. 147s.
——— Hand Book of Alphabets.......folio Lon. 15s.
——— Illuminated Ornaments.........4to Lon. 105s.
a. Taine, H. The Ideal in Art............12mo N. Y.   1 25
———— Philosophy of Art...........16mo Lond. 6s.
——— Art in Greece..............16mo N. Y.   1 25
——— Art in the Netherlands.......16mo N. Y.   1 25
b. ——— Italy, Florence and Venice.... 8vo N. Y.   2 50
b. ——— ——— Naples and Rome...... 8vo N. Y.   2 50
Taylor, W. B. S. Hist. of Fine Arts in Great
     Britain, 2 vols....   Lon. 7s. 6d.
Tymnes, R. Art of Illuminating... ....12mo Lond.   2 50
Thornbury, W. British Artists. Hogarth
     to Turner, 2 vols....12mo Lon. 21s.
a. Tuckerman, H. T. Book of the Artists ;
     American Artist Life.. 8vo N. Y.   5 00
———— The same. Illus. (Various cost.)
Turner, J. W. M. Life by Thornbury,
     Illustrated, 2 vols... 8vo Lon. 30s.
Waagen. Art Treasures in Gt. B., 4 vols. 8vo Lon. 72s.
Walker. Analysis of Beauty in Women.*r.* 8vo Lon. 42s.
Walpole. Anecd. of Painting in Eng.,3 v. 8vo Lon. 27s.
——— The same, cheap edition......12mo L. & N.   2 00
Westmacott. Schools of Sculpture, Ancient
     and Modern.... 8vo Lond.   3 75
Wedgewood (the Potter), Life of. Ill.,2 v. 8vo Lond.   12 00
b. Winckelmann. Hist. of Ancient Art,3 v. *r.* 8vo Bost.
——— ——— Ancient Art among Greeks.. 8vo Lond.   3 00
Wornum. Life and Works of Holbein..*r.* 8vo Lond.   8 00
——— Epochs of Paint'g from Early Ages. 8vo Lond.   5 00
——— Analysis of Ornament. Illust... 8vo Lond.   2 50
Wyatt, M. D. Fine Art ; a Course of Lect. 8vo Lond.   3 00

Fine Arts—ILLUSTRATED BOOKS.
   *** No attempt is made to classify these in the order of value
   or importance.
Art Publications, Illustrated with Autotypes, Heliotypes,
   Woodburytypes, etc., all published.in London.
Hogarth. Works, 150 photographs, 2 v.. 4to 105s.

Landseer. Great Works............... 4to 42s.
Mulready's Great Works............... 4to 42s.
Raphael. Great Works............... 4to 42s.
Rembrandt Etchings.................... 4to 42s.
Rembrandt Gallery.................... 4to 63s.
Reynolds, Sir Joshua. English Children. 4to 42s.
Titian. Portraits, 17 photographs....... 4to 105s.
Turner. Landscapes, 16 autotypes....... 4to 42s.
Velasquez. Works, 17 photographs..... 4to 105s.
Wilkie. Great Works................. 4to 63s.
Contemporary French Painters.......... 4to 42s.
Gems of the Dutch and Flemish Schools.. 4to 25s.
Gems of Modern Belgian Art.......... 4to 42s.
Masterpieces of English Art............. 4to 42s.
———— ———— — Italian Art............ 4to 42s.
———— ———— — Flemish Art .... 4to 42s.
Mountains and Lakes of Switzerland..... 4to 42s.
Shakespeare Gallery, from Boydell....... 4to 42s.
Sheepshank's Gallery.................. 4to 42s.
Wonders of Sculpture. By Viardot..... 4to 12s. 6d.
Wonders of European Art. ————.... 4to 12s. 6d.
Wonders of Italian Art. ————..... 4to 12s. 6d.
World-Noted Pictures. 15 photographs.. 4to 21s.

Art and Song. Ill. with Vignettes on Steel. 4to Lon. 21s.
Baronial Halls, etc., of Eng. By Hall, 2 v. folio L. (147s.)$30 00
Beautiful Women, with 16 photos. from
                    Reynolds, etc....folio Lond. 20 00
Beautiful Pic. by Eng. Artists, eng. on steel. 4to Lon. 21s.
Berlin and its Art Treasures, mor........ 4to Lond. 25 00
Booth. Characters in Trag. and Come. Ill. 8vo Bost.
Boissere Gallery at Munich, photog......folio Lond. 50 00
———— The same (original copy, folio, £105), 125 00
British Schools of Art, 2 vols. in 1........ 4to Lond. 40 00
Canova's Works in Sculpture, 3 v. Lond. r. 8vo (120s.) 18 50
Chamberlaine's Imitations of Drawings,
                    etc. Lond., folio. (£12 12s.) 30 00
Claude. Liber Veritatis, ½ mor., 3 vols.,
                    Lond., folio. (£31 10s.) 54 00
Claude, Beauties of ; 24 plates. Lon., folio. (£3 12s.)   7 50
Coesvelt. Picture Gallery. By Mrs. Jame-
                    son. Lond. 4to (105s.) 12 75
Constable. Graphic Works, ½ mor......folio Lond. 16 50
Cooper Vignettes. By Darley, mor....... 4to N. Y. 40 00
Cruikshank. Complete Catalogue of his
                    Works. Illust., 3 vols. Lon. 4to £12 12s.
Cutts. Scenes and Characters in Middle
                    Ages, Illustrated....   Lond.
Dell, C. H. Nature Pictures. 30 Ill. on wood.folio L. 73s. 6d.
Doré. Illustrated Bible, 2 vols........folio Lond. 64 00
———— Illus. Dante Inferno to Paradiso, 2 v.folio Lond. 50 00
———— ———— Milton's Paradise Lost.....folio Lond. 40 00

Doré. Illus. Don Quixote..............	4to	Lond.	$15 00
—— —— La Fontaine's Fables.......	4to	Lond.	15 00
—— —— Baron Munchausen........	4to	Lond.	6 00
—— —— Fairy Realm..............	4to	Lond.	9 00
—— —— Croquemitaine	4to	Lond.	8 50
—— —— Tennyson's Idyls.........folio		Lon. 75s.	
Fairholt. Homes, Haunts, and Works of			
Rubens, Illustrated....	4to	Lon. 42s.	
Flaxman. Classical Compositions com-			
plete, ½ mor....folio		Lond.	35 00
—————— Compositions from Dante....folio		Lond.	16 00
Folk Songs; Illustrated on wood........	4to	N. Y.	15 00
Foster, Birket. Pictures of Eng. Landscape.	4to	Lond.	10 00
Gal. of Landscape Painters, Amer. Scenery.	4to	N. Y.	18 00

GALLERIES.

Berlin Gallery, morocco..............	4to	Lond.	25 00
Dresden Gallery, mor.................	4to	Lond.	25 00
Dusseldorf Gallery (pho.), mor.........folio		N. Y.	30 00
Leuchtenberg Gallery (Munich), ½ mor.	4to	Lond.	18 00
Munich Gallery, mor.................	4to	Lond	25 00
New York Galleries (pho.), mor........folio		N. Y.	40 00
Turner Gallery, 2 vols. London.......folio		£10. 10s.	
Vernon Gallery, 4 vols. London......folio		£8 8s.	
Vienna Galleries, mor.................	4to	Lond.	25 00
Wilkie Gallery, mor. London........folio		50s	

Gems of European Art (from Art Journal.)			
half mor., 2 vols....	4to	Lond.	50 00
Gems of English Poetry. Illustrated by			
Millais, Gilbert, etc....	4to	Lond.	
Goethé Gallery (photographs), mor.......	4to	Stutt.	20 00
—— Female Characters by Kaulbach).folio		Stutt.	36 00
—— Faust; with Silhouettes by Ko-			
newka....	4to	Bost.	4 00
Gems of Art, 36, in portfolio............		N. Y.	9 00
Gruner. Italian Frescoes, with Text, 2 v.folio		Lond.	35 00
—— Specimens of Ornamental Art..folio		Lond.	60 00
Hamerton. The Unknown River. Illus.			
with etchings....	4to	L. & B.	6 00
Hogarth's Works, 150 Illust. in Photo. 2 v.	4to	Lon. 105s	
Hood. Poems, Wanstead edition Illus..r.	8vo	N. Y.	8 00
Homely Scenes from Great Painters, 24 Ill.	4to	Lond.	6 00
Hope. Costume of the Ancients, 2 vols.r.	8vo	Lond.	13 50
Irving. Sketch Book, artist's edition....r.	8vo	N. Y.	10 00
Italian School of Design..........Lond.	4to	(£10)	16 00
Japanese Manners and Customs........r.	8vo	Lond.	9 00
Joseph and his Brethren, Illuminated...r.	8vo	Lond.	12 50
Lacroix. Arts of Middle Ages, Illust....r.	8vo	Lond.	12 00
—— Mœurs, Usages et Costumes			
de Moyen Age, Illustrated...r.	8vo	Paris.	15 00
Leslie, C. R. Pictures from his Works...	4to	Lond.	15 00

Life of Man Symbolized, Illust. mor.....*r*.8vo   N. Y. $20 00
Lossing. The Hudson River, Illust.....*r*.8vo   N. Y.   10 00
Maclise Gallery of Illust. Lit. Portraits... 4to   Lon. 21s.
Mantz.   Chefs d'Œuvre de la Peinture
                Italienne, Illustrated....folio   Paris. 30 00
Martin. Civil Costumes in England..... 4to   Lond. 16 00
Michel Angelo, 60 Outlines from Works of. folio Lond.   7 50
Michelet. The Mountain, Illustrated....*r*.8vo Lond.
Millais. The Parables of our Lord, Illus. folio L & N. 10 00
Modes et Costumes Historiques, col. plts. 4to   Paris. 18 50
Moses' Antique Vases, &c............... 4to   Lon. 63s.
New York Central Park, Illustrated...... 8vo   N. Y.   10 00
Ottley. Florentine School, ½ mor.......folio Lond. 28 00
———— Italian School of Design........folio Lond. 30 00
Palgrave. Gems of Engl. Art in 19th cent. folio L. & N. 10 00
Penley. Sketches from Nature, in Water
                colors.... folio Lond. 10 50
Pictures and Painters. Gems of Mod. Art, (from Art
  Journal) with text by T. A. Richards..folio Lond. 30 00
Portfolio of Cabinet Pictures, after Turner,
             Constable, &c....folio Lon. 42s.
Raphael, Great Works of, (Photog.)......folio Lond. 15 00
Raphael of Urbino & his Father, with Ill. folio L. 31s. 6d.
Reynard, the Fox, with Kaulbach's des'ns. 4to Lond. 20 00
Roberts. Views in Holy Land, Egypt, &c.,
      4 vols.....................*imp*.8vo Lond. 30 00
Royal Victoria Gallery, half bound....... 4to Lon.84s. 7 00
Ruskin and Turner. Harbors of England. folio Lond. 10 00
Selected Pictures from Galleries of Great
      Britain, eng. on steel, proofs.2 v.folio Lond. 275 00
Shakspeare. Midsummer's Night Dream
      Illustrated by Konewka....*r*.8vo Bost.   5 00
———————— Merchant of Venice, Illus.
         on wood....*r*.8vo Lond.   6 00
Schiller. Song of the Bell, Ill. by Retsch.. 4to Stutt. 7 50
Sculpture Gallery, (from Art Journal).... 4to Lond. 42 00
Strutt. Dresses & Habits of the English. 4to Lond. 19 00
Sun Pictures. 20 Heliotype Illustations of
      Ancient and Modern Art.... 4to Lon. 21s.
Sheepshanks, Turner, Vernon, Wilkie. [*See Galleries.*]
Tennyson's Idylls, Illustrated by Doré....folio Lond. 35 00
Turner. Liber Fluviorum: Rivers of Fr.*r*.8vo Lond. 16 00
————— Liber Studiorum, autotyped.... 4to Lond. 50 00
————— Southern Coast of England..... 4to Lond. 18 00
————— Harbors of England...........folio Lond.   3 75
Waverley Gallery....................*r*.8vo N. Y.   10 00
Walton, E. Coast of Norw'y, 12 col'd plates.folio L. & B. 30 00
Walton & Cotton's Angler, Illust., 2 vols.*r*.8vo Lond. 20 00
Waring. Masterpieces of Industrial Art,
      richly illuminated, etc. Lond. folio (£27) 100 00
Werner, Carl. Nile Sketches, 6 col'd plates.folio L. & B. 28 00
Wightwick. Palace of Architecture, Ill.*r*.8vo Lond.   5 00

Wyatt. Industrial Arts of 19th century,
2 vols., Lond., folio   (£21) $50 00

Fish—FISH CULTURE.—[*See also Angling, Aquarium.*]

Bertram. Harvest of the Sea: Brit. Fishes. 8vo Lond.   9 00
b. Figuier. The Ocean. Trans. & Illust..... 8vo Lond.   4 50
Fry. Artificial Fish Breeding........... 12mo Lond. 4s.
Herbert ("Frank Forrester"). Fish and
                Fishing. Illus.... 8vo N. Y.   5 00
Green, Seth, Trout Culture...16mo, Caledonia, N. Y.   1 25
b. Hartwig. The Sea and its Living Wonders. 8vo Lond.   3 75
b. Mangin. Mysteries of the Ocean. Illust. *r.* 8vo Lond.   6 00
a. Norris, Thad. Fish Culture. 1868...... 8vo Phila.   6 00

Florida.

a. Bill, L. Winter in Florida.............12mo N. Y.   1 25
Brinton, D. G. Notes on Florida. 1859..12mo Phila.   1 00
b. Fairbank, G. R. Hist. of Florida to 1842.12mo Phila.   2 50
Fairbank. Spaniards in Florida ....,12mo N. Y.   1 50
a. Irving, Theo. Conquest of Flor. by De Soto.12mo N. Y.   2 00
Yelverton, Mrs. St. Augustine, etc......12mo N. Y.   75

Flowers.—[*See Botany, Gardening, etc.*]
Language of. [*See Language of Flowers.*]

Food.—[*See Cookery and Food; Health.*]

Fossils.—[*See Geology.*]

France—GENERAL HISTORY OF.

Bonnechose. Hist. of France, new ed....12mo Lond. 5s.
Calcott. Lady. Hist. of France. London.18mo 2s. 6d.
a. Chambers R. France and its Revolutions.12mo Edn. 3s. 6d.
Crowe, E. E. Hist. of France, 5 vols.....12mo Lon. 18s.
b. Godwin, Parke. Hist. of France, vol. 1... 8vo N. Y.   3 00
b. Guizot. Hist. of France. Illustrated...*r.* 8vo Lond.
                (Now in progress, Nov. 1871.)
Martin H. Hist. of France to 1789, 17 v. 8vo Paris.
c. ——— — Trans. by M. L. Booth, 1 and 2 v. 8vo Bost.   8 00
Markham, Mrs. Hist. of France.........12mo N. Y.   1 75
a. Michelet. Hist. of France. Trans., 2 v.. 8vo N. Y.   4 00
Stephen. Lects. on Hist. France, 2 vols.. 8vo Lond. 24s.
a. Student's Hist. of France...............12mo N. Y.   2 00
b. White, Jas. Hist. of France............ 8vo N. Y.   2 00
Yonge, C. D. Hist. of France, 1867, 4 vols. 8vo Lond. 30s.

France—EARLY HISTORY.

Commines. Memoirs of F. & Burgundy, 2 v.12mo Bohn.   3 50
Cousin, V. Secret History of the Court
        under Richelieu & Mazarin ...12mo N. Y.   1 25
Duclos. Hist. of Louis XI..............
b. Froissart. Chronicles, 2 vols... ....*r.* 8vo Lond.   12 00

Freer, Mrs. W.   Henry III., Henry IV.,
   Mary de Medici, 6 vols....16mo Lond. 63s.
———— ———— Married Life & Regency of
   Anne of Austria, 3 vols.... 8vo Lon. 42s.
b. James, G. P. R.   Hist of Henry IV.,2 vols.12mo N. Y. $3 00
a. ———————— Hist. of Charlemagne...18mo N. Y.   75
   ———————— Hist. of Louis XIV., 2 v.   Bohn.   3 50
   4 vols.... 8vo Lond. 10 00
b. Kirk. Hist. of Charles the Bold, 3 vols... 8vo Phila.   9 00
Monstrelet.   Chronicles (continuing Frois-
   sart), 2 vols.....*r.* 8vo L. &. N. 9 00
Pardoe, Miss. Hist. of Francis I........   Lon. 36s.
b. ———— ——— Hist. of Louis XIV., 2 vols.12mo N. Y.   4 00
Thierry. The Third Estate.............12mo Lond.   2 25
———————— The Merovingian Era.........12mo Lon. 4s. 6d.
Tocqueville, A. de. The Old Regime....12mo N. Y.
Voltaire. Age of Louis XIV.............12mo

France—THE REVOLUTION OF 1789.

 Abbott. History of French Revolution.. 8vo N. Y.   5 00
 Alison. Europe during French Rev. 4 v. 8vo N. Y.   8 00
a. Carlyle. Hist. French Revolution, 2 vols.12mo N. Y.   3 50
 ———— The same,3 v.,8vo,Lon., $10.50 ; 3 v.16mo Lond.   2 70
b. Lamartine. Hist. of Girondists,3 vols ...12mo N. Y.   4 50
 Landon, M. D. Franco-Prussian War....12mo N. Y.   2 00
a. Michelet. French Revolution...........12mo Lond.   1 75
a. Mignet. French Revolution..... ......12mo Lond.   1 75
 Smyth. Lectures on French Revolution. 8vo Lond. 7s.
b. Sybel, H. Von. The French Revolu., 4 v. 8vo Lon.48s.
b. Thiers. Hist. of French Revolution,5 v. 8vo Lond. 10 00
 ———— ———— ———— ———— 4 v. 8vo N. Y.   8 00

France—THE CONSULATE AND EMPIRE ; NAPOLEON I.—
   [*See also Biography of Napoleon.*]

 Alison. [*See Europe.*]
 Jomini. Hist. of Campaign of Waterloo.12mo N. Y.   1 25
 ———— Military Life of Napoleon. 4 v.. 8vo N. Y. 25 00
a. Lanfrey, P. Hist. of Napoleon I., vol. 1. 8vo Lond.   3 50
 Segur. The Expedition to Russia, 2 vols. 8vo Lond. 7s.
 Siborne. War in France & Belgium in 1815. 8vo Lon. 12s.
 ———— The Battle of Waterloo.......
 Thiers. The Consulate & Empire, hf. calf.
   20 vols. in 10 .... 8vo Lond. 35 00
 ———— The same, 5 vols............. 8vo Phila. 11 25
 Wilson, Sir R The Invasion of Russia.. 8vo Lon. 15s.

France—RECENT HISTORY ; 1815–1870.

 Blanc, Louis. History of Ten Years, 2 v. 8vo Lon. 26s.
 ———————— Fr. under Louis Philippe..
 ———————— Histor'l Revelations. Lon.12mo 10s. 6d.
 Guizot. Memoirs of my own Time....... 8vo Lond.   3 00
 ———— Last Days of Louis Philippe.... 8vo Lond. 18s.
 ———— Democracy in France.... ......12mo Lon. 3s. 6d.

Hozier.   History of Seven Weeks' War
           (with Austria), 2 v.... 8vo Lon. 28s.
a. Lamartine.   The Restoration, 4v. 12mo.,
                   N. Y. $6.00....   Bohn. **$7 00**
a. Revolution of 1848.....................12mo Bohn.   1 75
Michelet.   France before Europe........12mo Bost.   1 00
Mitchell. D. G.   The Battle Summer, 1848.12mo N. Y.   1 50
Renan, E.   Constitutional Monarchy in Fr.16mo Bost.   75
a. Ténot E.   Paris in 1851.................12mo N. Y.   2 00

France.—WAR WITH PRUSSIA, 1870-1.

Adams, W. D.   Franco-Prussian War: its
              Causes, &c., — vols.... 4to Lond.
Bowles.   Defence of Paris—As it was seen. 8vo Lon. 16s.
Guizot de Witt, Mad.   Book ab't the War.12mo N. Y.
Hozier, Capt.   Franco-Prussian War, 3 v.
                 London.... 4to *ea.*8s. 6d.
Pictures from Paris in War and Siege.
           By an American Lady.... 8vo L. 7s. 6d.
Rueston, Col.W. War for the Rhine Front'r 8vo Lond.   8 00
a. War Correspondene of Daily News...... 8vo Lon. 6s.

France.—THE COMMUNE OF 1871.
      *** French works on this theme are very numerous.
Brockett, L. P. Paris under the Commune.12mo Hartf.   1 25
a. Fetridge, W. P.   Hist. of the Commune..12mo N. Y.   2 00
Labouchere, H.   Diary in Paris, 1871.....12mo Lond.
b. Leighton.   Paris and the Commune......12mo Lond.   4 00

France.—TRAVELS IN, GEOGRAPHY OF, ETC.

American Family in Paris...............16mo N. Y.   1 50
American (The) in Paris, summer and win-
              ter, 2 vols.... 8vo Lon. 18s.
Bulwer, H. L.   France, Literary, Social
         and Political, 2 vols....   N. Y.   3 00
Buffum, E. G.   Sights and Sensations in
              France....12mo N. Y.   1 50
Craik.   Fair France. By author of John
             Halifax....12mo Lond.
Head, Sir F.   Faggot of French Sticks...12mo N. Y.
a. Jarves, J. J.   Parisian Sights and French
            Principles, 2 vols....   N. Y.   3 00
a. Murray.   Hand-Book for France.........12mo Lond.   4 00
Musgrave, G.   Nooks and Corners of Old
            France, 2 vols....   Lon. 24s.
————— By-Ways in Picardy......12mo Lond.
Robinson.   Parks and Gardens of Paris.. 8vo L. & B.   7 50
Tomes, R.   The Champagne Country....12mo N. Y.   1 50
Tuckerman, H. T.   Papers about Paris...18mo N. Y.   1 00

French Language.—[*See also Dictionaries.*]

Bolmar.   French Course of Study, 4 vols.12mo N. Y.   5 00
Collot.   French Course, 5 vols..........12mo N. Y.   5 00

De Fivas.   French Course, 3 vols........12mo N. Y. $3 50
De Vere.   French Course, 3 vols........12mo N. Y.   3 25
Fasquelle. French Course, 7 vols.......12mo N. Y.   0 00
Girard.   French Course, 5 vols.........12mo Phila. 4 40
Ollendorf. French Course, 3 vols........12mo N. Y.   3 25
Robertson. French Course, 3 vols.......12mo N. Y.   5 00

French Literature.—[See *Literature.*]

Free Masons.—[See *Secret Societies.*]

Free Trade—[See also *Political Economy.*]

    Bastiat.   Sophisms of Protective Policy..16mo N. Y.   30
    ——   Essays on Political Economy....12mo Chica. 2 00
    Cobden, R.   Political Writings, 2 vols.... 8vo Lond. 24s.
b. Grosvenor, W. M. Does Protection Protect? 8vo N. Y.   2 50
a. What is Free Trade? "By Emile Walter."12mo N. Y. 1 00

Fruits—[See *Agriculture.*]

Fuel—[See *Warming and Ventilation.*]

Furniture.

b. Eastlake, C. L.   Hints on Household Taste
                     in Furnishing ... 4to Lond.   7 50
    Hibberd.   Rustic Adornments of Homes of
                         Taste.... 8vo Lond. 10 50
    King.   Cabinet Maker's Guide.......... 4to Lon. 21s.
    Shaw.   Ancient Furniture. Illust....... 4to Lon. 42s.

Future State.

a. Alger.   Critical Hist. of Doctrine of Fu-
                   ture Life.... 8vo N. Y.   3 50
    Constable, H.   The Duration of Future
                  Punishment. 1868.... 8vo Lond.
    George, M. D.   Annihilation not of the
                      Bible....12mo Bost.   1 50
    Harbaugh. Heaven, 3 vols....... ......12mo Phila. 4 25
    Hudson. Human Destiny...............12mo N. Y.
    Kimball, J. W.   Heaven...............12mo Bost.   1 50
a. Phelps, E. S.   The Gates Ajar...........12mo Bost.   1 50
    Randolph, R. B.   After Death. 1868..... 8vo Bost.   1 50
    Wood.   The Gates Wide Open..........12mo Bost.   1 50

Galvanism.—[See also *Electricity; Magnetism.*]

    Hare.   Galvanism & Electro Magnetism. 8vo Phila.
    Harris, W. S.   Rudimentary Galvanism..16mo Lon. 1s. 6d.
    ——   ——   Animal Galvanism.......12mo Lon. 1s. 6d.

Gambling.

    Green, J. H.   Arts & Mysteries of Gam'lg.
    ——   ——   Gambling Unmasked. 1844.
    Steinmetz.   The Gaming Table. 1870, 2 v. 8vo Lon. 30s.

Games and Amusements.—[*See also Athletic Sports, Gymnastics, Chess, Draughts, etc., and Juveniles.*

	Art of Amusing...................?......12mo N. Y.	**$1 50**
a.	Boys' own Book........................16mo N. Y.	1 00
b.	Boys' Treasury of Sports and Pastimes... 8vo Lond.	1 75
	Cheney, Mrs. Social Games with Cards..24mo Bost.	1 00
a.	Dodge, M. E. A few Friends, and How	
	they Amused themselves....12mo Phila.	1 25
	Evening Amusements. Konewka's Des'ns.12mo Bost.	1 50
a.	Girls' Own Book....................16mo N. Y.	1 50
b.	Girls' Own Treasury.................... 8vo Lond.	2 50
	How to Amuse an Evening Party........18mo Phila.	1 25
b.	Home Book of Pleasure and Instruction.. 8vo Lond.	4 00
	Hoyle's Games, 18mo., London..........18mo Phila.	1 00
	Magician's Own Book...................12mo Phila.	1 50
b.	Mental Photographs.................... 4to N. Y.	1 50
	Sociable: or, 1001 Amusements.........12mo Phila.	1 50
	Secret Out: 1000 Tricks with Cards...... 8vo Lond.	3 00

Gardening.—[*See also Agriculture, Botany, Landscape Gardening.*]

Abell, L. G. Rose Culturalist, (Saxton)..	
Barnard, Chas. Simple Flower Garden... 8vo Bost.	25
Beecher, H. W. Fruits, Flowers & F"m'g.12mo N. Y.	1 50
Breck. New Book of Flowers.... ......12mo N. Y.	1 75
a.	Bridgman. Young Gardener's Assistant.12mo N. Y.	2 50
	Buist. Amer. Flower Garden Directory..12mo N. Y.	1 50
	—— Family Kitchen Gardener.......12mo N. Y.	1 00
	Fessenden. American Kitchen Gardener.12mo N. Y.	
	Fulton. On Peach Culture.............12mo N. Y.	1 50
	Field. Green Houses, and Green House	
	Plants....12mo N. Y.	75
a.	Henderson. Gardening for Profit........12mo N. Y.	1 50
	—— Practical Floriculture......12mo N. Y.	1 50
	Hibberd, S. Fern Garden..............12mo L. 3s. 6d.	
	Johnson, L. Every Lady her own Flower	
	Gardener....12mo N. Y.	
a.	Lindley. Horticulture. Ed. by Downing. 8vo N. Y.	2 00
b.	Loudon. Encyclo. of Gardening......... 8vo Lon. 21s.	
	—— Mrs. Gardening for Ladies....12mo N. Y.	2 00
	Parkman, F. Book of the Rose.........12mo Bost.	1 50
	Parsons, S. B. On the Rose............12mo N. Y.	1 25
	Quin. Pear Culture for Profit..........12mo Tribune 1 00
	—— Money in the Garden...........12mo Tribune 1 00
	Rand, E. S. Bulbs, Hardy and Tender...12mo Bost.	3 00
b.	—— Flowers for Parlor & Garden...12mo Bost.	3 00
	—— Seventy-five Popular Flowers..12mo Bost.	1 50
	Robinson. Gleanings from Fr. Gardens.12mo Lond.	3 00
b.	Thomas, J. J. Amer. Fruit Culturalist..12mo N. Y.	3 00
a.	Watson, A. American Home Garden....12mo N. Y.	2 00
	White. Gardening for the South. ......12mo N. Y.	2 00

Gas—GAS WORKS.

Bowditch, W. R. Analysis of Coal Gas.. 8vo Lon.12s.6d.
Clegg. Treatise on Coal Gas, London.. 4to 31s. 6d.
Gas Consumers' Guide.................12mo Bost. $1 00
Hughes. Treatise on Gas Works........16mo Lond. 1 50
Moore, A. The Gas Consumer's Guide...12mo 1 00
Newbigging. Gas Managers' Hand Book. 8vo Lond. 3 75
Perkins, E. E. On Gas and Ventilation..12mo 1 25
Sugg. On Gas Manipulation............ 8vo Lond. 7 00

Gazetteers.

Beeton. Dictionary of Geography....... 8vo Lond. 3 50
Blackie's Imperial Gazetteer, 4 v.Imp.8vo Glasg. £4 15s.
Harpers' Statistical Gazetteer........... 8vo N. Y. 5 75
a. Lippincott's Pronouncing Gazetteer...... 8vo Phila. 10 00
b. McCulloch's Geographical Dictionary, 2 v. 8vo Lond. 14 00
————— —————— ————— 4 v. 8vo N. Y. 10 00
Maunder's Treasury Gazetteer..........16mo Lond. 4 00
    ** There are Gazetteers of several of the States of the Union.

Gems.

a. Billing. Science of Gems, Jewels, etc., Ill. 4to Lond. 15 75
Emanuel, H. Diamonds and Precious
                    Stones. ...16mo Lond. 3 25
Feuchtwanger. Treatise on Gems, 1859.. 8vo N. Y. 5 00
Jeffries on Diamonds.................... 8vo Lond. 4 00
King, C. W. Nat. Hist. of Gems, 1867...12mo L. 10s. 6d.
————— Nat. Hist. of Precious Stones.12mo Lond.
————— Hand-B'k of Eng'd Gems,'66.12mo Lond.

Genealogy.

New Engl. Hist.—Geneal. Register, 18 v.. Bost.
b. Savage. Genealogical History of Settlers
         of New England, 4 vols.... Bost. 12 00
a. Whitmore. Hand-Book of Am. Genealog. 4to Alb. 3 00
    ** Family Genealogies are numerous, but copies for sale are *not*
      numerous.

Geography.—[*See also Atlases, Bible Geography, Gazetteers,*
               Physical Geography, Travels, and names of
               each country.]

Ansted, D. T. Science of Phys. Geog....12mo N. Y. 3 00
————— World we Live in; First
              Lessons in Geography.... N. Y. 75
Anthon, C. Ancient Geography......... 8vo N. Y. 3 00
Beeton. Dictionary of Geography....... 8vo Lond. 3 50
Bevan, W. L. Ancient Geog. (by Smith).12mo Lond.
————— Student's Mod. Geography.12mo Lond.
Fay, T. S. Great Outline of Geography
             and Atlas, 2 vols.,... N. Y. 2 50
a. Guyot. Earth and Man......... 12mo Bost. 1 75
Johnston, A. K. Dictionary of Geography. 8vo Lon. 30s.
Malte Brun & Balbi. Geography........ 8vo Lon. 15s.

Milner, Rev. T.   Gallery of Geography
    Pictures and Designs, 2 vols...*r*. 8vo Lond. $10 50
a. Reclus, E.   The Earth ; Phenomena of the
    Life of the Globe, 2 vols.... 8vo Lond. 10 00
b. Ritter.   Comparative Geography, 4 vols.. 8vo Edinb.
  ——— Geographical Studies..........12mo Bost. 1 50
Schmitz.   Ancient Geography...........12mo N. Y. 1 75
Student's Manual of Ancient and Modern
    Geography....*ea*.12mo Lond. 8 75
Woodbridge & Willard.   Universal Geog-
    raphy and Atlas, 2 vols.... N. Y. 2 75

Geology and Paleontology.

Agassiz.   Geological Sketches...........12mo Bost. 2 25
Ansted.   The Earth's History ; First Les-
    sons in Geology....12mo Phila. 1 25
  ——— Great Stone Book.   1863.......12mo Phila.
Blake, W. P.   Geol. Report of California. 4to N. Y. 8 00
Buckland.   Geology and Mineralogy Text.12mo Bohn. 2 50
—————— ——— ——— ———plates. 5 00
Catlin.   Subsidized Rocks of America. Lon. 8vo 7s. 6d.
Cotta.   Rocks Classified and Described...12mo Lond.
a. Dana, J. D.   Manual of Geology......... 8vo Phila.
  ——— ——— Text Book of Geology...... 8vo Phila.
  ——— ——— On Corals............... 8vo N. Y. 6 00
b. Figuier.   The World Before the Flood.. 8vo N. Y. 4 50
Geike.   Story of a Boulder.   1858 ......12mo Lond. 5s.
Gray.   Elementary Geology.............12mo N. Y. 1 50
b. Hartwig.   The Subterranean World..... 8vo Lond. 8 50
Hitchcock.   Elementary Geology........12mo N. Y. 1 60
Kobell.   The Mineral Kingdom.........12mo Bohn. 2 50
Loomis, J. R.   Elements of Geology......12mo Bost. 1 25
a. Lyell.   Elements of Geology (Lond. 9s.).. 8vo N. Y. 3 50
a. ——— Principles of Geology........... 8vo N. Y. 3 50
  ——— Principles of Geology, 10th ed., 2 v. 8vo Lond. 16 00
Mantell.   The Medals of Creation, 2 vols.12mo Bohn. 6 00
  ——— Wonders of Geology, 2 vols....12mo Bohn. 6 00
a. Miller, Hugh.   Footprints of the Creator.12mo B. & L. 1 75
a. ——— ——— Old Red Sandstone......12mo B. & L. 1 75
a. ——— ——— Testimony of the Rocks..12mo B. & L. 1 75
a. Molloy.   Geology and Revelation........12mo N. Y. 2 25
Murchison, R.   Siluria.   1854........... 8vo Lon. 18s.
Nicholson, H. A.   Text Book of Geology.12mo N. Y. 1 50
Owen, R.   Palæontology........Edinb. 8vo 7s. 6d.
b. Page, D.   Geology for General Readers..12mo N. Y. 3 00
  ——— Hand Book of Geol. Terms.Edin.16mo 1s. 6d.
  ——— Intro. Text Book of Geol..Edin. 8vo 7s. 6d.
  ——— Text Book of Geology....Edin. 8vo 7s. 6d.
  ——— Past and Present of the Globe.
    Edinburgh....12mo 7s. 6d.
Smith, Dr. J. Pye. Geology and Scripture.12mo Bohn. 2 50
b. St. John.   Elements of Geology........12mo N. Y. 1 50

Thoughts on a Pebble.................18mo

*** There are also extensive Official Reports on the Geology of Massachusetts, New York, Pennsylvania, Ohio, Indiana, California, and several other States, published (usually) in quarto volumes, illustrated.

Georgia.

- Carpenter. Hist. of Georgia............18mo Phila. $ 63
  Stevens. Hist. of Georgia, 2 vols........ 8vo Phila. 3 75

Germany.—[*See also Austria, Prussia, and names of separate States; also France.*]

- Bryce.   The Holy Roman Empire........12mo Lon.7s.6d.
  Carlyle.   Hist. of Frederick the Great, 6v.12mo N. Y. 12 00
               or 10 vols....16mo Lond. 9 00
- *a.* Hozier.   The Seven Weeks' War (Austria
          and Prussia), 2 vols.... 8vo Lon. 28s.
- *a.* Kolrausch.   History of Germany........ 8vo N. Y. 2 50
  Markham, Mrs.   History of Germany.....12mo Lon. 4s.
- *b.* Menzel.   History of Germany, 3 vols.....12mo Bohn. 5 25
- *b.* Schiller.   History of Thirty Years' War..12mo Bohn. 1 75
  ——— ——— — ——— ——— 12mo N. Y. 1 00
  Turner, D. W.   Analysis of Hist. Germ..16mo Lond.

Germany—TRAVELS IN.

- *a.* Brace, C. L.   Home Life in Germany....12mo N. Y. 1 75
- *a.* Browne, J. R.   Amer. Family in Germany 12mo N. Y. 2 00
  Head, Sir F. B. Bubbles from the Brunnen.12mo N. Y. 75
  Howitt, W.   Student Life in Germany... 8vo L. 10s. 6d.
  ——— Rural & Domes. Life in Ger. 8vo L. 7s. 6d.
  Kohl.   Travels in Germany............. 8vo Lond.
  Spencer, E.   Ger. from Baltic to Adriatic. 8vo Lon.7s. 6d.
- *b.* Stael, Mme. de.   Germany, 2 vols........12mo N. Y. 3 00

German Language.

- *a.* Adler.   Germ. & Eng. Dict.,abg'd. $2.50...*r*. 8vo N. Y. 6 00
  ——— German Reader.................12mo N. Y. 1 00
- *b.* Comfort's German Course, 3 vols.........12mo N. Y. 6 00
  Ollendorf's Method of Teaching German.12mo N. Y. 1 25
  Otto's German Grammar.................12mo N. Y. 1 75
- *a.* Preu.   German Primer, $1 ; First Steps.. 8vo N. Y. 1 25
- *b.* Whitney.   Ger. Reader, $1.25 ; Grammar.12mo N. Y. 1 75
  *** And many others.

German Literature.—[*See Literature.*]

Ghosts.—[*See Apparitions, Demonology.*]

Gift Books.—[*See Fine Arts, Illustrated Books, Juveniles, Natural History, Poetry, etc.*]

The following are some of those not otherwise classified.

Among the Trees. By Mary Lorimer. Ill. 4to N. Y. 1 75
Art and Song. Illus. by Painters and Poets. 4to L. & P. 10 00
Aubigne, J. H. Merle d'. History of Refor-
             mation. Illust.... 4to N. Y. 10 00

Barbauld. Hymns in Prose. Illust..:.	4to	L. & N.	$2	00
Bewick. Fables, with Illustrations from original blocks....	18mo	L. & N.	2	50
Book of Rubies; a Collection of Poems...	8vo	N. Y.	7	00
Browning. Lady Geraldine. Illust.....	8vo	N. Y.	5	00
Bryant. Song of the Sower. Illust......	4to	N. Y.	5	00
——— ——— Story of the Fountain.....	4to	N. Y.	5	00
Christmas Poems and Pictures. Illust...	4to	N. Y.	2	50
Christian Lyrics, from Mod. Authors. Ill.	8vo	L. & N.	6	00
Cooper Vignettes. By Darley, eng. on steel.	4to	N. Y.	40	00
Cotter's Saturday Night. Illustrated.....	8vo	N. Y.	5	00
Cowper. John Gilpin, Illust............	4to	L. & N.	2	50
Dickens. Christmas Carol, Illust........	8vo	Bost.	5	00
Dunkin. Midnight Sky, Illust.........r.	8vo	L. & N.	3	75
Favorite Authors, with Portraits........	8vo	Bost.	2	50
Forest Scenes, drawn by Hows...........	4to	N. Y.	7	00
Folk Songs, edited by Palmer, Illust....r.	8vo	N. Y.	15	00
Foster, Birket. Illustrated Poets, for Gifts, 12 vols....ea..	8vo	L. & N.	2	50
Good Company, with Portraits..........	8vo	Bost.	2	50
Golden Thoughts from Golden Fountains.r.	8vo	L. & N.	12	00
Holland ' Katrina,'—Bitter Sweet, Ill. ea.	8vo	N. Y.	9	00
Household Friends, Illustrated..........	8vo	Bost.	2	50
Home-Book of Pleasure and Instruc., Illust.	8vo	L. & N.	3	75
Irving. Sketch-Book, Artist's ed., Illust.r.	8vo	N. Y.	10	00
——— Rip Van Winkle, Illust.........r.	8vo	N. Y.	1	50
——— Sleepy Hollow, Illust..........r.	8vo	N. Y.	1	25
——— Knickerbocker. Illus. by Darley.r.	8vo	N. Y.	9	00
Konewka. Silhouette Ilustratious........				
——— Goethe's Faust................	4to	Bost.	4	00
——— Falstaff, etc.................	4to	Bost.	4	00
——— Shakespeare. Midsum. Nt. Dm.	4to	Bost.	5	00
Legend of St. Gwendoline, Illustrated by Ehninger....	4to	N. Y.	10	00
Light of the World and other Poems, etc., Illustrated....	4to	Lond.	5	00
New York Central Park, Illustrated......	4to	N. Y.	10	00
Picture Gallery of all Nations, Illust.....	4to	L. & N.	2	50
Poet and Painter; English Poets, Illust..r.	8vo	N. Y.	12	00
Poet's Gallery; 36 Ideals f'm Eug. Poetry.r.	8vo	L. & N.	7	50
Queens of England; 29 Portraits; text from Strickland....r.	8vo	L. & N.	15	00
Republican Court in days of Washington, Illustrated....r.	8vo	N. Y.	15	00
Songs of Life; Songs of Home; Songs of the Heart, Illustrated.....ea.	8vo	N. Y.	5	00
Spirit of Praise; Hymns Old & New, Illus.	8vo	L. & N.	3	75
Stratford Gall'y; Shakespeare Sisterhood.r.	8vo	N. Y.	15	00
Sunnyside Book, by popular Authors and Artists....r.	8vo	N. Y.	4	50
Swiss Pictures; Spanish Pictures, ea. Ill.r.	8vo	L. & N.	3	75
Tuckerman. Book of the Artists, (Ill. $30).	8vo	N. Y.	5	00

Watts. Divine and Moral Songs, Illust. . 4to L. & N. $2 00
Waverley Gallery ; Female Portraits...*r*.8vo N. Y.   7 50
Willmott's Poets of 19th Century, Illust. . 4to N. Y.   3 75
Winter Poems ; Longfellow, Whittier, etc.,
                          Illustrated. . . . 4to Bost.   5 00
World-Noted Women ; steel portraits...*r*. 8vo N. Y. 15 00

Glaciers.—[*See Alps.*]

Glass-Making.

Sauzany. Marvels of Glass-Making.....12mo N. Y.   1 50

Gold.—[*See Finance, Mineralogy.*]

Jukes. Lectures on Gold. 1852........12mo Lond.
Phillips. Mining in Gold and Silver. Lon. 8vo 12s. 6d.
Scoffern. Chemistry of Gold............16mo Lond. 1s.

Government.—[*See also Constitution, Internat'l Law, Law.*]

a. Alden. Science of Government.........12mo N. Y.   1 50
———— Citizen's Manual..............12mo N. Y.   50
   Bristed, C. A. Interference Theory of Gov't.12mo N. Y.   1 00
b. De Tocqueville. Democracy in Amer., 2 v. 8vo Camb.   5 00
   Gillett, R. H. Democracy in the U. S....12mo   1 50
   Guizot. Hist. of Constitutional Gov't....12mo Bohn.   1 75
. Holmes. Parties and their Principles...12mo N. Y.   1 50
   Humboldt, Wm. Sphere and Duties of
                          Government.... 8vo Lond. 5s.
   Jennings. Eighty Years of Republican
                   . Gov't in U. S . . 12mo   1 75
   Lewis, Sir G. C. Administration of Eng-
                   land. 1783-1830.... 8vo Lon. 15s.
b. Lieber. On Civil Liberty and Self Gov't. 8vo Phila.   3 25
   Louis Napoleon. Napoleonic Ideas...... 8vo Lond. 4s.
   Maine, H. S. Village Communities...... 8vo Lond. 9s.
a. Mill, J. S. On Liberty..............16mo Bost.   1 50
b. ———— Representative Government..12mo N. Y.   1 50
   Montesquieu. Spirit of Laws, 2 v., *scarce.* 8vo Lond.
b. Mulford, E. The Nation..............8vo N. Y.   3 00
   Munroe, Jas. The People the Sover'ns, etc.12mo Phila.   1 75
   Seaman. Amer. System of Government..12mo N. Y.   1 50
   Stern. Representative Government.....12mo Phila.   1 75
   Tileston. Hand Book of the Administrat.12mo Bost.
   Wedgewood, W. B. Gov't and Laws of U.S. 8vo N. Y.   5 00
   Yeaman, Geo. Study of Government.... 8vo Bost.   5 00

Grammar—ENGLISH.—[*See also Languages, separate.*]

a. Brown, Gould. Grammar of Grammars.. 8vo N. Y.   5 00

    ** Also about 30 other Elementary Grammars, used as text-books.

Grapes—WINE—[*See Agriculture.*]

Grasses.—Flint. Grasses and Forage Plants.. 8vo Bost.

Great Britain.—[*See England, Ireland and Scotland.*]

Greece—ANCIENT.—[*See also Athens; History, Anct.*]

	Arnold, Rev. F. History of Greece. Illus.12mo Lond.		
b.	Becker. Charicles: Manners, etc. of Gr.. 8vo Lond.	$3 50
	Boeck. Public Economy of Athens..... 8vo Lond. 18s.
	Bonner. Child's History of Greece, 2 vols.18mo N. Y.	2 50
	Bulwer, Sir E. L. Athens, its Rise and Fall, 2 vols.... 8vo L. 31s. 6d.
a.	Curtius. History of Greece, — vols..... 8vo N.Y. *ea.* 3 00
	Elton. Speci. of Greek Classic Poets, 3 v. 8vo Lond. 6 00
b.	Felton, Prof. Greece, Ancient & Modern. 8vo Bost. 5 00
	Finlay, G. History of Greece, 5 vols..... 8vo Edn. 66s.
	Gladstone, W. E. Ancient Greece in Providential order of the World.... 8vo Lond.
b.	Gladstone. Juventus Mundi............ 8vo Bost. 2 50
	———— Homer & the Homeric Age, 3 v. 8vo Oxfo. 33s.
a.	Grote. History of Greece, 12 vols........12mo N. Y. 18 00
	.——— ———— ———— 12 vols..... ..12mo Lond. 24 00
	Heeren. Politics of Ancient Greece..... 8vo Lond. 3 75
	Keightley. History of Greece, (element.).12mo Lon. 6s. 6s.
	Mitford. History of Greece, 10 vols...... 12mo Bohn. 40s.
	Muller, C. O. Athens and Attica........ 8vo Lon. 6s.
	St. John. Manners and Customs of Ancient Greece, 3 vols ... 8vo Lon. 21s.
	Schmitz. History of Greece............12mo L. 7s. 6d.
	Smith, W. Smaller History of Greece...12mo N. Y.
a.	———— Students' History of Greece.12mo N. Y. 2 00
	Thirlwall. Hist. of Greece (8 v. 60s.), 2 v. 8vo N. Y. 4 00
	Thucydides. Hist. Trans. by Smith, 2 v. N. Y. 1 50
b.	———— ———— — Dale......12mo N. Y. 1 50
	Wacksmuth. Polit. Antiq's of Greece, 2v. 8vo Oxfo. 30s.
	Xenophon. Whole Works. Trans. by Smith. 8vo N. Y. 2 00
	———— Anabasis, by Smith..........12mo Bohn. 2 25
	———— ———— — —— 2 vols.....18mo N. Y. 1 50
b.	———— Literally trans. by Watson..12mo N. Y. 1 50

Greece—MODERN.

	Baird, H. M. Modern Greece............12mo N. Y. 1 50
	Gordon. Hist. Greek Revolution, 2 vols..8vo Edn. 10s. 6.
	Keightley. Greek War of Independence. Lon. 7s.
	Leake. Topography of Athens, 2 vols.... 8vo Lon. 30s.
	———— Travels in Morea, 3 vols........ 8vo Lond.
	———— ———— Northern Greece, 4 v. 8vo L. 60s.
a.	Murray. Hand Book for Greece.........12mo Lon. 15s.
a.	Rangabe. Greece, Prog. and Pres. Condi. 4to N. Y. 75
b.	Wordsworth, C. Tour in Greece. Rich. ill. *r.* 8vo Lond. 10 50

Greek Literature.—[*See Literature.*]

Green Houses.—[*See Gardening.*]

Greenland.—[*See Arctic Regions.*]

Guatemala.—[*See America, Central.*]

Guide Books.—[*See names of Countries.*]

Gun—GUNNERY; GUNPOWDER.—[*See Ordnance.*]

Gymnastics and Calisthenics.

Beecher, Miss.   Physiolo. & Calisthenics..12mo N. Y. $ 75
a. Depping. Wonders of Bodily Strength..12mo N. Y.   1 50
Howard, J. H.   Gymnasts and Gymnastics.16mo L. 7s. 6d.
Kehoe, S. D.   Indian Club Exercise.... .. 4to   N. Y.   2 00
a. Lewis, Dio.   New Gymnastics.......... .12mo Bost.   1 50
Larpee, H. de.   Calisthenics............. 8vo Lond.   3 75
Maclaren, Arch.   Training in Theory and
                    Practice.... 8vo Lond.
————————— Syst. of Physical Educa. 8vo Oxfo.   ·
Ravenstein & Hulley. Hand Book of Gym-
                    nastics, etc.....8vo London.7s. 6d. & 2s. 6d.
Trall, R. F.   Family Gymnasium..... ..12mo N. Y.   1 75
Watson.   Hand Book of Calisthenics & G.. 8vo Lon. 8s.
Wilkinson.   Modern Athletes........... .12mo Lond.   50
Woods.   Manual of Physical Training...12mo N. Y.   1 50

Gypsies.

Borrow, Geo.   Romany Rye, paper....... 8vo N. Y.   75
b. ———— ———— Zincali, or Gypsies of Spain.12mo L. 3s. 6d.
———— ———— Lavengro, paper........... 8vo N. Y.   75
a. Simson, W.   History of the Gypsies...... 8vo N. Y.   3 00

Hayti.—[*See St. Domingo.*]

Health.—[*See also Cookery, Food, Maternity & Physiology.*]

Anstie.   Use of Wines in Health and
                    Disease....12mo Lond.   50
Banting.   Letter on Corpulence........ ... 8vo N. Y.   25
a. Bellows, A. J.   How Not to be Sick......12mo N. Y.   ·2 00
a. ———— ———— Philosophy of Eating.....12mo N. Y.   2 00
Bill, L.   Winter in Florida.............12mo N. Y.   1 25
Brown, Jno., M. D.   Plain Words about
                    Health....12mo Lon. 6s.
Chavasse.   Advice to a Mother on Health.12mo Phila.   1 50
Chambers, T. K.   The Indigestions...... 8vo L. 10s. 6d.
Combe, A.   Physiology app. to Health, etc.12mo Ed. 3s. 6d.
Clark, Sir J.   Sanative Infl'nce of Climate. 8vo L. 10s.6d.
Eyre, Sir J.   The Stomach & its Difficulties.12mo Phila.   75
First Help in Accidents and Sickness.....12mo Bost.   1 50
Good Health ; the Laws of Correct Living. 8vo Bost.   2 50
Hall, W. W.   Coughs and Colds..... ...12mo N. Y.   1 50
———————— Health and Disease........12mo N. Y.   1 50
a. ———————— Health by Good Living.....12mo N. Y.   1 50
———————— On Sleep.................12mo N. Y.   1 50
Haviland.   Influ. of Climate on Health, etc. 8vo Lon. 7s.
a. Hinton.   Health and its Conditions..,.....12mo N. Y.   1 50
a. Hope.   Till the Doctor Comes...........12mo N. Y.   60
Lee, Dr.   Influence of Climate on Pulmo-
                    nary Disease....12mo L. 4s. 6d.

•

Lewis, Dio.   Our Girls..................12mo N. Y. $1 50
——— ———   Talks ab't People's Stomachs.12mo Bost.   1 50
——— ———   Weak Lungs, and How to be
                              Strong....12mo Bost.   1 50
a. Macé.   Hist. of a Mouthful of Bread.....12mo N. Y.   1 75
———   Servants of the Stomach.........12mo N. Y.   1 75
Macpherson.   Baths & Wells of Europe..12mo L. 6s. 6d.
Mitchell, S. W.   Wear and Tear: the
                              Overworked....18mo Phila.
Murray, W. H. H.   The Adirondacks—for
                              Invalids....12mo Bost.   1 50
Nightingale, Florence.   Notes on Nursing.12mo N. Y.   75
Ordronaux.   The Code of Health of School
                              of Salernum... 8vo Phila.   5 00
Pereira.   On Food and Diet, edited by C.
                              A. Lee....12mo N. Y.   1 75
Ray.   Mental Hygiene.. ....12mo Bost.   1 50
Smith, South.   Philosophy of Health.... 8vo Lond. 5s.
Sweetser.   Human Life and its Duration.12mo N. Y.   1 50
Winslow.   Influence of Light on Health.12mo N. Y.   1 75

Heat.

a. Abbott, Jacob.   On Heat ....12mo N. Y.   1 50
Metcalfe.   Caloric: its Mechanical, &c.,
                              Agencies.... 8vo Phila.   5 00
Stewart, B.   Elementary Treatise on Heat.16mo L. & N.   2 50
a. Tyndall.   Heat as Mode of Motion.......12mo N. Y.   2 00
b. Wonders of Heat.... ....12mo N. Y.   1 50

Heathenism.

Chinese Classics, ed. by Legge, 8 vols....*r*. 8vo
a. ———   ———   ——— Rev. A. W. Loomis.12mo N. Y.   2 00
Döllinger.   Heathenism and Judaism, 2 v. 8vo Lon. 21s.
Fergusson.   Tree and Serpent Worship.. 4to Lon. 105s.
Gould, Baring.   Heathenism and Mosaism,
                    vol. 1 of Hist. of Religions.. 8vo Lon. 15s.

Heraldry.

b. Burke.   Encyclopedia of Heraldry......*r*. 8vo Lon. 21s.
Boutwell.   Heraldry; Hist. and Popular.*r*. 8vo Lond.   7 50
a. Clark.   Manual of Heraldry (col'd $7.50)..12mo Bohn.   2 25
Cussons.   Hand-Book of Heraldry........12mo Lond.   3 75
Fairbairn.   Crests of Families of Great
                    Britain, 2 vols....*r*. 8vo Lond.   15 00
Millington, E. J.   Heraldry; its History,
                    Poetry, etc.....16mo L. 7s 6d.
Whitmore.   Elements of Heraldry......*r*. 8vo Camb.   6 00

Hindostan.—[*See India.*]

History—(GENERAL) PHILOSOPHY OF.

Bissett, A.   Essays on Historical Truth..8vo Lon. 14s.
Bolinbroke.   Letters on Study of History.

Bunsen.   God in History................ 8vo Lon. 12s.
———   Philosophy of Univ'l Hist., 2 v.. 8vo Lon. 33s.
Hegel.   Philosophy of History...........12mo Bohn. $2 50
Knight, Chas.   Historical Parallels, 3 v..18mo L. 4s. 6d.
Miller.   Philosophy of History, 4 vols....12mo Bohn.   7 00
a.   Schlegel.   Philosophy of History........12mo Bohn.   1 75
a.   Smith, (Goldwin).   On Study of History..12mo N. Y.   1 50
Taylor, W. C.   Nat. Hist. of Society, 2 v..12mo Lon. 21s.
Volney.   Ruins; Revolutions of Empires.16mo N. Y.   1 25

History.—UNIVERSAL.—[*See also Chronology.*]

b.   Buckle.   History of Civilization, 2 vols... 8vo N. Y.   6 00
a.   Creasy.   Fifteen Decisive Battles of the   ·
                       World....12mo N. Y.   1 50
Dean, A.   History of Civilization, 7 vols.. 8vo Alb.   28 00
Dew.   Digest of Anc. & Mod. History....
Lieber, Dr. F.   Great Events by Great
                       Historians....12mo N. Y.   1 50
Muller.   Universal History, 4 vols.......12mo N. Y.
a.   Putnam.   The World's Progress........12mo N. Y.   3 50
Robson.   Great Sieges of History, Illust..12mo L. & N.   2 00
Smith.   Turner.   [*See Ancient History.*]
a.   Tytler.   Elements of Univ'l Hist., 6 vols...18mo N. Y.   4 50
Willard, Emma.   Univ'l Hist. in Perspec. 8vo N. Y.   2 25
Woodward, etc.   Histor. & Chron. Cyclo.. 8vo Lond.

History.—ANCIENT.   [*See also, Greece, Rome, etc.*]   ·

Baldwin.   Pre-Historic Nations..........12mo N. Y.   1 75
Baker.   Aryan Civilization..............12mo Lond.   ˙ 3 00
b.   Cæsar.   Trans. by Anth. Trollope........12mo Phila.   1 00
Heeren.   Hist. of Ancient Nations, 6 vols. 8vo Lon. 45s.
b.   Herodotus.   Trans. by Rawlinson, (best) 4 v. 8vo Lon. 48s.
———   Trans. by Beloe, 3 vols., $2.25
                       by Swayne....12mo N. Y.   1 00
———   Literal Trans. by Cary.......12mo Bohn.   1 75
b.   Le Normand & Chevalier.   Ancient His-
                       tory of the East, 2 vols.... 8vo Lond.   5 50
a.   Lord, John.   Ancient States and Empires. 8vo N. Y.   3 00
Morris, J. W.   Students' Chart of Ancient
                       History... 4to Lond. 5s.
Niebuhr.   Lectures on Anct. Hist., 3 v... 8vo Phil.   5 00
b.   Plutarch's Lives of Anc. Greeks & Romans,
                       trans. by Clough, best ed., 5 vols.... 8vo Bost.   15 00
or a.———   by Langhorne, 4 v. $5; 1 v. 8vo N. Y.   2 00
Putz & Arnold.   Manual of Ancient Geog-
                       raphy and History....12mo N. Y.   1 50
Prideaux.   Connection of Old and New
                       Testament, 2 vols.... 8vo. N. Y.   5 00
b.   Rawlinson.   Five Great Monarchies of the
                       Ancient World, 3 vols.... 8vo Lond.   15 00
———   The same cond. for Students.12mo Bost.
a. ———   Manual of Ancient History....12mo N. Y.   2 50

Rollin. Ancient History, 2 vols........ *r*.8vo N. Y.	$4 50
——— The same, 4 vols............... 8vo Phila.	8 00
——— Arts and Sciences of the Ancients.	
b. Smith,Ph. Ancient Hist. of theWorld,3 v. 8vo N. Y.	10 50
a. ——— — Students' Ancient History...12mo N. Y.	2 00
a. ——— — New Test. and Old Test. Hist.12mo N. Y. *ea*	2 00
Turner, Sharon. Sacred Hist. of World, 3v.18mo N. Y.	2 25
Thucydides. Translated by Smith, 2 vols.18mo N. Y.	1 50
a. ——————— ——— (literally) by Dale.12mo N. Y.	1 50
Wheeler. Life and Travels of Herodotus.	
2 vols....12mo N. Y.	3 50
Xenophon. Trans. by Spelman, 2 vols...18mo N. Y.	1 50
·a. ——————— ——— (literally) by Watson.12mo N. Y.	1 50
——————— ——— by Sir A. Grant......12mo	1 00

History—MODERN : GENERAL WORKS. [*See Europe.*]

b. Alison. Europe during French Revolution and to 1830, 8 vols.. N. Y.	16 00
a. Arnold. Lectures on Modern History....12mo N. Y.	1·50
b. Gage, W. L. Modern Historical Atlas...12mo N. Y.	3 50
Gervinus. Intro. to Hist. 19th Century... 8vo Lond. 1s.	
c. Merivale. Conversion of North. Nations. 8vo N. Y.	1 50
b. Schlegel. Lectures on Modern History...12mo Bohn.	1 75
b. Schlosser. History of 18th Century, 8 vols. 8vo Lond.	16 00
a. Smith, Goldwin. Lectures on Mod. Hist.12mo N. Y.	1 75
Smyth, Wm. Lectures on Mod. Hist., 2 v. Bohn.	3 50
b. Von Sybel. Europe during French Revolution, 4 vols.... 8vo Lon. 48s.	
Yonge, C. D. 3 Centuries of Mod. Hist... 8vo Lond.	

History of Literature.—[*See Literature.*]

Holland and Belgium.

Davies. History of Holland, 3 vols...... 8vo Lon. 36s.	
Esquiros. The Dutch at Home.........12mo Lon. 18s.	
Grattan. History of the Netherlands. Lon.12mo 3s. 6d.	
a. Motley. Rise of Dutch Republic, 3 vols. 8vo N. Y.	10 50
Murray's Hand Book for Holl'd & Belgium.12mo Lon. 9s.	
a. ——— The United Netherlands, 4 vols. 8vo N. Y	14 00
b. Schiller. The Revolt of the Netherlands.12mo Bohn.	1 75
Tennent, J. E. Belgium, 2 vols.. ....12mo Lond. 7s.	

Holy Land.—[*See also the East.*]

Barrows. Sac. Geography and Antiquities.12mo N. Y.	2 00
b. Bartlett. Walks about Jerusalem. Ill. *r*.8vo Lond.	6 00
——— Footsteps of our Lord. Illus. *r*.8vo Lond.	6 00
——— Forty Days in the Desert. Ill. *r*.8vo Lond.	6 00
Burt, Rev. Dr. The Land and its Story,	
Illust....*r*.8vo N. Y.	3 50
Dixon, W. H. The Holy Land ; a Record	
of Travel....12mo Lond.	2 50
Early Travels in Palestine... ....12mo Bohn.	2 50
Kitto. Physical Geography of Palestine.18mo Lond.	1 25
a. ——— History of Palestine............12mo Lond.	1 75

a. Kitto. Bible Hist. of the Holy Land, Ill.. 8vo L. & N. $3 00
Lynch. Exploration of Dead Sea, 1849... 8vo Phila. 8 00
Macleod, Norman. Eastward; Travels in
　　　　　　　　　　Holy Land.... 8vo L. & N. 5 00
Macgregor. The Rob Roy on the Jordan.. 8vo N. Y. 2 50
Newman, Rev. J. P. Dan to Beersheba 12mo N. Y. 1 75
Porter, J. L. The Giant Cities of Bashan,
　　　　　　　　etc., 2 vols....12mo Lond. *ea.* 1 50
a. Prime, W. C. Tent Life in Syria and Holy
　　　　　　　　　　　Land....12mo N. Y. 2 00
b. Robinson & Smith. Biblical Researches in
　　　　　　　　Palestine, in all 4 vols.... 8vo Bost. 12 00
b. Robinson, E. Phys. Geog. of Holy Land. 8vo Bost. 8 50
Spencer, J. L. The East; Egypt and
　　　　　　　　　　Holy Land....12mo N. Y. 2 00
b. Stanley, (Dean). Sinai and Palestine..... 8vo N. Y. 2 50
a. Thompson, W. M. The Land and the Book,
　　　　　　　　　　2 vols....12mo N. Y. 5 00
a. Warburton, E. The Crescent & the Cross. 12mo. Phila. 2 00
Wilson & Warren. The Recovery of Je-
　　　　　　　　　rusalem.... 8vo Lon. 21s.

Honduras.—[*See Central America.*]

Horse.—HORSEMANSHIP.

Bruce. American Stud Book, vol. 1... .. 8vo Chica.
Fleming. Horseshoes and Horseshoeing. 8vo Lon. 21s.
a. Herbert, H. W. Hints to Horsekeepers. .12mo N. Y. 1 75
b. Herbert, H. W. Horse and Horsemanship
　　　　　　　　　　2 vols.... 8vo N. Y. 15 00
Herschberger. The Horseman..........12mo N. Y. 2 50
Jennings. Horse Training made Easy...12mo N. Y. 1 25
Mayhew. Horse Management, Illust.....12mo N. Y. 8 00
McClung. The Gentleman's Stable Guide.
Miles. The Horse's Foot........... ...*r.* 8vo L. 12s. 6d.
Ryle, J. S. On Taming the Horse........
Stewart. Stable Book.................12mo N. Y. 1 50
Wallace. American Stud Book, Illust...*r.* 8vo N. Y. 10 00
b. Walsh, J. H. ("Stonehenge"). The Horse. 12mo N. Y. 2 50
Whyte. Hist. of the Brit. Turf, 2 vols... 8vo Lon. 12s.
Woodruff. Trotting Horse of America...12mo N. Y. 2 25
a. Youatt. On the Horse, by Spooner ..... 8vo Phil. 1 50

Horticulture.—[*See Gardening, Agriculture.*]

Huguenots.

Blackburn. Coligny and the Huguenots.
Martyn, W. C. History of the Huguenots. 12mo N. Y. 1 50
Maury. Memoirs of Huguenot Family...12mo N. Y. 1 50
a. Smiles. Huguenots in Engl'd & Ireland.. 8vo N. Y. 1 50

Humorous Works. [*See also Poetry, Comic.*]

A'Becket. Comic History of England.... 8vo Lond. 5 00
———　Comic History of Rome...... 8vo Lond. 5 00

" Awful," and other Jingles. By P. R. S.12mo N. Y. $1 25
Amer. Tour of Browne, Jones & Robinson. 4to   N. Y.   5 00
a. Bede, Cuthbert. Adven. of Verdant Green.12mo N. Y.   1 50
Brown, C. F. (Artemus Ward.) Humorous
                    Books, 4 vols....12mo N. Y.   6 00
a. Burton. Cyclopedia of Wit and Humor.
      •   Illustrated, 2 vols. r. 8vo N. Y.   8 00
Comic Blackstone. Illustrated..........12mo Phila.   1 50
Comic English Grammar. Illustrated...18mo Lond. 1s.
—— Latin Grammar. Illust. Lond..12mo 1s. 6d.
a. Combe. Dr. Syntax's Tours. Illust.....12mo Lond.   3 00
Cozzens. The Sparrowgrass Papers.....12mo N. Y.   1·75
Cruikshank. Omnibus. Illus.....Lond. 8vo 10s. 6d.
De Mille, Jas. The Dodge Club. Illust. 8vo N. Y.   1 25
Derby, G. H. Phœnixiana..............12mo N. Y.   1 25
Erasmus. Praise of Folly......... .....16mo Lond.   3 00
Father Tom and the Pope..............18mo Phila.   75
Haliburton, T. C. Sam Slick's Sayings, 2 v.12mo N. Y.   1 50
Harte, Bret. Condensed Novels........12mo Bost.   1 50
—— —— Luck of Roaring Camp....12mo Bost.   1 50
—— —— Sketches................12mo Bost.   1 50
Hood, Thos. Prose Works. Illus., 3 vols.12mo N. Y.   7 50
—— —— Up the Rhine; Whims and
            Oddities, etc., 3 vols....12mo N. Y.   4 50
—— —— ComicWorks, cheaper ed.4 v.12mo Phila.
Irving. Knickerbocker's N. Y. 16mo $1.25.12mo N. Y.   2 25
Jerrold. Mrs. Caudle's Lectures........12mo N. Y. .   1 25
" Joe Miller's" Jest Book................16mo Lond.   1 25
" Josh Billings." Humorous Works, 2 v.12mo N. Y.   3 00
Leland, C. G. " Hans Breitman's Ballads".12mo Phila.   2 00
Locke, D. R. " Petroleum C. Nasby."
            Works, 2 vols....12mo Bost.   3 00
" Miles O'Reilly." Book of Adventures..12mo N. Y.   1 50
New Gospel of Peace.................12mo N. Y.   2 00
Newell. "Orpheus C. Kerr" Papers, 3 v.12mo N. Y.   4 50
" Phenix." The Squibob Papers.........12mo N. Y.   1 50
Pomeroy ("Brick"). Sense, Nonsense,
            etc., 3 volumes....12mo N Y.   4 50
Prentice. Prenticeana.................12mo Phila.   1 50
Punch (Lond.), — vols. repub. (2 yrs. in 1 v.) 4to L. ea. 21s.
Rabelais. Works, 2 vols................12mo Bohn.   3 50
—— —— with Doré Illustrations.12mo L. 7s. 6d.
Scheffel. Gaudeamus. Trans. by C. G.
            Leland....12mo Lond.
Shaw, H. W. Sayings of Josh Billings..12mo N. Y.   1 50
Sherwood. Comic History of U. States..12mo Bost.   2 00
Shillaber. Mrs. Partington's Sayings....12mo Bost.   1 50
Smith, Seba. Jack Downing's Letters....12mo N. Y.
Swift. Gulliver's Travels..............12mo Phila.   1 50

Hungary.

Brace, C. L. Hungary in 1851...........12mo N. Y.   1 75

a. Hungary and Its Relations..............12mo Bohn. $2 25
Klapka. War of Independ. in Hung'y, 2 v. 12mo L. 10s. 6d.
Paget. Hungary and Transylvania, 2 v. . 12mo Phil.   2 00
Pardoe, Miss J. City of the Magyars, 3 v. 12mo L. 10s. 6d.
Pragay. Hungarian Struggle, 1850.....12mo N. Y.   1 00
Schlesinger. Hungary, 1850, 2 vols......12mo Lon. 21s.
Tefft, B. F. Hungary and Kossuth......12mo Phila.
Winkstein   Hist. of War in '48 and '49..

Hunting and Shooting.

Browning, M. 44 Years of Hunter's Life. 12mo Phila.   1 50
Bumstead. On the Wing; Book for
                                        Sportsmen..12mo Bost.   2 25
Dead Shot; or, Sportsman's Guide.. ....
Cumming. Wild Men and Wild Beasts..12mo N. Y.   1 50
Gillmore, P. Hunter's Adventures......12mo Lon. 15s.
Herbert, H. W. Hints for Young Sports'n. 12mo N. Y.
Hooper, J. J. Dog and Gun.............
Lewis. American Sportsman.... .... 8vo Phila.   2 75
a. Meunier, V. Great Hunts of the World..12mo N. Y.   1 50
Newhouse, S. Trapper's Guide......... 8vo N. Y.   1 25
Walsh, J. H. Shot-Gun and Rifle... ...12mo L. 10s. 6d.

Hydraulics.

Box. Practical Hydraulics..............12mo Lond.   2 00
Bressé. Hydraulic Motors..............12mo N. Y.   2 00
Downing. Practical Hydraulics....... .. 8vo Lond.   4 00
a. Ewbank. History of Hydraulics, etc... . 8vo N. Y.   6 00
Hughes. Water Works for Cities and
                                        . Towns....18mo Lond.   1 50
Humber. Water Supply of Cities and
                                        Towns.... 4to Lond.   40 00

Hydropathy.

Johnson. Domestic Hydropathy.........12mo Lond. 6s.
Trall. Hydropathic Encyclopædia.......12mo N. Y.   4 50

Hygiene.—[*See Health.*]

Iceland.

Chambers, R. Iceland and Faroe Islands.12mo Lond 5s.
a. Dufferin, Lord. Yacht Voy. to Iceland.....12mo Lond. 9s.
Gould, Sir Baring. Iceland; its Scenes
                                        and Passes.... 8vo Lond. 28s.
Henderson. Residence in Iceland, *o. p.* 2 v.   Edinb.
Pfeiffer, Ida. Iceland ; translated by C.
                                        F. Cooper....12mo N. Y.   1 00
b. Paijkull. A Summer in Iceland, Illust.. 8vo N. Y.   5 00

Ichthyology. [*See Fishes.*]

Iconography.

Didron. Christian Iconography, vol. 1...12mo Bohn.   2 50

Illinois.

 Carpenter. History of Illinois..........18mo Phila. $ 63
 Ford. History of Illinois, 1854.........12mo Chic.

Illuminating. [*See Decorative Art.*]

Illustrated Books. [*See Fine Arts, Illustrated Books.*]

Immigration. [*See Emigration.*]

Immortality. [*See Future Life.*]

Index Rerum; or Index of Subjects, by J. Todd. 4to North. 3 00

India.

 Allen. India, Ancient and Modern.....*r.* 8vo Lon. 14s.
 Chunder, B. Travels of a Hindoo in Ben-
  gal and Upper India, 2 v. 8vo Lond. 10 50
 Erskine. History of India, 2 vols........ 8vo Lond. 6 00
b. Hunter. Annals of Rural Bengal........ 8vo N. Y. 4 00
 India—Pictorial and Descriptive.........12mo Bohn. 2 50
 Malcolm. Hist. of British India.........
 Marshman. Hist. of Brit. India, 3 v. Lon. 22s. 6d.
b. Martin. The Indian Empire, 3 v....imp. 8vo Lond. 12 00
 Minturn, R. B. New York to Delhi.......12mo N. Y. 2 00
a. Murray, Wilson, etc. British India, 3 v..18mo N. Y. 2 25
 Nolan, E. H. History of British Empire
  in East, 2 vols.... Lond. 10 00
b. Taylor, Bayard. India, China and Japan.12mo N. Y. 1 50
b. Thornton, Edw. Hist. of British India, 6 v. 8vo Lon. 48s.
 Wheeler, J. T. History of India, 2 vols.. 8vo Lon. 42s.

Indiana.

 Dillon, J. B. Hist. of Indiana, vol. 1..... 8vo Ind.
 Smith, O. H. Early Indiana Trials, etc.. 8vo Cinc.

Indians—NORTH AMERICAN.

 Beckworth G. Life. 1856..............12mo N. Y. 1 50
 Browne, J. R. Advent in Apache Country.12mo N. Y. 2 00
b. Catlin. North American Indians, 2 vols.. 8vo 30s.
 Copway. Hist. of Ojibway Nation......12mo Bost.
 Domenech, Abbe. Seven Years in Desert
  of North America, 2 vols.... Lon. 36s.
 Eastman, Mrs. Dakotah. 1849......... 8vo N. Y.
 Morgan, L. F. League of the Iroquois. '51. 8vo Roch.
a. Parkman, F. Conspiracy of Pontiac, 2 v. 8vo Bost. 5 00
 Schoolcraft, H. R. Algic Researches. 2 v.12mo N. Y. 2 00
 ———————— Indian Tribes; Archives
  of Aborigi. Knowledge, 7 v. 4to Phila. 90 00
 ———————— Notes on the Iroquois.'47. 8vo Albany. 3 00
 ———————— Oneota, 1845........... 8vo N. Y. 1 50
 ———————— Personal Mem. of Resi-
  dence among Indians.... 8vo Phila. 3 00
a. Thatcher. Indian Biography, 2 vols.....18mo N. Y. 1 50

Indigestion.—[*See Health.*]

Infidelity—RATIONALISM.—[*See also Evidences of Christianity.*]

 Faber, G. S. Difficulties of Infidelity...12mo N. Y.
 Farrar. History of Free Thought....... 8vo N. Y. $2 00
 Hurst. History of Rationalism.......... 8vo N. Y. 3 50
a. Lecky. Hist. of Rationalism in Europe, 2 v. 8vo N. Y. 4 00
 Morel, C. Authority and Conscience; a
        free Debate, etc.... 8vo L 7s. 6d.
 Modern Skepticism; Course of Lectures.. 8vo L. 7s. 6d.
 Morgan, R. W. Christianity and Modern
         Infidelity....16mo Lond.
 Trench, R. C. Shipwrecks of Faith......16mo L. 2s. 6d
 Vaughan, C. J. Foes of Faith...........16mo Lond.

Inquisition.

 Limborch. History of the Inquisition....
 Llorente. History of Spanish Inquisition. 8vo Lond.
 Mackenna. Inquisition of America...... 8vo L. 7s. 6d.
 Rule, W. H. History of Inquisition...... 8vo L. 8s. 6d.

Insanity.

 Behind the Bars; Retrospect of Insane
        Asylums....16mo Bost. 2 00
a. Burton. Anatomy of Melancholy, 3 vols..12mo N. Y. 6 75
 Mayo. On Insanity...................12mo L. 3s. 6d.
a. Monro, H. Insanity; its Nature & Treatm't.12mo Lond. 6s.
 Pritchard. Insanity in Criminal Cases... 8vo Lond.
 Ray, I. Mental Hygiene................12mo Bost. 1 50
 Storer, H. R. Reflex Insanity in Women .12mo Bost. 1 50
 Winslow. Anatomy of Suicide. Lond... 8vo 10s. 6d.

Insects.—[*See Entomology.*]

Instinct.—[*See Natural History.*]

Instruction.—[*See Education.*]

Intemperance.—[*See Temperance.*]

Inspiration of the Bible.—[*See also Bible.*]

a. Curtis, T. F. The Human Element in In-
     spiration of Scripture....12mo N. Y. 2 00
 Gaussen. On Plenary Inspiration of Scrip-
     ture, 1850....12mo N. Y. 1 50
 Leifchild. Remarkable Facts on Inspira-
     ration of Scripture....12mo L. 3s. 6d.

International Law.—[*See also Copyright.*]

 Bernard. The Neutrality of Great Britain
     during American Civil War.... 8vo Lon. 16s.
 Boynton, C. B. The Four Great Powers..12mo Cincin. 3 00
 De Burgh. Maritime International Law. 8vo L. 10s. 6d.
 Wheaton. Internat'l Law, by Lawrence.. 8vo Bost.
b. ——— The same, ed. by R. H. Dana, Jr. 8vo Bost. 7 50
a. Woolsey, T. D. Introd'n to Intern'l Law .12mo N. Y. 2 50

Inter-Oceanic Communication.

Nourse, J. G. The Suez Canal, paper.... 8vo Wash.	$	75
Otis, F. N. Hist. of Panama Railroad....12mo N. Y.	2	00
Stephens, H. Tehuantepec, 1869........ 8vo N. Y.		
Stuckle. Inter-Oceanic Canals.......... 8vo N. Y.	2	00

Inventions.

Beckmann. History of Inventions, etc., 2 v.12mo Bohn. 3 50
Bakewell, F. C. Inventions in 19th Cent.12mo N. Y. 1 00
History of Wonderful Inventions........12mo N. Y. 1 50
a. Timbs, John. Hist. of Wonderful Inven.12mo N. Y. 2 50

Iowa.

Parker, N. H. Iowa as It is............12mo Phila. 1 50

Ireland.—[See also *Biography, Curran, etc.*]

Barrington, Sir J. The Irish Nation..... 8vo Lon. 12s.
Brett, J. Irish People and Irish Landlord. 8vo Lond.
Cusack, M. F. Student's Man'l Hist. Irel'd.   Lond. 6s.
Godkin, J. The Land War in Ireland.... 8vo Lond. 6s.
Jervis, Lt. Col. Ireland under Brit. Rule. 8vo Lon. 12s.
Lecky, W. E. H. Leaders of Opinion in
                                  Ireland.... 8vo Lond.
Madden, R. R. The United Irishmen, 2 v.12mo Lon. 12s.
McGee, T. D. History of Ireland, 2 vols..12mo N. Y. 3 00
b. Moore, Thos. Hist. of Irel'd (4 v. Lond.), 2 v. 8vo N. Y. 4 00
Smith, Goldwin. Irish Hist. & Irish Church.12mo Oxf. 5s.
a. Taylor, W. C. History of Ireland, 2 vols.18mo N. Y. 1 50
Thackeray. The Irish Sketch Book......12mo Bost. 1 00
a. Trench. Realities of Irish Life..... ...16mo Bost. 1 00

Iron and Steel.

Bauerman. Treatise on Metallic Iron....12mo Lond. 2 50
Fairbairn. Iron; its Hist. and Properties. 8vo L. & B. 4 50
——— Application of Iron to Building. 8vo Lond. 8 00
Francis, J. B. On Strength of Cast Iron
                               Pillars.... 8vo N. Y. 2 00
Hewitt, A. S. Rep. on Production of Iron. 8vo Wash. 2 00
Kohn. Iron and Steel Manufacture...... 4to L. & N. 15 00
Landrin. Treat. on Steel & its Properties.12mo Phila. 3 00
Osborn. Metallurgy of Iron and Steel... 8vo Phil. 10 00
Tredgold. On Strength of Cast Iron and
                          other Metals.... 8vo Lond. 6 00
Truran, W. Iron Manuf. of Gt. Britain.r.8vo Lond. 10 00
Turner. On Manufacture of Iron, 2 vols. 8vo N. Y. 10 00

Italy.—[See also *Rome, Florence, Naples, Venice, etc.*]

Adams, W. H. Queen of the Adriatic,
                          (Venice) ...12mo L. & N. 2 00
——————— Buried Cities of Campania.12mo L. & N. 1 50
Butt, I. History of Italy, 1860, 2 vols ... 8vo Lon. 36s.
Eustace. Classical Tour in Italy, 3 vols..16mo L. 10s. 6d.
Gould, W. M. Letters from Italy & Sicily.12mo N. Y. 1 00

Guicciardini.   Civil Wars in Italy, trans..
a. Hawthorne, Mrs.   England and Italy.....12mo N. Y. $2 00
a. Hillard, Geo. J.   Six Months in Italy.....12mo Bost.   2 00
a. Howell, W. D.   Italian Journeys.........12mo N. Y.   2 00
a. ——————————   Venetian Life...........12mo N. Y.   2 00
Jarves, J. J.   Italian Lights and Papal
                      Principles....12mo N. Y.   1 50
Machiavelli.   History of Florence........12mo Bohn.   1 75
Mariotti. Italy, Past and Present, 2 v. Lon. 12mo 10s. 6d.
—————— Italy in 1848..............12mo Lon. 12s.
—————— Scenes from Italian Life. Lond. 12mo 10s. 6d.
Murray.   Hand Book of Northern Italy..12mo Lon. 10s.
————— Central Italy and Rome........12mo Lon. 12s.
————— Southern Italy and Naples.....12mo Lon. 10s.
Napier.   Florentine History, 6 vols......12mo Lond.   7 50
Norton, C. E.   Travel and Study in Italy. 12mo Bost.   1 25
Proctor, G. History of Italy.   1844.'..... 8vo Lond. 6s.
b. Ranke.   History of the Popes, 3 vols.....12mo Bohn.   5 25
a. Sismondi.   Italian Republics.... ....12mo Lond. 5s.
—————— Literat. of So. of Europe, 2 v.. 12mo Bohn.   3 50
Spalding.   History of Italy and Italian
                      Islands, 3 vols.   Edinb....18mo 7s.6d.
b. Story, W. W.   Roba di Roma, 2 vols.....12mo Phila.   5 50
—————— —————— Graffiti d'Italia.....Lond. 16mo 7s. 6d.
a. Taine.   Florence and Venice ; Rome and
                      Naples....ea. 8vo N. Y.   2 50
b. Trollope, T. A.   Hist. of Florence, 4 vols. 8vo Lond. 10 00
—————— —————— Italian Revolution......12mo Lond.
Trinity (The) of Italy.   Pope, Bourbon and
                      Victor.... 8vo Lon. 14s.

Fiction, illustrative of History of Italy :
Bulwer.   Rienzi ; Last of Tribunes; Pompeii.
"Geo. Elliot ;" " Romola," etc. [*See Fiction.*]

Jamaica.

Bigelow, John.   Jamaica in 1850.........18mo N. Y.   1 50

Japan.

Alcocke.' The Capitol of the Tycoon..... 8vo Lond.   3 50
Foublanque.   Two Years in Japan and N.
                      China....   Lond.   2 00
Hoffman, Dr.   Japanese Grammar in Eng.   Lond.   7 50
b. Japanese Manners and Cust., col'd plates. folio Lond.   9 00
Jephson & Elmhurst.   Life in Japan..... 8vo Lond.
Perry, Com. U. S.   Exped. to Japan, 3 v.. 4to U. S.
—————— —————— Conden. & ed. by Dr. Hawks, r. 8vo N. Y.   5 00
Siebold, P. von.   Japan and the Japanese. 8vo Lond. 6s.
b. Taylor, Bayard.   India, China and Japan. 12mo N. Y.   1 50
—————— Japan in our Day (a compilation). 12mo N. Y.   1 50
Tomes, R.   The Americans in Japan.....12mo N. Y.

Java.
    Raffles' History of Java. 1830. 2 vols.. 8vo Lond.

Jerusalem.—[*See Holy Land.*]

Jests.—[*See Humorous Works.*]

Jesuits.
    Niccolini. History of the Jesuits........12mo Lond. $2 25
a. Parkman, F. The Jesuits in N. America. 8vo Bost. 2 50
    Pascal, Blaise. Provincial Letters.......12mo N. Y. 1 75
    Steinmetz. History of the Jesuits, 2 vols. 8vo Lon. 24s.

Jesus.—[*See Christ.*]

Jews.—[*See also Holy Land; History, Ancient, etc.*]
b. Ewald. History of Israel. Translated by
                    Carpenter, 3 vols.... 8vo Lon. 63s.
    Edeisbeirn. History of Jewish Nation... 8vo Lon. 6s.
    Finn. The Sephardria; Jews of Spain
                    and Portugal....12mo L. 8s. 6d.
    Geiger, A. Judaism and its History, v. 1. 8vo N. Y.
    Herder. Spirit of Hebrew Poetry, 2 vols.12mo Andover.
    Jahn. Hebrew Commonwealth...... ... 8vo Andover.
    Jennings. Jewish Antiquities.......... 8vo 10s. 6d.
a. Josephus. Works. Whiston's trans., 4 v. 8vo Phila. 8 00
  ——   —— Illustra. edition.... *r.* 8vo L. &. N. 12 00
    Lewis. Antiquities of Hebrew Republic.
a. Milman. History of the Jews, 3 vols....18mo N. Y. 2 25
  ——   —— best ed., 3 v.12mo N. Y. 5 25
    Raphall. Post Bible Hist. of the Jews, 2 v.12mo N. Y. 4 00
    Rule, W. H. History of Karaite Jews...12mo L. 1s. 6d.
    Smith, Geo. The Hebrew People, 2 vols. 8vo Lon. 12s.
    Smucker, S. M. History of Modern Jews.12mo Phila. 1 75
    Strauss, F. Helon's Pilgrimage; Glory of
                 House of Israel....
    Wines, E. C. Hebrew Commonwealth... 8vo Phila, 3 00

Jurisprudence.—[*See Law.*]

Juvenile Books.—[*See Appendix.*]

Kaleidoscope.—[*See Optics.*]

Kentucky.
    Collins, L. Historical Sketches of Ken'y. 8vo Maysv. 6 00

Kindergarten.
    Adler. Kindergarten Occupations....... 50c. to 2 50
    Peabody, Miss. Kindergarten Guide....12mo N. Y. 1 25

Kitchen Garden.—[*See Agriculture, Gardening.*]

Knighthood.—[*See Chivalry.*]

Labor.—[*See Co-operation, Political Economy, Sociology.*]
    Carey, H. C. On the Rate of Wages..... 8vo Phila,

Cassagnac. History of Working and Bur-
    gher Classes.... 8vo Phila. $2 50
Fawcett. Economical Position of British
     Laborer....16mo Lond.   1 50
Le Play. Organization of Labor, translated
     by Emerson....12mo Phila.   2 00
Mayhew. Lond. Labor & Lond. Poor, 3 v. *r.* 8vo L. 22s. 6d.

Landscape Gardening.

Copeland, W. T. Country Life, etc...... 8vo Bost.   6 00
Downing. Lands. Gardening & Rural Orn. 8vo N. Y.   6 50
Kemp. Landscape Gardening...........12mo N. Y.
Weidenmann. Beautifying Country Homes 4to N. Y.   15 00

Language.—[*See Dictionaries, English Language, Grammar, Synonymes.*]

Beames. Compar. Grammar of Modern
    Aryan Languages.... 8vo Lond.
Blake. Comp. Grammar of South African
    Languages, vol. 1.... 8vo Lon. 16s.
——— Origin of Language............. 8vo N. Y.   50
b. Bopp. Comp. Grammar of Sanscrit (and
    9 other) Languages, 3 vols.... 8vo Lond.   15 75
De Vere. Comparative Philol. (1854, *o.p.*).12mo N. Y.
——— Americanisms...............12mo N. Y.   3 00
Dwight, B. W. Modern Philology, 2 vols. 8vo N. Y.   6 00
Earle. Philology of the English Tongue.12mo Lond. 6s.
Edkins. China, Place in Modern Philol.. 8vo Lond.
Farrar, F. W. Families of Speech. Lon. 12mo 5s. 6d.
Kavanagh, M. Origin of Language and
    Myths....12mo Lond.   10 50
Kraitsir. Language of Nature and Nature
    of Language....12mo N. Y.   1 50
Marcel. The Study of Languages: True
    Principles....12mo N. Y.   1 25
a. Muller, Max. Lect. on Language, 2 vols. 8vo N. Y.   5 00
——— Stratification of Language. Lon.. 8vo 2s. 6d.
Wedgewood, H. Origin of Language. '66.18mo Lond.
Whitney, W. D. On Language........ 8vo N. Y.   2 50

Language of Flowers.

Hale, Mrs. S. J. Flora's Interpreter......12mo Phila.
Ildrewe, Mrs. Language of Flowers.....12mo Bost.   3 00
Language of Flowers. Ed. by H. G. Adams.12mo Phila.   1 50
Tyas. Language of Flowers.......... 4to Lond.   5 00

Law.—[*See also Constitution, Government, International Law and Municipal Government.*]

** Technical Treatises, Reports, etc., not included.
Anthon, J. The Law Student.........: 8vo N. Y.   8 50
Austin, J. Lectures on Jurisprudence, 3 v. 8vo Lon. 24s.
Bigelow, L. J. The Bench and the Bar;
    Anecdotes.... 8vo N. Y.   2 00

Blackstone. Commentaries. Ed. by Chitty,
      Christian, &c., 2 vols.... 8vo Phila. $7 00
Bouvier, J. Law Dictionary, 2 vols...... 8vo Phila. 12 00
Butler, W. A. Lawyer and Client.......12mo N. Y.   1 00
Dumphy & Cummins. Remarkable Trials. 8vo Lon. 18s.
Gaius. Commentaries on Roman Law, 2 v.. 8vo Lon. 52s.
Grotius. Rights of War and Peace, by
        Whewell.... 8vo Lond. 12 00
Kent. Commentaries on Amer. Law, 4 v. 8vo Bost. 20 00
Mackenzie, A. Studies in Roman Law... 8vo Lon. 12s.
Maine. Ancient Law................. 8vo Lon. 12s.
Ortolan. History of Roman Law. Trans.
     by Pritchard & Nasmith.. 8vo Lond.
Phillimore, J. G. Principles and Maxims
      of Jurisprudence.... 8vo Lon. 12s.
Short. Law relating to Literature and Art. 8vo Lond. 12 50
Student's Blackstone (The).............12mo Lond.   3 75
Warren, Samuel. Duties of Attorneys..16mo Edin. 9s.
Woolsey. Introduc. to International Law.12mo N. Y.   2 50

Legends.—[*See also Fables, Fairy Stories, Demonology,
    Mythology, etc.*]

Brinton, D. G. Myths of the New World.12mo N. Y.   2 50
Bulfinch, T. The Age of Fable.........12mo Bost.   3 00
———— Age of Chivalry; Charlemagne.*ea*.12mo Bost.   3 00
Burton, R. F. Vikram and the Vampire.. 8vo Lond. 9s.
Gould, S. Baring. Book of Were-Wolves.12mo Lond. 6s.
———— —— Curious Myths of Mid. Ages.12mo L. 9s. 6d.
Kennedy. Legendary Fic. of Irish Celts.12mo Lond.

Letters.—[*See Correspondence.*]

Levant.—[*See Mediterranean.*]

Levees.

Hewson on Embanking Lands........... 8vo N. Y.   2 00

Lexicons.—[*See Dictionaries.*]

Liberty.

Elliot, Samuel. History of Liberty, 4 vols. 8vo N. Y.   6 00
Mill, J. Stuart. On Liberty.............12mo Bost.   1 50

Libraries and Collections.

Ancient Classics for English Readers, ed.
    by Collins, now publishing....12mo L. & P.*ea*.1 00
Arber's Reprints of Old Eng. Literature..18mo L. & N. var.
Bohn's Antiquarian Library, 27 vols......12mo Lon. *ea*. 2 00
———— British Classics, 21 vols... ..... 12mo Lon. *ea*. 1 40
———— Classical Library, 90 vols.........12mo Lon. *ea*. 2 00
———— Ecclesiastical Library, 8 vols.....12mo Lon. *ea*. 2 00
———— Historical Library, 19 vols........12mo Lon. *ea*. 2 00
———— Illustrated Library, 74 vols.......12mo Lon. *ea*. 2 00
———— French Memoirs, 6 vols... ......12mo Lon. *ea*. 1 40

Bohn's Philolog'l and Philos., 16 vols....12mo Lon. *ea.*$2 00
—— Scientific Library, 67 vols........12mo Lon. *ea.* 2 00
—— Standard Library, 167 vols........12mo Lon. *ea.* 1 40
—— Extra volumes, 7 vols...........12mo Lon. *ca.* 1 40
Brit. Essayists, (Spectator, Tattler, etc.)38 v18mo Bost. *ea.* 1 25
—— —— Modern, 8 vols........ 8vo N. Y. 16 00
—— Poets, edited by Child, 130 vols...18mo Bost. *ea.* 1 25
—— —— Aldine edition, 52 vols.....18mo Lond. *ea.* 75
Golden Treasury Series, — vols.........16mo Camb.*ea.*1 25
—— —— Eng. ed.,' — vols.16mo Lond. *ea.* 1 25
Harper's Classical Library, 37 vols.......18mo N. Y. *ea.* 75
—— New do., (literal trans.) 22 vols..12mo N. Y. *ea.* 1 50
—— Family Library, (about) 150 vols.18mo N. Y. *ea.* 75
—— School Library, 25 vols.... ....12mo N. Y. *ea.* 1 50
—— New Miscellany, 26 vols........12mo N. Y. *ea.* 1 00
—— Select Library, (includ'g Family)
300 vols....18mo N. Y. *ca.* 75
Library of Entertaining Knowledge, *o. p.*18mo Lond.
—— of Wonders, published by Scribner
& Co., 20 vols....16mo N. Y. *ea.* 1 50
—— of Travel and Adventure, edited
by.Bayard Taylor....16mo N. Y. *ea.* 1 50
Tauchnitz. Collection of British Authors,
now comprising about 1100 vols.16mo Leipsic. *ea.* 60
—— Collection of German Authors,
translated, about 20 vols....16mo Leipsic. *ea.*60
₊ These two series are bound in paper. Price of binding
them in half roan, 60 cents to $1 00 per vol. In most
instances 2 vols. can be bound in one. Full lists
printed separately.
Weale's Series of Rudimentary Works on
Engineering, Build'g, Drawing, etc., 148v.16mo L. & N.
₊ Prices from 40 cents to 90 cents.

Light.—[*See Optics.*]

Light-Houses.

Adams. Light-Houses and Light-Ships..16mo N. Y. · 1 50

Literature—HISTORY AND OUTLINES OF.—[*For Drama,
Fiction and Poetry, see those titles ; also
names of Countries ; also Language.*]

Literature—HISTORY, GENERAL.

Botta, Mrs. Hand Book of Universal Lit.12mo Bost. 2 50
Schlegel, A. W. History of Literature...12mo Bohn. 1 75

Literature—HISTORY OF—SANSKRIT.

Muller, Max. Anc't Sanskrit Literature. 8vo Lon. 21s.

Literature—CLASSICAL.

Anthon. Greek Literature.........:...12mo N. Y. 1 50
Browne, R. W. Hist. of Greek Classical
Literature, 2 vols.... 8vo Lon. 12s. ·
—— —— Hist. of Roman Literature. 8vo Lon. 12s. ·

Cleveland. Compend. of Class. Literat...12mo Phila.
Donaldson. Lit. of Ancient Greece, 2 vols. 8vo Lond. $6 00
Dunlop. Hist. of Roman Literature, 3 v. 8vo Lond.
Hamilton & Clark. Interlinear Transla.
    of Cæsar, Ovid, Sallust, Cicero, etc., 6 v.12mo Phila.*ea.*2 25
Mills, Abm. Poets & Poetry of Greece. *o. p.* 8vo Bost.   3 50
Mure. Literature of Ancient Greece, 3 v. 8vo Lond. 12 00

Literature—SCANDINAVIAN.

Howitt, W. & M. Literature and Romance
    of Northern Europe, 2 v....12mo Lon. 12s.

Literature—SLAVIC.

Robinson, Mrs. Language and Literature
    of the Slavic Nations.....*o. p.*12mo N. Y

Literature—EUROPEAN.

Cleveland. Litera. of the 19th Century..12mo Phila. 2 50
Foster. Hand Book of Mod. Europ. Liter.12mo Bohn 2 50
Hallam. Literature of Europe, 4 vols...12mo N. Y. 7 00
————— ————————— —— Students' ed.12mo Lond. 2 50
Sismondi. Lit. of South of Europe, 2 v.12mo Bohn 3 50

Literature—ITALIAN.

Chambers. Italian Literature.....Edinb.16mo 3s. 6d.
Mariotti. Italy, its Hist. and Liter., 2 v..12mo Lon. 24s

Literature—FRENCH.

Agell, J. R. Introduc. to French Litera.12mo Phila.
Half Hours with best French Authors.... 8vo Lon. 14s.
Vericour. Course of French Literature.. 8vo Lond. 2s.

Literature—SPANISH AND PORTUGUESE.

Bouterwek. Span. and Portug. Lit.....12mo Lond. 1 75
Ticknor. Hist. of Spanish Litera., 3 vols.12mo Bost. 10 00

Literature—GERMAN.

Austen, Mrs. Fragments from Ger. Lit..12mo Lon. 10s.
Chambers. Course of German Literature.16mo Ed. 2s. 6d.
Hedge. Prose Writers of Germany.....*r.*8vo Phila. 5 00
Menzel. History of German Litera., 4 v.12mo Oxf.40s.
Metcalfe. History of German Literature.12mo L. 7s. 6d.

Literature—ENGLISH.

    [Botta, Cleveland, etc. *See European.*]

Allibone. Dictionary of Authors, 3 vols.*r.* 8vo Phila. 22 50
Angus. Hand Book of English Literature.16mo Lond. 2 00
————— Specimens of English Literature.16mo Lond.
Arnold, Thos. Manual of English Litera. 8vo L. 10s. 6d.
Chambers. Cyclo. of English Litera., 2 v. 8vo L. & P. 8 00
————— Readings in English Litera..16mo L. & P. 1 75
Craik. Hist. of the English Language, 2 v. 8vo N. Y. 7 50
————— Outlines of ————— —————.....16mo L. 2s. 6d.
Day, H. N. Introd. to Eng. Literature...12mo N. Y. 2 25

D'Israeli. Curiosities of Literature, 4 vols.12mo N. Y. $7 00
Five Centuries of Eng. Language and Lit.16mo Lond.   1 25
Gilman.   First Steps in English Litera..12mo N. Y.   1 00
Hannay.   Course of English Literature..12mo Lond.
Hunt.   Literature of English Language..12mo N. Y.   2 50
Hazlitt, W. C.   Hand Book to Litera. of
           Great Britain (Bibliography).. 8vo L. 31s. 6d.
Knight. Half Hours with Best Authors, 6 v.12mo Lond.   9 00
        6 vols., Phila, $9 ; 2 vols. 8vo Lond.   6 00
Mills, Abm.   Litera. of Gt. Britain, 2 vols. 8vo N. Y.   4 00
Morley.   Tables of English Literature...folio Lon. 12s.
Shaw.   Manual of English Literature... 12mo N. Y.   2 50
Smith.   English Synonyms Explained... 8vo Lond.   6 50
Spaulding.   Hist. English Literature....12mo N. Y.   1 50
Taine.   Hist. of Engl. Literature, 2 vols.. 8vo N. Y. 10 00
Townsend.   Every Day Book of Modern
           Literature, ... 8vo L. & N.   3 75

Literature, Celtic.

Arnold, M.   Study of Celtic Lit'ture, 1867. 8vo L. 8s. 6d.

Literature, American.

Allibone.   [*See Lit., English Bibliography.*]
Cleveland.   Compendium of Amer. Liter.12mo Phila.   2 00
Duyckinck.   Cyclo. of Amer. Liter., 2 v.r.8vo N. Y. 10 00
————   Supplement to same.......r.8vo N. Y.   2 50
Griswold.   Prose Writers of America.... 8vo Phila.   5 00
————   Poets and Poetry of America. 8vo Phila.   5 00
Hart.   Female Prose Writers of America. 8vo Phila.   5 00
Raymond, Ida.   Southland Writers, 2 v. 8vo Phila.   6 00

Logic.

Bain, A.   System of Logic.......Lond..12mo 10s. 6d.
Everett, C. C.   Science of Thought: Sys-
          tem of Logic....12mo   2 00
Hamilton, Sir W.   Lectures on Logic.... 8vo Bost.   3 50
————   Lectures, ab'd by Day..12mo Bost.   1 00
McCosh, James.   Logic.................12mo N. Y.   1 50
Mill, J. Stuart.   System of Logic........ 8vo N. Y.   2 00
Tappan, H. P.   Elements of Logic......12mo N. Y.   1 50
Ueberweg.   System of Logic, and System
          of Logical Doctrines ... 8vo Lon. 16s.
Whately, R.   Elements of Logic ....12mo Bost.   1 75
————   Lessons in Reason........
————   Hist'c Doubts on Napoleon. 8vo N. Y.   50
Wilson.   Elementary Treatise on Logic..12mo N. Y.   1 50

London.

Dixon, W. H.   Her Majesty's Tower..... 8vo Phila.   1 50
Greenwood.   Seven Curses of London.,...12mo Bost.   1 50
Jesse, J. H.   London; its Celebrated Char-
          acters and Places, 3 vols.... 8vo L. 31s. 6d.
Knight, Chas.   London, Illust., 8 vols...r.8vo Lon. 38s.

London: a Pilgrimage.　By Gustave Doré
　　　　and Blanch. Jerrold....folio Lon. 60s.
Mayhew.　The Great World of London..*r.* 8vo Lond.
—————　London Labor & London Poor,
　　　　　　　　　　4 vols.... 8vo Lon. 33s.
Meteyard.　Hallowed Spots of Ancient
　　　　　　　London.... 4to L. 10s. 6d.
Murray's Hand Book of London.........12mo L. 3s. 6d.
—————　London, Past and Present......12mo L. 16s.
Ritchie, J. E.　Night Side of London....12mo L. 7s. 6d.
Thornbury.　Haunted London........... 8vo Lon. 21s.
Timbs, J.　Curiosities of London........ 8vo Lon. 21s.
—————　Walks and Talks ab't London. 16mo Lond. 6s.
————— London & Westminster, 2 vols. 12mo Lon. 21s.

Louisiana.

French Hist'l Collections of Louisiana.... 8vo N. Y.　4 00
Gayarre.　Hist. of Louisiana, 3 vols...... 8vo N. Y. $12 00

Machinery.—[*See also Inventions, Mechanics, Railroads,
　　　　　　Steam Engines,etc.*]

Abel.　Rudimentary Construct. of Mach. 16mo Lond.　75
Appleton's Dictionary of Mechanics, Ma-
　chines and Engineerings, etc., 2 v.....*r.* 8vo N. Y.　21 00
Appleby.　Illus. Hand Book of Machinery. 8vo L.12s. 6d.
Baker.　Practical Mech. & Machine Tools.12mo Lond.　1 25
Browne.　507 Mechanical Movements....12mo N. Y.　1 25
Burn, R. S.　Self Aid Cyclopedia.　Illust. 8vo Lond.　4 00
Fontain, W.　Mills and Mill Work, 2 v.　　 Lon. 32s.
Fitzgerald.　The Boston Machinist.......18mo Bost.　75
Johnson.　Cyclo. of Machinery, half mor. 4to Lon.　50 00
Joynson.　Construction of Gearing....... 8vo Edinb.　2 00
Tomlinson.　Cyclo. *See Manufactures.*
Watson.　Modern Practice of Am. Machs.12mo Phila.　3 50

Madagascar.

Ellis, Rev. W.　Hist. of Madagascar, 2v.. 8vo Lon. 25s.
—— ——　Three Visits to Madagascar. 8vo Lon. 16s.
a. Sibree.　Madagascar and its People......12mo Lond.　2 75

Madeira.

Dix, John A.　Winter in Madeira & Spain. 12mo N. Y.　1 50

Magazines.—LITERARY.—[*See Appendix.*]

Magic.—[*See Demonology.*]

Sargent.　Planchette; the Despair of Scien.12mo Bost.　1 25
Magician's Own Book, with Illust........12mo Phila.　1 50

Magnetism.—[*See also Electricity.*]

Harris, W. S.　Exposition of Magnetism. 16mo Lond.　1 75
Reichenbach.　Physiological Researches
　　　　　　on Magnetism 8vo Lond.　3 50

Mahomet.—[*See Mohammed.*]

Maine.—UNITED STATES.

Sullivan. History of Maine, 1795....*o. p.* 8vo Bost.
Thoreau. Maine Woods................12mo Bost. $2 00
Williamson. History of Maine, 1839, 2 v. 8vo

Maine Law.—[*See Temperance.*]

Malta.—[*See Mediterranean.*]

Porter. Hist. of the Knights of Malta, 2 v. 8vo Lon. 24s.
Vertot. Achievements of Kn'ts of Malta.

Mammoth Cave.

Binkherd. Mammoth Cave, 1869........ 8vo Cincin.
Forward. Mammoth Cave, 1870........12mo Phila. 2 00

Man.—[*See Ethnology, Mental Philos., Morals, Physiology.*]

Manners.—[*See Etiquette.*]

Manufactures and Mechanics.—[*See Machinery, etc.*]

Amateur Mechanics' Workshop......... 8vo Lond. 3 00
Bishop, J L. Hist. of Am. Manufact., 3 v. 8vo Phil. 12 00
Bischoff. Hist. of Woolen and Worsted
     Manufactures, 2 vols... 8vo Lon. 26s.
Byrne, Oliver. Practical Mechanics.....12mo Phila. 3 50
Dodd. Dictionary of Manufactures, Mining
     and Mechanics....12mo L. & N. 2 00
England's Workshops. By G. L. M....12mo Lond. 1 50
Geldard. Hand Book on Cotton Manf, 1867.12mo N. Y. 2 50
Gilroy, C. G. Art of Weaving, Hist'l & Prl. 8vo N. Y. 8 50
Goodeve. Elements of Mechanism......12mo Lond. 1 75
Harrison. Mechanics' Tool Book........12mo N. Y. 2 50
Hist. of Silk, Cotton, Linen, and Woolen
     Manufactures.... 8vo N. Y. 8 00
Hyde. Science of Cotton Spinning, 1867. 8vo Lond. 5 25
Mason. On Art Manufactures, Illust....12mo N. Y. 8 50
Tomlinson. Cyclopædia of Useful Arts;
    Mechanical, Chemical, Manufactur-
    ing, Mining, etc., 3 vols.,.....*imp.* 8vo Lond. 40 00
Timbs, Jno. Year Book of Facts, (in
     Mechanics, &c.,) 20 vols......12mo Lon. *ea.* 2 50
Ure. Cotton Manufac. of Gt. Britain, 2 v. 8vo Bohn. 4 50
—— Dict. of Arts, Manuf. & Mines, 3 v. *r.* 8vo N. Y. 15 00
—— Philosophy of Manufactures.....12mo Lond. 3 75
Watson. Memoirs of the Hand Lathe...12mo Phila. 1 50
Willis. Principles of Mechanism, 1871.. 8vo Lond. 6 50

Maritime Adventure.—[*See Travels.*]

Marriage and Divorce.—[*See also Woman; Woman's Rights.*]

McLennan, J. Primitive Marriage......12mo Edinb.
Pendleton, Mrs. H. Parents' Guide; Hu-
     man Development....12mo N. Y. 1 50

Wells, S. R.   Wedlock; or, Relations of
                              Sexes....12mo N. Y. $1 50
Wood, E. J.   The Wedding Day in all
                              Countries....12mo N. Y.   1 25
Woolsey, T. D.   Essay on Divorce.......12mo N. Y.   1 75

Martyrs.

Fox. Book of Martyrs. Several editions..   L. 5s. to 96s.
Tayler, C. B. Memorials of Eng. Martyrs.12mo N. Y.   1 50

Maryland.

McSherry. History of Maryland........ 8vo Balt.   1 25
Onderdonk. History of Maryland....... 8vo

Masonry.—[*See Secret Societies.*]

Massachusetts.—[*See also New England, Puritans and
                      United States.*]

Carpenter. History of Massachusetts....18mo Phila.   68
Massachusetts in the Rebellion. ByHeadly. 8vo Bost.   4 50
Minot. History of Massachusetts Bay... 8vo Bost.
Thoreau. Cape Cod; The Merrimack. ea.12mo Bost.   1 50
Winthrop, R. C. Early History of Massa. 8vo Bost.
Young. Chroni. of the Pilgrim Fathers. 8vo Bost.

Maternity.—[*See Health.*]

Combe. On Management of Infancy.....12mo N. Y.   1 50
Chevasse. Counsel to a Mother.........16mo Phila.   1 00
————   Advice to a Mother.........16mo Phila.   1 50
————   To a Wife.................16mo Phila.   1 50
————   Physical Training of Children.
Storer. On Nurses and Nursing, & 4 others.12mo Bost. ea. 1 00
Verdi, T. S. Maternity (Homœopathic)..12mo N. Y.   2 25

Mathematics.—[*Not including Elementary Text-Books.*]

Bledsoe. Philosophy of Mathematics.... 8vo N. Y.   2 00
Compte. Philosophy of Mathematics....12mo N. Y.   1 50
Davies. Mathematical Dictionary....... 8vo Bost.   5 00
———— Logic of Mathematics.......... 8vo N. Y.   1 50
Young. Advantages Mathematical Study.12mo L. 4s. 6d.

Mauritius.

Boyle, C. I.   Far Away; Sketches in
                      Mauritius. 1867....12mo Lond. 9s.

Maxims, etc.—[*See also Table Talk.*]

Colton, C. C. Lacon; or Many Things in
                      Few Words....12mo N. Y.   2 00
La Rochefoucault. Maxims......Lond.12mo 4s. 6d.
Napoleon I. Maxims..............16mo L. & N.   1 25

Mechanics—ENGINEERING.—[*See also Machinery, Inven-
                      tions, and Steam Engines.*]

Ball, R. S. Experimental Mechanics.... 8vo L. & N.   6 00
Hamson. Mechanics' Tool Book........12mo   2 50

Haswell. Engineer's and Mec. Pocket B'k.18mo N. Y. $3 00
Knight. The Mechanician and Construc-
          tor, for Engineers.... 4to Lond. 20 00
Lardner. On Mechanics.... ....12mo Lond. 5s.
Mahan, D. H. Civil Engineering........ 8vo N. Y.   4 00
Morin. Prac. Treatise on Mech. Trans.. 8vo   3 00
Moseley. Mechanical Principles of Civil
          Engineering. By Mahan.. 8vo N. Y.   5 00
Overman. Mechanics for Engineers, etc. 12mo Phila. 1 50
Rankin, W. J. M. Applied Mechanics... 8vo Lond.   6 25
Trautwine, J. C. Civil Engin. Pocket Bk.12mo Phila. 5 00
Wiesbach. Mechanics of Engineering... 8vo Lond. 10 00
Young Mechanic, The.................12mo N. Y.   1 75

Medals.—[*See Numismatics.*]

Medicine.—[*See Health, Maternity.*]

Meditations.—[*See Devotion.*]

Mediterranean.—[*See Levant.*]

Mediterranean and Islands.—[*See also Molta, Crete, &c.*]

Adams, A. The Nile and Malta......... 8vo Lond.
Bennet*, H. J. Winter and Spring on the
          Shores of the Mediterranean....12mo N. Y. 3 50
Cox, S. S. Search for Winter Sunbeams. 8vo N. Y. 3 00
Newton, C. F. In the Levant, 2 vols....r. 8vo Lond. 7 00

Memoirs.—[*See Biography.*]

Mental Philosophy.—[*See Metaphysics.*]

Mercantile.—[*See Business.*]

Mesmerism.—[*See Animal Magnetism.*]

Metallurgy.—[*See Iron Mining, Precious Metals, etc.*]

Blake, W. P. Report on Precious Metals. 8vo Wash. 2 00
Bloxam. On Metals—their Properties, etc.12mo Lond. 1 75
Kerl. Practical Treatise on Metallurgy, 3 v. 8vo Lond. 30 00
Lamborn. Metallurgy of Copper........12mo L. & N. 1 00
————   ————— — Silver and Lead.12mo L. & N. 1 00
Watt, A. Electro-Metallurgy...........12mo Lond. 2s.

Metaphysics.—[*See also Mind and Body.*]

Abercrombie. The Intellectual Powers..18mo N. Y.   75
————   Moral Feelings..........18mo N. Y.   75
Aristotle. Works Translated, 7 vols.....12mo Bohn. 16 00
Bacon, Lord. Novum Organum.........12mo Bohn.   2 50
———— ———— Whole works, 15 vols.....12mo N. Y. 33 75
Bain, P. Mental and Moral Science...ca.12mo Bost. 1 75
Boethius. Consolations of Philosophy...12mo Bohn.   2 50
Burton. Anatomy of Melancholy, 3 vols.12mo N. Y.   5 25
————   The same, new edition, 1 vol... 8vo Lond.   4 25
Brown. Philosophy of Human Mind, 4 v. 8vo Lond. 18 00

Clark. Mind in Nature................ 8vo Lond. $3 50
Combe, Geo. Moral Philosophy.........12mo N. Y. 1 75
Comte. General View of Positivism..... 8vo Lond. 4 50
——— Philosophy of the Sciences. By
     Lewes, 2 vols ...12mo Bohn. 5 00
Cousin, Victor. Psychology.............12mo N. Y. 1 75
——— ——— Course of Mod. Philos., 2 v. 8vo N. Y. 4 00
Cudworth. Intellectual System of the
     Universe, 3 vols.... 8vo Lon. 24s.
Fichte. Science of Knowledge..........12mo Lond. 2 00
——— Science of Right...............12mo Lond. 2 00
Fleming. Vocabulary of Philosophy....12mo L. 4s. 6d.
Grote. Plato and Compan's of Socrates, 3 v. 8vo Lon. 45s.
Hamilton, Sir W. Metaphysics..... .... 8vo Bost. 3 50
——— ——— Same, edit. by Bowen. 8vo Bost. 2 00
——— — Philos. of. By O. W. Wight, 8vo N. Y. 2 00
——— Outlines of. Murray & McCosh.12mo Bost. 1 50
Haven. Mental Philosophy.............12mo Bost. 2 00
——— Moral Philosophy..............12mo Bost. 1 75
Hazard. Freedom of the Will..........12mo 2 00
Henry, C. S. History of Philosophy, 2 v.18mo N. Y. 1 50
Hickok. Empirical Psychology.........12mo N. Y. 1 60
Hopkins, Mark. Moral Science........12mo Bost. 1 50
——— ——— Love as a Law........12mo N. Y. 1 75
Lewes, G. H. Biograph'l Hist. of Philos. 8vo N. Y. 3 50
Locke. Philosophical Works, 2 vols....12mo Bohn. 3 50
——— On the Understanding...........: 8vo N. Y. 2 00
Maudsley, H. Physiology and Pathology
     of the Mind.... 8vo Lon. 16s.
Masson. Recent British Philosophy.....12mo Lond. 1 25
McCosh. Metaphysics................. 8vo Lon. 12s.
——— Outlines of Moral Philosophy..12mo Lond.
——— Examination of Mill's Philos..12mo Lond.
——— Intuitions of the Mind........ 8vo Lond. 12s.
——— Philosophical Papers.......... 8vo L. 3s. 6d.
——— Laws of Discursive Thought.. 8vo Lond. 12s.
Melancholy Anatomized, (from Burton)... 8vo 2 50
Mill, J. Stuart. Comte and Positivism...12mo Phila. 1 50
Paley. Moral and Political Philosophy..12mo Bost. 1 50
Plato. Dialogues, translated and edited by
     Jowett, 4 vols.... 8vo N. Y. 12 00
——— Translated by Cary.............12mo Bohn. 2 50
——— Works, translated, 6 vols.........12mo Bohn. 15 00
Porter, Noah. The Human Intellect..... 8vo N. Y. 5 00
Reid, T. Essays on the Intellect'l Powers. 8vo Lond. 5s.
——— Collected Works, by Hamilton.. 8vo Lond. 25s.
Ritter. Hist. of Ancient Philosophy. 4 v.. Oxf. 42s.
Rush, Jas., M. D. Anal. of Human Intel't. 8vo Phila. 7 50
Smith, Sydney. Sketches of Mor. Philos. 8vo Lond. 7s.
Spencer, Herbert. Psychology, vol. 1.... 8vo N. Y. 2 50
Stewart, Dugald. Philos., ed. by Bowen.12mo Bost. 1 50
Taylor, Isaac. Nat. Hist. of Enthusiasm.12mo N. Y. 1 50

Taine. On Intelligence, trans. by Haye.. 8vo N. Y. $5 00
Ueberweg. History of Philosophy, trans.
                by Morris.... 8vo N. Y. 3 50
Upham. Mental Philosophy, 2 vols.....12mo N. Y. 3 00
———— The same, abridged..........12mo N. Y. 1 50
Watts. On the Mind..................18mo N. Y. 50
Wayland. Moral Science....... ....12mo Bost. 1 75
Whateley, R. Lessons on the Mind.....12mo 90

Meteorology.

Arago. Meteorological Essays.......... 8vo Lond. 9 00
Brocklesby. Meteorology..............12mo Lond. 5s.
Buchan. Hand Book of Meteorology.... 8vo Lond. 4 50
Butler, T. B. Atmospheric System......12mo Norw'k
Lackland. Meteors and Aerolites.......16mo N. Y. 1 50
Zurcher & Margolle. Meteors, &c.......12mo N. Y. 1 50

Methodism.—[See *Church History.*]

Metric System.

Davies. Report on Metric Syst. (against).12mo N. Y.
Lamotte. Metric System (for)..........16mo Phila. 40

Mexico.

Abbott, G. D. Mexico and the U. S...... 8vo N. Y. 3 50
Bartlett, J. R. Explora. in Mex. and Texas. 8vo N. Y. 5 00
Bernal-Diaz. True Hist. of Conquest of Mex.
Calderon de la Barca, Madame. Life in
                Mexico.... 8vo Lond. . 3 00
Cortes, Hernan. Life of. By Helps.....12mo N. Y. 2 00
————Letters and Despatches. By Folsom. 8vo N. Y.
Elten, J. E. With the French in Mexico. 8vo N. & P. 2 75
Hall, F. Maximilian I. 1868..........12mo N. Y. 2 00
Keratry. Maximilian : His Rise and Fall. 8vo
Mansfield. The Mexican War with U. S. 8vo N. Y. 1 50
Mayer, Brantz. Mexico as it Was and Is. 8vo N. Y.
Prescott. Hist. of Conquest of Mexico, 3 v. 8vo Phila. 7 50
Ripley, R. S. The War (of U. S.) with
                Mexico, 2 vols.... 8vo N. Y. 4 00
Ruxton. Mexico and the Rocky Mount..12mo L. 3s. 6d.
Salm-Salm, Prince. Diary in Mexico, 2 v. 8vo Lond. 24s.
Taylor, Bay. Eldorado: Mex. and Califor.12mo N. Y. 1 50
Thompson, Waddy. Life in Mexico.....12mo N. Y.
Wilson, R. A. New Hist. of Conq. of Mex. 8vo Phila.
——— ——— Mexico and its Religions..12mo N. Y.
Wise, H. A. Los Gringos : Mex. and Cal.12mo N. Y.

Michigan.

Lanman. History of Michigan..........16mo N. Y. 75

Microscope.

b. Beale. How to Work with the Microscope. 8vo Lond. 7 50
Brocklesby, J. Views of Microsc. World. 8vo N. Y. 1 25

b. Carpenter, W. B.   The Microscope and its
 Revelations.... 8vo Lond. $5 25
 Clarke, L. L.   Objects for the Microscope.12mo Lond.   1 75
 Davies, Thos.   Preparations, etc., of Micro-
 scopic Objects....12mo Lond.   1 50
 Griffith & Henfrey.   Micrographical Dict. 8vo Lond. 22 50
 —— —— Element. Text B'k of Micro.12mo Lond.   3 75
 Hogg, Jas.   Hist., etc., of the Microscope. 8vo Lond.   3 50
 Josse, P. H.   Evenings with the Micro...12mo Lond.   1 50
 Lankester.   Half Hours with the Micro..18mo Lond.   2 50
 Martin, J. H.   Microscopic Objects....... 8vo Lond.   .
a. Quekett.   Use of the Microscope........ 8vo Lond.   2 25
 Slack, H. J.   Marvels of Pond Life (Infuso.).12mo Lond.   2 50
 Somerville, Mary.   Microsco. Science, 2 v. 8vo Lond. 10 00
 Ward, Mrs.   The Microscope........... 8vo Lond.   1 75
 Wood, J. G.   Objects for the Microscope.12mo Lond.   1 25
 Wood, Han., Mrs.   Microscopic Teachings. 4to Lond.   5 00

"Middle Ages"—OF EUROPE.

 Baring, Gould. Myths of the Mid. Ages, 2 v.12mo L. & P.   2 50
b. Froissart.   Chronicles.   Illustrated, 2 v. *r.* 8vo Lond. 12 00
b. Hallam.   Europe during Mid. Ages, 3 v.12mo N. Y.   5 25
a. —— —— —— Cheap ed., 1 v.12mo Lond.   2 50
 Koeppen.   The World in the Mid. Ages, 2 v.   N. Y.   7 50
 Maitland.   The Dark Ages.............. 8vo Lon. 12s.
 Putz & Arnold.   Mediæval History.......12mo N. Y.   1 50
 Schmitz.   The Middle Ages, 2 vols ..... 8vo L. 7s. 6d.
 Wright.   The Homes of the Mid. Ages. Ill. 8vo Lon. 21s.
 —— —— —— —— —— 12mo N. Y.   1 50

 Fiction : Illustrative of Middle Ages, viz:
 Scott's Ivanhoe, Talisman, Quentin Dur-
 ward and Anne of Gierstein: Tasso's
 Jerusalem, etc. *See Fiction and Poetry.*

Military Dictionary. By H. L. Scott........ 8vo N. Y.   5 00

Mind and Body.—[*See also Metaphysics.*]

a. Galton, F. Hereditary Genius.......... 8vo N. Y.   3 50
 Holland, Sir H. Chapts. on Ment. Physiol.12mo Lond.   3 00
 Holmes, O. W. Mechanism in Thought
 and Morals....12mo Bost.   50
 Laycock.   The Mind and Brain, 2 vols... 8vo Edin. 21s.
b. Maudsley.   Physiology and Pathology of
 the Mind.... 8vo N. Y.   3 50
a. Moore, Geo.   The Body and Mind.... .. 12mo N. Y.   1 00
 —— —— The Soul and Body........12mo N. Y.   1 00

Mineralogy.—[*See also Gems.*]

b. Dana, J. D.   System of Mineralogy...... 8vo N. Y. 10 00
a. —— —— Manual of Mineralogy......12mo Phila.   2 00
 —— —— Corals and Coral Islands.... 8vo N. Y.   6 00
 Hooker.   Mineralogy and Geology.......12mo N. Y.   1 50

Overman, F.   Mineralogy, Assaying and
                Mining....12mo Phila. $1 00
Ramsay.   Rudiments of Mineralogy......18mo   1 50
Wohler.   Hand Book of Mineral Analysis..12mo Phila   3 00

Mines, Mining.—[*See also Coal, Iron, etc.*]

Crustell. Metallurgy................... 8vo   5 00
Hollister, O. J.   Mines of Colorado......12mo Spring. 2 00
Overman. (See above.)
Phillips.   Mining and Metallurgy of Gold
               and Silver....r. 8vo Lond.   10 50
Raymond.   Statist. of Mines west of Rocky
   Mountains, (8vo N. Y. $1.75) ½ mor. '70. 8vo Wash.   4 50
Rickard.   Practical Mining............12mo Lond.   1 25
Simonin.   Underground Life; or Mines
             and Miners....r. 8vo L. & N. 16 00
Ure. Dictionary. [*See Manufactures.*]
Whitney.   Metallic Wealth of the U. S.. 8vo Phila.   3 50

Minnesota.

Bond, J. W.   Minnesota and its Resources.12mo Phila.   1 50
McClung.   Minnesota in 1870..........12mo St. Paul
Minnesota; its Advantages to Settlers.... 8vo St. Paul
Neill, E. D.   History of Minnesota. 1858. 8vo Phila.

Missions.

Anderson, R.   Foreign Missions; their
              Claims, etc....12mo N. Y.   1 50
————— History of American Board of
             Com. Foreign Missions.. 8vo
Mailen.   Christian Miss. in Middle Ages.
              Camb....12mo 10s.6d.
Marshall, T. W.   Christian Missions, 2 v. 8vo N. Y.   5 00
Newcomb, H.   Cyclopedia of Missions... 8vo

Mississippi—River and Valley.

a. Foster, J. W.   The Mississippi Valley... 8vo Chica.
Gale.   The Upper Mississippi..........12mo Chica.
Humphries & Abbott. Report on Missi. Riv. 4to Phila. 15 00
Monette. Hist. of the Mississippi Val., 2 v. 8vo N. Y.
Shea, J. G. Discov. of the Mississippi Val. 8vo N. Y.
——— ——— Early Voyages on the Missi.. 4to Alb'y

Missouri—State of.

Parker, N. H.   Missouri in 1867........ 8vo Phila.   3 50

Mohammedanism.

Bush, Geo.   Life of Mahomet..........18mo N. Y.   75
Green, S.   Life of Mahomet............18mo Lond.
a. Irving.   Mohammed & his Successors, 2 v.12mo N. Y.   4 50
Koran.   Translated by Sale............, 8vo Phila.   3 00
Neale, F. A.   Islamism, 2 vols.......... 8vo Lon.21s.
Ockley.   History of the Saracens........12mo Bohn.   1 75
Taylor, W. C.   Hist. of Mohammedanism.12mo Lon. 4s.

Molluscs.—[*See Conchology.*]

Money.—[*See also Banks, Business.*]
Bagehot. A Universal Money.......... 8vo Lond.
McCulloch, J. R. Money and Banks .... 8vo Edin. 5s.
Spaulding. History of Legal Tender.....8vo Buffalo. 1 50

Monograms.—[*See Decorative Art.*]
A Book of Monograms. (Sabin's).........r. 8vo N. Y. $7 50

Moral Science.—[*See also Metaphysics.*]
Abercrombie. Philos. of Moral Feelings.18mo N. Y.   75
Alden. Christian Ethics................12mo N. Y.   1 25
Antoninus, Marcus Aur. Thoughts of...12mo Bost.   1 50
Beattie. Moral Science................. 8vo
b. Coleridge. Aids to Reflection...........12mo N. Y.   1 75
— ———— The Friend, (8 v. Lond)......12mo N. Y.   1 75
b. Cousin, Victor. The Good, Beautiful and
                and True, trans. by Wright.... 8vo N. Y.   2 00
Dymond. Principles of Morality........ 8vo N. Y.   1 25
Haven. Moral Philosophy..............12mo Bost.   1 75
b. Hopkins, Mark. Moral Science.........12mo Bost.   1 75
———— Law of Love.................12mo Bost.   1 75
a. Lecky. Hist. of European Morals, 2 vols. 8vo N. Y.   6 00
Paley. Moral Philosophy...............12mo Bost.   1 50
Tupper. Proverbial Philosophy, var. ed.L.&N. 75c. to 6 00
a. Wayland, F. Moral Science......... ...12mo Bost.   1 75
———— The Same, abridged......16mo Bost.   70
Whewell. Elements of Morality, 2 vols.12mo N. Y.   2 00

Mormons and Utah.
Burton, R. F. The City of the Saints, '62. 8vo N. Y.   8 50
Dixon, W. H. New America, $2.75 ; Spir-
                itual Wives.... 8vo Phila.   2 50
Ferris, Mrs. Mormons at Home, 1856....12mo N. Y,
Gunnison, J. W. The Mormons.
Tucker. Origin, Rise and Progress of
                Mormonism....12mo   1 25

Morocco.—[*See Africa, Northern.*]

Municipal Government.
Herrick, W. A. Town & Parish Officers.. 8vo Bost.   8 00
Maine, H. S. The Village, East & West. 8vo Lon.9s.
Pomeroy, M. Introd. to Municipal Law.. 8vo N. Y.   8 50

Music.
Bowman & Dana. Household B'k of Songs. 4to N. Y.   2 00
Burney. History of Music, 4 vols....o. p. 4to Lond.
Chapel. British Music, 1838............ 4to Lond.
Chorley, H. F. Modern German Music,
                (1854), 2 vols....16mo Lon. 21s.
Hogarth. History of Music............. 8vo N. Y.
Hullah. History of Modern Music......12mo L. 6s. 6d.

Moore, J. N.   Encyclopædia of Music...*r*. 8vo Bost.
Weber, Godfrey. Musical Comp'n, 2 v.. 8vo Bost.
Zundel, J.   Harmony and Composition... 8vo N. Y.

Mysticism.—[*See Supernaturalism.*]
Hours with the Mystics. ....
Keble. Mysticism of the Fathers.......

Mythology.—[*See Classical Dictionaries, Fables, &c.*]
Adams. Roman Antiquities............. 8vo Phila. $2 50
Bulfinch. (See Fable.)
Cox. G. W. Hand Book of Mythology....16mo L. 3s. 6d.
————— Mythology of the Aryan Na-
tions, 2 vols....   Lon. 28s.
Dwight, M A. Ancient Mythology...... 8vo N. Y.   3 00
b. Gladstone, W. E. Juventis Mundi; Gods
and Men.... 8vo Bost.   2 50
a. Keightley. Fairy Mythology...........12mo Bohn.   2 50
a. ————— Ancient Mythology......... 8vo N. Y.   2 25
Pritchard. Egyptian Mythology........
Thorpe. Northern Mythology, 3 vols.... 8vo Lon. 24s.
White. Student's Manual of Mythology .12mo N. Y.   1 25

Names.
b. Lower. Dictionary of Family Names.... 8vo Lon. 25s.
Salverte. History of Names, 1864, 2 vols. 8vo Lond.
Thomas, R. Hand Book of Fict's Names. 8vo Lond.
a. Wheeler. Dict. of Noted Names of Fiction.12mo Bost.   2 50
Yonge, C. M. Hist. of Christian Names, 2 v. 8vo Lon. 21s.

Naples.—[*See Italy.*]
Napoleon.—[*See Biography ; France.*]
Narcotics—OPIUM.

a. Beard. Stimulants and Narcotics... ... 12mo N. Y.   75
Calkins. Opium and the Opium Habit...12mo Phila.   1 75
Cooke, M. C. Seven Sisters of Sleep....12mo L. 7s. 6d.
b. Fiske. Tobacco and Alcohol............16mo N. Y.   1 00
Lizars. Use and Abuse of Tobacco......12mo Phila.   1 50
Opium Habit: with suggest'ns as to Reme.12mo N. Y.   1 75
b. Parton. Smoking and Drinking.........16mo Bost.   1 00

Natural History.—[*See also Names of its Departments ;
Botany, Ornithology, etc.*]
Adams, H. G. Hum. Birds Described Ill.16mo Lon.   1 60
————— W. H. Picturesque Objects of
Natural History.... 8vo Lond.   3 00
a. Agassiz, L. Structure of Animal Life.... 8vo Bost.   2 50
————— Mrs. Actœa; First Lessons in
Natural History....12mo Bost.
a. ————— L. Methods of Study in Natural
History....12mo Bost.   1 75
————— — Contributions to the Nat. Hist.
of the U. States, vols. 1 to 4.... 4to Bos. *ea.* 12 00

b. Agassiz, E. C. & A. Seaside Studies in
                    Natural History.... 8vo Bost. $3 00
—— & Gould. Principles of Zoology..12mo Bost. 1 50
b. Audubon. Quadrupeds of America, 3 v. r. 8vo N. Y. 60 00
—————— —————— with fol. plates, 5 v. N. Y. 300 00
Baird, S. F. The Mammals of N. A. Ill. r. 8vo Phila. 15 00
Biart. Adventures of a Young Naturalist.12mo N. Y. 1 75
Broderip. Leaves from Note Book of a
                    Naturalist....12mo L. 10s. 6d.
Buckland, F. Curiosities of Nat. History,
                3 series....ea.12mo Lon. 5s.
Burroughs, John. Wake Robin.........16mo N. Y. 1 50
b. Carpenter, W. B. Zoology. Illust. 2 v.12mo Bohn 6 00
Cassel's Popular Natural History, 2 vols. r. 8vo N. Y. 12 00
Chadbourne, P. A. Lectures on Nat. Hist.12mo N. Y. 1 00
Cassin. Birds of West Coast of North
                America. Illust....r. 8vo Phila. 13 00
—— Mammology and Ornithology of
                U. S. Explor. Exped., 2 v. folio Phila. 50 00
Coan, T. Curious Facts in Hist. of Insects.12mo Phila.
Cooper, Miss. Rural Hours (Naturalists).12mo N. Y. 2 50
Darwin. Voyages of a Naturalist. Lon.12mo 8s. 6d.
a. —— Naturalist's Researches in the
                Voyage of the Beagle....12mo N. Y. 2 00
b. De Vere. Leaves of the Book of Nature.12mo N. Y. 1 50
b. —— Wonders of the Deep (Ill., $2).12mo N. Y. 1 50
Dulcken. Animal Life the World over.. 4to L. & N. 4 00
Duncan. Sacred Philos. of Seasons, 4 v..12mo L. & N. 6 00
—— Transformations of Insects.... 4to Lond. 7 50
Edwards, H. M. Zoology. Trans. by Knox.16mo L. 8s. 6d.
b. Figuier. The Ocean World. Illustrated. 8vo L. & N. 4 50
b. —— Earth and Sea. Trans. by Adams. 8vo L. & N. 8 00
b. —— Mammalia. Illustrated....... 8vo L. & N. 4 50
b. —— Reptiles and Birds. Illustrated. 8vo L. & N. 4 50
b. —— Insect World................. 8vo L. & N. 4 50
Garrett, G. Marvels of Instinct. Lond..12mo 3s. 6d.
Girard. Herpetology of U. S. Exploring
                Expedition, 2 vols. 4to Phila. 30 00
Goldsmith. Earth and Animated Nat., 2 v. 8vo Phila. 5 00
Good, J. Mason. The Book of Nature.... 8vo Hartf. 3 00
Gosse. Romance of Natural History.....12mo Bost. 1 75
Gould's Descript. of Shells & Mollusks, 2 v. folio Bost. 55 00
Hartung. The Sea and its Liv'g Wonders. 8vo Lond.
Hartwig. The Subterranean World..... 8vo Lond. 8 00
—— Harmonies of Nature......... 8vo Lond. 10 00
Hooker, W. Child's Book of Nature.....12mo N. Y. 2 00
———— Natural History..........12mo N. Y. 1 50
Huxley, T. Classification of Animals.... 8vo Lon. 6s.
Jaeger. North American Insects........12mo N. Y. 1 50
Jesse. Gleanings in Natural History....12mo Lon. 6s.
Jones. The Broad Ocean and its Inhabit.12mo L. & N. 2 50
Journal of a Naturalist.................12mo

a. Kirby.   The Sea and its Wonders....... 4to L. & N. $3 00
Kingsley, C. Glaucus: Wond. of Sea Shore.12mo Bost.
Lannoy.   The Sublime in Nature........12mo N. Y.   1 50
Leroy. The Intelligence of Animals (1870). 8vo L. 7s. 6d.
Lewes, G. H.   Sea Side Studies......... 8vo L. 6s. 6d.
——— ———   Studies in Animal Life....12mo N. Y.   1 00
Mangin.   The Desert World. Illust..... 8vo L. & N. 8 00
Martin.   Natural History, 2 vols........12mo N. Y.   4 00
Maunder.   Treasury of Natural History..18mo L. & N. 4 00
Maynard, C. J. Naturalist's Guide, Illust.12mo Bost. 2 00
Menault. Intelligence of Animals.......12mo N. Y.   1 50
Milne—Edwards. Manual of Zoology.... 8vo Lond.   5 00
a. Milner.   The Gallery of Nature. Illust..*r.* 8vo Lond.   8 00
Natural Hist. of the State of N. Y., 21 v.. 4to Alb.   120 00
Nicholson.   Adv. Text Book of Zoology..12mo N. Y.   1 75
b. Pouchet.   The Universe ; the Infinitely
          Great and Infinitely. Little, Illust....*r.* 8vo L. & N. 12 00
Reeve.   Pop. Nat. Histories, Illust., 16 v.16mo Lond. *ea.* 2 75
Siebold, C. T. Von.   Comparative Anatomy
          of the Animal Kingdom.... 8vo Bost.   8 50
Tenney.   Manual of Natural History....12mo N. Y.   2 00
———   Elements of Zoology..........12mo N. Y.
Warterton. Wanderings of a Naturalist..12mo Lond. 5s.
Watson.   Reasoning Power of Animals.12mo Lon. 9s.
Westwood, J. O.   Modern Classification of
          Insects, 2 vols.... 8vo Lon. 18s.
White, Gilbert.   Nat. Hist. of Selbourne.12mo Lond.   2 25
          [And various other editions.]
Wood, J. G.   Houses without Hands..... 8vo N. Y.   4 50
b. ———   Natural History, 8 vols...*r.* 8vo L. & N. 21 00
a. ———   ——— ——— abridged...12mo L. & N. 1 50
———   Bible Animals............... 8vo N. Y.   5 00
———   Insects at Home. Illust... 8vo N. Y.   5 00

Natural Science—GENERALLY.**—***Including Natural Philosophy. [See also Astronomy, Cosmology, Mechanics,
Optics, Geology, etc., etc.]*

a. Annual of Scientific Discovery, edited by
          Wells and others, vols 1 to 20....12mo Bost. *ea.* 2 00
Arnott, N. Elements of Physics........12mo L. & N.
Box. Treatise on Heat................12mo Lond.   4 25
Brande & Cox. Dict. of Science and Art.. 8vo N. Y.   6 00
——— ——— ——— new edition.. Lond.
Brewster, Sir D. Natural Magic........18mo N. Y.   75
——— ——— ——— new ed..... 8vo Lond.   8 75
Büchner. Force and Matter.............12mo Lond.   4 00
Correlation and Conservation of Forces, ed.
          Youmans,...12mo N. Y.   2 00
Dircks, H. Nature Study.........Lond. 8vo 12s. 6d.
Euler. Natural Philosophy, 2 vols......18mo N. Y.   1 50
Faraday.. The Various Forces of Matter.12mo N. Y.   1 00

Frost and Fire, or Natural Engines—Chips
and Tool Marks, 2 vols.. 8vo Lond. $12 00
a. Ganot. Elements of Physics, by Atkinson.12mo L. & N. 6 00
———— ———— ———— ed. by Peck...12mo N. Y.
Grove, W. R. Correlation of Phys. Forces.
1867.... 8vo Lond.
Half Hours with Modern Scientists .....12mo N. Hav.
Hardwicke. Science Gossip...........
Hartwig, G. Harmonies of Nature. Ill.. 8vo L. & N. 7 50
" Haydn Series"—Dictionary of Science.. 8vo Lon. 18s.
Henry. Glossary of Scientific Terms.... 8vo
Herschel. Familiar Lect. on Scien. Subj.12mo L. 10s. 6d.
———— Natural Philosophy.........12mo N. Y. 1 50
———— Preliminary Disc. on Nat. Phil. 8vo Lon. 18s.
———— Manual of Scientific Enquiry.. 8vo Lond. 4 50
b. Humboldt, A. von. Cosmos, 5 vols......12mo N. Y. 6 25
———— ———— Aspects of Nature...
Hunt, R. Researches on Light......... 8vo Lond. 2 50
a. Huxley, T. H. Lay Serm. and Addresses. 8vo N. Y. 1 75
———— ———— Organic Nature (63)...... 8vo Lond.
Lardner, D. Hand Book of Nat. Phil., 4 v. Lond. 10 00
b. Library of Wonders. Scribner's, v. 1 to 22.18mo N. Y. ea.1 50
Mayhew, H. Wonders of Familiar Things.12mo N. Y. 1 25
Olmsted, D. Natural Philosophy........ 8vo N. Y. 4 00
Pepper, J. H. Play Book of Metals. Lon. 8vo 7s. 6d.
———— Scientific Amusements......... 8vo Lon. 2s.
———— Cyclopedic Science Simplified...12mo 9s.
Proctor. Light Science for Leisure Hours.12mo N. Y. 1 75
Schonn. Earth, Plants and Minerals... 16mo Lond. 5s.
a. Somerville, Mrs. Connexion of Phy. Sci.12mo Lond. 9s.
Spencer, H. Principles of Biology, 2 vols.12mo N. Y. 5 00
Timbs, J. Things not generally Known, 2 v.16mo Lon. 5s.
———— Things to be remembered in
Daily Life....16mo L. 3s. 6d.
a. Tyndall, J. Fragments of Science.......12mo N. Y. 2 00
———— Imagination and Science....18mo Lon. 3s.
———— See Acoustics, Alps, Heat, Light.
Vestiges of Natural History of Creation..12mo N. Y. 75
Whewell. History of the Inductive
Sciences, 2 vols.... 8vo N. Y. 5 00
Warne. Series of Books for the Country,
viz.: Shells, Seaweeds, Ferns, Micro-
scope, etc....ea.18mo L. & N. 50
Wells, D. A. Science of Common Things.12mo N. Y.
Winslow, C. F. Force of Nature........ 8vo Phila. 5 00
Year Book of Facts. Edited by John
Timbs. 1839–71....ea..12mo Lon. 5s.
Youmans, E. L. Correlation and Conserva-
tion of Forces....12mo N. Y. 2 50

Natural Selection.—[See Darwinism.]

Natural Theology.—[*See also Religion & Science.*]
b. Bascom.   Science, Philosophy & Religion.12mo N. Y. $1 50
    Bushnell, H.   Nature & Supernatural.... 8vo N. Y.   2 25
b. Butler.   Analogy of Religion... ....12mo N. Y.   1 50
a. Chadbourne. P. A.   Natural Theology....12mo N. Y.   1 50
    Bridgwater Treatises on Power and Wis-
                dom of God in Creation, 5 v..12mo Bohn. 23s.
    Chalmers, T. Adaptation of Nature to Man. 8vo Phila.   2 50
    ———— — Natural Theology, 2 vols...12mo N. Y.   2 50
    Child.   Benedicite: Power, Wisdom and
                Benevolence of the Creator..12mo N. Y.   2 00
    McMillan.   Bible Teaching in Nature....12mo N. Y.   2 00
    Paley, W.   Natural Theology...........16mo Bost.   1 75

Navigation.
    Adams, W. H. D.   Light-Houses and Light-
                        Ships....18mo N. Y.   1 50
    Bowditch.   American Navigator......... 8vo N. Y.
    Dana, R. H., Jr.   The Seaman's Friend...12mo Bost.   1 50
    Folkard.   The Sailing Boat.......Lond..12mo 12s. 6d.
    Totten, C. J.   U. S. Naval Text Book.... 8vo N. Y.   3 00

Navy.—[*See under England, France, United States, etc.*]

Needlework.
    Hand-Book of Needlework (Murray)..... 8vo L. 7s. 6d.
    Plain Needlework.....................18mo Lond.
    Palliser, Mrs. B.   History of Lace....... 8vo Lond.
    Stephens, Mrs.   Ladies' Guide to F'cy W'k.12mo N. Y.
    Warren, Mrs.   Treasures in Needlework.12mo L. 7s. 6d.

Nestorians.
    Grant, A.   The Nestorians: The Lost
                        Tribes.   1845....12mo N. Y.
    Laurie, T.   Dr. Grant and Nestorians....12mo Bost.   1 75
    Perkins, J.   Residence among Nestorians. 8vo Andov.

Netherlands.—[*See Holland.*]

New England.—[*See also Puritans.*]
    Hubbard, W.   History of Indian Wars in
                        New England, 2 vols.... 4to Roxb.
    Oliver, Peter.   Hist. of Pur. Commonw'lth. 8vo Bost.   2 00
    Martyn, W. C.   The Pilgrim Fathers of
                        New England....12mo N. Y.   1 25
b. Palfrey, J. G.   Hist. of N. England, 3 vols. 8vo Bost.   10 00
a. ————————   The same, condens., 2 vols.12mo N. Y.   5 00
    Savage.   Geneal. Hist. of N. Eng., 4 vols. 8vo Bost.   12 00
    Uhden.   New England Theocracy.......12mo Bost.

Newfoundland.
    Bonnycastle.   Newfoundland in 1842, 2 v. 8vo Lon. 21s.

New Grenada.
    Holmes.   New Grenada..........,.,.,,.... 8vo   8 00

New Hampshire.

Barstow.   Hist. of New Hamp. to 1818...
Belknap, J.   Hist. of New Hamp., 3 vols. 8vo Bost.
Chase, F. E.   Early Hist. of New Hamp. .12mo Claremt.

New Jersey.

Carpenter & Arthur.   Hist. of N. Jersey. .18mo Phila. **§** 63
Gordon.   History of New Jersey.........
Mulford.   History of New Jersey........
Sypher & Apgar.   Hist. of New Jersey. ..12mo Phila.   1 25

Newspapers.

Andrews.   British Journalism, 2 vols.... 8vo Lon. 21s.
Grant, Jas.   Hist. of Newspapers, '71, 2 v. 8vo Lon. 24s.
Hunt.   The Fourth Estate.............. 8vo Lon. 21s.

New York—STATE OF.

b. Brodhead.   History of New York, 2 vols. 8vo N. Y.   6 00
Dunlap.   History of New York. 1840, 2 v. 8vo N. Y.
. ——— Same, abridged......... ....12mo N. Y.
Hammond.   Political Hist. of N. York, 2 v. 8vo N. Y.
Macauley.   Hist. of New York. 1829, 3 v. 8vo N. Y.
O'Callaghan.   History of New Nether-
lands, 2 vols.... 8vo N. Y.   6 00
a. Randall.   Hist. of New York, for Schools.12mo N. Y.   1 75

New York City.

Booth, Mary L.   Hist. of N. York City, 2 v. 8vo N. Y.   6 00
Valentine.   Hist. of N. York City. 1853. 8vo N. Y.   3 00

New Zealand.

a. Barker, Lady.   Station Life in N. Zealand.12mo L. &. N. 2 50
Fox.   The Maori War. 1866............ 8vo Lond.
Swainson, W.   New Zealand. 1859..... 8vo Lon. 18s.
Thompson.   Story of New Zealand.

Nicaragua.—[*See Central America.*]

Nile, The.—[*See Egypt.*]

Nineveh.

Bonomi.   Nineveh and its Palaces.......12mo Bohn.   2 50
Fergusson, J.   Nineveh and its Palaces.. 8vo Lon. 16s.
Layard, A. H.   Nineveh and its Remains,
2 vols.... 8vo Lon. 32s.
———— The same, abridged (12mo N. Y.,
$1.75). Lond....12mo 7s. 6d.
———— Nineveh and Babylon; 2d Visit. 8vo Lond.   5 00
8vo N. Y.   4 00
———— The same, abridged.....Lond..12mo 7s. 6d.
———— The same, abridged...........12mo N. Y.   1 75

North America.—[*See America.*]

North Carolina.

Hawks, History of North Carolina...... 8vo N. Y.
Wheeler. Hist. Sketch of North Carolina. 8vo Phila. $2 00
Williamson. Hist. of N. Carolina. 1812. 2 v. 8vo Phila.

Norway.—[*See Scandinavia.*]

Browne, J. R. The Land of Thor.......12mo N. Y.   2 00
Laing, S. Residence in Norway. Lond..12mo 2s. 6d.
———— Chronicles of Kings of Nor., 3 v. 8vo Lon. 36s.
Mugge. Afraja; Life & Love in Norway.12mo L. 10s. 6d.
Norway and its Scenery, Illust..........12mo Bohn.   2 50

Notabilia.—FACTS, STATISTICS, MISCELLANIES.

Timbs, J. Notabilia; or, Curious and
          Amusing Facts....12mo L. & N. 8 00
————   Things not generally known,
          edited by Wells....12mo N. Y.   1 75
————   Popular Errors Explained..12mo Lond.
————   Year Book of Facts in Science
          and Art, 1839–70.....12mo L. *ea.* 5s.

Nova Scotia.

Haliburton. Hist. of Nova Scotia, 2 vols. 8vo Halif.
Martin. Colonial Library, [vol. vi.].....12mo L. 3s. 6d.

Novels.—[*See Fiction.*]

Nubia.—[*See also Africa, Egypt.*]
Burckhardt. Travels in Nubia, 1819..... 4to Lond.

Numismatics.

Ackerman, J. V. Anc. and Mod. Coins...16mo Lon. 6s.
Dickerson, M. W. Numismatic Manual.. 4to Phila. 10 00
Mickley. Hist. of United States Coins...
Snowden, J. R. Anc. and Mod. Coins.... 8vo Phila. 8 50

Nursing.—[*See Health.*]

Object Lessons.

Calkins, N. A. New Prim. Object Lessons.12mo N. Y.   1 50
Sheldon. Object Lessons...............12mo N. Y.   1 75

Ocean.—[*See Natural History.*]

De-Vere. Wonders of the Deep. Illus..12mo N. Y.   2 00
Gosse, P. H. The Ocean...............12mo L. 4s. 6d.
Kirby. The Sea, and its Living Wonders. 4to L. & N. 8 00
Maury. Physical Geography of the Sea.. 8vo N. Y.   4 00
Mangin. Mysteries of the Ocean, Illust.. 8vo L. & N. 6 00
Michelet, J. The Ocean, Illust..........12mo N. Y.   1 50
Moquin—Tandon; World of the Sea.....
Sorrel, L. The Bottom of the Sea.......18mo N. Y.   1 50

Oceanica.—[*See Islands.*]

Ohio.

Atwater. History of Ohio.............8vo Cinc.

Carpenter & Arthur. History of Ohio....18mo Phila. **$** 63
Lossing, B. J. Pictorial Description of
                    Ohio. (1850).... 8vo N. Y.

Opium.—[*See Narcotics.*]

Optics.—[*See also Spectroscope.*]

Airy, G. B. Undulatory Theory of Optics.12mo Lond.   2 50
Brewster, Sir D. Treatise on Optics.....12mo L. 3s. 6d.
——————— ——— Kaleidoscope..........12mo L. 5s. 6d.
Goblet, H. F. Theory of Sight.......... 8vo Lond.
Hunt, R. Researches on Light.......... 8vo Lond. 5s.
Nugent, E. Treatise on Optics..........12mo N. Y.   2 00
Tyndall, J. On Radiation..............12mo N. Y.   50
Wonders of Optics (Lib. of Wonders.)...18mo N. Y.   1 50

Oratory.—[*See also Elocution.*]

American Oratory ; P. Henry, Ames, Pink-
                  ney, etc.... 8vo Phila.   2 75
American Eloquence, Cyclop. of, 2 vols.. 8vo N. Y.   7 00
Ames, Fisher. Works (Speeches, &c.)... 8vo Bost.   2 00
Bantain. Extempore Speaking........12mo N. Y.   1 20
Bright, John. Speeches. By Thor. Rogers. 8vo Lon. 25s.
—————— ———— ———— 16mo, 2s. 16mo L. 3s. 6d.
Burke. Works (Speeches, etc.), 12 vols.. 8vo Bost. 30 00
Calhoun, J. C. Speeches and Works, 6 v. 8vo N. Y. 15 00
Cicero. Orations, etc., 4 vols...........12mo Bohn 10 00
————— Oratory & Orators.............12mo Bohn   2 50
Chatham, Burke & Erskine's Speeches, 1 v. 8vo Phila.   2 75
Clay, Henry. Speeches & Life, by Colton, 2 v. 8vo N. Y.   4 50
Demosthenes. Orations. Trans., 5 vols..12mo Bohn 11 75
—————————— ——————Trans. by Leland, 2 v.18mo N. Y.   1 50
—————————— —————— Literal trans. 2 vols.12mo N. Y.   3 00
Dix, John A. Speeches, etc., 2 vols...... 8vo N. Y.   5 00
Dickinson. D. J. Speeches, 2 vols...... 8vo N. Y.   5 00
Erskine, Lord. Speeches & Life, 2 vols... 8vo Lond.   8 00
Everett, Edw. Works, chiefly Orations, 3 v. 8vo Bost.   9 00
Gladstone. Speeches on Parl. Reform...16mo Lond.   1 00
Goodrich. Select British Eloquence..... 8vo N. Y.   4 00
Household Book of Irish Eloquence. Ill. 8vo N. Y.   5 00
Kirkland. Mrs. Patriotic Eloquence.....12mo N. Y.   1 75
Macaulay. Speeches, 2 vols............. 8vo N. Y.   4 50
Magoon. Living Orators in America.....12mo N. Y.   1 50
————— Orators of the Revolution.....12mo N. Y.   1 50
Marshall. First Book of Oratory........12mo N. Y.   1 50
Maury. Principles of Eloquence........18mo N. Y.   75
Peel, Sir Robert. Speeches, 4 vols...... 8vo Lon. 42s.
Phillips, W. Speeches............. ....16mo Bost.   2 50
Phillips, Curran & Grattan. Speeches.. 8vo Phila.   2 00
Quintillian Institutes of Oratory, trans., 2 v.12mo Bohn.   5 00
Sargeant. Standard Speaker........... 8vo Phila.   2 50
Sheil. Speeches and Life..............12mo Dub. 4s.

Sumner, Charles. Speeches and Works,
    now publishing, 10 vols.... 8vo Bost. $30 00
Webster, Daniel. Speeches, 6 vols...... 8vo Bost. 18 00
Winthrop, R. C. Speeches & Addresses.. 8vo Bost. 3 50

Ordnance.—[*See Arms and Armor.*]
     (Professional Works omitted.)

Oregon.
Bulfinch, F. Oregon and Eldorado......12mo Bost. 2 50

Origin of Species.—[*See Darwinism.*]

Ornithology.—[*See also Cage Birds, Natural History, etc.*]
Audubon. Birds of America, Illust., 8 v.r.8vo N. Y. 165 00
——— ——— with folio plates, 5 v.r.8vo N. Y. 250 00
Bailey. Our Own Birds............. ..12mo Phila. 1 50
Baird, S. F. and others. Birds of North
     America, 2 vols.... 4to Phila.
Cassin. Birds of Western Coast of North
     America....r. 8vo Phila. 13 00
Figuier. Birds and Reptiles, Illust...... 8vo Lond. 4 50
Michelet. The Bird, Illust............r. 8vo L. & N. 6 00
Nichols. Ornithology and Oology of New
     England.... 4to Bost.
Samuels, E. A. Birds of New England.. 8vo Bost. 4 00
——— ——— larger ed. col'd. Bost. 4to $9 to 25 00
Stanley, E. History of Birds...........12mo L. 5s. 6d.
Wilson. American Ornithology, 3 vols.r.8vo Phila. 75 00

Pacific Ocean.
Beechey. Voyage to the Pacific. 1828.. 4to Lond.
Jones. Adventures in So. Pacific Ocean..12mo 1 50
Melville. Typee; Mardi; Omoo; etc. (*See Fiction.*)
Pritchard. Polynesian Reminiscences... 8vo Lond.
Reynolds & Ruschenberger's Voyages, o. p.
Wilkes. U. S. Exploring Exped., 5 vols. r. 8vo Phila. 25 00
——— ——— ——— abridg., 1 vol. 8vo Phila. 3 50

Paganism.—[*See Heathenism.*]

Painting—TREATISES ON.—[*See also Fine Arts.*]
Barnard, Geo. Landscape Painting.....r. 8vo Lond. 8 00
Benson. On the Science of Color........ 4to Lond. 15 00
Burnet. Treatises on Painting.......... 4to Lond. 22 50
Cavé, Madame. Du Color........... ..12mo N. Y. 1 00
Chevreul. On Color..................12mo Lond. 5s.
Eastlake. History of Oil Painting...... 8vo Lon. 16s.
Field. Rudiments of Color............12mo Lond. 2 00
Fuseli. Lectures on Painting, 3 vols., o. p. Lond.
Gulick & Timbs. Painting, Popularly Ex-
     plained....12mo Lond. 2 50
Hamerton. The Painter's Camp....;...16mo Bost. 1 50
——— Painting in France. 1869... 4to Lond.
——— Thoughts about Art..........16mo Bost. 1 50

Haydon. Lectures on Painting, 2 vols... 8vo Lon. 15s.
Hand B'k on Oil Paint., for Young Artists 12mo N. Y. $2 00
Hazlitt, Criticisms on Art. [*See Fine Arts.*]
Howard. On Color as Means of Art.....12mo Lond.
Jameson, Mrs. Works. [*See Fine Arts.*]
Kugler. Hand Books. Trans. by Eastlake.
                    [*See Fine Arts.*]
O'Neill. Lectures on Painting..........12mo Lond. 2 50
Penley. English School of Painting in
                    Water Colors....folio Lond. 42 00

Paleontology—[*See Geology.*]

Palestine.—[*See Holy Land.*]

Paper Making.

Herring. Paper and Paper Making, Anc't
                    and Modern.... 8vo Lond. 5 00
———— Guide to Varieties and Value
                    of Paper.... 4to Lond. 10 00

Paraguay.

Burton, R. F. Battle-Fields of Paraguay. 8vo Lon. 18s.
Masterman. Seven Years in Paraguay.. 8vo Lon. 5s.
Washburn, C. C. Hist. of Paraguay, 2 v. 8vo Bost.   7 50

Paris.—[*See France.*]

Parliamentary Law.

Cushing. Law & Pract. of Legisl. Assem.   N. Y.   75
Jefferson. Manual of Parl. Practice.....18mo N. Y.

Parodies.—[*See Poetry and Humorous Works.*]

Patent Law.

Curtis, G. T. The Law of Patents....... 8vo
Law, S. D. Patent and Copyright Laws.. 8vo N. Y. 2 50

Pauperism.—[*See also Charities.*]

Fawcett. Pauperism; its Causes and
                    Remedies ...12mo L. & N. 2 25
Ginx's Baby; (satire on English Poor
                    Laws, etc.)....12mo N. Y.   50

Peace and War.

Dymond, J. War and Christianity......12mo Phila.
Upham, T. C. Manual of Peace........ 8vo N. Y.

Peninsular War.

Napier. Hist. of the Peninsular War, 5 v.   N. Y.   12 50
Southey. Hist. of the Penins. War, 6 v.. 8vo Lon. 63s.

Pennsylvania—PHILADELPHIA.

Bowen. Pictorial Sketch Book of Penn'a. 8vo Phila.
Gordon. History of Pennsylvania. 1829. 8vo Phila.
Sypher. School History of Pennsylvania.12mo Phila.   1 50

Watson.   Annals of Philadelphia, 2 vols. 8vo Phila. $7 50

Perfumery.

Dussance.   Treatise on Perfumery....... 8vo   7 50
Pease.   The Art of Perfumery..........12mo   1 25

Periodicals.—[*See Appendix.*]

Perpetual Motion.

Dircks.   Perpetuum Mobile, 2 vols......12mo Lond.

Persia.

Eastwick, E. P. Three Years in Persia, 2 v. 8vo Lon. 18s.
Frazer.   History of Persia ....18mo N. Y.   , 75
Watson, R. G.   History of Persia to 1858. 8vo Lond.

Perspective.—[*See Drawing; Fine Arts.*]

Peru.

Hill, S. S. Travels in Peru and Mexico, 2 v. 8vo Lon. 21s.
Prescott.   History of Conquest of Peru, 2 v. 8vo Phila.   5 00
Tschudi.   Travels in Peru..............12mo N. Y.   1 50

Petroleum—AND OIL WELLS.

Cone & Johns.   Petrolia (in Pa.).........12mo N. Y.   3 00
Wright.   The Oil Regions of Pa.... ...12mo Phila.   1 50

Philology.—[*See Language.*]

Philosophy—MENTAL.—[*See Metaphysics.*]

Philosophy—NATURAL.—[*See Natural Philosophy.*]

Phonography.

Graham.   Outline of Standard Phonog...12mo N. Y.   2 00
———   Hand Book of Phonography...12mo N. Y.   2 00
———   Phonographic Dictionary......12mo N. Y.   4 00
  a. Munson, J. E.   Complete Phonographer.12mo N. Y.   2 00
Pittman.   Manual of Phonography......12mo L. & N. 1 00
———   Reporter's Manual......Lond.18mo 2s. 6d.

Photography.

Ayres.   How to Paint Photographs......12mo Phila.   1 50
Delamott.   Photographic Practice.......12mo N. Y.   50
Hunt, R. Photographic Manual.......... 8vo Lon. 6s.
Lea, H. C. Manual of Photography..... 8vo Phila.   3 00
Price.   Manual of Photographic Manipu.12mo Lond.   3 25
Sutton & Dawson.   Dict. of Photography.12mo Lond.   3 00
Fowler, J.   The Silver Sunbeam........12mo N. Y.   2 50

Phrenology.

Boardman.   Defence of Phrenology.....12mo   .   1 50
Browne, J. P. Phrenology; its application,
      ... ... etc., to Education....12mo L. 12s. 6d.

Combe.   Lectures on Phrenology........12mo N. Y. $1 50
Phrenology ; Proved, Illust. and Applied.12mo N. Y.   1 50

Physics.—[See *Natural Science.*]

Physical Education.—[See *Calisthenics, Gymnast., etc.*]

Physical Geography.—[See *also Ocean, Volcanoes, etc.*]

a. Ansted, D. T.   Physical Geography......16mo Lond.   8 00
———————— World We Live in.......16mo N. Y.   75
Figuier.   The Earth and the Sea.   Illus. 8vo Lond.   4 50
Hartwig, G.   The Tropical World.   1862. 8vo Lon. 21s.
Herschell, J. W. F.   Physical Geography.12mo Ed. 7s. 6d.
Mangin.   The Desert World......Lond. 8vo 12s. 6d.
Marsh, G. P.   Man and Nature.......... 8vo N. Y.   8 00
Pouchet.   The Universe...............*r.* 8vo L. & N. 12 00
b. Reclus.   The Earth : Physical Phenomena
of Life of the Globe, 2 v.. 8vo L. & N. 10 00
——— ——————— Cheap edition......... 8vo N. Y.   5 00
Somerville, Mrs.   Physical Geography..12mo Lond. 9s.
——— — American edition (*o. p.*)..12mo Phila.

Physiognomy.

Lavater.   Essays on Physiognomy....... 8vo Lon. 12s.
Redfield, J. W.   Comparative Physiogno. 8vo N. Y.   8 00

Physiology and Anatomy—POPULAR.—[See *Protoplasm.*]

Beecher, Miss.   Physiology and Calis-
thenics.....12mo N. Y.   1 00
Brinton & Napheys.   Personal Beauty...12mo Spring. 2 00
b. Carpenter, W. B.   Human Physiology... 8vo Phila.   5 50
———————— Comparative Physiolo. 8vo Phila.   5 00
a. Combe, Geo.   The Constitution of Man..12mo N. Y.   1 00
Dalton, J. C.   Human Physiology .... 8vo N. Y.   5 25
——— —— Physiology and Hygiene...12mo N. Y.   1 50
a. Draper, J. W.   Anato., Phys. & Hygiene. 8vo N. Y.   8 75
———————— Physiology.............. 8vo N. Y.   5 00
——— ——— The same abridged......12mo N. Y.   1 50
Huxley & Youmans.   Elementary Physi-
ology and Hygiene....12mo N. Y.   1 75
a. Lewes, G. H.   Phys. of Common Life, 2 v.12mo N. Y.   8 00
Loomis.   Elements of Anatomy & Physiol.12mo N. Y.   1 25
Marshall, J.   Outlines of Physiology, 8 v.16mo Lon. 82s.
Morgan, J. E.   Deterioration of the Race
in Great Cities.   '66......16mo Lond.
Napheys, G. H.   Physical Life of Woman.12mo Phila.   1 50
Roget, Ph.   Animal and Vegetable Physi-
ology, 2 vols....12mo Bohn.   5 00
Wonders of the Human Body...........12mo N. Y.   1 50

Plays.—[See *Drama.*]

Plurality of Worlds.—[See *Astronomy.*]

Poetry.—Divided into: I. *History of Poetry, etc.;* 2. *Collections;* III. *Poetical Works;* IV. *Humorous and Satirical Poetry.* [*See also Ballads.*]

—— HISTORY AND CRITICISM.

Everett, Erastus.   English Prosody and
                  Versification....12mo N. Y.
Fauriel.   Hist. of Provençal Poetry, trans.
                 by Adler.... 8vo N. Y. $3 00
Johnson, Dr.   Lives of the British Poets,
               2 vols....12mo Phila.   3 00
Lowth.   Lectures on Hebrew Poetry..... 8vo L. 3s. 6d.
Reed, Henry.   Lectures on Brit. Poets, 2v.12mo Phila.   3 50
Tuckerman.   Thoughts on the Poets.....12mo N. Y.   1 50
Walker, J.   Rhyming Dictionary........12mo Lond.   3 00
Warton.   History of English Poetry.....12mo L. & N.   4 25

—— (2) COLLECTIONS OF POETRY.

Alger, W. R.   Poetry of the East........12mo Bost.   2 00
British Poets, from Chaucer to Wordsworth.
      Edited by Prof. Child, 130 vols.
    * Akenside, 1 vol.; Ballads, 8 vols.;
    * Beattie; 1 vol.; * Butler, 1 vol.;
    * Burns, 3 vols. ;   Byron, 10 vols.;
    Campbell, 1 vol; Chatterton, 1 vol.;
    * Churchill, 1 vol.; Coleridge, 3 vols.;
    * Collins, 1 vol.; * Cowper, 3 vols.;
    Donne, 1 vol.; * Dryden, 5 vols.;
    * Falconer, 1 vol.;   Gay, 2 vols.;
    * Goldsmith, 1 vol.; * Gray, 1 vol.;
    Herbert, 1 vol.; Herrick, 2 vols.;
    Hood, 5 vols.; Keats, 1 vol.; Marvell,
    1 vol.; * Milton, 3 vols.; Montgomery,   } ea. 18mo Bost. 1 25
    5 vols.; Moore, 6 vols.; * Parnell,
    etc., 1 vol.; * Pope, 3 vols.; * Prior,
    2 vols.; Scott, 9 vols.; * Shakespeare,
    1 vol.; Shelley, 4 vols.; Skelton, 3
    vols.; Southey, 10 vols.; * Spencer,
    5 vols.; * Surrey, 1 vol.; * Swift, 3
    vols.; * Thompson, 2 vols.; Vaughan,
    1 vol.; Watts, 1 vol.; * White, 1 vol.;
    Wordsworth, 7 vols.; * Wyatt, 1 vol.;
    * Young, 2 vols...................

British Poets; Aldine ed'n (reprint), 53 v.16mo L. & P. *ea.* 75
(This set contains the authors in previous set marked * and, in
  addition, Chaucer. in 6 vols., edited by Morris ; the other works
  are edited by Milford, Dyce, Collier, Hannay and Sir H. Nicolas.
Beeton.   Book of English Poetry, 2 vols. *r.* 8vo Lond.   10 00
Book of Gems.   Ed. by S. C. Hall. Ill. 2v. 8vo L. & P.   7 50
Brooks, C. T.   Lays, etc., from Uhland,
              Korner, etc....12mo N. Y.   1 00
Bowman & Dana.   Household B'k of Songs. 4to N. Y.   2 50
a. Bryant, Library of Poetry and Song...... 8vo N. Y.   6 00

Campbell, Thos.   Speci. of British Poets. 8vo L. & P. $2 75
Carter, P.   Scotia's Bards.   Illustrated... 8vo N. Y.   4 50
Companion Poets.   Illustrated, 2 vols....12mo Bost.   5 00
a. Dana, C. A.   Household Book of Poetry,
                    half morocco....r. 8vo N. Y.   7 00
——— ——— Illustrated ed., morocco.... 4to N. Y. 20 00
Duffy.   Poetry of Ireland..... ....
Ellis.   Metrical Romances...............12mo Bohn   2 50
Griswold, R. W.   Poets & Poetry of Amer. 8vo Phila. 5 00
——— ——— Female Poets of America. 8vo Phila. 5 00
a. Golden Treasury Series, 7 vols.........ea. 16mo Camb. 1 25
Hymns of the Ages, 3 vols............. 8vo Bost. 7 50
Kendrick, A. C.   Our Poetical Favorites.12mo N. Y. 2 00
b. Longfellow.   Poets and Poetry of Europe. r 8vo Phila. 6 00
Lyra Americana..................... 12mo N. Y. 1 50
Lyra Anglicana................... ....12mo N. Y. 1 50
Lyra Germanica......... ....12mo N. Y. 1 50
——————— Christ. year : Christ. Life ; ea. 4to Lon. 10 50
Mackay, Chas.   Book of English Songs..12mo Lond. 5s.
——— Illus. Book of Scottish Song...16mo L. 3s. 6d.
——— 1001 Gems of English Poetry.. 8vo Lond. 5 00
——— Home Affections Portrayed by
               Poets.   Illust.... 8vo L. & N. 9 00
Morgan.   Hymns of the Latin Church... 8vo Lond.
——— J. A.   Macaronic Poetry.........12mo N. Y. 2 75
Motherwell.   Minstrelsy, Anct. and Mod.12mo
Palmer, J. W.   Folk Songs.   Ill., mor., r. 8vo N. Y. 15 00
——— ——— Poetry of Compliment and
              Courtship....12mo Bost. 4 00
——— ——— ——— ——————— ———16mo Bost. 1 50
Palmer, Roundell.   Book of Praise (8vo L.)16mo Camb. 1 25
Parton, J.   Humor. Poetry of Eng. Lang. 8vo Bost. 3 00
Parnassus : a Poetical Hand Book.   Notes
              by Emerson....12mo Bost.
a. Percy.   Reliques of Old English Poetry .. 8vo Phila. 3 50
——— The same, 3 vols.... ....16mo Lond. 3 75
Read, T. B.   Female Poets of America... 8vo Phila. 3 00
Schaff, P.   Christ in Song.... .. ..12mo N. Y. 2 25
Somers.   Selections from Modern French
              Poets.... L. 10s. 6d.
Universal Songster.   Illustrated.   3 vols. 8vo Lond. 9 00
Willmott.   Sacred Poets of the 19th Cent. 4to L. & P. 3 75
——— English Sacred Poetry....... 4to L. & N. 9 00

Poetry.—WORKS OF INDIVIDUAL POETS.

Akenside.   Poetical Works..............18mo Bost. 1 25
Akers, Elizabeth.   Poetical Works......16mo Bost. 1 50
Allingham, W.   Poetical Works.........16mo Bost. 1 50
Aldrich, T. B.   Poetical Works..........10mo Bost. 1 50
Allston, Wash.   Poetical Works.........12mo N. Y.
Ariosto.   Trans. by Hoole, 2 vols........ 8vo Lond.
——— Trans. by Rose, 2 vols..........12mo Bohn. 3 50

Aristophanes. Trans., 2 vols............	Bohn.	$5 00
Arnold, Matthew. Poetical Works......12mo Bost.		2 00
——— George. Poetical Works........12mo Bost.		2 00
Aytoun, Prof. Bothwell; a Poem.......12mo Bost.		1 25
——————— Lays of the Cavaliers....32mo N. Y.		
Bailey, P. J. Festus; a Poem...........12mo Bost.		1 00
————— The Mystic...............12mo Bost.		1 00
Barnes, William. Poems..............16mo Bost.		1 00
Barnes. Poems in the Dorset Dialect....12mo Bost.		2 50
Beattie. The Minstrel, and other Poems.18mo Bost.		1 25
Beranger. Poems. Trans. by Young... 12mo N. Y.		1 50
Bickersteth, E. H. "The Rock of Ages."		
Poems....12mo N. Y.		2 50
——————— Yesterday, To-Day and Forever.12mo N. Y.		2 00
Brownell, H. H. War Lyrics............16mo Bost.		1 50
Browning, Robert. Poetical Works, 2 v.16mo Bost.		8 00
——————— Mrs. Poems, 2 vols.........16mo N. Y.		5 00
——————— — (Dia. ed., 24mo. 1.50).12mo N. Y.		4 50
Bryant. Poetical Works, 3 vols.........12mo N. Y.		5 25
——— ——— Red line ed. 16mo $4.50.		
blue and gold...	N. Y.	1 50
——— ——— Illust. ed., calf........r. 8vo	N. Y.	12 00
Bulwer, R. L. ("Owen Meredith.") Poems.24mo N. Y.		1 50
Burns. Poetical Works, 3 vols..........18mo Bost.		8 75
——— Several editions in 1 vol.........	8vo N.Y.&P.	
——— Several editions in ....12mo N.Y.&P.		
——— Several Illust. editions........ ...	L. & N.	
Butler, Wm. Allen. Poems; Nothing to		
Wear, etc....16mo Bost.		2 00
Byron. Poetical Works, 10 vols........18mo Bost.		12 50
——— 1 vol. 8vo, N. Y. $3; Illustrated. 8vo Phila.		2 00
——— 1 vol. 12mo, L. & P. $2; Globe Ed.16mo L. & P.		1 50
——— 8 vols. 16mo Lond. $10; 16 vols.16mo Lond. £4.		
Camoens. Lusiad. Trans. by Quilliman.12mo Lond.		
Campbell, Thos. Poems, with Life by		
Sargent....12mo N. Y.		2 00
——— —— Poems, 18mo, Bost. $1.25...16mo N. Y.		1 25
——— —— Poems Illustrated.........; 8vo Phila.		
Cary, Alice. Ballads, Hymns, etc........12mo N. Y.		2 25
——— Phœbe. Poems of Faith, Hope and		
Love....12mo N. Y.		1 50
Catullus. Translated..................12mo Bohn.		2 50
Chatterton. Poems....................18mo Bost.		1 25
Chaucer. Poet'l Works, ed. by Morris, 6 v.16mo L. & P.		4 50
——— 1 vol. 8vo, Lond. $5.00; edited		
by Bell, 8 vols....16mo		6 00
Churchill. Poetical Works, 3 vols......18mo Bost.		8 75
Clough, A. H. Poems............'......12mo L. & N.		2 00
Coleridge. Poetical Works, 1 v. $1.50; 3 v.18mo Bost.		8 75
Collins. Poetical Works..............18mo Bost.		1 25
Collins, Gray & Goldsmith, by Sargent...12mo N. Y.		2 00
Crowley. Poetical Works, 3 vols.......18mo Lond.		8 75

Cowper. Poetical Works, (1 vol. $1.50) 3 v.18mo Bost. $3 75
————   ———— by Grimshaw, 8 v., $14.00
                by Cowper, 8 vols....12mo Lon. 25s.
Crabbe. Poetical Works, (1 vol. 8s 6d) 8 v.16mo Lon. 40s
Dana, R. H. Poems, 2 vols.........o. p.12mo N. Y.
Dante. Trans. by Cary.................12mo N. Y.   1 50
———— Inferno. Trans. by Parsons..... 8vo Bost.   5 00
———— Complete. By Longfellow, 3 vols.,
      r. 8vo.. $15.00 ; 3 vols...........16mo Bost.   6 00
De Vere, Aubrey. Poems, 3 vols........16mo Lon. 16s.
Dies Iræ. With various translations.....12mo N. Y.
Dobell, Sydney. Poems.................32mo Bost.   1 50
Donne. Poetical Works.................18mo Bost.   1 25
Drake, J. R. The Culprit Fay, Illust....18mo N. Y.   1 00
Drummond of Hawthornden. Poems....16mo Lond.
Dryden. Poetical Works, 5 vols.........18mo Bost.   6 25
———— Works, 1. 8vo, Lond. $5.00 ; 2 v. 8vo N. Y.   4 00
Elliott, E. Corn Law Rhymes, etc......r. 8vo Lond. 3s.
Emerson, R. W. Poems.................32mo Bost.   1 50
Faber, F. W. Hymns, Illust..........12mo North.   2 00
Falconer. Shipwreck, and other Poems..18mo Bost.   1 25
Frenau, Ph. Poems of the Revolution...12mo N. Y.   1 75
Gay. Poetical Works, 2 vols........... 18mo Bost.   2 50
Goethe. Reynard, the Fox, trans........   N. Y.   2 00
———— Faust. Trans. by Bayard Taylor,
            2 vols....r. 8vo Bost.   10 00
———— ———— cheaper ed., 2 vols....16mo Bost.   5 00
———— First part, trans. by Hayward..12mo Bost.   1 50
———— ———————— trans. by Brooks....12mo Bost.   1 50
Goldsmith. Poetical Works............18mo Bost.   1 25
———————— ————Illust. 8vo Lond. & 8vo L. & P.   2 75
———————— With Gray and Collins.....12mo N. Y.   2 00
———————— With his Prose W'ks, Globe
                edition....12mo L. & P.   1 50
Gray. Poetical Works..................18mo Bost.   1 25
——— ———— ———— Illust...........24mo L. & N.   1 25
——— ———— ———— Illust.......... 8vo Phila.
——. With Collins and Goldsmith.....12mo N. Y.   2 00
——— Elegy. Various Illust. editions..
Grun. The Last Knight. Trans. by Sargent. 8vo N. Y.   2 50
Halleck. Poetical Works (32mo, $1).....12mo N. Y.   2 50
Harte, Bret. Poems, 2 vols..........ea.12mo Bost.   1 50
Heber. Poems..............18mo Lond. 6s.
———— ———— with Crabbe, &c......... 8vo Phila.   1 50
Heine, H. Poems. Trans. by Leland....12mo Phila.   2 50
Hemans, Mrs. Poems (1 vol., $1.50), 2 v.16mo N. Y.   3 00
Herbert. Poetical Works (Lon., $1.50)...18mo Bost.   1 25
Herrick. Poetical Works, 2 v...........18mo Bost.   2 50
Hervey, T. K. Poems...............32mo Bost.   1 50
Hesiod. Callimachus and Theognis, Trans.12mo Bohn.   2 25
Hogg, Jas. Poet. W'ks (2 v. r. 8vo) 5 v.Glas.16mo 17s. 6d.
Holmes, O. W. Poems (32mo, $1.50). ...16mo Bost.   2 00

Holland, J. G.　Bitter Sweet; Katrina..*ea*.12mo N. Y.　$1 50
Homer.　Trans. by Cowper, 2 vols.......12mo Bohn.　3 50
————　———— by Pope, 3 vols......16mo N. Y.　2 25
————　———— —————— 2 vols........12mo Bohn.　5 00
————　literally translated, 2 vols......12mo N. Y.　3 00
————　Iliad.　Trans. by Bryant, 2 v...*r*. 8vo Bost.　10 00
————　———— ———— —— small ed., 2 v.16mo Bost.　5 00
————　Odyssey.　By the same, 2 vols..*r*. 8vo Bost. *ea*. 5 00
Hood, Thos.　Poetical Works, 3 vols.....12mo N. Y.　7 50
———— ————　Chief Poems, 2 vols. in 1...12mo N. Y.　3 00
———— ————　Poems. Illustrated edition. 4to N. Y.　8 00
———— ————　Poems, 5 vols...........18mo Bost.　6 25
Horace.　Literally trans. by Smart......12mo N. Y.　1 50
————　Odes, trans. by Martin........32mo Bost.　1 50
Hunt, Mrs. ("H. H.")　Poems.....:.....16mo Bost.　1 25
Hunt, Leigh.　Poems, 2 vols..........32mo Bost.　3 00
———— ————　Book of the Sonnet, 2 vols.16mo Bost.　3 00
Ingelow, Jean.　Poems (1 vol., $2.25), 2 v.16mo Bost.　3 50
"Jerningham," Mrs.　Journal (in verse)..12mo N. Y.　75
Juvenal and Persius.　Trans. literally...12mo N. Y.　1 50
Landor, W. S.　(In his Works.)
Larcom, Lucy.　Poems.................16mo Bost.　1 50
Lessing.　Nathan the Wise, a Poem.....16mo N. Y.　1 50
Lockyer.　Land Lyrics...............16mo Bost.　1 50
Lockhart.　Anc't Spanish Ballads........16mo N. Y.　1 00
Longfellow.　Poetical Works, fine ed., 4 v.16mo Bost.　10 00
———————　————— Cabinet ed., 2 v.16mo Bost.　4 00
———————　————— Red line ed. 1 v.16mo Bost.　4 50
———————　————— Diamond ed...32mo Bost.　1 50
———————　————— Illust. ed...... 8vo Bost.　12 00
———————　Separate Poems; do Illust.... Bost.
Lowell.　Poetical Works, 2 v...........16mo Bost.　4 00
————　———— —— Red line ed........16mo Bost.　4 50
————　———— —— Blue & gold ed., 2 v.32mo Bost.　3 00
Lucan, Pharsalia.　Trans...............12mo Bohn.　2 25
Lucretius.　Trans ....12mo Bohn.　2 25
Lytton, Lord Bulwer.　King Arthur. ... 12mo Lond.　1 50
————New Timon. Lost Tales of Miletus.12mo N. Y.　1 50
Macaulay.　Lays of Ancient Rome.......12mo N. Y.　1 00
Marvell, A.　Poetical Works...........18mo Bost.　1 25
Massey, Gerald.　Poetical Works, (32mo
　　　　　　　$1.50,) 2 vols....16mo Bost.　4 00
Meredith, Owen.　(Bulwer.) Poems. (32mo
　　　　　　　$7.50,) 5 vols....18mo Bost.　10 00
Miller, Joaquin.　Poems...............16mo Bost.　1 50
Millman, H. H.　Poetical Works, 3 vols..18mo Lon. 18s.
Milton.　(18mo, $1.50) 3 vols...........18mo Bost.　3 75
————　Fine ed'n, ed. by Brydes, 6 vols.. 8vo Lon. 30s.
————　———— —— by Mitford, 2 vols. 8vo Lon. 21s.
Montgomery, Jas.　(Br. P.) 5 vols.......18mo Lond.　6 25
Moore, Thos.　Poetical Works, 6 vols....18mo Bost.　7 50
————　————1 vol. 8vo N. Y. $3.00.12mo Lond.　50

Moore, Thos. Poetical Works, Globe ed..12mo L.& P.	$1	50
Morris, (Wm.) The Earthly Paradise, 3 v.16mo Bost.	4	50
———————— Life and Death of Jason..16mo Bost.	1	50
———————— Loves of Gudrun........16mo Bost.	1	00
Motherwell. Poems...................32mo Bost.	1	50
Muloch, Dinah. Poems, (32mo, $1.50)...18mo Bost.	2	00
Ossian. Poems.......................18mo L. 3s. 6d.		
Ovid. Translated, 3 vols.. ....12mo Bohn.	6	75
Palgrave, F. T. Lyrical Poems.........12mo L. & N.	1	75
Parnell. Poetical Works. (B. P.).......18mo Bost.	1	25
Parsons, T. W. Poems...............16mo Bost.	1	25
Petrarch. Trans. by Campbell.........12mo Bohn.	2	25
Pindar. Translated..................12mo Bohn.	2	50
Poe. Poetical Works, (Illust. $6.00).... 16mo N. Y.	1	75
Pollok. Course of Time, (24mo 75c.).....16mo N. Y.	1	25
Pope. Poetical Works, 3 vols...........18mo Bost.	3	75
———— (1 vol. 16mo $1.25; Illus. $1.50) 4 v.16mo Lon. 10s.		
Praed, W. M. Poetical Works, 2 vols.....12mo N. Y.	3	50
Prior. Poetical Works, (B. P.,) 2 vols....18mo Bost.	2	50
Proctor. ("Barry Cornwall.") Poems...12mo Bost.		
———— Adelaide. Poems, (32mo $1.50)..16mo Bost.	2	00
Propertius, Petronius and Secundus......12mo Bohn.	2	25
Ramsay, Allan. Edited by Mackay, 2 v..4to	32	00
Read, T. T. Poems, 3 vols..............16mo Phila.	5	25
Rogers, Samuel. Poetical Works, edited		
by Sargent....12mo N. Y.	2	00
———— ——— ————Illustrated.... 4to Phila.		
Rosetti, Chris. G. Poems..............16mo Bost.	1	75
———— Dante G. Poems................16mo Bost.	1	50
Saadi. Rose Garden of Persia. Trans...16mo Bost.	2	50
Sargent, Epes. "The Woman who Dared."12mo Bost.	1	50
Saxe, J. G. Poems. 32mo, $1.50; 16mo, $2.16mo Bost.	2	50
Schiller. Poems and Plays. Trans., 2 v.12mo Bohn	3	50
The same, trans. by various persons, 2v. r 8vo N. Y.	6	00
Schiller. Poems & Ballads. Tr. by Lytton.16mo N. Y.	1	60
Scott, Sir W. Poetical Works, 9 vols....18mo Bost.	11	25
————1 vol. 8vo, $3.00; 6 vols...........12mo N. Y.	7	50
————Red line ed., 16mo, $4.50; Globe ed.16mo Lond.	1	50
Shakespeare. Poems and Sonnets.......18mo Bost.	1	25
Shelley. Poetical Works, 4 vols.........18mo Bost.	5	00
———— Poems. Edited by Rosetti.....12mo Lond.	1	75
Shenstone. Poetical Works... ....18mo Bost.	1	25
Sigourney, Mrs. Poems................12mo		
Skelton. Poetical Works (B. P.), 3 vols..18mo Bost.	3	75
Smith, Horace & Jas. Rejected Addresses,		
etc....12mo N. Y.	2	00
Somerville. The Chase................		
Southey. Poetical Works (B. P.), 10 vols.18mo Bost.	12	50
———— ———— complete in 1 v. 8vo N. Y.	3	00
Spenser. Poetical Works (B. P.), 5 vols.18mo Bost.	6	25
———— Select, 18mo, $1.50; complete, 1 v.r.8vo L.& N.	4	00
Sprague, Chas. Poems................12mo Bost.	1	25

```
Stedman, E. C.  Poems, 3 v............12mo Bost.   $4 50
Stoddard.  Poems, 12mo, $1 ; new Poems,
                            2 vols....12mo Bost.    2 50
Stowe, Mrs.  Religious Poems..........16mo Bost.   2 00
Surrey, Earl of.  Poems (B. P.).........18mo Bost.   1 25
Swain, Chas.  Poems....... ..........16mo Bost.    1 50
Swift.  Poetical Works (B. P.), 3 vols....18mo Bost. .   3 75
Swinburne.  Atlanta in Calydon, etc., 2 v.12mo Bost.   4 00
Tasso   Translated by Fairfax...........12mo N. Y.
————— — Wiffen............16mo N. Y.    1 25
Taylor, Bayard.  Poems, 32mo, $1.50.....16mo Bost.   2 00
Taylor, H.  Philip Van Artevelde.......18mo Bost.   1 50
Tegner (Swedish).  Frithiof's Saga, ed. by
                      Bayard Taylor....16mo N. Y.   1 50
Tennyson.  Poetical Works, 2 vols.......16mo Bost.   4 00
—————     —————  Fireside ed., 10 v.16mo Bost.  10 00
—————     —————  12mo, $1.75 ; 2 v.32mo Bost.    3 00
—————     —————  Cheap ed., 8vo, N.Y. $1.25.24mo Bost.   1 50
—————     ————Various Illustrated ed's.
—————     ————The Last Tournament..12mo Bost.   1 25
—————·    ———— Separate Works, ea. $1. to     1 50
Terry, Rose.  Poems...................16mo Bost.   1 25
Thackeray.  Poems ...................12mo Bost.   1 25
Theocritus.  Trans. by Chapman........16mo Lond. .
Thompson.  Poetical Works (B. P.) 2 v...18mo Bost.   2 50
Tickell.  Poems ............... .......
Trowbridge.  The Vagabond & other Poems.16mo Bost.   1 50
Tuckerman, H. T.  Poems..............12mo Bost.   1 25
Tupper.  Proverbial Philosophy, various
                     editions.....N. & P. 75c. to   6 00
Vaughan.  Poems (B. P.)...............18mo Bost.   1 25
Virgil.  Trans. by Dryden, etc., 2 vols....18mo N. Y.   1 50
—————  Literal translation..........12mo N. Y.   1 50
Waller.  Poems, ed. by Bell...........16mo L. 2s. 6d.
Watson.  Beautiful Snow & other Poems.12mo Phila.   2 00
Watts.  Poetical Works (B. P.)..........18mo Bost.   1 25
Wesley, Chas.  Poems.................16mo N. Y.   1 50
White, H. K.  Poetical Works (B. P.)....18mo Bost.   1 25
Whitman, Walt.  Poems (Leaves of Grass),
                       2 vols....12mo N. Y.   2 50
Whittier.  Poetical Works (2 v., $5), 2 v.16mo Bost.   4 00
—————     ————— Red line edition..16mo Bost.   4 50
—————     ————— Blue and gilt, 2 v.16mo Bost.   3 00
—————     ————— various Illus. ed.
—————  Separate works..... .. ..ea.Bost.   $1 to 1 50
Wieland.  Oberon.  Trans. by Sotheby..
Willis, N. P.  Poems (Illust. ed., $6)....16mo N. Y.   1 60
Wilson, John.  Poems (in his works)....12mo Lond. 6s.
Wordsworth.  Poetical Works, 7 vols....18mo Bost.   3 75
—————     —————    1 vol..... 8vo Phila.   4 00
—————     ————— Choice Poems...........12mo Lond.   1 75
Wyatt, Sir Thos.  Poetical Works (B. P.).18mo Bost.   1 25
```

Young. Night Thoughts, and other Poems,
2 vols....18mo Bost. $2 50

Poetry.—HUMOROUS, COMIC, SATIRICAL, ETC.

Aytoun, W. E. Fermillian.............12mo
———— ———— . Bon Gaultier's Ballads...12mo L. 8s. 6d.
"Awful" and other Jingles. By P. R. S.12mo N. Y. 1 25
Barham. Ingoldsby Legends..........12mo N. Y. 2 25
Butler,(Saml). Hudibras,(16mo $1.25)2 v.18mo Bost. 2 50
———————————— various Eng. ed's.
Gilbert, W. S. The Bab Ballads.......12mo Phil. 1 75
Harte,(Bret.) Poems (in dialect),2 vols..12mo Bost. 3 00
————— —— ———— Red line ed. Illust.16mo Bost. 4 50
Hay, John. Pike County Ballads.......12mo Bost. 1 50
Juvenal and Persius. Satires, trans.....12mo Bohn. 2 25
Lear. A Book of Nonsense, Illust.......12mo N. Y. 1 50
Leland, C. G. Hans Breitmann Ballads,etc.12mo Phil. 2 00
Lowell, J. R. Fable for Critics.........12mo Bost. 75
———————— Bigelow Papers, 2 vols....12mo Bost. 3 00
Parton. Humorous Poet. of the Eng. Lang. 8vo Bost. 3 00
Trumbull, J. McFingal, an Epic........16mo N. Y. 1 50

Poisons.

Christisson. Treatise on Poisons........ 8vo Lon.10s.
Horsley. Toxicologists' Guide..........12mo Lond. 3s. 6d.

Poland.

Corner. History of Poland and Russia..18mo L. 3s. 6d.
Day. Russian Gov't in Poland. 1867... 8vo Lond.
Dunham. History of Poland......Lond.16mo 3s. 6d.
Edwards. Polish Insurrec. of 1863, 2 vols.16mo Lond.
Fletcher. History of Poland...........18mo N. Y. 75
Van Zandt. History of Poland.........

Polar Regions.—[*See Arctic.*]

Political Economy.—[*See also Banking, Free Trade, Money,*
Protection, Taxation.]

Bentham, Jer. Works, 11 vols......... 8vo Edinb. 28 00
Bowen, F. Political Economy.......... 8vo Bost. 2 50
Carey. Political Economy, 3 vols........ 8vo Phila. 10 00
Cairnes, J. E. Political Economy....... 8vo Lond. 6s.
Champlin. Political Economy........12mo N. Y. 1 25
Colton, C. C. Public Economy of U. S... 8vo N. Y. 2 25
De Quincey. Logic of Political Economy.12mo Bost. 1 50
Elder, Wm. Questions of Pub. Policy, etc. 8vo Phila.
Gevons, W. S. Theory of Polit. Econ. 1871.12mo Lon. 9s.
Greeley. Science of Political Economy..12mo Bost. 1 50
Malthus, T. Political Economy....Lond.12mo 3s. 6d.
———— — On Population, 2 vols....... 8vo Lond.
McCulloch. Literature of Political Econ. 8vo Lon. 14s.
———————— Indust'l Hist. of Free Trade. 8vo Lond.
———————— Political Economy.........12mo Lond. 1 75

Portraits.—

Gallery of Portraits. Edited by Charles
Knight, 7 vols....*r*. 8vo Lond.
National Portrait Gallery (Amer.). Edited
by Duyckinck, 2 v... 4to N. Y.
———————————— (English) 5 vols. ...*r*. 8vo L. £8.

Portugal.—[*See Spain.*]

Positivism.—[*See Metaphysics.*]

Comte, A. Positive Philosophy......... 8vo N. Y.
Mill, J. S. Comte and Positivism........12mo Lond.

Poultry.—[*See also Agriculture.*]

Bement. Poulterer's Companion.........12mo N. Y. $2 00
Cooper, J. W. Game Fowls............
Doyle. Illust. Book of Poultry, col. plates. 8vo Lond. 2 50
Piper, H. Profits. & Ornamental Poultry.12mo Lond. 1 75
Poultry Yard..........................18mo Lond. 50
Richardson. Domestic Poultry.........18mo N. Y.
Saunders. Domestic Poultry...........12mo N. Y. 75
Tegetmeir, W. B. Poultry Book col'd...*r*. 8vo Lond. 9 00
Wright L. Practical Poultry Keeper....12mo N. Y. 2 00

Prayers.—[*See Devotion.*]

Preaching and Preachers.—[*See also Sermons.*]

Gould, S. B. Post Mediæval Preachers..16mo Lond.
Hood, E. P. Lamps, Pitchers & Trumpets.12mo L. 10s. 6d.
Hoppin, J. M. Office & Work of Christian
Ministry....12mo N. Y. 3 50
Jackson. Curiosities of Pulpit Literature.12mo Lond. 2 00
Pulpit Themes & Preacher's Assistant...12mo N. Y. 2 00
Ramsay, E. B. Pulpit Table Talk.......16mo L. 3s 6d.
Zincke. Extempore Preaching.........12mo N. Y. 1 50

Precious Stones.—[*See Gems.*]

Printing.

Humphrey. History of Printing. Illust. folio Lond. 26 00
Mackellar, T. American Printer.........12mo Phila. 1 50
Pearson, E. C. Güttenberg & the Art of
Printing ...12mo Bost. 2 00
Ringwalt. American Cyclo. of Printing.. 8vo N. Y. 10 00
Savage. Dictionary of Printing........ 8vo Lon. 12s.

Prisons.—[*See Crimes and Punishments.*]

Protoplasm.

Beale, L. S. Protoplasm ; Life, Force, etc.12mo L. 6s. 6d.
———————— Mystery of Life...........
Sterling, J. H. As Regards Protoplasm..
Tyson, Jas. The Cell Doctrine.........12mo Phila. 2 00

Proverbs.

Fielding. Proverbs of all Nations.......16mo Lond. $1 25
Hand Book of English Proverbs.........12mo Bohn. 2 50
Kelly, W. K. Proverbs of all Nations,
       Exp'd, etc....12mo Andov. 1 25
Polyglott of Foreign Proverbs...........12mo Bohn 2 50
Proverbs of Solomon, in Eng., Fren. & Ital.16mo L. 3s. 6d.

Prussia.—[*See Germany.*]

Carlyle. Frederick the Great, 6 vols.....12mo N. Y. 12 00
History of Prussia. By M. A. D....:....16mo Lond.
Ranke. Memoirs of House of Branden-
       burg, 3 vols.... 8vo Lon. 36s.
Vehse. Memoirs of Court of Prussia....12mo L. 6s. 6d.

Psychology.—[*See Metaphysics.*]

Punctuation.

Wilson, J. Punctuation................12mo Bost. 1 50

Puritans.—[*See also New England.*]

Felt, J. Ecclesiast. Hist. of N. England, 2 v. 8vo
Hall. The Puritans & their Principles.. 8vo N. Y. 2 50
Martyn, W. C. Hist. of English Puritans.12mo N. Y. 1 25
———— ———— Pilgrim Fathers of N. E.12mo N. Y. 1 25
Neal. History of the Puritans, 2 v...... 8vo N. Y. 5 00

Puzzles.—[*See Conundrums, etc.*]

Pyramids.—[*See Egypt.*]

Pyrotechnist's Compan. By G. W. Mortimer.12mo 1 25

Quotations.—[*See also Extracts, Selections.*]

a. Bartlett. Dictionary of Quotations .....12mo Bost. 3 00
Ballou, M. M. Treasury of Thought; En-
    cyclopedia of Quotations ... 8vo Bost.
Dictionary of Latin Quotations.........:..12mo Bohn 2 50
a. Great Truths from Great Authors....... 8vo Phila. 2 00
Ramage. Beautiful Thoughts from Greek,
   Lat., Fren., Ger., Span. & Ital. authors,
   with orig. text, 4 vols...............12mo Lond. 12_00
Southgate. Many Thoughts of Many
        Minds.... 8vo L. 10s. 6d.
      Second Series......... 8vo L. 12s. 6d.
Thompson. Sentences f'm Gr'k Dramatists.16mo Edinb.
Things Old and New, or Storehouse of
        Similes.... 8vo Lond. 7 00

Railroads.

Chambers, W. About Railways.........12mo Lond.
Dodd, G.W. Railways, Steamers & Telegs.12mo Lond.
Poor, H. V. Manual of Railroads in U. S. 8vo N. Y. 5 00

Rationalism.—[*See Infidelity.*]

Reading.—[*See also Bibliography and Literature.*]

Moore, C. H.   What to Read & How to Read.16mo N Y.   **$**   75
Porter, Noah.   Books and Reading......12mo N. Y.   2 00
Potter, Bishop.   Hand Book for Students
                              and Readers....18mo N. Y.   75
Poole, W. F.   Index to Periodicals...... 8vo Bost.
Pycroft.   Course of Reading (by Spencer).12mo N. Y.   1 25
Todd, John.   The Student's Manual......12mo North.   1 50
Willmot, R. A.   Pleasures of Literature.   Lond. 5s.

Rebellion.—[*See under England & United States.*]

Reference Books.—[*See Dictionaries, Encyclopedias and under names of Subjects.*]

Reform.—[*See Sociology, Temperance & Women's Rights*]

Reformation.—[*See Church History.*]

Religion.—[*See also Bible, Christianity, Church History, Devotion, Evidences of Christianity, Heathenism, Science & Religion.*]

Beard, J. R.   Progress of Relig. Thought. 8vo Bost.   1 75
Beecher, H. W.   Lecture Room Talks...12mo N. Y.   2 50
Clarke, J. F.   Ten Great Religious Beliefs.12mo Bost.   3 00
Goulburn, E. M.   Thoughts on Personal
                                       Religion ...12mo N. Y.   1 00
——————— Pursuit of Holiness..12mo N. Y.   75
Gould, S. B.   Origin of Religious Belief, 2 v.12mo N. Y.   4 00
Hunt, J.   Relig. Thought in England, 2 v. 8vo L. 42s.
Moffatt.   Comparative Hist. of Religions.12mo N. Y.   1 75

Revenue.—[*See Free Trade, Political Economy, Protection, and Taxation.*]

Revolution.—[*See under France and United States.*]

Rhetoric.—[*See also Elocution and Oratory.*]

a. Bain.   Composition and Rhetoric.......12mo N. Y.   1 75
Bascom.   Philosophy of Rhetoric........12mo N. Y.   1 50
Blair.   Treatise on Rhetoric............. 8vo N. Y.   3 00
——— ——————— Edited by A. Mills.12mo N. Y.   1 50
Campbell.   Philosophy of Rhetoric...... 8vo N. Y.   1 50
Coppee.   Elements of Rhetoric.........12mo Phila.   1 60
Kerl.   Composition and Rhetoric.......12mo N. Y.   1 25
Whately.   Elements of Rhetoric.......12mo Bost.   1 75

Rhode Island.

Arnold, S. G.   History of Rhode Island, 2 v. 8vo N. Y.   6 00
Peterson.   History of Rhode Island...... 8vo N. Y.

Romance.—[*See Fiction.*]

Romanism.—[*See also Church History.*]

Burk.   Mediæval Popes, 4 vols.......... 8vo Lon. 42s.

Dollinger.   Fables about Popes of Middle
                   Ages.... 8vo Lon. 14s.
Dowling, J.   History of Romanism...... 8vo N. Y.
Moehler, J. A.   Symbolism.............. 8vo N. Y. $4 00
Pressensé.   Rome and Italy; Opening of
                 Council....12mo N. Y.   1 50
a. Ranke.   History of the Popes, 3 vols....12mo Bohn   5 25
Rome and the Popes.   From the German
             of Brandes....12mo N. Y.   1 25
Spalding.   (Roman Catholic) History of
             the Reformation.... 8vo N. Y.   3 50
———— Review of D'Aubigne's Refor.12mo Lon. 3s.6s.
———— Lect. on Evid. of Catholicity. 8vo N. Y.   2 00
Wiseman, Cardinal.   Mem'ls of Four Popes. 8vo N. Y.   1 50
———— —— Doctrines of the Cath. Ch'h.12mo N. Y.   2 00

Rome—(Ancient)—Roman Empire.

(1.) Ancient Writers.

Livy.   History.   Trans., 4 vols..........12mo Bohn   9 00
Plutarch.   Civil Wars of Rome.   Trans.
                 by Long....
Polybius.   General History............
Sallust.   Trans. by Rose. ....12mo Bohn   2 25
Suetonius. Trans. by Thompson........12mo Bohn   2 25
Tacitus.   Literally translated........2 v.12mo Bohn   4 50
———— Trans. by Murphy.........1 v. 8vo N. Y.

(2.) Modern Writers.

a. Arnold, Thomas.   History of Rome...... 8vo N. Y.   4 50
———— —— Later Rom. Com'nwealth, 2 v. 8vo Lon. 24s.
Bonner.   Child's History of Rome, 2 v...16mo N. Y.   2 50
De Quincey.   The Cæsars..............16mo Bost.   1 25
b. Dyer, T. H.   History of Kings of Rome.. 8vo Lond.   5 00
———— History of the City of Rome. 8vo Lond.
b. Gibbon.   Decline & Fall of Rom. Emp., 8 v. 8vo Lon. 60s.
———— The same, 6 vols..............12mo N. Y.   9 00
a. ———— The same, complete in 3 vols...12mo N. Y.   7 50
———— The Student's edition, condensed.12mo N. Y.   2 00
Goodrich.   Pictorial History of Rome...12mo Phila.   1 75
Liddell.   Student's History of Rome.....12mo N. Y.   2 00
Long.   Decline of Roman Republic......
Lord, John.   The Old Roman World.... 8vo N. Y.   3 00
Merivale.   Hist. of Roman Empire, 7 v.. 8vo N. Y.   14 00
———— Conversion of Roman Empire. 8vo N. Y.   1 50
Michelet.   History of Roman Republic...12mo Bohn   1 75
b. Mommsen.   History of Rome, 4 vols....12mo N. Y.   8 00
Niebuhr.   History of Rome, 3 vols...... 8vo Lon. 36s.
———— Lectures on Hist. of Rome, 3 v.12mo Phila.   5 00
Pictorial History of Rome, 3 vols...:.....12mo Glasg.   9 00
Schmitz.   Roman History.............. 8vo L. 7s. 6d.
Sewell.   Child's History of Rome.......16mo N. Y.   75
b. Sismondi.   Fall of the Roman Empire, 2 v.   Lond.   4 00

Smith. Smaller History of Rome.......16mo N. Y. $1 00
a. —— Student's Gibbon..............12mo N. Y. 2 00

Rome.—(3) MANNERS AND CUSTOMS.

Arnoy, M. d'. Private Life of the Romans.
a. Becker. Gallus; or Life among the Romans.12mo N. Y. 3 50
Forsyth. Life of Cicero, &c. [See Biog.]
Knight. Social Life of the Romans.....
Novels Illustrating Roman Life, viz :
Croly—Salathiel. De Mille—Helena's Household. Kingsley's Hypatia. Lockhart's Valerius. Ware's Probus or Aurelian. [See Fiction.]

—— MODERN (CITY).

Butler, C. M. Inner Rome.............12mo Phila. 1 75
—————— St. Paul in Rome........12mo Phila. 1 75
Eaton. Rome in the 19th Century, 2 vols.12mo Bohn 5 00
Eustace. Classical Tour in Italy, 3 vols.16mo L. 10s. 6d.
b. Gell. Topography of Rome, new ed., 2 v. 8vo Lond. 4 50
b. Hawthorne, Mrs. England and Italy ...12mo N. Y. 2 00
a. Hare. Walks in Rome. 1871...........12mo Lond. 3 50
Kip, Bishop. Christmas Holidays in R.12mo N. Y. 1 75
—— The Catacombs of Rome...........18mo N. Y.
Murray. Hand Book to Rome........12mo Lond. 9s.
Roma Sotteranea. Trans. by Northcote. 8vo L. 31s. 6.
a. Story, W. W. Roba di Roma......... 8vo L. & P. 4 00
a. Taine. Rome and Naples............. 8vo N. Y. 2 50

Rural Sports.—[See also Hunting, Angling, etc.]

Blaine. Encyclopedia of Rural Sports... 8vo Lon. 42s.
Strutt. Sports and Pastimes of People of
England.... 8vo Lond. 3 00
Walsh ("Stonehenge"). Cyclo. of Rural
Sports.... 8vo Lond. 7 00
White. History of British Turf, 2 vols... 8vo Lond. 6 00

Russia.—[See also Crimean War, Siberia.]

b. Bell, R. History of Russia, 3 vols. Lond.18mo 10s. 6d.
Bremner, R. Interior of Russia, 2 vols.. Lon. 21s.
Bush. Reindeer Dogs and Snow Shoes... 8vo N. Y. 3 00
, Dixon, W. H. Free Russia .... 8vo N. Y. 2 00
Gurowski, A de. Russia as it Is.........12mo N. Y. 1 00
Jermann. Pictures from St. Petersburg.12mo N. Y. 1 00
a. Kelly, W. R. History of Russia, 2 vols..12mo Bohn. 3 50
Kohl, J. G. Russia and the Russians.... 8vo Lon. 5s.
Maxwell. The Czar, his Court and People.12mo N. Y.
Morley, H. Sketches of Russian Life ('66).16mo Lond.
Oliphant, L. Russian Shores of the Black
Sea.... 8vo Lon. 14s.
Proctor, Edna D. A Russian Journey....12mo Bost. 1 25
Schmitzler. Secret History of the Court
of Russia, 2 vols.... 8vo Lon. 28s.
Schmucker. Life of Catherine II........12mo Phila. 1 75
—————— Life of Nicholas I..........12mo Phila. 1 75

Stephens, J. L.   Greece, Russia, Poland,
                 etc., 2 vols....12mo N. Y. $3 00
a. Taylor, Bayard.   Greece and Russia.....12mo N. Y.   1 50

Sacred History.—[*See Bible, Christianity, Church History, Religion, Romanism, Monastic Orders.*]

Sacred Poetry.—[*See under Poetry.*]

St. Domingo.

Chazotte.   Insurrection in St. Domingo...
Franklin.   Present State of Hayti........

Sandwich Islands.

Cheever, H. T.   Life in Sandwich Islands.12mo N. Y.   1 50
Jarves, J. J.   Hist. of Sandwich Islands.. 8vo L. 3s. 6d.
Simpson, A.   Sandwich Islands........ 8vo Lond. 4s.

Saracens.—[*See Arabia, Arabs, Africa, and Mohammed (Biography).*]

Sardinia.

Murray.   Hand-B'k for Sardinia, Genoa, etc.12mo Lond. 9s.
Tyndale, J. W.   Island of Sardinia, 3 vols. 8vo L. 31s. 6d.

Satire.—[*See under Comic Poetry, Humorous Works.*]

Scandinavia.—[*See also Denmark, Norway, Sweden.*]

Browne, J. Ross.   The Land of Thor. Ill.12mo N. Y.   2 00
Crichton, A., & Wheaton, H.   History of
           Scandinavia, 2 vols....18mo N. Y.   1 50
a. Mallett.   Northern Antiquities.........12mo Lond.   2 50
Sinding, Paul.   History of Scandinavia..12mo N. Y.
a. Taylor, Bayard.   Northern Travel: Den-
           mark, etc....12mo N. Y.   1 50
b. Wheaton, H.   History of the Northmen.. 8vo Phila

Schools.—[*See Education.*]

School Architecture.

Johannot, Jas.   School Houses......... 8vo N. Y.

Schleswig-Holstein.

Bunsen, C. C. J. von.   Schleswig and Hol-
           stein. Lond.... 8vo 3s. 6d.
Dicey, E.   The Schleswig-Holstein War, 2 v.16mo Lond.

Science.—[*See Natural History, Natural Philosophy, Natural Science, Natural Theology, and names of Sciences.*]

Science and Religion.—[*See also Natural Theology.*]

Adams.   Elements of Christ. Science '50..   Phila.
a. Argyll, Duke of.   The Reign of Law,....12mo L. & N.   2 00
Babbage, C.   Ninth Bridgewater Treatise. 8vo L. 9s. 6d.
a. Bascom, John.   Science, Philosophy and
           Religion....12mo N. Y.   1 75

Bremer, Rev. Dr.   Theology in Science...12mo L. & N. $2 00
a. Chadbourne, P. A.   Natural Theology...12mo N. Y.   1 75
b. Child, G. C.   Benedicite : The Power, Wis-
          dom, etc., of God in Creation..12mo N. Y.   2 00
Cooke, J.   Religion and Chemistry......12mo Lond.   1 00
Excelsior.   Helps to Prog. in Relig., 6 v.12mo Lon. 14s.
Hitchcock, E.   Religion and Geology....12mo Bost.   1 75
Morris, Rev. H. W.   Science and the Bible. 8vo Phila.   3 75
Pater Mundi, or Modern Science and a
          Heavenly Father....12mo Bost.   1 50
Porter, Noah.   The Sciences of Nature vs.
          The Science of Man....12mo N. Y.   1 00
b. Rawlinson.   Historical Evidences of Scrip-
          ture Records....12mo Bost.   1 75
Sidney, Rev.   Conversations on the Bible
          and Science....12mo L. & N.   2 00
Sutton, G.   Faith and Science.......... 8vo Lond. 9s.
Thompson, J. P.   Man in Genesis and Geol.12mo N. Y.   1 00
Walker, J. B.   God Revealed in Nature
          and Christ....12mo N. Y.   1 50

Scotland.—[*See Biography, Mary Queen of Scots, etc.*]
Abbott, Jacob.   A Summer in Scotland...12mo N. Y.   1 75
Boswell, J.   A Tour to the Hebrides.....12mo L. 3s. 6d.
Buchanan (and others).   Hist. of Scotland. 8vo Glasg. 15s.
b. Burton, J. H.   History of Scotland, 2 v.. 8vo L. 26s.
Chambers.   Hist. of Rebellions in Scot...18mo Edin. 4s.
Hunnewell.   The Lands of Scott........12mo Bost.   2 50
Laing.   History of Scotland, 4 vols...... 8vo. Lond.
Mackenzie.   History of Scotland........ 8vo L. & N.   3 50
Maxwell.   The Battle Hist. of Scotland..12mo L. & N.   2 50
Mignet.   Hist. of Mary Queen of Scots... 8vo Lon. 6s.
Ramsay.   Scottish Life and Character....16mo Bost.   1 50
a. Robertson.   Hist. of Scotland under Mary. 8vo N. Y.   2 00
Rogers, C.   Scotland, Social & Domestic. 8vo Lon. 21s.
a. Scott, Sir.   Hist. of Scotland, 2 vols.....12mo Lon. 7s.
—— ——   Tales of a Grandfather, 6 vols.   Bost.   7 50
—— ——   The same, 4 vols...........   Phila.   5 00
Sinclair.   Scotland and the Scotch......12mo Ed. 2s. 6d.
b. Strickland, Miss.   Lives of the Queens of
          Scotland, 8 vols....12mo N. Y.   12 00
Stuart, G.   Scotland under Mary........
Tytler.   History of Scotland, 4 vols in 2.. 8vo Edn. 9s.

Scriptures.—[*See Bible.*]

Sculpture.—[*See Fine Arts.*]

Secession.—[*See Rebellion*—under *United States.*]

Secret Societies.

Findell.   History of Freemasonry....... 8vo L. 10s. 6d.
Fox, T. L.   Freemasonry in England....16mo Lond.

Greene, S. D.   Broken Seal, or the Morgan
                              Abduction....12mo Bost. $1 50
James, G. P. R. History of Secret Societies
                          of the Middle Ages....
Jennings, H. The Rosicrucians.........12mo Lond.
Rebold, E. Freemasonry in Europe.....8vo Cincin.
Stearns, J. G. Inquiry into Freemas. 1858.18mo Utica
——— —— Letters on Freemasonry. 1860.12mo Utica

Selections—EXTRACTS.—[*See also Quotations.*]

a. Knight. Half Hours with best Authors,
              etc. [*See Literature and History.*]
    Laconics ; or, the best Words of the best
                          Authors, 3 vols....16mo L. 7s. 6d.
b. Landor. Selections from. By Hillard...8vo Bost.   2 50
    Milton. Treasures from Prose Writings of.18mo Bost.   2 50
    Montagu, Basil. Selections from Taylor,
                          Hooker, Barrow, etc..12mo N. Y.   1 50
    Parton. The Words of Washington, se-
                          lected, etc...16mo Bost.   1 00
    Saunders. Salad for the Solitary, etc....12mo N. Y.   4 00
    Selections from Jeremy Taylor.........16mo Bost.   1 25
a. Smith, Sydney. Wit and Wisdom of.
                          Edited by Duyckinck..12mo N. Y.   2 25
    Southgate. Noble Thoughts in Noble
                          Language....8vo Lond.
    ——— —— Many Thoughts of Many Many
                          Minds, 2 series, *ea.* 8vo L. 12s. 6d.
    Townsend. Everyday Book of Mod. Lit. sq. 8vo Lond.   4 00

Sermons.—[*See also Preaching and Preachers.*]

⁎⁎⁎ This selection is obviously meagre.

Arnold, Thos. Serms. on Christ. Life, 2 v.12mo N. Y.   4 00
Beecher, H. W. Sermons, 4 vols........8vo N. Y. *ea.*2 50
Blair, Hugh. Sermons................8vo N. Y.   2 00
Burns. ,Cyclopedia of Sermons.........8vo N. Y.   2 50
Bushnell. Sermons for the New Life....12mo N. Y.   2 00
Butler, Bp. Sermons.................12mo Bohn.   2 50
Collyer, Robert. Nature and Life......12mo Bost.   1 50
Hall, Newman. Sermons..............12mo N. Y.   1 75
Melville, Henry. Sermons, 2 vols......*r.* 8vo N. Y.   5 00
Murray, W. H. H. Music Hall Sermons..12mo Bost.   1 50
Pulpit Cyclopedia & Ministers' Companion. 8vo N. Y.   2 50
Robertson, F. W. Sermons, 4 vols. in 1..8vo Bost.   2 00
South, Bishop. Sermons, 5 vols........8vo N. Y.   20 00
Spurgeon. Sermons, 8 series.........*ea.*12mo N. Y.   1 50
Sketches and Skeletons of 500 Sermons..8vo N. Y.   2 00
Taylor, Jeremy. Sermons (select).......12mo L. 3s. 6d.

Servia. Ranke. History of Servia.....:...12mo Bohn   1 75

Sewing Machine.
    Green. History of Sewing Machines, '64. 8vo Lond.   3 75

Shakespeare.—[*See under Drama.*]

Sheep.

Jennings. Sheep, Swine and Poultry....12mo N. Y. $1 75
Morrell. American Shepherd...........12mo N. Y.   1 75
Randall. Sheep Husbandry........ ...12mo N. Y.   1 50
———— Fine Wool Husbandry........12mo N. Y.   1 00
Youatt. On Sheep............ ....12mo Phila. 1 00

Shetland—THE ORKNEYS, ETC.

Sinclair, Cath. Shetland and Shetlanders.12mo L. 2s. 6d.
Weld, C. R. Highlands, Orcadia and Skye. 8vo L. 12s. 6d.

Ships.—[*See Navigation.*]

Shipwrecks, etc.

Barrow. The Mutiny of the Bounty.....18mo N. Y.   75
Belcher, Lady. Mutiny of the Bounty... 8vo L. 12s.
Goodrich. Man upon the Sea.......... 8vo Phila. 2 25
Perils of the Sea......................18mo N. Y.   75
Redding, C. Shipwrecks and Disasters at
                    Sea, 4 vols....16mo Lon. 14s.

Shooting.—[*See Hunting.*]

Short Hand.—[*See Phonography.*]

Siam.

Bowring, Sir J. People and Kingdom of
                    Siam, 2 vols.... 8vo Lon. 32s.
Leonowens, Mrs. A. H. English Governess
                    at the Court of Siam....12mo Bost.   3 00
Mouhot, H. Trav. in Siam. 1858–60. 2 v. 8vo Lon. 32s.

Siberia.

Atkinson, T. W. Orien. and West. Siberia. 8vo N. Y.   3 50
———— ———— The same..............12mo Phila. 1 75
———— ———— Amoor River......r. 8vo Lon. 42s.
Bush. Reindeer Dogs and Snow Shoes.. 8vo N. Y.   3 00
Erman. Travels in Siberia, 2 vols. ..... 8vo L. 31s. 6d.
Kennan. Tent Life in Siberia.........12mo N. Y.   2 00
Muller & Pallas. Conquest of Siberia...
Pallas. Travels in Siberia.............

Sicily.—[*See also Italy.*]

Amari. Hist. of the Sicilian Vespers, 3 v.12mo L. 31s. 6d.
Tuckerman, H. T. Sicily : a Pilgrimage..12mo N. Y.   75

Skating.

Anderson, G. Art of Skating..........12mo L. 2s. 6d.
Vandervell & Witham. System of Figure
                    Skating....12mo Lond. 6s.

Singing.

Seiler. The Voice in Singing, from the
                    German....12mo Phila. 1 50

Skepticism.—[*See Infidelity.*]

Sketches.—[*See Essays.*]

Sleep.—[*See also Dreams.*]

    Hall, W. W.   On Sleep................⸱.......12mo N. Y. $1 50
    Macnish.   Philosophy of Sleep........,.12mo Glasg. 1s.

Social Science—" SOCIOLOGY."—[*See also Charities, Coopera-*
                 tion, Labor, Political Economy, Women's Rights.]

    Booth, A. T.   St. Simon and St. Simonians. 8vo L. 7s. 6d.
    Carey, H. C.   Past, Present and Future.. 8vo Phila.   2 50
    ———— ——   Princip. of Soc. Science, 3 v. 8vo Phila. 10 50
    ———— ——   The same, ab'd by McKean. 8vo Phila.   2 50
    Coxe, A. C.   Moral Reforms Suggested..12mo Phila.   1 00
    Chapin, E. H.   Moral Aspects of City Life.12mo N. Y.   1 00
    Dall, C. H. The College, Market and Court.12mo Bost.   2 50
    Elder, Wm.   Questions of the Day, Econ-
                 omic and Social.... 8vo Phila.   3 00
    Foote, E. B.   Social Life Analyzed and Ill.12mo N. Y.   3 25
    Galton, F. Heredit'y Genius, its Laws, etc. 8vo N. Y.   2 00
    Ginx's Baby : His Birth and other Misfortunes. (Satire
          on London Charities, by Jenkins)..12mo N. Y.   1 50
    Greenwood, J. The Seven Curses of Lond.12mo Bost.   1 50
    Hamley, Col.   Our Poor Relations. Lon.12mo 3s. 6d.
    Lord Bantam.   By the Author of Ginx's
                   Baby....12mo L. & N.
    Mackinnon, W. A. Hist. of Civilization, 2 v. 8vo Lond.   7 50
    Spencer, Herbert.   Social Statics........12mo N. Y.   2 50

Solar System.—[*See Astronomy.*]

Songs.—[*See Ballads, Poetry.*]

Sound.—[*See Acoustics.*]

South America.—[*See America, South, and names of*
                 each Country.]

    Grimshaw.   History of South America..12mo Phila.   1 00
    Hassaurek.   Four Years among Spanish
                   Americans....12mo N. Y.   1 75
    Head. Journey across the Pampas & Andes.12mo L. 2s.
    Paez, R.   Travs. in So. & Cent'l Am.*plates.* 8vo N. Y.   3 00
    Waterston.   Travels in South America..12mo L. 5s.

South Seas.—[*See East Indies, Pacific, Polynesia, etc.*]

Southern States.—[*See United States and Separate States.*]

South Carolina.

    Ramsay.   Hist. of Revolution in S. Caro. 8vo
    Simms, W. G.   Hist. of South Carolina..

Spain and Portugal.—[*See also Peninsular War.*]

    Abbott, J. S. C. Romance of Spanish Hist.12mo N. Y.   2 00
    Andersen, Hans C.   In Spain............12mo N. Y.   2 25

Attaché at Madrid ; Court of Isabella II..12mo N. Y. $1 00
Byrne, Mrs.W. P. Cosas de Espana, lll. 2v. 8vo Lond.   7 50
Baxter, W. E.   Portugal, Spain & Italy, 2 v. 8vo L. 21s.
Callcott, Mrs.   History of Spain & Port., 2v.12mo L. 12s.
Condé.   The Arabs in Spain, 3 vols......12mo Bohn   5 25
Dunham.   Hist. of Spain & Portugal, 5 v.12mo L. 17s. 6d.
Florian.   The Moors in Spain..........18mo
Ford, R.   The Spaniards & their Country.12mo N. Y.   1 50
———   Hand Book for Spain, 2 vols...12mo L. 30s.
Gautier.   Wanderings in Spain. 1853...12mo Lond.
Hay, John.   Castilian Days..........:...12mo Bost.   2 00
Herbert, Lady.   Impressions of Spain... 8vo N. Y.   2 00
Historical Sketches of Portugal... ......12mo L. 5s.
Irving, Wash.   The Conquest of Granada.12mo N. Y.   2 25
——— ——— Same, cheaper ed'n, $1.25 and   1 75
——— ——— Alhambra, $1.25, $1.75..12mo N. Y.   2 25
Mackenzie, A. Slidell. A Year in Spain, 3v.12mo N. Y.   3 75
——— ——— Spain Revisited, 2 v.12mo N. Y.   3 50
Mahon, Lord.   War of Succession in Spain. 8vo L. 15s.
——— ——— Spain under Charles II.... 8vo L. 6s.
March, C. W.   Madeira & Portugal......12mo N. Y.
Murray. Hand Book for Portugal.......12mo L. 7s. 6d.
Prescott, W. H.   Reign of Ferdinand and
                    Isabella, 3 vols.... 8vo Phila.   7 50
——— ———   Phillip II., 3 vols....... 8vo Phila.   7 50
——— ——— — Ed. of Robertson's Chas.V., 3v. 8vo Phila.   7 50
Spanish Pictures, drawn with Pen and
                    Pencil....r. 8vo Lond.   3 75
Thornbury.   Life in Spain, 2 vols........12mo N. Y.   1 50
Ticknor.   Hist. of Spanish Literature, 3 v.12mo Bost. 10 00
Wallis, S. T.   Glimpses of Spain........12mo N. Y.   1 50
——— ——— Spain, her Institutions, &c.12mo Bost.   1 50
Wells, N. A.   Picturesque Antiqs. of S. r. 8vo L. 8s. 6d.

Spectroscope.

Huggins.   Spectrum Analysis..........12mo Lond.
Roscoe, W. E.   Spectrum Analysis......12mo L. 21s.
Schellen.   Spectrum Analysis. Notes by
                    Huggins.... 8vo Lon. 28s.

Speeches.—[*See Oratory.*]

Spiritualism.—[*See also Demonology and Witchcraft, Super-
                    natural.*]

Ashburner, J.   Animal Magnetism and
                    Spiritualism....12mo L. 12s. 6d.
Brittan, S. B.   Man and his Relations.... 8vo N. Y.   4 00
Davis, J.   Death and After Life........12mo Bost.   75
———   Other works, 7 vols..........12mo Bost.   8 00
Hammond, W. A.   Physics & Physiology
                    of Spiritualism....12mo N. Y.   1 00
Hardinge, Emma.   Modern American
                    Spiritualism.... 8vo N. Y.   3 50

Owen. R. D.   Footfalls on the Boundary
                 of another World....12mo Phila. $2 00
—— —— The Debatable Land between
                 this World and the Next..12mo N. Y.   2 00
Report on Spiritualism, of the London
                 Dialectic Society.... 8vo L. 15s.

Sports.—[*See Rural Sports.*]

Stammering and Stuttering.   By James Hunt.12mo L. 5s.

Statistics.

American Year Book. 1869.............. 8vo Hart. 3 50
American Almanac. 1831 to 1861. *scarce.*12mo Bost.
British Almanac & Companion. 1828 to '70.12mo L. *ea.* 4s.
Homans.   Bankers' Magazine. [*See Periodicals.*]
Martin. Statesman's Year Book,'67,'68,'70. *ea.* L.10s. 6d.
a. Macculloch.   Dictionary of Commerce... 8vo L. 50s.
———— Stat'l acct. of Brit. Empire, 2 v. 8vo L. 42s.
Nat'l Hand Book of Facts and Figures..12mo N. Y.   1 50
Tribune Almanacs,1843–1870, Reprint,2 v.12mo N. Y. 10 00
United States Blue Book Annual.........12mo Wash.
U. S. Commercial Reports—Annual...... 8vo Wash.

Steam Engine.—[*Many Technical Works not included.*]

Bourne.   Catechism of the Steam Engine.18mo Phila. 2 00
———— Hand Book of Steam Engine...18mo Phila.   2 00
———— Treatise on Steam Engine ..... 4to Lond. 21 00
King, W. H.   Pract. Notes on Steam Eng. 8vo   2 00
Marten.   Rec. of Steam Boiler Explosions. 8vo Lond. 2 50
Robinson.   On Explosion of Steam Boilers.12mo Bost. 1 25
Wallace.   On Constructing Steam Engines.16mo Pittsb. 5 00
Young.   Econ. of Steam on Com. Roads.12mo Lond.   2 50

Stenography.—[*See Phonography.*]

Stereoscope.

Brewster, Sir D.   On the Stereoscope.....

Stimulants.—[*See Temperance.*]

Storms.—[*See Meteorology.*]

Submarine Warfare.

Barnes, J. S.   Submarine Warfare....... 8vo N. Y.   5 00
Scheliber, Col. von.   Coast Defence.....*r.*8vo Lond. 15 00

Suez Canal.—[*See Inter-Oceanic Communication.*]

Sugar.

Grant, E. B.   Beet Root Sugar and Culti-
                 vation of Beet....12mo Bost.   1 25
Reed, W.   The Hist. of Sugar and Sugar
                 Plants....12mo Lond.   2 75
Porter.   History of the Sugar Cane..... 8vo Lond.   4 50

Sumatra.

Marsden. History of Sumatra .... 4to L. 31s. 6d.

Supernaturalism.—[See also Spiritualism.]

a. Bushnell. Nature and the Supernatural. 8vo N. Y. $2 25
   Dendy. Philosophy of Mystery.........12mo N. Y.   1 50
   Elliott. Mysteries, or Glimpses of the
                       Supernatural....12mo N. Y.   1 00
   Howitt, Wm. Hist. of the Supernat'l, 2 v.12mo Phila.   3 00
b. Owen, R. D.   The Debatable Land between
              this world and the next....12mo N. Y.   2 00

Superstition and Extravagances.—[See Demonology and
                                    Witchcraft.]

   Dixon, W. H. Spiritual Wives........12mo Phila.   2 50
a. Gould, J. B. Curious Myths of Mid. Ages.12mo Bost.   2 50
   Gould, S. Baring. Book of Were-Wolves.12mo Lond.   1 50
   Gray, G. Z. The Children's Crusade....12mo N. Y.   1 50
b. Lea, H. C. Superstition and Force.......12mo Phila.   2 75
   Mackay Chs. Popular Delusions, 2 vols.12mo Lond. 5s.
   Madden, R. R. Phantasmagoria, 2 vols.. 8vo Lond. 28s.

Sweden.—[See also Scandinavia.]

a. Andersen, Hans C. Pictures of Travel in S.12mo N. Y.   1 75
   Fryxell, A. History of Sweden. Trans.
              by M. Howitt, 2 vols.... 8vo Lond. 21s.
b. Laing. Tour in Sweden................ 8vo Lond. 5s.
   Lloyd. Peasant Life in Sweden........ 8vo Lond.
   Vertot. Revolutions in Sweden........ 8vo L. 2s. 6d.
a. Voltaire. Hist. of Charles XII.........12mo Phila.   1 00

Swedenborgianism.

   Ferrold. New Age of the New Church. '60.   Bost.
   Giles, H. The Nature and Spirit of Man.12mo N. Y.   1 25
   ————— Man as a Spiritual Being......12mo N. Y.   1 25
   James, H. Substance and Shadow......12mo Bost.   2 00
   Swedenborg. Angelic Wisdom; Divine
                       Love.... 8vo Phila.   2 00
   ————————— Concerning Providence. 8vo Phila.   2 25
   ———————— Doct. of Life for New Jerus.12mo Phila.   75
   ———————— Heaven and Hell........ 8vo Phila.   2 50
   ———————— The Divine Attributes.... 8vo Phila.   2 00
   ———————— The True Christian Re-
                       ligion, 2 vols.... 8vo Phila.   5 00
   ———————Economy of the Animal
                  Kingdom, 2 vols.... 8vo Bost.   6 00
   ————————— Doctrines of the New Jeru-
                  salem Church....12mo Bost.   60
   ————————— Gems from Writings of. By
                       Heller, 2 vols....12mo Bost.   2 00
   ————————— Heaven Opened .. ..12mo Bost.   1 25

Swimming.

 Frost. Art of Swimming.............

Switzerland.—[*See also Alps; Glaciers.*]

 Agassiz, L. Tours in Switzerland. 1833. Lond.
b. Berlepsch. The Alps; Sketches of Life
        and Nature.... 8vo Lon. 15s.
 History of Switzerland (Lardner)........12mo L. 3s. 6d.
 Jones, Rev. H. The Regular Swiss Round. 8vo L. & N. $1 75
 Morell, J. R. Scientific Guide to Switz'ld.12mo L. 10s. 6d.
 Muller. History of Switzerland.........
 Murray. Hand Book for Switzerland....12mo Lon. 9s.
a. Swiss Pictures, drawn with Pen and Pencil.
        Illustrated....folio Lond. 3 75
 Vieusseux. Hist. of Switzerland, S. U. K. 8vo L. 7s. 6d.
 Zschokke. History of Switzerland......12mo N. Y.

Synonymes.

b. Crabbe, Geo. English Synonymes.. .... 8vo N. Y. 2 50
 Doederlein. Hand-Book Latin Synonymes.12mo Lond. 4s.
 Graham. English Synonymes..........12mo N. Y. 1 50
 Ramshorn. Latin Synonymes......... .12mo L. 4s. 6d.
a. Roget, P. M. Thesaurus of Eng. Words.12mo Bost. 2 00
b. Smith. Synonymes Discriminated....... 8vo L. & N. 6 00
 Soule. English Synonymes.............
 Trench, R. C. Synonymes of N. Testam't.12mo N. Y. 1 25
b. Wedgewood. Dict. of English Synonymes. 8vo Lond.
 Whately, R. English Synonymes......12mo Lond. 3s.

Syria.—[*See also Holy Land.*]

a. Curtis, G. W. The Howadji in Syria ...12mo N. Y. 1 50
 Kelly, W. K. Syria and the Holy Land.. 8vo L. 8s. 6d.
 Porter, J. L. Five Years in Damascus, 2 v. 8vo Lon. 21s.
b. Prime, S. J. Trav. in Syria, Egypt, etc., 2 v.12mo N. Y. 3 00

Table Talk.

a. Coleridge, S. T. Table Talk...........12mo Lond. 6s.
 Doran. Table Traits.................. 8vo N. Y. 1 75
b. Hazlitt, W. C. Table Talk, 2 vols.......12mo Lon. 10s.
 Luther. Table Talk..................12mo Bohn. 1 75
 Rogers, Samuel. Table Talk.... ....12mo N. Y. 1 00
 Selden. Table Talk....... ....12mo Lond. 1 50

Tales and Novels.—[*See Fiction.*]

Tariff.—[*See Free Trade, Protection.*]

Tartary.—[*See China. See also Asia: Pumpelly, etc.*]

a. Huc. Travels in Tartary and China, 2 v.12mo N. Y. 3 00
 —— —— — Tartary and Thibet....12mo L. 2s. 6d.
 Shaw. Explor. Journey in High Tartary. 8vo Lon. 16s.

Tasmania.—[*See Australia.*]

Taste.—[*See Criticism.*]

Taxation.—[*See Finance, Revenue, Protection,
Political Economy.*]

Taxidermy.
Brown. Taxidermist's Manual.........12mo Glasg. $1 25
Swainson. Taxidermy...... .....Lond.12mo 3s. 6d.

Teachers—Teaching.—[*See Education.*]

Technology.—[*See Inventions, Mechanic Arts, etc*]
Bigelow, Jacob. Technology, 2 vols.....12mo N. Y.
Craig. Technol. Dictionary, 2 vols..Glasg. 4to   42s.
Hazen. Popular Technol.: Trades, etc., 2 v.18mo N. Y.   1 50

Tehuantepec.—[*See Inter-Oceanic.*]

Telegraphing.
Bright, E. B. Electric Telegraph.......16mo Lond.
a. Cooke, W. F. Electric Telegraph...Lond. 8vo 3s. 6d.
Field, II. M. Hist. of Atlantic Telegraph.12mo N. Y.   2 00
Prescott, G. B. Hist. of Elect. Telegraph.12mo Bost.   2 50
Pope. Mod. Practice of Elect. Telegraph.12mo N. Y.   2 00
Russell, W. H. Hist. of Atlantic Teleg..folio Lond.   15 00
Sabine. Hist. and Progress of Elect. Tel.12mo Lond.   1 75
Van Choate. Ocean Telegraphing.......

Temperance—INTEMPERANCE.
Beecher, Lyman. On Intemperance.....
a. Beard, G. E. Stimulants and Narcotics.12mo N. Y.   75
Carpenter. Use and Abuse of Alcohol...12mo Phila.   60
Day, A. Methomania; Alco. Poison.....16mo Bost.   75
b. Fiske. J. Tobacco and Alcohol..........16mo N. Y.   1 00
Lear, F. R. Text Book of Intemp.(U.T.S.).12mo N. Y.   1 50
Macnish. Anatomy of Drunkenness.....12mo N. Y.
Miner and Andrew. Discussion on..... 8vo Bost.
Miller, Jas. Alcohol; its Place and Power.12mo Phila.   1 00
———— Alcohol. (U. T. Soc)... ...12mo N. Y.   1 50
Parton, J. Smoking and Drinking......16mo Bost.   1 00

Tennessee.
Carpenter. History of Tennessee........16mo Phila.   63
Ramsay. History of Tennessee ....

Texas.
Maillard. History of Texas. 1842....... 8vo Lon. 15s.
Olmstead, F. L. Tour in Texas.........
Yoakum. History of Texas. 1856...... N. Y.

Theatre.—[*See Drama.*]

Theism.—[*See Infidelity.*]

Theology.—[*See Bible, Church History, Devotion, Religion.*]
Aids to Faith: Theological Essays......12mo N. Y.   2 00
Blunt, J. H. Dictionary of Doctrinal and
Historical Theology..imp. 8vo Lon. 42s.

Dagg.　Manual of Theology............. 8vo　N. Y.　$4 00
Encyclopedia of Religious Knowledge..*r.* 8vo　Phila.　6 00
b. Hodge.　System of Theology............ 8vo　N. Y.　5 00
Knapp.　Christian Theology........... 8vo　Andov.
Philosophy of the Plan of Salvation.....12mo Bost.　1 25
Pond, E.　Pastoral Theology............12mo Andov.　1 75
Theologia Germanica, ed. by Prof. Stowe..12mo Andov.　1 50
Tyler, Prof. W. S.　Theol. of Greek Poets.12mo Andov.　1 75
Venema.　Institutes of Theology....... 8vo　Andov.　2 50
Vinet.　Outlines of Theology........... 8vo　L. & N.　3 00

Tobacco.—[*See Narcotics.*]

Torpedoes.

Toxicology.—[*See Poisons.*]

Trade and Commerce.—[*See Business.*]

Tragedy.—[*See Drama.*]

Trade Unions.—[*See Co-operation.*]

Travels and Voyages—GENERALLY.
　　　　(For those in particular Countries, see their names.)
——(1.) ART OF TRAVEL.
a. Galton.　The Art of Travel......Lond..18mo 7s. 6d.
Heine.　Pictures of Travel, by Leland...12mo Phila.　1 50
Lord & Baines.　Shifts and Expedients of
　　　　　　　　Camp Life.　1871....*r.* 8vo　Lond.
Marcy, R. B.　Instruc. for Prairie Travel.16mo N. Y.　1 00
——(2.) GUIDE BOOKS, ETC.
Appleton's Hand-Books for Travellers:
————　——— —— Northern States.12mo N. Y.　2 00
————　·——— —— Middle States....12mo N. Y.　2 00
————　·——— —— Southern States.12mo N. Y.　2 00
——————　Hand-Book for Europe.......12mo N. Y.　6 00
Harper.　Hand-Book for Europe........12mo N. Y.　5 00
Murray's Hand-Books for Europe and the East,
　　each 12mo, London, viz.: Berks, Bucks, etc.,
　　7s. 6d.; Bombay and Madras, 2 volumes, 24s.;
　　Continent (Europe), 10s.; Devon and Cornwall, 7s.
　　6d.; France, 10s.; Germany, North, 10s.; Germany,
　　South, 10s.; Greece, 15s.; Italy, Northern, 12s.;
　　Italy, Central, 10s.; Italy, Southern, 10s.; Kent
　　and Sussex, 10s.; London, Modern, 3s. 6d.; London,
　　Past, etc., 16s.; Malta, Turkey, etc., 15s.; Norway,
　　Sweden, etc., 15s.; Portugal, 9s.; Rome, etc., 9s.;
　　Russia, Iceland, etc., 12s.; Spain, 2 vols., 30s.;
　　Surrey, Hants, etc., 7s. 6d.; Syria and Palestine,
　　2 vols., 24s.; Turkey, Asia, etc., 10s.; Wales, 2 v.,
　　12s.; Wilts, Dorset, etc., 7s. 6d.
Sargent, H. W.　Skeleton Tours.........18mo N. Y.　1 00

Travels and Voyages—GENERALLY.

——(3.) COLLECTIONS OF ADVENTURES, ETC.

Adventures of Hunters and Travellers...12mo Phila. $1 75
Cleveland. Voyages and Com. Enterprises.12mo Camb.
Illustrated Travels ; Record of Discov. and
     Adventure. Ed. by Bates, 3 v..*r.* 4to L. & N. *ea.*
Library of Travel, 2 vols................ 8vo L. 17s. 6d.
a. Taylor, Bayard. Cyclopedia of Mod. Trav. 8vo Cincin. 5 00
——————————— Library of Travel (edited
     by B. T.), — vols.....*ea.*12mo N. Y. 1 50
a. ————————— Travels in Europe, Asia,
     Africa & America, 10 v.12mo N. Y. 15 00

——(4.) CIRCUMNAVIGATIONS AND JOURNEYS.

Abbott. Rollo Books................⎫   *See*
——— Marco Polo Books..........⎬ *Juveniles.*
Browne, J. Ross. Etchings on a Whaling
     Cruise.... 8vo N. Y.
——— ——— Crusoe's Island, Cal., 2 v.12mo N. Y. 1 75
Clemens (Mark Twain). The Innocents
     Abroad (Europe and Palestine).... 8vo Hartf. 3 50
b. Coffin, C. C. Our New Way Round the
     World.... 8vo Bost. 3 00
Cook's Voyages round the World, 2 vols.*r.* 8vo Lon. 24s.
——— ——— ——— abridged. Illust....12mo Lond. 2 00
a. Dana, R. H., Jr. Two Years Before the Mast.12mo Bost. 1 50
b. Dilke, C. W. Greater Britain..........12mo Phila. 3 00
Dufferin, Lord. Let'rs from High Latitud. 8vo Lond. 9s.
Earth (The) ; Delineated with Pen and
     Pencil. By W. F. Ainsworth. Plates
     by Doré.... 4to Lon. 21s.
Goodrich, F. B. Man upon the Sea ; Hist.
     of Maritime Adventure.. 8vo Phila. 2 25
Macgregor. The Rob Roy on Baltic.....12mo Bost. 2 50
a. ——— 1,000 Miles in the Rob Roy.12mo Bost. 1 25
Minturn. New York to Delhi. by Rio,
     Australia and China....12mo N. Y. 2 00
Mountain Adventures in various Lands .12mo Bost. 2 50
Pfeiffer, Ida. 2d Jour. round the World.12mo N. Y. 1 50
a. Pumpelly, R. Across America and Asia.. 8vo N. Y. 2 50
Smiles. A Boy's Journey round the World.12mo N. Y. 1 50
Wanderings in every Clime ; Voyages, etc.
     Edited by W. F. Ainsworth. Illust. by
     Doré.... 4to Lond. 21s.
Wilkes. U. S. Exploring Expedition
     Round the World, 5 vols..*r.* 8vo Phila. 20 00
——— The same, condensed in 1 vol..*r.* 8vo Phila. 3 00

Trees.

Browne. The Forester................
Browne, D. J. The Trees of America.... 8vo N. Y. 5 50
Flagg. Wood Scenery of New England..

Fuller. Forest Tree Culturalist........12mo N. Y.
a. Hooper. Book of Evergreens..........12mo N. Y. $3 00
London. Encyclo. of Trees and Shrubs.. 8vo Lond. 15 00
b. Michaux & Nuttall. North Amer. Sylva,
      colored plates, 6 vols..*r.* 8vo Phila. 65 00
Meehan. Hand-Book of Ornamen. Trees.
Warder. Hedges and Evergreens. 1858. 8vo N. Y.

Trials.—[*See Law.*]

Tripoli.—[*See Africa, North.*]

Tunis.—[*See Africa, North.*]

Turkey.

Benjamin, S. G. W. The Turk & the Greek.12mo N. Y. 1 75
a. Creasy. History of the Ottoman Empire. 8vo L. 7s. 6d.
Jacob & others. Hist. of Ottoman Empire.12mo L. 7s. 6d.
Lamartine. History of Turkey........
b. Macfarlane. Turkey and its Destiny....12mo Phila. 2 00
Mavor. Ottoman Empire in Asia........
Mackenzie and Irby. The Turks, Greeks
      and Slavons.... 8vo Lon. 24s.
Ranke. Ottoman and Spanish Empire in
    16th and 17th Centuries.... 8vo Lond. 2s.
Smyth, W. W. A Year with the Turks.. 8vo Lond. 8s.
Toser. Highlands of Turkey, 2 vols..... 8vo Lon. 24s.
Turkish Empire ; Annals of. (Oriental
      Fund).... 4to L. 31s. 6d.
b. Urquhart. Turkey and its Resources.... 8vo L. 9s. 6d.
Wise. Scampavias ; Gebeltarek to Stam-
      boul....12mo Phila. 1 75

Turning.

Campin. Hand Turning................12mo Phila. 3 00
Turner's Companion.................12mo Phila. 1 50
a. The Lathe and its Uses......... .... 8vo Lond. 6 00
Watson. Manual of the Hand Lathe....12mo Phila. 1 50

Tuscany.—[*See Italy.*]

Typography.—[*See Printing.*]

Tyrol.—[*See Switzerland.*]

United States.—[*See also America, North ; Mexico ; New
    England ; and Names of States.*]

The Sub-divisions below are :
(1.) *General History,* (2.) *Revolution,* (3.) *War of
1812,* (4.) *Rebellion,* (5.) *Travels, etc.*

——(1.) GENERAL HISTORY.

Adams, John. Works, Letters, etc., 10 v. 8vo Bost. 30 00
———— Life by J. Q. & C. F. Adams, 2 v.12mo Phila. 3 00
Adams, John Q. Diary and Memoirs..... 8vo Phila. 3 00
Adams, Samuel. Works and Life, 3 vols. 8vo Bost. 12 00

b. Bancroft. Hist. of the United States, 9 v. 8vo Bost. $27 00
Bartlett & Woodward. History of U. S.
        Illustrated, 3 vols.... 4to L. & N. 17 50
Benton. Debates in the U. S. Senate, 16 v. 8vo N. Y. 80 00
—— 30 Years' View of Pub. Affairs, 2 v. 8vo N. Y. 10 00
Bowen, J. Child's History of U. S., 3 v. .18mo N. Y. 3 75
Cooper, J. F. Hist. of the Navy of U. S.. 8vo N. Y. 3 75
Cooke, W. A. Constitutional Hist. of U. S. 8vo Phila. 2 50
Draper, J. W. American Civil Policy... 8vo N. Y. 2 50
Franklin, B. Writings, 10 vols......... 8vo Phila. 30 00
Gibbs, Geo. Administrations of Washing-
     ton and Adams ('46), 2 v.. 8vo N. Y. 5 00
Goodrich, S. G. Hist. of the United States.12mo Phila. 1 75
Hamilton. Republic of the United States ;
     Writings of Hamilton, 7 v.. 8vo Phila. 24 50
b. Hildreth, R. Hist. of the United States, 6 v. 8vo N. Y. 18 00
Howitt, Mary. American History, 2 v...12mo N. Y. 3 50
Jefferson. Writings, 9 vols............ 8vo Phila. 27 00
Jennings, L. J. 80 Years of Rep. Gov. ('68).12mo N. Y.
b. Lossing. Pictorial History of U. S......12mo N. Y. 2 00
—————— —————— Common School Hist.12mo N. Y. 1 75
McPherson, E. Polit. Hist. of the U. S.. 8vo Wash. 3 00
Madison, Jas. Papers, Letters, etc., 4 v.. 8vo Phila. 16 00
Madison. Writings........ .... 8vo Bost. 3 00
National Hand-Book of Facts and Figures.12mo N. Y. 1 50
a. Parkman, F. Conspiracy of Pontiac..... 8vo Bost. 3 00
a. ———— — Jesuits in North America.. 8vo Bost. 3 00
Patton. History of the United States... *r.* 8vo N. Y. 3 00
Quackenboss. Hist. of the United States.12mo N. Y. 2 00
Smith & Watson. Historical and Literary
        Curiosities.... 4to Phila. 7 00
Sargent, W. Hist. of the Braddock Exped. 8vo Phila. 5 00
a. Swinton, Wm. Hist. of the United States.12mo N. Y. 1 25
a. Tocqueville. Democracy in America, 2 v. 8vo Camb. 5 00
Tomes, Robt. Battles of America by Sea
     and Land. Illust., 3 v.... 4to N. Y. 24 00
Van Buren, M. Polit. Parties in the U. S. 8vo N. Y. 3 00
Washington's Writings. By Sparks, 12 v. 8vo Bost. 24 00
———————— Life & Times. By Irving, 5v.12mo N. Y. 11 25
—————— —————— Various other ed'ns.
—————— —————— 1 v. $5.00 ; cond'nsd.12mo N. Y. 2 50
Willard, Jas. Hist. of Repub. of Amer.. 8vo N. Y. 2 25
Willson, M. Am. Hist. (chiefly U. S.)....12mo N. Y. 2 00
Wise, Henry A. Seven Decades of Am. Hist. 8vo Phila.

—(2.) THE AMERICAN REVOLUTION.

Bancroft. [*See United States General History.*]
Botta, C. History of Amer. Revolu., 2 v. 8vo
Campbell, W. W. Annals of Tryon County. 8vo N. Y.
Ellett, Mrs. Women of the Am. Rev., 3 v.12mo N. Y. 5 25
———— Domestic Hist. of Am. Rev..12mo N. Y. 1 50
Garden. Anecdotes of the Revol., 2 vols. 4to Brook.

Greene, G. W. Hist. View of Amer. Rev.12mo N. Y. $1 50
—————— Life of General Greene, 3 v. 8vo N. Y. 12 00
a. Irving. Washington ; Life and Times;
　　　　　　the Revolution, 5 vols... 12mo N. Y. 11 25
Lee. War in the Southern Department.. 8vo Phila.
b. Lossing. Field-Book of Amer. Rev., 2 v. r. 8vo N. Y. 14 00
————— Lives of Signers of Decl. Inde..12mo Phila. 1 50
Moore, G. H. Treason of Gen. Lee...... 8vo N. Y.
Riedesel, Mrs. Gen. Letters and Journals;
　　　　　　American Revolution.... 8vo Alb. 3 00
Rhoads. Battle-Fields of the Revolution.12mo Phila. 1 75
Sabine, L. American Loyalists, 2 vols... 8vo Bost. 7 00
 * Sparks. Diplomatic Correspondence of
　　　　　　the Amer. Revolu. 1824, 12 v. 8vo Bost.
Washington and his Generals.... ......12mo Phila. 2 50
Watson. Men & Times of the Revolution.12mo Phila. 1 50
————— Camp Fires of the Revolution.12mo N. Y. 2 00

——(3.) WAR OF 1812–14, AND WITH MEXICO, 1847.

 * Armstrong. General Notices of War of
　　　　　　1812, 2 vols. 1836....12mo N. Y.
 * Brackenbridge. War of 1812 ....
 * Dwight. Hist. of the Hartford Convention. 8vo
 * Ingersoll, C. J. Second War between
　　　　　　United States and Great Britain.... 8vo
a. Lossing. Field-Book of War of 1812, Ill. r. 8vo N. Y. 7 00
 * Porter. Cruise in the Pacific........... 8vo
Ripley. History of War with Mexico, 2v. 8vo N. Y.

——(4.) REBELLION—OF 1861–5.—[See also Neutrality,
　　　　　　　　　　　　International Law.]

(s.) Abbott, J. S. C. History of the Rebellion. 8vo Hart.
Appleton's History of the Rebellion....r. 8vo N. Y. 4 00
Adams, F. C. Story of a Trooper; Siege
　　　　　　of Washington....ea. N. Y. 2 00
Bartlett, J. R. Bibliography of the Re-
　　bellion and of Slavery. 1866....r. 8vo Bost.
　　₊ This volume contains no less than 6,073 titles of books
　　and pamphlets, published on this subject, up to 1866.
Boutwell, G. S. Speeches, etc., on the
　　　　　　Rebellion.... 8vo Bost. 2 50
Botts, J. Minor. The Great Rebellion...12mo N. Y. 2 50
Boynton, C. B. American Navy during
　　　　　　Rebellion, 2 vols.... 8vo N. Y. 8 00
Buchanan, J. Hist. of his Administration. 8vo N. Y. 1 50
Calhoun, J. C. Political Writings, 6 vols. 8vo N. Y. 15 00
Coffin, C. C. My Days and Nights on the
　　　　　　Battle-Field....12mo Bost. 1 50
a. Draper, J. W. History of the American
　　　　　　Civil War, 3 vols.... 8vo N. Y. 10 50

* Out of print and scarce.　　　　(s.) Subscription books.

Foote, H. S.   War of the Rebellion......12mo N. Y.   \$2 50
(s.) Greeley, H. Hist. of the Amer. Conflict, 2 v. 8vo Hartf.   10 00
Harper's Pictorial Hist. of Rebellion, 2 v.folio N. Y.   12 00
(s.) Headley, J. T.   History of Rebellion..... 8vo Hartf.   5 00
(s.) Lossing.   Pictorial Hist. of the Civil War
          of the United States, 3 vols.. 8vo Hartf.   15 00
Lunt, G.   Origin of the Late War.......12mo N. Y.   1 50
McPherson, E.   Political History of U. S.
          during Reconstruction.   1871. 8vo Wash.
Nichols, G. W.   Story of the Great March.12mo N. Y.   2 00
Pollard, E. A.   Southern Hist. of the War,
          4 vols. in 2.... N. Y.
(s.) ——— —— The Lost Cause......... 8vo N. Y.   5 00
(s.) ——— —— Lost Cause Regained.....12mo N. Y.   1 50
(s.) ——— —— Life of Jeff. Davis, and Se-
          cret History.... 8vo Phila.   3 00
b.   Rebel'n Record, ed. by Frank Moore, 12 v.r. 8vo N. Y.   60 00
Russell, W. H.   Diary in America....... 8vo N. Y.   1 00
Semmes, R.   Service Afloat.   1869....... 8vo Balt.   5 00
(s.) Stephens, A. H.   History of the War be-
          tween the States, 2 v.. 8vo Phila.   6 75
Stille.   History of the Sanitary Commiss. 8vo Phila.   3 50
(s.) Swinton, W.   History of the Army of the
          Potomac.... 8vo N. Y.   4 00
a.   ——— — Twelve Decisive Battles... 8vo N. Y.   3 50
(s.) Tomes & Smith.   The War with the South.
          Illustrated, 3 vols ... 4to N. Y.   45 00

——(5.) TRAVELS, ETC., IN U. S.; GEOGRAPHY, STATISTICS.

Agassiz, L.   Tour to Lake Superior ..... 8vo Bost.   3 50
Bowles, Sam.   Across the Continent.....12mo Spring.   1 50
Bremer, Fred'a.   Homes of the New World.
          2 vols....12mo N. Y.   3 00
Butler, Mrs. F. Kemble.   Journal in Amer.
          1835....12mo Phila.
Chevalier, M.   The United States.   1839. 8vo Bost.
b.   Coffin, C. C.   The Seat of Empire........12mo Bost.   1 50
Dickens, Chas.   American Notes........12mo N. Y.
Dilke, C. W.   Greater Britain ....:12mo N. Y.   1 00
Dixon, W. H.   New America.... ...... 8vo Phila.   2 00
Hall, Rev. N.   Liverpool to St. Louis....12mo L. & N.   1 75
a.   Irving.   Bonneville's Adven. in Far West.12mo N. Y.   2 25
a.   ——— Astoria—Enterprise beyond Rocky
          Mountains....12mo N. Y.   2 25
Jennings.   United States.............   1 75
Kohl, J. G.   Travels in the United States.
Laboulaye, E.   Paris in America........12mo N. Y.   1 50
Lewis & Clarke.   Trav. in Rocky Mts., 2 v.18mo N. Y.   1 50
Lyell, Chas.   Travels in the U. S.   1841..
——— —— Second Visit to U. S. 1849. 2 v.12mo N. Y.   3 00
McCrea, D.   Americans at Home.   '71. 2 v.12mo Lond.

* Out of print and scarce.   (s.) Subscription books.

Marcy, R. B.   Thirty Years' Army Life on
                      the Border.... 8vo N. Y. $2 00
Marryatt, F.   Diary in America.   1839..12mo N. Y.
Martineau, H.   Society in America.   1837.12mo N. Y.
Murray, C. A.   Travels in America.   1839.
Murray, Hon. Miss.   Letters from U. S..12mo N. Y.   1 00
Olmsted, F. L.   The Back Country.   1860.12mo N. Y.   1 50
———— ——   The Cotton Kingdom, 2 v.12mo N. Y.   2 00
———— ——   The Slave States.   1861..12mo N. Y.
Parkman, F.   The California and Oregon
                      Trail.   1849 ...12mo N. Y.
Peto, Sir S. M.   Resources and Prospects
                      of America....12mo L. & N.   2 00
Poussin, G. T.   The United States.   1851. 8vo Phila.
Ruxton.   Life in the Far West.   1851...12mo N. Y.
Rae.   Westward by Rail; the New Route
                      to East....12mo L. & N.
Sala, G. A.   Diary in America, 2 vols.... 8vo Lond.
Shaw, J.   Twelve Years in America....12mo Lon. 5s.
Towle, G. M.   Society in America, 2 vols.   Lon. 21s.
Tuckerman, H. T.   America and her Com-
                      mentators....12mo N. Y.   2 50

Universities.—[See *Colleges.*]

Useful Arts.—[See *Mechanics, Technology, and Names of
          Arts.*]

Usury.   Murray, B. C.   History of Usury..:. 8vo Phila.   2 00

Utah.—[See *Mormons.*]

Venice.

Flagg, E.   Venice.   1853, 2 vols........12mo N. Y.   2 00
a. Howell, W. D.   Venetian Life..........12mo N. Y.   2 00
Smedley.   Sketches of Venetian Hist., 2 v.18mo N. Y.   1 50

Ventilation and Warming.

a. Ainslee, A. C.   Smoking Fires.   1869....   Lond. 3s.
Edwards.   Our Domestic Fire-Places..*r.* 8vo Lon. 12s.
Gouge, H. A.   New Syst. of Ventilat'n. '70. 8vo N. Y.   2 00
Hood, C.   Warming by Hot Water, etc.. 8vo Lond.   5 25
Leavitt, T. H.   Facts about Peat........12mo   1 75
a. Leeds, F. W.   Treatise on Ventilation... 8vo Lond.   2 50
Reed, D. B.   Theory and Pract. of Ventil. 8vo Lond.   3 00
b. Ruttan.   On Ventilation of Buildings, R.W.
                      Cars, etc....*r.* 8vo N. Y.   5 00
Tomlinson, C.   Warming and Ventilation.16mo Lon. 3s.
Wyman, M.   On Ventilation.   1846......12mo Bost.

Vermont.

Carpenter & Arthur.   Hist. of Vermont..18mo Phila.   63
Hall, H.   History of Vermont.   1868..... 8vo Alb'y   4 00
Thompson.   Hist. of Vermont.   1842....   Burl'g.
Williams.   Hist of Vermont.   1809......   Burl'g.

Virginia.

Campbell, Ch. Hist. of Virginia. 1860.. 8vo Phila. $2 50
Dabney, R. L. Defence of Virginia......12mo N. Y.   1 50
Dodge, J. R.   Western Virginia, its Farms,
     etc., 2 vols....   N. Y.   1 50
Foote. Sketches of Va. Hist. and Biogr.. 8vo Phila.   2 00
Pollard, E. A. Virginia Transit........12mo Phila.   1 75
Howison. History of Virginia...8vo ⎫
Smith. do.   do. ...8vo ⎬ o. p. and scarce.
Stith. do.   do. ...8vo ⎭
Virginia Illustrated. By "Porte Crayon." 8vo N. Y.   3 50

Volcanoes and Earthquakes.—[See Natural
       Science, Geology.]

Daubeny, C. Earthquakes and Volcanoes. 8vo Lon. 24s.
Pouton. Earthquakes and Volcanoes....18mo L. 2s. 6d.
Truche & Margolle. Earthq. and Volc..12mo Lond. 6s.

Voyages.—[See Travels.]

Wages.—[See Labor, Political Economy.]

Wars.—[See each Country.]

Warming.—[See Ventilation.]

Watches.—[See Clocks.]

Weather.—[See Meteorology.]

Weights and Measures.—[See Metric System.]

West Indies.—[See also Cuba, Jamaica, etc.]

Baird. West Indies and North America.12mo Phila.   75
Kingsley, C. At Last; Christmas in West
       Indies....12mo N. Y.   1 50
Trollope, A. The W. Indies & Span. Main.12mo N. Y.   1 50

Whist.

Baldwin. On Short Whist.............16mo N. Y.   1 00
Cavendish. On Whist.................18mo N. Y.   75
Matthews. On Whist..................18mo N. Y.
Poole. Modern Game of Whist.........
Routledge. Hand-Book of Whist.......18mo L. & N.   20

White Mountains.

King, T. Starr. The White Mount's. Ill. 8vo Bost.   3 50

Wines.—[See also Agriculture.]

Flagg. European Vineyards............12mo N. Y.   1 50
Haraszthy. Grape Cult. and Wine-Making. 8vo N. Y.   5 00
Meade, P. B. American Grape Culture and
      Wine-Making.... 8vo N. Y.   3 00
Mulder. Chemistry of Wine, translated
     by Jones....12mo Lond. 6s.
Redding, C. Hist. and Descrip. Mod. Wines.12mo Bohn.   2 25

Reemelin. Wine Maker's Manual. .....12mo Cincin. $1 25
Thudichum. Treatise on Wines........ 8vo Lond.

Wisconsin.
Ritchie, J. S. Wisconsin and its Resources.
1857....12mo Phila   1 25
Smith, W. R. History of Wisconsin, 2 v. 8vo Mad., W.

Witchcraft.—[*See Demonology.*]

Wit.—[*See Humorous Works.*]

Women—WOMEN'S RIGHTS—SUFFRAGE, ETC.
Bliss, W. W. Woman ; her 30 Years' Pil-
grimage....12mo Bost.   2 00
Brockett, L. P. Woman; her Rights,
Wrongs, etc....12mo Hart.   2 00
——— —— Woman's Work in the
Civil War.... 8vo Phil.   3 75
b. Bushnell, H. Woman's Suffrage; against
Nature....12mo N. Y.   1 50
Butler, Josephine. Woman's Work and
Culture.... 8vo L. & N.   3 50
a. Cobbe, F. P. The Pursuits of Women... 8vo L. 3s. 6d.
b. Craik, Mrs. (Muloch). Woman's Thoughts
about Women....12mo Lond. 5s.
Dall, Mrs. C. H. College, Market & Court. 8vo Bost.   2 50
a. Dodge, Miss (Gail Hamilton). Woman's
Wrongs....12mo Bost.   1 50
——— —— —— Woman's Worth and
Worthlessness....12mo N. Y.   1 75
Hale, Mrs. Woman's Record.......... 8vo N. Y.   5 00
Linton. Ourselves; Essays on Women..12mo L. & N.   1 50
Logan, Olive. Women and Theatres....12mo N. Y.   1 50
Lowell, Mrs. A. C. The Educat'n of Girls.16mo Bost.
Ludlow, J. M. Woman's Work in the
Church....12mo L. & N.   1 75
Marryatt, Florence. Woman against
Woman.... 8vo Bost.   75
a. Mill, J. S. The Subjection of Women...12mo Phila.   1 00
Modern Women ; What is said of them.
[From Saturday Review], 2 v.12mo N. Y.   4 00
Ossoli, March. d'. Woman in the 19th
Cent. [See Margaret Fuller's Works].6 v.12mo N. Y. 10 50
Parks, Bessie. Essays on Woman's Work.16mo L. & N.   1 50
b. Penny, V. 500 Employments for Women.12mo Phila.   1 75
Saunders, F. Woman, Love & Marriage.12mo N. Y.   1 50
Social & Political Dependence of Women. 8vo L. 3s. 6d.
Southgate, H. What Men have said about
Women....12mo L. & N.   2 50
Sprague, W. B. The Excellent Woman
in Proverbs....12mo Bost.   1 50
Todd, J. Woman's Rights.............18mo Bost.   15

Wade, J. Woman, Past and Present....12mo L. 3s. 6d.
Weaver, Rev. G. S. Aims and Aids for
    Girls and Women....12mo N. Y. $1 50
Women of the Bible. By Mrs. T. S. Martyn.12mo N. Y. 3 50
Women of the Gospels. By author of
    Schönberg Cotta....12mo N. Y. 1 75
Women's Rights Tracts. By Phillips,
  Parker, Higginson, and others.... Bost.
Woods, C. H. Woman in Prison........16mo N. Y. 1 25
Wright. Womankind in Western Europe.
    Illustrated.... 8vo Lond. 10 00

Wood Engraving.—[*See Engraving.*]

Zoology.—[*See Darwinism, Cage Birds, Natural History,
  Ornithology.*]

Yachting.—[*See Navigation.*]

Yucatan.—[*See Central America.*]

ADDENDA.

(Including recent publications, and others accidentally omitted in their proper place.)

Abyssinia.

Plowden, W. C.   Travels in Abyssinia... 8vo Lon. 18s.

Africa—NORTH.

Du Chaillu, The Country of the Dwarfs.12mo N. Y. $1 75
Hodgkin, T. Journey to Morocco. 1865. 8vo Lond.

Agriculture.

Copeland, S. Agricul., Anc. and Mod.,2 v.r. 8vo Lond.

America—NORTH AND SOUTH—EARLY HISTORY.

Beamish. Discovery of America by Northmen in 10th Century.... 8vo Lond. 1 75
Charlevoix.   History of New France;
translated by Shea, 3 v.. 8vo N. Y. 15 00
Davis, W. H. Span. Conquest of New Mex. 8vo Doylest. 3 00

America—SOUTH.

Baxby.   What I saw on W. Coast S. Am. 8vo N. Y. 3 50
Myers.   Life and Nature in the Tropics of
South America....12mo N. Y. 2 00

Anglican Church.

Vaughan, R. Ritualism in Church of Eng.16mo Lond.

Anglo-Saxon.

Anglo-Saxon Chronicle, ed. by B. Thorpe. 8vo Lond.
2 vols. r. 8vo Lon. 17s.

Architecture.

Eastlake, C. L. Hist. of the Gothic Revival. 8vo Lond.
Otis, C. N.   Sacred and Constructive Art.12mo N. Y. 1 25
Woodward, G. E.   National Architect... 4to N. Y. 12 00
———————— F. W.   Landscape Gard. and
Rural Architecture....12mo N. Y. 1 00

Astronomy.

Leach. God's Glory in the Heavens ('67).16mo Lond.
Lyle. What are the Stars ? Illust..... 4to Lond. 5s.
Rosser, W. H.   The Stars ; How to Know
Them, etc. : ..r. 8vo Lond.

Autograph—FAC-SIMILES.

Book of Signers of Declarat. of Independ. 4to Phila. 5 00

Bible—ITS HISTORY.

Conant, W. C.   History of English Bible.12mo N. Y.
Hengstenberg.   Genuineness of the Penta-
         teuch, 2 vols.... 8vo Edin. 21s.
Scott, W. A.   Moses and the Pentateuch;
         Reply to Colenso....12mo L. 3s. 6d.
Stowe, C. E.   Origin and History of Books
         of the Bible.... 8vo Hartf. $3 50
Tischendorf.   Origin of Four Gospels....16mo L. 3s. 6d.

Bible—AIDS TO STUDY OF.

Cowles.   Notes on the Prophets, 5 vols..   N. Y. 1I 00
Fairbairn, W.   Imp. Bible Dictionary, 2 v.r. 8vo Lond.
Girdlestone.   Synonymes of the Old Test. 8vo Lon. 15s.
King.   Concordance to the Bible........12mo Bost. 1 75

Bibliography.

Bartlett.   Literature of the Rebellion
         (6,065 titles)....r 8vo Provid.
Berjeau.   Early Printers' Marks .. .... 8vo Lond.
Kelly.   American Catalogue of Books,
         original and reprint. 1866–1871.. 8vo N. Y. 7 50
Sabin, J.   Dictionary of Books relating to
         America—part 1 to 21..ea. N. Y. 2 00
—— —   American Bibliopolist, 2 vols.. 8vo N. Y. 6 00

Biography—COLLECTED—AMERICAN.

American Medi. Biography.   By Williams. 8vo Greenfi.
Drake.   Dictionary of Amer. Biography.. 8vo Bost.
✦Homes of American Authors........... 8vo N. Y. 5 00
Homes of American Statesmen......... 8vo Hartf. 5 00
Sanderson.   Biography of Signers of Dec-
         laration of Independence.. 4to Phila.
Stowe, C. E.   Men of our Times........ 8vo Hartf. 3 50

Biography—COLLECTED WORKS—WOMEN.

Female Sovereigns.   By Mrs. Jameson... 8vo L. & N. 2 50
Good Women.   By C. M. Yonge........16mo Lon. 6s.
Heroic Women of History.   By Watson..12mo Phila. 1 75
Queens of France.   By Mrs. Bush.......12mo Phila. 1 75
Queens of England.   By Lancelot, 2 vols. 8vo L. & N. 5 00

Biography—COLLECTED—SCIENTIFIC.

Distinguished Men of Science.   By Walker.16mo L. 3s. 6d.

Biography—COLLECTED—MISCELLANEOUS.

Archbishops of Canterbury.   By Hook, 5 v. 8vo L. 78s.
Character; a Companion to Self-Help.   By
         Smiles....12mo Lon. 6s.
Early Italian Poets.   By D. G. Rosetti...12mo Lon. 12s.
English Merchants.   By Bourne, 2 vols.16mo Lond.
Essays in Biography and Criticism.   By
         P. Bayne....12mo Bost. 1 75

Extraordinary Men. By W. H. Russell..12mo L. & N. $1 25
Extraordinary Women. By W. H. Russell.12mo L. & N. 1 25
Great Men; Last Hours of. By Karnes.. 8vo L. & N. 2 00
French Academy; Biog. Hist. of. By
      Edwards.... 8vo Lon. 6s.
Men of Our Day. By L. P. Brockett..... 8vo Phila. 3 00
Twelve Judges of England. By Town-
     send, 2 vols.... 8vo L. 28s.

Biography—INDIVIDUAL.

Aikin, Lucy. Memoirs and Miscellanies. 8vo L. 8s. 6d.
Cicero. Life and Letters. By Abeken.
      Trans....12mo L. 9s. 6d.
Franklin. By O. L. Holley............12mo Phila. 1 75
Guerin, Mad. de. Life. By St. Beuve...12mo N. Y. 1 25
Horner, Francis. By his Brother, 2 vols. 8vo Lond. 4 50
Huss, John. By E. H. Gillette.........12mo Bost. 1 75
Jackson, Geo. T. J. By Dabney......... 8vo N. Y. 4 00
Jefferson. By Schmucker.............12mo Phila. 1 75
Knox, John, and his Times. By Miss
      Warren....16mo Lond.
Lacordaire, Abbe. By Count Montalembert. 8vo Lon. 12s.
Lee, Gen. R. E. By John E. Cooke..... 8vo N. Y. 4 00
Louis Napoleon. By Schmucker........12mo Phila. 1 75
Mackintosh, Sir James. By his Son, 2 v. 8vo L. & B. 4 50
Mazzini. Life and Writings, 6 vols......12mo Lon. 54s.
Mather, Cotton. By S. G. Drake........ 8vo Bost.
Miller, Rev. S. By S. Miller, 2 vols.....12mo Phila. 4 50
Milton. Life and Times. By W. C. Martin.12mo N. Y. 1 25
Nicholas I. of Russia. By Schmucker...12mo Phila. L.75
Richard I. By Aytoun...............12mo L. 3s. 6d.
St. Chrysostom. Life and Times. By Rev.
     W. R. Stephens.... 8vo Lon. 16s.
St. Paul. Life and Work of. By A. Roberts.16mo Lond. 5s.
Voltaire. By F. Espinasse.......... ... 8vo Lond.
——— By Morley.................. 8vo Lon. 14s.
Warburton, Bp. By J. S. Watson....... 8vo Lon. 18s
Watt, Jas. By Muirhead.............12mo N. Y. 2 00
Weber, C. M. Von. By C. L. Von Weber,
     2 vols....12mo Lond.
Webster, Daniel. By Lyman...........12mo Phila. 1 75
Wellington, Duke of. By C. D. Yonge, 2 v. 8vo Lon. 42s.
Wilberforce. By his Son. New ed., cond. 8vo Lond. 6s.

Book-Keeping.

Haswell, C. H. Book-Keeping by Double-
     Entry, 4 vols.... N. Y. 5 50

Botany.

Wooster. Alpine Plants, with col'd Illus.r.8vo L. & N. 10 00

Business—COMMERCE.

Levi, Leone. History of Brit. Commerce. 8vo Lond.
Lewing. History of Savings Banks..... 8vo 5 00

Martin. Commercial Hand-Book of France.12mo L. 7s. 6d.
Moran. On Money.....................12mo N. Y. $1 25

Caricature.

Wright. History of Caricature and Gro-
            tesque, etc.... 8vo Lond. 9 00

Caucasus.

Freshfield, D. W. Caucasus and Bashan. 8vo Lon. 18s.

Chemistry.

Bloxam. Organic and Inorganic Chemistry. 8vo Lon. 16s.
Bowman. Practical Chemistry..........12mo Phila. 2 25
Brande & Taylor. Chemistry........ .. 8vo L. 12s. 6d.
Farraday, M. Researches in Chemistry.. 8vo Lon. 15s.
Graham. Inorganic Chemistry.......... 8vo Phila. 5 50
Knapp. Chemical Technology, 2 vols.... 8vo Phila. 6 00
Pelouze & Ferny. Gen'l Notions of Chem.12mo Phila. 1 75
Wagner. Hand-Book of Chemical Tech-
            nology,....12mo N. Y.

Christ.

Gethsemane; the Last Hours of Christ...12mo Bost. 1 25
Krummacher. The Suffering Saviour..12mo Bost. 1 75
Lange, J. P. Life of Jesus, 6 vols........ 8vo Edin.35s.
March, D. Walks and Homes of Jesus...12mo Phila. 2 50
Plumptree, E. H. Christ and Christen-
            dom ('66).... 8vo Lond.
Scott, W. A. The Christ of the Apos. Creed. 8vo N. Y. 3 00
Stier, R. The Words of the Lord Jesus, 8 v. 8vo Edin. 84s.
Stroud. Physical Cause of the Death of
            Christ....12mo N. Y. 2 00
Vaughan. Christ the Light of the World.16mo L. & N. 1 50
————— Charac. of Christ's Teachings.16mo L. & N. 1 50
Young, J. The Christ of History........12mo L. & N. 2 00

Christianity.

Blunt. Christ'n View of Christ'n History.16mo Lond.
Bryant, J. H. Christ'y & the Stoic School.12mo Lond.
Guizot. Christ'y in relation to Society...12mo N. Y. 1 75
————— Essence of Christianity.......12mo 1 75

Church History.

Collier, J. Ecclesiast'l Hist. of Gt. Brit., 4 v. 8vo L. 94s. 6d.
Jervis, Rev. W. H. History of Church of
            France, 2 vols.... 8vo Lond.
Jones, Rev. C. C. Hist. of Church of God. 8vo N. Y. 3 50
Macduff, Rev. J. R. St. Paul in Rome, etc.12mo L. 4s. 6d.
Neale, J. M. Hist. of East'n Church, 4 v. 8vo L. £4.
Pressensé, E. de. The Church during the
            French Revolution....16mo Lond.
Skeats. Hist. of Free Churches of Engl'd. 8vo Lon. 16s.

Conchology.

    Adams, H. G.   Beautiful Shells.........12mo L. & N. $1 60
    Say, J. B.   Conchology of the Uni. States. 8vo N. Y.   6 00

Constitution—UNITED STATES.

    Pomeroy, J. N.   Constitu'l Law of U. S.. 8vo N. Y.   3 50

Confectionery.

    Francatelli.   Royal Confectioner........12mo Lond.   1 50

Coal.

    Lesley, J. P.   Manual of Coal & its Topog.12mo Phila.   1 50

Correspondence.

    Berry, M.   Jour. and Correspondence, 3 v. 8vo Lond.

Corsica.

    Morris, E. J.   Corsica and Early Life of
                             Napoleon....12mo Phila.   1 75

Darwinism.

    Darwinian Theory Examined............ 8vo L. 10s. 6d.
    Huxley.   More Criticisms on Darwin....12mo N. Y.

Decorative Art.

    Art of Illumination.................... 8vo N. Y.   3 00

Devotion.

    Bayne, P.   The Christian Life.........12mo Bost.   1 75
    Christian Daily Treasury..............12mo Bost.   1 50
    Cowles, Miss M.   Rosary for Lent.......12mo N. Y.   1 50
    Fletcher.   Guide to Family Devotion.... 4to Lond.   10 00
    Muller.   Life of Trust................12mo Bost.   1 75

Dictionaries.

    Chinese and English.   By Morrison...... 8vo Lond.
    Japanese and English.   By Hepburn...r. 8vo Lond.

Dogs.

    Morris.   Dogs and their Doings.   Illust.. 4to N. Y.   1 75

Domestic Animals.

    Ross, C. H.   Book of Cats..............12mo L. 4s. 6d.

Domestic Economy.

    Cooley, A. J.   Cyclopedia of Receipts.... 8vo N. Y.   1 5)

Drama.

    Ford.   Dramatic Works by Gifford, 3 v.. 8vo Lon. 36s.
    Shakespeare.   Edited by H. G. Bell, 6 v..12mo L. & N.   9 00

Drawing-Books.

    Metz.   Drawing-Book of Human Figure..folio Phila.   7 50

East (The).

    McLeod, Norman.   Peeps at the Far East.12mo L. & N.   3 00

Education.

Abbott, J.   Gentle Measures for Training
                        of the Young....12mo N. Y. $1 75
Sewell.   Principles of Education........12mo N. Y.   2 00
Virchow.   Injurious Influence of Schools.
                        Trans. from German.... 8vo

Egypt.

Gordon, Lady Duff.   Letters from Egypt.16mo Lond.
Hengstenberg.   Egypt and Books of Moses.12mo Andov.
Hill, S. S.   Travels in Egypt and Syria.. 8vo   Lond.
Lane, E. W.   Modern Egyptians.   Illus.
                        New edition, 2 vols....12mo Lon. 12s.
Osburn.   Monumental Hist. of Egypt.... 8vo   Lond.
Thompson, J. P.   Egypt, Past and Present.
·   Wilkinson.   Anct. Egyptians, new ed., 2 v.12mo Lon. 12s.
Zincke.   Egypt of Pharaohs & the Khédive. 8vo   Lon. 18s.

England—HISTORY OF.

Lancelot.   Queens of England and their
                        Times, 2 vols.... 8vo L. & N.   5 00
Molesworth, W. N.   History of England
                        from 1830, vol. 1.... 8vo   Lon. 15s.

England—SPECIAL PERIODS.

Burton.   Cromwellian Diary, 4 vols...... 8vo   Lond.
Hall, Mrs.   Queens of England before the
                        Conquest.... 8vo L. & N.   2 50
Hallam.   Constitutional Hist. of England,
                        with May's Continuation, 5 v.12mo N. Y.   8 75
Pearson, C. H.   History of England ; Early
                        and Middle Ages, 2 v.. 8vo Lon. 30s.
Turner, Sharon.   Hist. of Anglo-Saxons, 3 v. 8vo   Lond.
Vaughan.   Revolutions of English Hist.3 v. 8vo Lon. 45s.
————   England under the Stuarts...

English History—ILLUSTRATIVE WORKS.

Browne, N.   Chaucer's England, 2 vols.. 8vo Lon. 24s.
Bulwer.   Last of the Barons...........12mo Phila.   1 50
Charles, Mrs.   Daytons and Davenants...12mo N. Y.   1 75
————   Both Sides of the Sea.....12mo N. Y.   1 75
Diary of Lady Willoughby, etc.........
Kingsley.   Hereward ; Westward, Ho!...⎫
Scott.   Ivanhoe, Kenilworth, Woodstock, ⎪   *See*
            Nigel, Peveril, Old Mortality, etc. ⎬ *Fiction.*
Thackeray.   Henry Esmond, Virginians. ⎪
Youth of Shakespeare, etc. (3 works).....⎭

English Language.

Morris, R.   Specimens of Early English.16mo Oxfd.

English Literature.

Yonge, C. D.   Three Centuries of English
                        *   Literature.... 8vo Lond.

Essays—MISCELLANEOUS.

Buckle. Posthumous Works, 3 vols..... 8vo Lond.
Frere, J. Hookham.　Works in Prose and
Verse, 2 vols.... 8vo Lon. 38s.
Goldsmith.　Works.　Edited by Cunning-
ham, 4 vols ..... 8vo Lond. 30s.
Osgood, Sam'l.　Milestones in our Life's
Journey....12mo N. Y.　$1 25
———— —— The Hearthstone.......12mo N. Y.　1 25
Rogers, H.　Essays from "Good Words".12mo L. & N. 1 75
Rosetti, M. F.　The Shadow of Dante... 8vo L. 10s. 6d.
Sidney, Sir Ph.　Miscel. Works and Life. 8vo Bost.　2 50
Spencer, Herbert.　Essays.............12mo N. Y.　2 50

Ethnology.

Harris, J.　Man Primeval.............12mo Bost.　1 50
———— The Pre-Adamite Earth......12mo Bost.　1 50
Heyworth, L.　The Origin, Mission and
Destiny of Man.... 8vo Lond.
Moore, J. S.　Pre-Glacial Man......... 8vo Dubl. 6s.
Smith, C. H.　Natural History of Human
Species....12mo L. 7s. 6d.
Thompson, J. P.　Moral Unity of Human
Race....12mo N. Y.

Europe—HISTORY.

Koch.　Revolutions in Europe (tables)....

Europe—TRAVELS.

Calvert, G. H.　First Year in Europe....16mo Bost.　1 75

Evidences of Christianity.

Cooper, T.　Bridge of History; Evidences
of Christianity.....16mo Lond.　1 25

Fiction.

Baring-Gould.　Gabrielle André; Histor.
Novel, paper.... 8vo N. Y.　60
Blanche, A.　The Bandit, from Swedish.
By S. Borg.... 8vo N. Y.
Douglas, Amanda.　Lucia; her Problem.12mo N. Y.　2 00
"Dorothy Fox" (Author of).　John Thomp-
son, Blockhead....12mo N. Y.　2 00
———— ———— The Blue Bell....16mo N. Y.　1 25
Erckman-Chatrain.　Story of the Peasant.12mo L. 3s. 6d.
Five Hundred Majority.　A Tale of the
Times.... 8vo N. Y.
Heywood, J. C.　How will it End? a ro-
mance....12mo Phila.　2 00
Higher Law; a Romance.　By author. of
Pilgrim and Shrine....12mo N. Y.　1 75
Howells, W. D.　Their Wedding Journey.12mo Bost.　2 00
"Lyndon."　Margaret........... .....12mo N. Y.　1 50

Macdonald, Geo. The Princess and the
     Goblin. Illust..12mo Phila.
Melville, G. J. W. Sarchedon ; a Legend. 8vo N. Y.
Morton House. By Author of Valerie
      Aylmer.... 8vo N. Y. $1 50
Muhlbach. Mohammed Ali and his House. 8vo N. Y. 1 50
Myself ; a Romance....................12mo N. Y. 2 00
Prentiss, Mrs. E. Fred, Maria and Me...16mo N. Y. 1 20
———— ——— — Aunt Jane's Hero.... 12mo N. Y. 1 50
Whitney, Mrs. Real Folks............12mo Bost. 1 50

Fine Arts—ILLUSTRATED WORKS.

Art Studies from Nature. Illust........ 4to Lon. 12s.
Cabinet Pictures. By Turner, Calcott, etc.
    6 engravings, in........ folio Lond.
Chef d'Œuvres of Art ; Masterpieces of
  Engraving, reproduced in photog. 4to Lond.
Crowe & Cavalcasselle. Paint'g in N. Italy :
 1st Series, 2d to 14th Century, 3 vols.. 8vo Lon. 63s.
 2d Series, 14th to 16th Century, 2 vols. 8vo Lon. 42s.
Cruikshank. 82 Illustra. from his Works. 4to Lond. 5 00
  2 parts....................Lond. folio 8s. 6d. ea.
Doré Gallery—250 Drawings selected from
     his Works....folio L. & N. 60 00
—— —— Atala. Illustrated........folio L. & N. 18 00
—— —— Wandering Jew..........folio L. & N. 6 50
Durer, Albert. Life and Works. By Mrs.
     Heaton. Illust.....r. 8vo Lond. 10 00
———— Passio Christi, reproduced in fac-
    simile, ed. by W. C. Prime. 4to N. Y. 15 00
English School of Painting in Water
     Colors....folio Lond. 40 00
Etchings and Engrs. from Old Masters, 20
     plates....folio Lon. 70s.
Finden's Gallery of Mod. Art., 31 engrs..folio Lon. 21s.
Hoppin, Augustus. Ups and Downs, by
    Land and Water..folio Bost. 10 00
Landseer, T. Life and Letters of Wm.
    Bewick, Artist, 2 vols.... 8vo Lon. 24s.
Maclise. Pict. from his Works, on steel. 4to Lon. 15s.
Nash. Mansions of England in Olden Time
    tinted plates, new ed., 3 v. Lond. folio ea. 31s. 6d.
New Test. Illust. with engrs. on wood,
    from old Masters.... 4to Lond. 50 00
New Test. Edited by Churton, etc., 115
    Illust., 2 vols.... 8vo Lond. 12 00
Scott. W. B. British School of Sculpture,
    steel plates.... 4to Lon. 25s.
Turner. His Celebrated Landscapes, 16
    Autotypes.... 4to Lon. 42s.
Woltman. Holbein and his Times, 60 Ill. 4to Lond.
World's Pictures (The), 15 photographs.. 4to Lon. 21s.

Fish Culture.

Francis. Fish Culture................12mo Lond. $2 00

France—REVOLUTION; AND WAR OF 1870.

Abbott. Hist. of French Revol. of 1789.. 8vo N.Y.

Loudon, M. D. Franco-Prussian War ...12mo N. Y. 2 00

France—THE COMMUNE.

Vésinier. History of the Commune...... 8vo L. 7s. 6d.

Geography.

Encyclopedia of Geography, by Murray

and others. 3 vols... *r.*8vo Phila. 5 00

Gift Books.

Andersen. Fairy Tales, 12 designs in color.folio Lond. 10 00

Bailey. Festus. Illust. by Billings..... 8vo N. Y. 5 00

Beauties of Waverley, 45 steel plates.... 8vo Phila. 5 00

Bickersteth. Yesterday, To-day, etc., large

paper.... 8vo N. Y. 4 00

Bryant. Forest Hymn. Illust. by Hows. 4to N. Y. 4 00

Century of Queens. Litera. and Art. Illus. 4to N. Y. 6 00

Christian Lyrics. Illust., new edition....12mo L. 7s. 6d.

Coles. Dies Iræ; 13 versions, with plates. 8vo N. Y. 6 00

Festival of Song. Illust. Ed. by Saunders.*r.* 8vo N. Y.

Gallery of Fine and Useful Arts. By

Knight, 2 vols....folio Lon. 35s.

Gallery of English and American Famous

Poets. Illus. with Vignettes on steel.

Edit. by Prof. Coppee..............*r.* 8vo Phila. 15 00

Goethe Gallery, 50 plates on steel....... 4to L. & N. 20 00

Harte, Bret. Sketches. Illust. by Eytinge. 4to Bost. 10 00

Herbert, Geo. Poems. Illust.......... 4to L. & N. 6 00

Howells. Their Wedding Journey......12mo Bost. 2 00

In the Woods, with Bryant, &c. Illustrated

by Hows.... 8vo N. Y. 4 00

Kneeland. Wonders of Yosemite Valley. 4to Bost. 4 00

Macaulay. Lays of Anc't Rome, red line

edition. Illust....18mo N. Y. 3 50

Michelet. The Mountain; Nature, its

Poetry, etc., *each* illust.... 8vo L. & N. 6 00

Mighty Works of Jesus Christ. Illustra.

with Photo's from Great Artists.... 8vo L. & N. 6 00

Ministering Children and Sequel. Illust. 8vo N. Y. 4 00

Parables of our Lord. Illust. on Steel.... folio L. & P. 10 00

Pictorial Sunday Book (Knight's). Illust. folio Lon. 25s.

Pictures from English Literature. Illust. 4to L. & N. 10 00

Proverbs of Solomon. Illustrated ...... 8vo Lond.

Retzsch. Outlines to Shakespeare...... folio Bost. 9 00

Saunders. Salad for the Social & Solitary.12mo N. Y. 4 00

Schiller Gallery. 50 Illustrations....... L. & N. 20 00

Sermon on the Mount. Illustrated...... folio L. & B. 12 00

Warner. Summer in a Garden, Illust..16mo Bost. 3 00

Wood, L.V. West Point Scrap-Book. Illus. 8vo N. Y, 5 00

Gold.

Chevalier. On Prob. fall in val. of Gold..12mo N. Y. $ 50

Government.

Helps, Arthur. Thoughts on Government. 8vo Lond.

Greece.

Arnold, Rev. F.   History of Greece, with
        Maps....12mo Lon. 6s.

Health.

Gardner, A. R.   Our Children: their Physi-
   cal and Mental Development....12mo Hartf.
Howe, J. W., M. D.   Emergencies, and
      How to Treat Them.... 8vo N. Y.   3 00
Maudsley.   Body and Mind; Mutual In-
      fluence, etc....16mo N. Y.   1 00

History—ANCIENT.

Niebuhr.   Lectures on Roman Hist. 3 v. 8vo Phila.   5 00

Holy Land.

Besant & Palmer.   Jerusalem; the city of
     Herod and Saladin.... 8vo L. 7s. 6d.
Hughes.   Outline of Scripture Geography
     and History....18mo Phila.   1 00
Palmer.   The Desert of the Exodus, 2 v. 8vo Lon. 28s.
Ritter.   Comparative Geog. of Palestine
     (by Gage), 4 vols.... 8vo L. & N. 14 00

Huguenots.

Marsh, Mrs.   Hist. of the Huguenots, 2 v.12mo Phila.   2 00

Humorous Works.

Cruikshank.   Comic Almanac.. 1835–43, 2v.12mo Lond.   7 00
Halliburton's Sam Slick................12mo N. Y.   1 25
Maginn.   Reliques of Father Prout. Ill.12mo Lond.   2 50
Munchausen's Travels.   Illustrated by
     Cruikshank....12mo L. & N.   1 75
Wit and Wisdom of Don Quixote........

India.

Butler, Rev. W.   Land of the Veda...... 8vo N. Y.   4 00

Infidelity.

Modern Scepticism.   Lectures.   By English
     Clergymen.... 8vo L. 7s. 6d.

Iron.

Lesley, J. P.   The Iron Manufacturer's
     Guide.... 8vo N. Y.

Italy.

Elliott, Mrs. Diary of Idle Woman in Italy.12mo Lond.
Gruner.　Terra　Cotta　Architecture　of
　　　　　　　　North Italy.... folio L. 105s.
Hawthorne.　Passages　from　Italian　and
　　　　　　French Note Books, 2 vols.12mo Bost.　$4 00

Jews.

Rothschild, C. & A. de.　History and Litera-
　　　　　　ture of the Israelites....12mo L. 3s. 6d.
Wilberforce, Sam'l.　Heroes of Hebrew
　　　　　　　　History.... 8vo L. & N.　2 50

Landscape Gardening.

Scott, F. J. Suburban Home and Grounds.r. 8vo N. Y.　8 00

Law.

Bryant & Stratton.　Commer. Law for Busi-
　　　　　　　　ness Men.... 8vo N. Y.　4 00
Handy Book of Property Law, by Lord &
　　　　　　　　Leonards....12mo N. Y.　1 00
Smith.　Compend. of Mercantile Law.... 8vo N. Y.　6 00
Tracy, W.　Hand-Book of Law...... ... 8vo N. Y.　5 50

Legends.

Baring-Gould, S.　Legends of Old Test.
　　Characters, from the Talmud, &c., 2 v.12mo Lon. 16s.

Mechanics.

Brown, H. T.　507 Mechan'l Movements..18mo N. Y.　1 00
Nystrom.　Pocket-Book of Mechanics and
　　　　　　　　Engineering....12mo Phila.　2 50

Metaphysics.

Mansell, Dean.　Metaphysics............12mo N. Y.　2 00
Munsell, Rev. O. S.　Psychology........12mo N. Y.　2 00
Payne, Martin.　Physiology of the Soul
　　　　　　and Instinct.... 8vo N. Y.　5 00
Potter, Alonzo.　Religious Philosophy... 8vo Phila.　8 00
Ueberweg.　History of Philosophy, 2 v.. 8vo N. Y.　7 00

Metallurgy.

Kustell, E.　Metallurgy of Silver Ores... 8vo San Fr.
──── ── Concentration of Ores....... 8vo San Fr.　7 50
Overman, F.　Treatise on Metallurgy.... 8vo N. Y.
Lieber, O. M.　Assayer's Guide..........12mo Phila.　1 25
Pigott, A. S.　Chemistry and Metallurgy
　　　　　　　　of Copper....12mo Phila.　1 50

Money.

Moran, C.　Money....................12mo N. Y.　1 25

Music.

Warner.　Rudimental Lessons in Music..12mo N. Y.　1 00

Natural History.

Cassell. Book of Birds. By T. R. Jones.
Illustrated, 2 vols.... folio L. & N.
Chadbourne, P. A. Lect's on Instinct. '71.12mo N. Y. $1 50
Dana, J. D. On Zoophytes.............. 8vo Phila. 4 00
Darwin. Origin of Species........cloth.12mo N. Y. 2 00
———— Descent of Man, 2 vols........12mo N. Y. 4 00
Huxley. Manual of Anatomy of Verte-
brated Animals. 8vo N. Y.
Jardine. Naturalist's Library. Illustrated
with col'd plates, 40 vols..12mo Lond. £9
Kirby & Spence. Introd. to Entomology,
7th edition.... 8vo Lond. 5s
Mivart. Genesis of Species......... ...12mo N. Y. 1 75
Morris. Brit. Moths, 4,000 col'd plates, 4 v. 8vo Lond.
Museum of Natural History, with Illus.
on wood, 2 vols....folio Lon. 34s.
Nicholson, H. A. Text-Book of Zoology,
for Colleges, etc....12mo N. Y. 1 75

Natural Sciences.

Arnott. Elements of Physics........... 8vo Phila. 2 25
Clark. Mind in Nature; Origin of Life, etc. 8vo N. Y. 3 50
Deschanel. Natural Philosophy. Trans.
4 vols.... 8vo N. Y. 8 00
Ganot. Elementary Treatise on Physics. 8vo Lon. 15s.
Maxwell, J. C. Theory of Heat........12mo L. 3s. 6d.
Muller. Physics and Meteorology....... 8vo Phila. 4 50
Schoedler & Medlock. Wonders of Nature. 8vo Phila. 3 00
Small Books on Great Subjects, 3 vols...18mo Phila. 1 50
Wonders of Water. Wonder Library...18mo N. Y. 1 50
Wonders of Vegetation. Wonder Lib'y.18mo N. Y. 1 50
Wonders of Electricity. Wonder Lib'y.18mo N. Y. 1 50

New England.

Elliott, C. W. Hist. of New England, 2 v. 8vo N. Y. 5 00

Notabilia.

Milledulcia; 1000 Pleasant Things......12mo N. Y. 1 50
Ten Thousand Wonderful Things.......12mo N. Y. 1 50
Wells. Things Not Generally Known...12mo N. Y. 1 75

Painting.

Kauffman, T. Amer. Painting Book..... 4to Bost. 5 0)

Patagonians.

Musters. At Home with the Patagonians. 8vo Lon. 16s

Physiognomy.

Lavater. Physiognomy. Condensed ed.12mo N. Y. 1 25

Physiology.

Brillat-Savarin. Hand-Book of Dining,
Corpulence, etc....12mo N. Y. 1 00

Poetry—COLLECTIONS.

Poets of the 19th Century; edited by
Willmott and Duyckinck. Illust.... 4to N. Y. $5 00
[*₊* This is erroneously called " Sacred Poets," on page 161.]

Poetry.

Randolph, A. D. F. Hopefully Waiting, etc.12mo N. Y.   1 50

Poetry—HUMOROUS, ETC.

Combe. Dr. Syntax's Three Tours......12mo L. & N. 2 00

Reformation.

Ranke. History of the Reformation .... 8vo Phila.   2 00

Rome—THE MODERN CITY.

Burn. Rome and the Campagna; History
and Topography.... 4to Lon. 63s.

Spain.

Street, G. R. Gothic Architecture in Spain. 8vo Lon. 30s.

Supernaturalism—DEMONOLOGY.

Burton. R. T. Vikram, and the Vampire:
Hindoo Deviltry.... 8vo Lond.   2 50
Credo; a Supernatural Book... ....12mo Lon. 5s.
McRae, Rev. Th. Lectures on Satan....12mo N. Y.

Theology.

Hodge, Chas. Systematic Theology, 2 v. 8vo N. Y.   10 00

Turkey.

Harney, Mrs. Turkish Harems and Cir-
cassian Homes.... 8vo Lon. 15s.

United States—TRAVELS IN.

Todd, John. The Sunset Land; the Pacific
Slope....12mo N. Y.   1 50

COLLECTED WORKS (MISCELLANEOUS)

OF

STANDARD AUTHORS.

(Embracing only uniform editions of works of leading Authors who have written in more than one department.)

Adams, John. Collected Works, 10 vols. 8vo Bost. $30 00
Addison. Works. Ed. by Greene, 6 vols.12mo Phila. 9 00
———— Works, 6 vols ....12mo Bohn. 8 40
Bacon, Lord. Complete Works, 15 vols..12mo N. Y. 33 75
Bentham, Jer. Works, 11 vols.......... 8vo Lond.
Brougham, Lord. Works, 11 vols.......12mo Glas. 55s.
British Essayists, 38 vols.................18mo Bost. 47 50
———— ———— Modern, 6 vols......... 8vo N. Y. 12 00
Burke, Edmund. Works, 12 vols........ 8vo Bost. 30 00
Burns—Byron. [See Poetry.]
Calhoun, J. C. Works, 6 vols........... 8vo N. Y. 15 00
Channing, W. E. Works, 3 vols........12mo Bost. 3 00
Chesterfield, Lord. Works.............12mo N. Y. 2 50
Coleridge, S. T. Works, 7 vols........12mo N. Y. 10 50
Cowper. Works. (Poems and Corresp.)
                By Southey, 15 vols.12mo Lon. 75s.
———— ———— By Grimshaw, 8 vols.12mo Lond. 11 20
De Foe. Works, 7 vols.................12mo Bohn. 9 80
De Quincey. Works, 22 vols............12mo Bost. 33 00
— ———— ———— 16 vols. ....12mo Lon. 72s.
Dickens. Works. Household edit., 56 v.12mo N. Y. 56 00
———— ———— Riverside edit., Ill., 28 v.12mo N. Y. 56 00
———— ———— Globe edit., Illust., 15 v.12mo N. Y. 22 00
———— ———— Illust. Library ed., 29 v.12mo Bost. 58 00
———— ———— Household ed., 15 vols..12mo Bost. 22 50
———— ———— Chas. Dickens' ed., 15 v.12mo Bost. 22 50
———— ———— The same, bound in 8 v.12mo Bost. 14 00
———— ———— Diamond edit., 14 vols..18mo Bost. 21 00
———— ———— Plum Pudding edit., 6 v.12mo N. Y. 10 50
———— ———— Handy vol. edit., 14 vols.12mo N. Y. 10 50
Dryden. Complete Works, 2 vols....... 8vo N. Y. 4 00
Edgeworth, Miss. Complete Works, 10 v.12mo N. Y. 15 00
———— ———— ———— ———— 10 v.12mo L. & B. 15 00
Fielding. Complete Works, fine ed., 10 v. 8vo L. & B. 30 00
———— ———— ———— cheap ed., 1 v.r. 8vo Lon. 18s.
Franklin, Benj. Writings, 10 vols...... 8vo Phila. 25 00
Goethe. Poetical and Prose Works, 5 v..12mo Bohn. 7 00
Goldsmith. Poetical and Prose Works.
                By Prior, 4 vols....12mo Phila. 6 00
———— The same, 4 vols .... 8vo Lon. 30s.
Hamilton, Alex. Political Works, 7 vols. 8vo Phila. 22 50
Hazlitt, W. Writings, 5 vols...........12mo Phila. 7 50

Hood, Thos.   Prose and Poet'l Works, 6 v. 12mo N. Y. $15 00
Irving.   Works.   Knickerbocker ed., 27 v. 12mo N. & P. 67 50
——— ———   Sunnyside ed., 28 vols. 12mo N. & P. 63 00
——— ———   Riverside edit., 26 vols. 18mo N. Y.   45 50
——— ———   People's edit., 26 vols.. 18mo N. Y.   32 50
Jefferson.   Works.   Edit. by H. A. Wash-
                      ington, 9 vols.... 8vo Phila. 27 00
Jerrold, Douglas.   Works and Life. 5 v.. 8vo L. & P. 12 50
Johnson, Dr. Sam.   Works.............
Lamb, Chas.   Works.   Best Edition, 5 v. 8vo N. Y.   9 00
Landor, W. S.   Whole Works, 2 v.....r. 8vo Lond.   10 00
Locke, Jno.   Philosophical Works, 2 v..   Bohn   2 80
Longfellow.   Prose & Poetical Works, 7 v. 12mo Bost. 17 50
Macaulay.   Complete Works, 16 vols.... 12mo N. Y.   36 00
Milman, Dean.   Prose Works, 14 vols.. 12mo N. Y.   24 50
Milton.   Prose and Poetical Works, 7 v.. 12mo Bohn.   9 80
Montaigne.   Works.   Edited by Wright, 4v. 8vo N. Y.   9 00
More, Hannah.   Works, 7 vols.........12mo N. Y.   8 75
Poe, Edgar A.   Prose and Poet'l Works, 4 v. 12mo N. Y.   9 00
Pope.   Prose and Poetical Works.   By
                      Elwin, 6 vols.... 8vo Lon. 63s.
Rabelais.   Works, 2 vols..............12mo Bohn.   2 80
Schiller.   Prose and Poetical Works, 4 v. 12mo Bohn.   5 60
——— ——— ——— ——— ———2 v. r. 8vo N. Y.   6 00
Schlegel.   Works, 6 vols..............12mo Bohn.   8 40
Scott, Sir W.   Whole Works, 100 vols... 12mo Edn. £20
——————   *₊* See also Fiction.
Seward, W. H.   Works (chiefly Polit'l) 4 v. 8vo N. Y.   16 00
Smith, Sydney.   Works and Life. New ed.
                      2 vols.... 12mo Lon. 12s.
——— ——— ——— ——— ———1 vol.... 8vo N. Y.   2 00
Smollett.   Works, 1 vol..............r. 8vo Lon. 18s.
Sterne.   Works (2 vols., Phila., $3), 1 vol. 8vo Lond.   1 75
Swift.   Works, 2 vols..............r. 8vo Lond. 24s.
——— ——— 19 vols. (scarce)........ 8vo Lond.
Thackeray.   Works.   Illust., 22 vols.... 8vo L. & P. 66 00
——— ——— ——— New ed.. 11 vols.. 8vo L. & P. 33 00
——— ——— · ——— 11 vols ....12mo Bost. 13 75
Washington.   Writings, 12 vols........ 8vo Bost.   24 00
Webster, Dan'l.   Works (Speeches) 6 v.. 8vo Bost.   18 00
Whittier.   Prose and Poetical, 4 vols ... 18mo Bost.   10 00
Wilson, John.   Works (Essays)........ 8vo. N. Y.   2 00

APPENDIX.

Young People's Books.

(See also Fairy Tales, Games, etc.)

(More than 1,000 different volumes of Juvenile and Sunday-School books may be selected from the Catalogues of the American S. S. Union, Tract Society, Methodist Book Concern, and numerous other "Publication Societies;" and from those of H. Hoyt, Lee & Shepard, Lothrop & Co., Boston; Randolph, Pott, Young & Co., Dutton, Sheldon, Dodd & Mead, Nelson, Leavitt & Allen, Hurd & Houghton, and others, New York, and many other publishers—we mention a few only.)

a. A. L. O. E. (Miss Charlotte Tucker) Juvenile Library in a wood case........... $28 00
b. Abbott, J.
  The Rollo Books, 14 vols., 16mo 12 60
  The Rollo Story Books, 12 vols., 16mo... .... 3 75
  Rollo's Tour in Europe, 10 vols., 16mo. 9 00
  Franconia Stories, 10 vols., 16mo, each............ 90
  Little Learner Series, 10 vols, 16mo, each... 90
  Marco Polo Series, 10 v., 16mo, each............ 90
  Rainbow & Lucky Series, 10 vols., 16mo, each..... 90
  Story Books, 12mo, each.. 1 75
  August Stories, 18mo, N. Y., each...... .... 1 50
  Florence Stories, 6 vols.. 6 00
  Science for the Young, ea. 1 50
  American Hist., 8 vols... 10 00
b. Adams, W. T. (Oliver Optic.)
  Young America Series; No. 1 and No. 2, 12 vols., 16mo, each............ 1 50
  Soldier Boy Series, 3 v., ea. 1 50
  Sailor Boy Series, 3 v., ea. 1 50
  Woodville Stories, 6 v., ea. 1 25
  Boat Club Series, 6 v., ea. 1 25
  Riverdale Stories, 12 v., ea. 45
  Starry Flag Series, 6 vols., each 1 25
a. Aikin, Dr. J. & Mrs. Barbauld.
  Evenings at Home, 12mo, N. Y.................. 1 50
a. Alcott, Miss L. M.
  Little Women, 2 vols..... 3 00
  Little Men, 1 vol.......... 1 50
  Old Fashioned Girl 1 50

a. Alcott, Miss L. M.
  Aunt Jo.'s Scrap Book, Bost........ .... $1 00
  Morning Glories, N. Y.... 1 50
a. Aldrich, T. B.
  Story of a Bad Boy, 16mo, 1 50
b. Alger, H., Jr.
  Juveniles, 13 vols., per vol. 1 25
  Strong and Steady, 16mo.. 1 50
a. Andersen, Hans C.
  Fairy Tales, 5 v., 16mo, ea. 1 25
  Wonder Stories, 12mo..... 2 25
  Stories and Tales, Illust'd. 12mo............... 2 25
a. Arabian Nights (and various other editions) 12mo..... 1 75
Aunt Fanny.
  [*See* Mrs. Barrow.]
Aunt Louisa.
  Nursery Books, with large colored plates, each..... 2 50
  Aunt Mattie's Library, 4 v. 18mo................... 3 60
b. Baker, S. W.
  Cast up by the Sea, 12mo.. 1 50
b. Ballantyne, R. M.
  Away in the Wilderness, 12mo................... 75
  Chasing the Sun, 12mo. .. 75
  Coral Islands, 12mo....... 1 25
  Dog Crusoe, 12mo........ 1 25
  Floating Light, 16mo...... 1 50
  Gascoygne, 12mo......... 1 25
  Gorilla Hunters, 12mo ... 1 25
  Fast in the Ice, 12mo..... 1 25
  Fighting the Whales, 12mo. 1 25
  Freaks on the Fells, 12mo. 1 25
  Martin Rattler, 12mo...... 1 25
  Red Eric, 12mo........... 1 25
  Shifting Winds, 12mo..... 1 25
  Ungava, 12mo....... ..... 1 25
  Wild Man of the West,12mo 1 25

a. Alcott, Miss L. M.	
World of Ice (The) 12mo..	$1 25
Young Fur Traders, 12mo.	1 25
Barbauld, Mrs.	
Things by their Right	
Names, 18mo..........	75
a. Barrows, Mrs. F.	
Aunt Fanny's Stories, 6 v.	5 00
Night Cap Stories, 6 vols..	5 00
Barrows, Rev. W.	
Twelve Nights in the Hunt-	
ers' Camp, 12mo........	1 25
b. Beckoning Series, 3 vols....	3 75
Belmont Series, 5 v., Bost..	6 25
a. Biart, L.	
Young Naturalist, 12mo..	1 75
Boy's Globe Library, 3 series,	
each 4 vol., Phila., per vol.	1 50
b. Bréhart, A de.	
Adventures of a Little	
French Boy.............	
Busch, W.	
Max and Maurice, 12mo..	1 50
a. Carroll, Louis.	
Alice's Adventures........	1 50
Behind Looking-Glass....	1 50
Castlemon, H.	
Frank on a Gunboat......	1 25
" on the Lower Missis.	1 25
" on the Prairies.....	1 25
" in the Woods.......	1 25
" the Young Natur'list	1 25
" before Vicksburg...	1 25
Go Ahead; No Moss, each.	1 25
Tom Newcombe..........	1 25
Cecil and His Dog, 16mo...	1 25
Chambers' Libr'y for Young	
People, 20 vols.; 2d series,	
7 vols., each	75
a. Charlesworth, Miss.	
Minister'g Children, 12mo.	1 75
Sequel to Ministering Chil-	
dren, 12mo..............	1 75
Both vols. in 1, red line ed.	4 00
England's Yeoman, 12mo.	1 75
Charlotte Elizabeth.	
[*See* Tonna, Mrs.]	
Child, Lydia Maria.	
Rainbows for Children....	1 50
Children's Album, etc......	
Child's Book of Song and	
Praise, with Music......	3 50
a. Clarke, R. S. (Sophie May).	
Dotty Dimple Books, 7 v.,	
each	75
Prudy Books, 7 vols., each.	75
b. Conant, Mrs.	
Butterfly Hunters, 16mo..	1 50
Crossland, Mrs.	
Memorable Women, Illus.	1 50
Dall, Mrs. C. H.	
Patty Gray's Journey to the	
Cotton Islands, 3 v., each	1 25
Daltou, W.	
Lost among the Wild Men,	
8vo ....3s. 6d.	
Tiger Prince, 16mo.......	1 50
Wolf Boy of China, 12mo.	1 25

a. Dana, R. H.	
Two Years before the Mast,	
16mo	$1 50
a. Day, Thos.	
Sandford & Merton, 16mo.	1 25
a. De Foe.	
Robinson Crusoe, 18mo...	1 50
(And various other edit.)	
De Mille, J.	
B. O. W. C., 16mo, Bost...	1 50
Boys of the Grand Pré	
School, 16mo Bost......	1 50
Lost in the Fog, 16mo Bost.	1 50
a. Diaz, Mrs. A. M.	
William Henry Letters,	
16mo Bost....	1 50
King's Lily and Rosebud..	1 50
a. Dickens. Child Pictures	
from............	1 50
Child's Hist. of Eng., 2 v...	1 50
Same in 1 vol.............	1 00
a. Dodge, M. E.	
Hans Brinker's Skates,	
12mo N. Y.............	2 00
Irvington Stories, 12mo	
N. Y...................	1 50
b. Du Chaillu, P.	
Travels and Adventures, 4	
vols., each...........	1 75
Country of Dwarfs, 12mo..	1 75
a. Edgeworth, Miss M.	
Frank, 2 vols., 18mo......	1 50
Harry & Lucy, 2 v., 12mo.	3 00
Moral Tales, 2 vols., 18mo.	1 50
Parents' Assistant, 12mo..	1 50
Popular Tales, 2 v., 18mo.	1 50
Rosamond, 12mo.........	1 50
Works complete, 10 vols..	15 00
Edgar.	
Books for Boys, 5 v., each.	1 20
Everett, Wm.	
Changing Base, 16mo.....	1 25
Double Play, 16mo.........	1 25
Fairy Book. Illust., 12mo..	1 50
Frolich. Picture Book, 4to.	2 00
Farming for Boys, 16mo,	
Bost.....................	1 50
Frontier Series.	
Hunter's Camp, etc., 5 v.,	
each	1 25
Gatty, Mrs.	
Alice and Adolphus, 16mo.	90
Aunt Judy's Tales, 16mo..	90
Parable from Nature, 16mo	90
Girl's Own Treasury, Illust.,	
4to....................	2 50
Girl's Own Book, 16mo....	1 00
a. Golden Treasury Series.	
Book of Golden Deeds....	1 25
Fairy Book..............	1 25
Robinson Crusoe	1 25
Goulding, F. R.	
Marooner's Island.......	
Nacoochee.............	
Sal-O-Quat	3 50
Sapelo................	
Young Marooners.... ..	
In set, 3 vols...... ....)	

Mackarnen, Mrs. M. A.
  Cloud with Silver Lining ⎫
  Dream Chintz........... ⎪
  Home on the Rock...... ⎪
  Merry Christmas........ ⎬
  Old Jolliffe............. ⎪
  Sequel to Old Jolliffe.... ⎪
  Only a Shilling.......... ⎪
  Star in the Desert ...... ⎭
    Above in set, 4 vols., 16mo $4 25
  Sibert's Wold........, ...
  Sunbeam Stories ....
McKeever, Harriet B.
  Breakers Ahead..........
  Edith's Ministry, 16mo....   75
  Eleanor's Three Birthdays,
    16mo 1 00
  Flounced Robe...........
  Lucy Forester's Triumphs,
    16mo 1 00
  Mary Leslie's Trials, 16mo. 1 00
  Silver Threads, 12mo..... 1 50
  Westnook Parsonage ....
  Woodcliff Children........
Mackintosh, Miss M. J.
  Conquest and Self-Con-
    quest, 18mo............. 75
b. Magnet Stories, 4 v., 16mo.. 5 00
Mann, Mrs.
  The Flower People........ 1 00
b. Mannering, May.
  Billy Grimes' Favorite,
    16mo.................. 1 00
  Climbing the Rope, 16mo. 1 00
  Cruise of the Dashaway,
    16mo.................. 1 00
  Little Maid of Oxbow,16mo 1 00
  Little Spaniard, 16mo.... 1 00
  Salt Water Dick, 16mo.... 1 00
Martineau, Harriet.
  Crofton Boys, etc., 4 vols.,
    16mo..................
a. Marryatt, Capt. F.
  Children of the New For-
    est, 12mo.............. 1 25
  Masterman Ready. Scenes ⎫
    in Africa. Settlers in ⎬ 2 25
    Canada, 3 vols., 16mo... ⎭
Mateaux.
  Home Chat with our Young
    Folks.................. 2 50
Max and Maurice. Trans.
  by Brooks..... ...... 1 50
May, Sophie.
  [See Clarke, R. S.]
Mayhew Bros.
  Good Genius that Turned
    Everything to Gold.:.... 75
  Magic of Kindness........ 75
a. Mayhew, Hy.
  Boyhood of Martin Luther,
    16mo. 1 25
  Peasant Boy Philosopher,
    16mo.................. 1 25
  Wonders of Science, 16mo. 1 25
  Young Benjamin Frank-
    lin, 16mo.............. 1 25
  The same, fine ed , gilt edg. 1 50

Men who have Made Them-
  selves. Illust........... $1 50
"Men who have Risen,"
  Library, each....... 1 50
  Men who have Risen......
  Small Beginnings... ....
  Steady Aim ....
  London Merchants........
"Ministering Children"
  Series, 4 vols........... 5 00
Miller, Thos.
  Boys' Book of the Seasons. 2 00
Morris.
  Dogs and their Doings.... 2 00
Munchausen, Baron, 16mo.. 1 25
Musset, Paul de.
  Mr. Wind and Madame
    Rain, square 4to....... 75
Oliver Optic's Books.
  [See Adams.]
Opie, Mrs., Works.
a. Our Young Folks (monthly)
  per vol 3 00
Paul Preston's Voyages, etc.,
  16mo.................. 1 25
Pepper. Boy's Play Book of
  Science.... .... 2 00
  Boy's Play Book of Metals. 2 25
  Popular Fairy Tales, 16mo. 1 25
Penniman, Maj. The Tan-
  ner Boy, Life of Grant,
    16mo.................. 1 50
  Pictures of Eng. Hist., 4to.. 2 50
  Pleasure Book of the Year,
    4to 2 50
a. Phelps, Miss E. S.
  Gypsey Breynton Series, 4
    vols., 16mo 5 00
  Trotty Book, 4to......... 1 50
  Philip Quarll's Emblems...
a. Picture Gallery of all Na-
  tions, Illustrated, 4to.... 2 50
a. Prentiss, E.
  Flower of the Family, 16mo 1 25
  The Little Susy Library, 3
    vols., 16mo............. 2 60
  The Percys, 16mo........ 1 25
  Nidworth & Magic Wands,
    16mo. 1 25
b. Reid, Mayne.
  Tales for Boys....,.......
    First Series, 12 vols, each 1 50
    Second Series, 4 v. each. 1 75
  Riverside Magazine, Illustra-
    ted, 4 vols., each....... 3 00
Rosetti. Sing Song (for
  Nursery)............... 2 00
Samuels, Mrs. P. C.
  Eric; or, Little by Little,
    12mo......... .... 1 25
  St. Winifreds, 12mo...... 1 25
  Springdale Stories, 6 vols. 4 50
Saxe, J. G.
  Clever Stories of Many Na-
    tions................... 3 50
Scudder, H. E.
  Dream Children, etc., 3 v.. 4 00
  Seven Little Sisters, 12mo.. 1 25

a. Sedgwick, Miss C. M.
 Boy of Mount Rhigi, 18mo. $1 25
 Live and Let Live, 18mo.. 75
 Poor Rich Man and Rich
  Poor Man, 18mo......... 75
 Love Token.............. 75
 Means and Ends, Self-
  Training..... 75
 Stories for Youth......... 75
Sherwood, Mrs.
 Whole Works, 16 vols..... 24 00
 Choice Works, Lady Manor,
  etc., 11 vols............. 16 50
Smith, Mrs. C.
 American Home Book, In-
  door Games............. 1 50
Stoddard.
 Adventures in Fairy Land. 1 25
Stolz, Mad. de.
 House on Wheels......... 1 25
Story Without an End, 16mo
 (Mrs. Austen)...........
a. Stowe, Mrs. H. B.
 Pussey Willow, small 4to. 1 50
 Queer Little People, small
  4to.................... 1 50
Sunshine Series. 6 v., 18mo. 3 00
a. Swiss Family Robinson,
 16mo.... .... 1 50
Thayer, Wm.
 Tanner Boy (Lincoln).....
 Printer Boy (Franklin)....
 Tale of a Nest, 12mo...... 1 50
 Things Worth Knowing.... 1 00
Thurston, Miss Louise M.
 Forest Mills, 16mo 80
Tonna, Mrs.
 The Charlotte Elizabeth
  Stories, 8 vols., 16mo ... 7 20
Treasury of Fairy Stories,
 Illust. (H. & H.)........ 1 75
a. Trowbridge, J. T.
 Lawrence's Adventures
  among the Ice-Cutters,
  Glass-Makers, etc....... 1 50
 The Brighthope Series, 5
  vols., 18mo............. 4 00
 Jack Hazard, 16mo....... 1 50

Tuthill, Mrs. L. C.
 Tip-top Story Book for
  Boys, 16mo, 3 vols., ea.. $1 25
 Tip-Top Story Book for
  Girls, 3 vols., 16mo, ea.. 1 25
Tyng, Rev. S. H.
 The Spencers......... ... 1 25
Tytler, Miss.
 Sweet Counsel for Girls... 1 50
Uncle Sam Series, 4 vols.,
 paper, col'd, each....... 60
Vieux Moustache.
 That Good Old Time, 16mo. 1 25
 Two Lives in One, 16mo.. 1 25
a. Warner, Miss.
 Carl Krinken, 16mo....... 1 00
 Casper, 16mo............. 1 00
 Hard Maple, 16mo........ 1 00
 Rutherford Children, 16mo. 1 00
 Sybil and Chryssa, 16mo.. 1 00
 Waste Not, Want Not, Series,
  8 vols., 16mo........... 2 50
 Watts' Songs for Children,
  Illustrated 2 50
Wells, Mrs. Kate G.
 In the Clearings, 16mo.... 80
Winter Evening Library (D.
 A. & Co.), 8 vols........ 8 00
Wood. The Modern Play-
  mate. Illust.....Lond. 4 50
 What Makes me Grow, 16mo. 1 00
a. Whitney, Mrs.
 Leslie Goldthwaite........ 1 75
 We Girls, 12mo 1 50
 Real Folks, 12mo 1 50
 Women of Worth Library,
  4 vols., each............ 1 50
Whittier, J. G. Child Life,
 Illustrated 3 00
Yonge, Miss C. M.
 Caged Lion, 12mo......... 1 25
 Castle Builders, 12mo..... 1 00
 Countess Kate............
 Richard the Fearless, 16mo. 75
 Six Cushions, 16mo....... 1 00
 Book of Golden Deeds.... 1 25
 Young American's Library,
  9 vols.................. 4 50

PERIODICALS—LITERARY.

[We refer only to the leading Periodicals of high class, literary, popularly scientific, or artistic; and we do *not* include theological, religious, medical, or technical publications.]

QUARTERLIES.—AMERICAN.

			PER ANNUM.
North American Review....	8vo	Bost.	$6 00

BRITISH.*

British Quarterly (Liberal)...................	8vo	Lond.	9 00
Edinburgh Review, " (reprint, $4).......	8vo	Lond.	9 00
London Quarterly (Lit., Theol., Sci.)	8vo	Lond.	12 00
Quarterly Review (Conservative), reprint, $4..	8vo	Lond.	9 00
Westminster and For. Quart. (Liberal), reprint, $4.....................................	8vo	Lond.	9 00

MAGAZINES.—AMERICAN.

"Aldine," The. (Illustrated Literary).......	folio	N. Y.	5 00
Atlantic Monthly (Literary).................	8vo	Bost.	4 00
Bookseller's Guide, Am. News Co. (Literary)..	8vo	N. Y.	1 00
City, The. (Literary)......................	8vo	N. Y.	4 00
Galaxy (Literary)...........................	8vo	N. Y.	4 00
Harper's Magazine (Literary, Illustrated).....	8vo	N. Y.	4 00
Lippincott's Magazine (Literary).............	8vo	Phila.	4 00
Literary Bulletin, Leypoldt's.........	8vo	N. Y.	1 00
Old and New (Literary).....................	8vo	Bost.	4 00
Publisher's Circular, Child's (Lit.) semi-month.	8vo	Phila.	2 00
Scribner's Magazine (Literary, Illustrated) ...	8vo	N. Y.	4 00

REPRINTS.

Blackwood's Magazine.......................	8vo	N. Y.	3 00
Good Words...............................	8vo	L.&P.	3 75
Sunday Magazine	8vo	L.&P.	3 50
Eclectic Magazine (Literary and Scientific)....	8vo	N. Y.	5 00
Every Saturday (Literary Weekly)........ ..	8vo	Bost.	4 00
Living Age (Literary Weekly)...............	8vo	Bost.	8 00

BRITISH.

Academy, The. (Scientific).................	4to	Lond.	3 00
Art, Pictorial and Industrial (Illustrated).....	4to	L. & N.	13 50
Art Journal (Illustrated)....................	4to	L. & N.	15 00
Athenæum (monthly parts)...................	4to	Lond.	9 00
Bookseller, The. (Literary News)..........	8vo	Lond.	4 00
Chambers' Journal (for families) ....r.	8vo	Lond.	4 00

* The present high duty and expenses of exchange, etc., add largely to the cost of imported periodicals. January, 1872.

			PER ANNUM.
Cornhill Magazine (Literary)................	8vo	Lond.	$6 00
English Society (light Literature)...........	8vo	Lond.	7 00
"Fortnightly" Review (Radical), pub. monthly.	8vo	Lond.	12 00
Gentleman's Magazine (Literary).............	8vo	Lond.	6 00
Journal of Travel and Natural History.......	8vo	Lond.	14 00
London Society (light Literature)...........	8vo	Lond.	7 00
Macmillan's Magazine (Literature)..........	8vo	Lond.	6 00
Portfolio, edited by Hamerton (Artistic, Illust.).	4to	Lond.	15 00
Punch (monthly parts)......................	4to	Lond.	7 00
St. James' Magazine (Literary)..............	8vo	Lond.	6 00
St. Paul's Magazine "	8vo	Lond.	6 00
Tinsley's Magazine "	8vo	Lond.	6 00

LITERARY WEEKLIES.—AMERICAN.

Appleton's Journal. Illustrated............	4to	N. Y.	4 00
Christian Union (Beecher's)................folio		N. Y.	2 50
Harper's Bazar. Illus. (Lit. and Fashions.)..folio		N. Y.	4 00
Harper's Weekly. Illustrated...............folio		N. Y.	4 00
Hearth and Home. Illustrated.............folio		N. Y.	4 00
Independent (Literary and Religious).........folio		N. Y.	2 50
Literary World............................	4to	Bost.	1 50
The Nation (Literary, Critical, Political).....	4to	N. Y.	5 00

ENGLISH.

Athenæum (Literary and Sci.)...............	4to	Lond.	9 00
Examiner (Literary)......................folio		Lond.	9 00
Field (Sporting)..........................folio		Lond.	15 00
Fun (Comic).............................	4to	Lond.	4 00
Graphic (Artistic). Illustrated.............folio		Lond.	14 00
Illustrated London News..................folio		Lond.	14 00
Illustrated Times........................folio		Lond.	9 00
Nature (Scientific)........................r. 8vo		Lond.	6 00
Notes and Queries (Liter. and Antiquarian)...	4to	Lond.	12 00
Pall Mall Budget (Liter. and Polit.).........folio		Lond.	15 00
Punch (Comic). Illustrated.................	4to	Lond.	7 00
Public Opinion (Eclectic)...................folio		Lond.	7 00
Saturday Review (Literary, Political and Crit.) folio		Lond.	15 00
Spectator (Literary, Political and Critical)....folio		Lond.	15 00
Vanity Fair (with Political Caricatures)......folio		Lond.	15 00

FORTNIGHTLY.

Publisher's Circular......................r. 8vo		Lond.	5 00

YOUNG PEOPLE'S PERIODICALS.

Little Corporal...................monthly	8vo	Chica.	1 00
Merry's Museum.................monthly.	8vo	Bost.	1 50
Our Young Folks.................monthly.	8vo	Bost.	2 00
Oliver Optic's Magazine............weekly.	4to	Bost.	2 50
The Nursery....................monthly.	8vo	Bost.	1 50

PART SECOND.

PREPARED BY FRED. B. PERKINS.

READINGS ON READING.

I. The Duty of Owning Books.

BY HENRY WARD BEECHER.

WE form judgments of men from little things about their houses, of which the owner, perhaps, never thinks. In earlier years, when travelling in the West, where taverns were scarce, and in some places unknown, and every settler's house was a house of entertainment, it was a matter of some importance and some experience to select wisely where you would put up. And we always looked for flowers. If there were no trees for shade, no patch of flowers in the yard, we were suspicious of the place. But, no matter how rude the cabin or rough the surroundings, if we saw that the window held a little trough for flowers, and that some vines twined about strings let down from the eaves, we were confident that there was some taste and carefulness in the log cabin. In a new country, where people have to tug for a living, no one will take the trouble to rear flowers unless the love of them is pretty strong; and this taste, blossoming out of plain and uncultivated people, is itself like a clump of harebells growing out of the seams of a rock. We were seldom misled. A patch of flowers came to signify kind people, clean beds, and good bread.

But in other states of society other signs are more significant. Flowers about a rich man's house may signify only that he has a good gardener, or that he has refined neighbors, and does what he sees them do. But men are not accustomed to buy *books*, unless they want them. If, on visiting the dwelling of a man of slender means, we find that he contents himself with cheap carpets and very plain furniture, in order that he may purchase books, he rises at once in our esteem. Books are not made for furniture, but there is nothing else that so beautifully furnishes a house. THE PLAINEST ROW OF BOOKS THAT CLOTH OR PAPER EVER COVERED IS MORE SIGNIFICANT OF REFINEMENT THAN THE MOST ELABORATELY CARVED *étagère* OR SIDEBOARD.

Give us a house furnished with books rather than furniture! Both, if you can, but books at any rate! To spend several days in a friend's house, and hunger for something to read, while you are treading on costly carpets, and sitting upon luxurious chairs, and sleeping upon down, is as if one were bribing your body for the sake of cheating your mind.

Is it not pitiable to see a man growing rich, augmenting the comforts of home, and lavishing money on ostentatious upholstery, upon the table, upon everything but what the soul needs? We know of many and many a rich man's house where it would not be safe to ask for the commonest English classics. A few garish annuals on the table, a few pictorial monstrosities, together with the stock religious books of his "persuasion," and that is all! No poets, no essayists, no historians, no travels or biographies, no select fictions, or curious legendary lore. But the wallpaper cost three dollars a roll, and the carpets four dollars a yard!

Books are the windows through which the soul looks out. A home without books is like a room without windows. No man has a right to bring up his children without surrounding them with books, if he has the means to buy them. It is a wrong to his family. He cheats them! Children learn to read by being in the presence of books. The love of knowledge comes with reading and grows upon it. And the love of knowledge, in a young mind, is almost a warrant against the inferior excitement of passions and vices.

Let us pity these poor rich men who live barrenly in great, bookless houses! Let us congratulate the poor that, in our day, books are so cheap that a man may every year add a hundred volumes to his library for the price of what his tobacco and his beer would cost him. Among the earliest ambitions to be excited in clerks, workmen, journeymen, and, indeed, among all that are struggling up in life from nothing to something, is that of owning, and constantly adding to, a library of good books. A little library growing larger every year, is an honorable part of a young man's history. It is a man's duty to have books. A library is not a luxury, but one of the necessaries of life.—"*Eyes and Ears.*" 12mo. Boston, 1862.

II. Value and Pleasure of Books and Reading.

Books are the food of youth, the delight of old age; the ornament of prosperity; the refuge and comfort of adversity; a delight at home, and no hindrance abroad; companions by night, in travelling, in the country.—*Cicero.*

Books are a guide in youth and an entertainment for age. They support us under solitude, and keep us from becoming a burden to ourselves. They help us to forget the crossness of men and things, compose our cares and our passions, and lay our disappointments asleep. When we are weary of the living, we may repair to the dead, who have nothing of peevishness, pride, or design in their conversation. It is chiefly through books that we enjoy intercourse with superior minds; "and these invaluable communications are within the reach of all."—*Madame de Genlis.*

"—— the great minds of former ages. The debt which he owes to them is incalculable. They have guided him to truth. They have filled his mind with noble and graceful images. They have stood by him in all vicissitudes; comforters in sorrow, nurses in sickness, companions in solitude. Their friendships are exposed to no danger from the occurrences by which other attachments are weakened or dissolved; time glides on; fortune is inconstant; tempers are soured; bonds which seemed indissoluble are daily sundered by interest, by emulation, or by caprice. But no such cause can affect the silent converse which we hold with the highest of human intellects. That placid intercourse is disturbed by no jealousies or resentments. There are the old friends who are never seen with new faces, who are the same in wealth and in poverty, in glory and in obscurity. With the dead there is no rivalry. In the dead there is no change. Plato is never sullen. Cervantes is never petulant. Demosthenes never comes unseasonably. Dante never stays too long. No difference of political opinion can alienate Cicero. No heresy can excite the horror of Bossuet."—*Lord Macaulay: Review of Montagu's Bacon.*

Books ? The only bodies are they, for noble spirits, that have no ailments or annoyances. Books talk to you, not through the ear, but another way. They shout their silent meaning at the soul through the eye. They never importune, and are never reluctant. They are always full without eating. They are still, but never sleep. They grow old without infirmity. They are neither sick nor weary ; they outwatch the watcher, and greet the morning, and wait for the stars at evening. For every other guest we make a couch and spread a table. But strange are the manners of books and pictures, that bring rest to our perturbations, and are guests that perform all the offices of hospitality for the host.—*H. W. Beecher, " Eyes and Ears,"* page 397.

[Note the coincidence of expression, as well as thought, in the above four extracts.]

It is nearly an axiom, that people will not be better than the books they read.—*Dr. A. Potter.*

It is as important that we should have good books as that we should keep good company, as the one will make the other.— *" An Old Bookseller."*

We cannot linger in the beautiful creations of inventive genius, or pursue the splendid discoveries of modern science, without a new sense of the capacities and dignity of human nature, which naturally leads to a sterner self-respect, to manlier resolves, and higher aspirations. We cannot read the ways of God to man as revealed in the history of nations, of sublime virtues as exemplified in the lives of great and good men, without falling into that mood of thoughtful admiration, which, though it be but a transient glow, is a purifying and elevating influence while it lasts. The study of history is especially valuable as an antidote to self-exaggeration. It teaches lessons of humility, patience, and submission. When we read of realms smitten with the scourge of famine or pestilence, or strewn with the bloody ashes of war ; of grass growing in the streets of great cities ; of ships rotting at the wharves ; of fathers burying their sons ; of strong men begging their bread ; of fields untilled, and silent workshops, and despairing countenances,—we hear a voice of rebuke to our own clamorous sorrows and peevish complaints. We learn that pain and suffering and disappointment are a part of God's providence, and that no contract was ever yet made with man by which virtue should secure to him temporal happiness.

In books, be it remembered, we have the best products of the best minds. We should any of us esteem it a great privilege to pass an evening with Shakespeare or Bacon, were such a thing possible. But, were we admitted to the presence of one of these illustrious men, we might find him touched with infirmity, or oppressed with weariness, or darkened with the shadow of a recent trouble, or absorbed by intrusive and tyrannous thoughts. To us the oracle might be dumb, and the light eclipsed. But, when we take down one of their volumes, we run no such risk. Here we have their best thoughts embalmed in their best words; immortal flowers of poetry, wet with Castalian dews, and the golden fruit of wisdom that had long ripened on the bough before it was gathered. Here we find the growth of the choicest seasons of the mind, when mortal cares were forgotten, and mortal weaknesses were subdued; and the soul, stripped of its vanities and its passions, lay bare to the finest effluences of truth and beauty. We may be sure that Shakespeare never out-talked his Hamlet, nor Bacon his Essays. Great writers are indeed best known through their books. How little, for instance, do we know of the life of Shakespeare; but how much do we know of him ! . . . .

For the knowledge that comes from books, I would claim no more than it is fairly entitled to. I am well aware that there is no inevitable connection between intellectual cultivation, on the one hand, and individual virtue or social well-being, on the other. "The tree of knowledge is not the tree of life." I admit that genius and learning are sometimes found in combination with gross vices, and not unfrequently with contemptible weaknesses; and that a community at once cultivated and corrupt is no impossible monster. But it is no overstatement to say, that, other things being equal, the man who has the greatest amount of intellectual resources is in the least danger from inferior temptations,—if for no other reason, because he has fewer idle moments. The ruin of most men dates from some vacant hour. Occupation is the armor of the soul; and the train of Idleness is borne up by all the vices. I remember a satirical poem, in which the Devil is represented as fishing for men, and adapting his baits to the taste and temperament of his prey ; but the idler, he said, pleased him most, because he bit the naked hook. To a young man away

from home, friendless and forlorn in a great city, the hours of
peril are those between sunset and bedtime; for the moon and
stars see more of evil in a single hour than the sun in his whole
day's circuit. The poet's visions of evening are all compact of
tender and soothing images. It brings the wanderer to his home,
the child to his mother's arms, the ox to his stall, and the weary
laborer to his rest. But to the gentle-hearted youth who is thrown
upon the rocks of a pitiless city, and stands, "homeless amid a
thousand homes," the approach of evening brings with it an ach-
ing sense of loneliness and desolation, which comes down upon the
spirit like darkness upon the earth. In this mood his best im-
pulses become a snare to him; and he is led astray because he is
social, affectionate, sympathetic, and warm-hearted. If there be
a young man thus circumstanced within the sound of my voice,
let me say to him, that books are the friends of the friendless,
and that a library is the home of the homeless. A taste for reading will always carry you into the best possible company, and
enable you to converse with men who will instruct you by their
wisdom, and charm you by their wit; who will soothe you when
fretted, refresh you when weary, counsel you when perplexed,
and sympathize with you at all times.—*George S. Hillard.*

If I were to pray for a taste which should stand me in stead
under every variety of circumstances, and be a source of happiness and cheerfulness to me through life, and a shield against its
ills, however things might go amiss, and the world frown upon
me, it would be a taste for reading. . . . Give a man this
taste, and the means of gratifying it, and you can hardly fail of
making a happy man, unless, indeed, you put into his hands a
most perverse selection of books. You place him in contact with
the best society in every period of history—with the wisest, the
wittiest, the tenderest, the bravest, and the purest characters who
have adorned humanity. You make him a denizen of all nations,
a cotemporary of all ages.—*Sir J. Herschel.*

Employ your time in improving yourself by other men's documents; so shall you come easily by what others have labored
hard for. Prefer knowledge to wealth; for the one is transitory,
the other perpetual.—*Socrates.*

He that will inquire out the best books in every science, and
inform himself of the most material authors of the several acts

of philosophy and religion, will not find it an infinite work to acquaint himself with the sentiments of mankind concerning the most weighty and comprehensive subjects.—*Locke.*

Reading maketh a full man.—*Bacon.*

Read, and you will know.—*Mrs. Jones.*

TREASURES OF LIBRARIES.

My days among the dead are passed ;
　Around me I behold,
Where'er these casual eyes are cast,
　The mighty minds of old :
My never-failing friends are they,
With whom I converse day by day

With them I take delight in weal,
　And seek relief in woe ;
And while I understand and feel
　How much to them I owe,
My cheeks have often been bedewed
With tears of thoughtful gratitude.

My thoughts are with the dead ; with them
　I live in long-past years ;
Their virtues love, their faults condemn,
　Partake their hopes and fears,
And from their lessons seek and find
Instruction with a humble mind.

My hopes are with the dead ; anon
　My place with them will be,
And I with them shall travel on
　Through all futurity ;
Yet leaving here a name, I trust,
That will not perish in the dust.—*Southey.*

I no sooner come into the library, but I bolt the door to me, excluding Lust, Ambition, Avarice, and all such vices, whose nurse is Idleness, the mother of Ignorance and Melancholy. In the very lap of eternity, among so many divine souls, I take my seat with so lofty a spirit, and sweet content, that I pity all that know not this happiness.—*Heinsius.*

A book is good company. It is full of conversation without loquacity. It comes to your longing with full instruction, but pursues you never. It is not offended at your absent-mindedness, nor jealous if you turn to other pleasures, of leaf, or dress, or mineral, or even of books. It silently serves the soul without recompense, not even for the hire of love. And yet more noble, it seems to pass from itself, and to enter the memory and to hover in a silvery transformation there, until the outward book is but a body and its soul and spirit are flown to you, and possess your memory like a spirit. And while some books, like steps, are left behind us by the very help which they yield us, and serve only our childhood or early life, some others go with us, in mute fidelity, to the end of life, a recreation for fatigue, an instruction for our sober hours, and a solace for our sickness or sorrow. Except the great out-doors, nothing that has no life of its own gives so much life to you.—*H. W. Beecher, " Eyes and Ears," p. 292, 3.*

No such treasure as a library.—*Whitlock.*

———— Books are yours,
Within whose silent chambers treasure lies
Preserved from age to age; more precious far
Than that accumulated store of gold
And orient gems, which, for a day of need,
The Sultan hides deep in ancestral tombs.
These hoards of truth you can unlock at will.
— Wordsworth.

Dreams, books, are each a world; and books, we know,
Are a substantial world, both pure and good;
Round these, with tendrils strong as flesh and blood,
Our pastime and our happiness will grow.
— Wordsworth : Personal Talk, 56. 1.

Books make up no small part of human happiness.—*Frederic the Great, in youth.*

My latest passion will be for literature.—*Frederic the Great, in old age.*

For books are not absolutely dead things, but do contain a progeny of life in them as active as that soul whose progeny they are; nay, they do preserve, as in a vial, the purest efficacy and extraction of that living intellect that bred them.—*Milton : Areopagitica.*

As good almost kill a man as kill a good book: who kills a man kills a reasonable creature, God's image; but he who destroys a good book kills reason itself, kills the image of God, as it were, in the eye.—*Same.*

Knowledge is proud that he has learned so much ;
Wisdom is humble that he knows no more.
Books are not seldom talismans and spells.
        —*Cowper : Task, bk.* vi. *line* 96.

Of the things which man can do or make here below, by far the most momentous, wonderful, and worthy, are the things we call books.—*Carlyle.*

Every great book is an action, and every great action is a book.—*Luther.*

Nothing can supply the place of books.—*Channing.*

A book's a book although there's nothing in't.—*Lord Byron.*

Nothing is more delightful than to lie under a tree, in the summer, with a book, except to lie under a tree, in the summer, without a book.—*C. J. Fox.*

III. How to Read Books.

The substance of Bishop Potter's "Cautions and Counsels," from his "Handbook for Readers and Students," New York, 1843.

1. Always have some useful and pleasant book ready to take up in " odd ends " of time.

2. Be not alarmed because so many books are recommended.

3. Do not attempt to read much or fast.

4. Do not be so enslaved by any system or course of study, as to think it may not be altered.

5. Beware, on the other hand, of frequent changes in your plan of study.

6. Read always the best and most recent book on the subject which you wish to investigate.

7. Study subjects rather than books.

8. Seek opportunities to write and converse on subjects about which you read.

9. Refer what you read to the general head under which it belongs; if a fact, to the principle involved; if a principle, to the facts which follow.

10. Try to use your knowledge in practice.

11. Keep your knowledge at command, by reviewing it as much as you can.

12. Dare to be ignorant of many things.

There is no business, no avocation whatever, which will not permit a man, who has an inclination, to give a little time, every day, to the studies of his youth.— *Wyttenbach.*

Nothing, in truth, has such a tendency to weaken, not only the powers of invention, but the intellectual powers in general, as a habit of extensive and various reading without reflection. The activity and force of mind are gradually impaired in consequence of disuse ; and, not unfrequently, all our principles and opinions come to be lost in the infinite multiplicity and discordancy of our acquired ideas.—*Dugald Stewart.*

Books have brought some men to knowledge, and some to madness. As fullness sometimes hurteth the stomach more than hunger, so fareth it with wits, and, as of meats, so, likewise, of books, the use ought to be limited according to the quality of him that useth them.—*Petrarch : Twyne's tr.*, 1579, *f.* 62.

Books cannot always please, however good ;
Minds are not ever craving for their food.
   Crabbe : The Borough, Letter xxiv.: *Schools.*

Some books are to be tasted, others to be swallowed, and some few to be chewed and digested; that is, some books are to be read only in parts; others to be read, but not curiously; and some few to be read wholly, and with diligence and attention.— *Lord Bacon.*

Histories make men wise; poets, witty; the mathematics, subtile; natural philosophy, deep; morals, grave; logic and rhetoric, able to contend.—*Same.*

Read, not to contradict and confute, nor to believe and take for granted, nor find talk and discourse, but to weigh and consider. —*Same.*

How should we read? First, thoughtfully and critically; secondly, in company with a friend, or your family; thirdly, repeatedly; fourthly, with pen in hand.—*Dr. A. Potter.*

Study subjects rather than books: therefore, compare different authors on the same subjects; the statements of authors, with information collected from other sources; and the conclusions drawn by a writer, with the rules of sound logic.—*Same.*

All who would study with advantage, in any art whatsoever, ought to betake themselves to the reading of some sure and certain books oftentimes over; for to read many books produceth confusion, rather than learning, like as those who dwell everywhere are not anywhere at home.—*Luther : Table-Talk.*

Those who have read of everything are thought to understand everything too; but it is not always so. Reading furnishes the mind only with materials of knowledge; it is thinking that makes what we read ours. We are of the ruminating kind, and it is not enough to cram ourselves with a great load of collections; unless we chew them over again, they will not give us strength and nourishment.—*Locke.*

The thoughts of our deliberation are most accurate; these we vent into our papers. What a happiness it is, that without all offence of necromancy, I may here call up any of the ancient worthies of learning, whether human or divine, and confer with them of all my doubts! that I can at pleasure summon whole synods of reverend Fathers and acute doctors from all the coasts of the earth, to give their well-studied judgments in all points of question which I propose! Neither can I cast my eye casually upon any of these silent masters but I must learn somewhat. No law binds us to read all; but the more we can take in and digest, the better-liking must the mind needs be.—*Bishop Hall.*

—who reads
Incessantly, and to his reading brings not
A spirit and judgment equal or superior,
Uncertain and unsettled still remains,
Deep versed in books, but shallow in himself.
                  —*Milton : Paradise Regained.*

To call him well read who reads many authors is improper.—
Shaftesbury.

As concerns the quantity of what is to be read there is a single
rule,—Read much, but not many works (multum non multa).—*Sir
W. Hamilton.*

Multum legendum esse non multa.—*Quintilian.*

In reading authors, when you find
Bright passages that strike your mind,
And which, perhaps, you may have reason
To think on at another season,
Be not contented with the sight,
But take them down in black and white.
Such a respect is wisely shown
As makes another's sense one's own.

IV. How to Choose Books.

Under our present enormous accumulation of books, I do affirm
that a most miserable distraction of choice must be very generally
incident to the times; that the symptoms of it are in fact very
prevalent, and that one of the chief symptoms is an enormous
"gluttonism" for books.—*De Quincey.*

A wise man can sooner gather gold out of the drossiest volume than a fool wisdom out of Scripture.—*Milton.*

Non refert quam multos libros sed quam honor HABEAS.—
Seneca.

For out of the old fieldes, as men saithe,
Cometh al this new corne fro yere to yere,
And out of old bookes, in good faithe,
Cometh al this new science that men lere.
—Chaucer : Assembly of Foules, l. 22.

Old wood to burn! Old wine to drink!
Old friends to trust! Old books to read!
—Alonzo of Aragon.

Books that you may carry to the fire and hold readily in your hand are the most useful, after all.—*Johnson.*

We ought to regard books as we do sweetmeats, not wholly to aim at the pleasantest, but chiefly to respect the wholesomest; not forbidding either, but approving the latter most.—*Plutarch, as quoted by Felltham.*

A love of books can be acquired only by those who find pleasure in using them; and hence, whoever would cultivate in himself or others this most desirable taste, should select, especially at first, such works as can be read with sustained and quickened attention. *—Dr. Potter.*

Blessings be with them, and eternal praise,
Who gave us nobler loves, and nobler cares,
The Poets, who on earth have made us heirs
Of truth and pure delight by heavenly lays!
(See further of it.)   *— Wordsworth : Personal Talk,* st. 4.

The novel, in its best form, I regard as one of the most powerful engines of civilization ever invented.—*Sir J. Herschel.*

Novels are sweets. All people with healthy literary appetites love them—almost all women; a vast number of clever, hardheaded men. Judges, bishops, chancellors, mathematicians, are notorious novel-readers, as well as young boys and sweet girls, and their kind, tender mothers. *— Thackeray : Roundabout Papers.*

BOOK-BUYING.

In starting a library, select from the accompanying list fifty, or a hundred, or more, volumes, and take your list to some responsible bookseller, and he will fill it for you at a fair discount from the retail prices; he can, of course, and will, furnish the whole list cheaper than he could by a single volume at a time. Then, by all means, keep an open account with him, and in the course of your reading, when you come across some volume you want, or some fact that should be hunted up, make a note of it, and procure the volume. A book read at the time your interest is excited will possess not only double its interest, but the facts it contains will be much more firmly impressed upon the mind. An account at your bookseller's is one that you should take pride in maintaining, in making it as large as your means will allow, and in paying promptly and willingly when due.

Never buy books published in numbers; it is the most expensive form, because the same book can generally be had bound, when finished, for the same price as published at in numbers; because, also, numbers will get lost and have to be replaced, at the additional cost; or they will get torn or soiled; and often, when sent to the binder's, they are returned bound in an unsatisfactory manner.—" *An Old Bookseller*." Phila.: Porter & Coates.

[The " Old Bookseller" also puts in a warning against buying books at Auction, and of "Canvassing Agents;" but as the evils and dangers of these are not wholly unmixed with advantage in some cases, we do not quote his advice on these points.—ED.]

READING

AND

COURSES OF READING.

BY FRED. B. PERKINS.

Twenty thousand editions of books had issued from the press before the year 1500. In one public library (the Bibliothèque Impériale of Paris) there were, in 1858, it was claimed, only 142,000 volumes short of two million printed books, besides 86,000 MSS. A single separate collection of pamphlets in the British Museum about the English Rebellion only, contains 40,000 publications. Probably not less than 25,000 new books appear every year now. This does not include periodicals or newspapers.

Now, an able and experienced old reader of the hard-going sort, Lenglet du Fresnoy, made a calculation that convinced him that nobody could read more than 900 folio volumes in a life-time. Roughly, this would allow 2,700 quartos, 8,100 octavos, and about 16,000 duodecimos—so that your life is gone in reading eight months' books—two-thirds the present annual reinforcement to literature of books alone. To keep up, alone, would require the reading of about sixty-eight volumes a day, without allowing for reading up such arrears as the classics, etc.

It is obvious enough, therefore, that any one who desires to read, or to buy books to the best advantage, will need to select with all the care and judgment he can muster, both within himself, or from friends, or paid experts.

Is reading your most useful mental employment, after all? There are speakers to hear; conversation and debate to maintain; thinking of your own to elaborate. Are not there more real and profitable mental activities; and is not reading rather to be made a last resort, when these are not practicable?

Plausible arguments may be found in favor of those suggestions, but weighty ones against them. Careful and thorough thinking to the utmost of our ability should underlie and accompany the hearing of a speaker, conversation, debate and reading. Thinking—that is, the pursuit and attainment of truth on whatever subjects are before us—is indeed the object of them all. They are all useless without it, and entirely subordinate to it (except, of course, the care of mere amusement).

Now, Reading is the best means of nourishing Thought. Oratory, on the other hand, is the worst, since it depends on moving the feelings, which disturbs the reason. And even if the hearer can keep his feelings untouched, yet he may not object nor question. He is to sit unresisting, and drink in whatever is put down his throat. This is well enough for young robins and babies, but it is a ludicrous way of dieting for a grown man—for an enlightened mind. Debating and conversation are better discipline than oratory, since they allow a comparison of views. Conversation especially, and most of all that form of it so highly prized by open minds, where one can resort to some wise friend and ask questions, and discuss them, is extremely useful. It is greatly superior to debate in this, that it is not so liable to excitements of the external sort, such as anger, desire to win, or desire to show off.

But if only one of these kinds of mental exercise might be had, it should be books, books, books, a thousand times to one. Compared with books, public speaking is a war-dance, conversation a beating bushes for wild fruit; well enough for savages and strays, but having small place or power in the discipline of a cultured mind. And accordingly we find that they have been valued most when there were few books or no books, and that as books have multiplied and reading has become general, they have fallen from the rank of great civic and philosophic engineers, to mere accomplishments and public shows. To-day, it is Reading that furnishes both news and knowledge to the people at large, and that determines their opinions and their action. Conversation is a meagre appendix to the use of books, periodicals, and newspapers, and seldom much besides a retailing of what they have furnished. Oratory exists only in the sermon, which is substantially assented to beforehand; the political speech, which is more for amusement than for instruction; and the lecture, which is for nothing but amusement.*

What shall I read? Shall I pursue a general course? Or shall I work at some department of knowledge exclusively? What book shall I begin with? What books shall I go on with?

Answer: Do you want to read as work or as relaxation? for accomplishment, or for knowledge? What do you know already? What have you read already?

The answer is only another question, for the questions supposed—they are the usual ones—could not be answered otherwise. They are like the well-known queries: How long is a string? How much does a horse cost? There are a great many people for whom the profundities of Tupper and Tompkins are the solidest reading that can be endured, and Southworth is splendid! There are others who want Plato in the Greek and Kant in the German; who, like Queen Caroline, take Butler's Analogy for their light reading. I beg pardon; that is not abreast

---

* Mr. Perkins' position in this may be questioned.—ED.

with the Spirit of the Age. I ought to say, who read
the Vedic hymns in the original Sanscrit for amusement,
and decipher inscriptions in the arrow-headed character
when they have five minutes' leisure, and as they ride in
the street-cars.

Among the gayly variegated mosaic stuff that con-
stitutes a certain well-known pavement, I suppose there
are as many Courses of Reading as good resolutions of
any other kind   Perhaps as good a rule as any to begin
reading with is :

Don't pursue a course of reading. Or, rather, don't
try to; there's very little danger that you *will*.

And yet it is very agreeable to sit down and plan out
a full and rounded series of noble books, which shall
train the mind into strength and swiftness and beauty.
There is something extremely attractive, for instance, in
the conception of a series of masterpieces, or monumental
Course of Reading, which shall acquaint the student with
the great thoughts of the great men in historic order,
and thus set before him a history of mankind in its
noblest representations. Thus, for instance :

[Filled out with a few titles in parentheses, as being
either out of chronological order, or as connectives, etc.
Translations are always meant, of non-English books.
Epithets and estimates are taken for granted.]

First seize a few pictures of the pre-historic civiliza-
tions, executed in the modern manner; by reading Rawlinson's Five Great Monarchies and Wilkinson's Ancient
Egyptians. This background laid in, read Bryant's
Homer, and, along with it, dictionary-wise, Gladstone's
Juventus Mundi. Follow with Greek historians: Herodotus (Rawlinson's), Thucydides, Xenophon's Anabasis.
Now add the leading Greek philosophies of mind and
action; the Ethics and Politics of Aristotle, Plato's Dialogues (Jowett's), and Xenophon's Memorabilia (Supple-

ment with Grote's Plato, and his Companions of Socrates). Add the greatest Greek dramatists and an orator: Æschylus, Sophocles, Euripides; Aristophanes, most wondérful of all; and Demosthenes. Then read Plutarch's Lives. Lastly, round up and vivify your knowledge of the Greek nation and spirit by reading Grote's magnificent History of Greece.

Next comes Rome. Read of the historians, Livy, Sallust, Cæsar, Tacitus; of poets, Virgil (Conington's), Horace (Francis' is as good as any); for oratory, philosophy, and belles-lettres, Cicero's writings. (Supplement Greek and Roman antiquity together with Becker's Charicles, and his Gallus; then revise and solidify your Rome by reading Mommsen, as Grote for Greece. But you will find it, though good, far inferior to Grote.)

Now comes the transition from heathen to Christian history. Read Gibbon's Decline and Fall. To keep your balance against the often denounced innuendoes of Mr. Gibbon, don't quiddle with the goody little notes to Gibbon, by Milman and others, but having let Gibbon poison you as much as he can—he won't hurt you if you have much intellect of your own—turn away and master at once the right side of the main question of Christ in History, by a thorough study and mental appropriation of Horne's Introduction to the study of the Sacred Scriptures. I mean not the obsolete old edition, still obstinately and improperly kept in the American market to the exclusion of the proper one, but the last edition, with Horne's own latest revisions, and with the addition, by first-class evangelical English scholars, of all the recent learning on the subject. No man of sound mind, having mastered Horne, will ever be materially troubled by such little snips and sneers as Gibbon's, or by any other attempt to destroy the historical argument for the substantial truth of the Bible.

To further familiarize yourself with this great turning-point in the history of mankind, read Augustine's Confessions, and his City of God, as specimens of the best effects of the new religion upon a fervid, and powerful, and noble nature. (Add for completeness Milman's First Three Centuries of the Christian Church, Merivale's Conversion of the Roman Empire, and his Conversion of the Northern Nations.)

Now, grasp at once the beginnings of modern history, by reading carefully Hallam's Middle Ages and Guizot's History of Civilization. Turn back a moment and surrender yourself to one of the latest phases of heathen romance, in reading the Nibelungen Lied. (If you like to add a prose romance of the same key, but having also the transition to Christianity in it, read Fouqué's Thiodolf the Icelander.) Now, for two narrower pictures, yet full of bright, sharp drawing and character, read Thierry's Merovingians, and his Norman Conquest. Add Froissart; for the chivalric romances, read Morte d'Arthur and Amadis de Gaul; and for the times of the Crusades, take (history quite as much as romance) Ivanhoe, The Talisman, and Quentin Durward.

Next comes the Great Awakening of the 15th Century. Yet Dante belongs earlier. Read, then, Dante (Longfellow's); after him Ariosto (Rose's), and Tasso (Wiffen's). (Now take d'Aubigné's spirited and graphic History of the Reformation, and follow it with Schiller's Thirty Years' War, and you have the transition from Catholic Europe to the Catholic-Protestant Europe of to-day. For glimpses into ways of thought and speech, read Luther's Table-Talk; and to fill out the whole with its immense and indispensable Fine Art portion, read Eastlake's and Kugler's Hand-Books.) As the Nibelungen Lied marked in some sense a close of heathen national epics, so now read Don Quixote, to mark the

extinction of the romance of chivalry. Follow it with
Gil Blas, which establishes the transition to the earliest
period of modern Fiction Proper, viz., the string-of-ad-
ventures and character novel. (To fill out the historical
impressions of that imperial time, read Prescott's Ferdinand and Isabella, Philip II., Mexico and Peru, and
Motley's Dutch Republic and United Netherlands.)

Cross the channel, and come into the splendid blaze of
the Elizabethan period. But it will bear, and, indeed,
requires, ample introduction. This is the place to ascer-
tain your views of English History; you may come down
well past it in that department, and then, returning, set
your Elizabethan jewels all the more distinctly in the
middle of the broad field. Read, therefore, Hume and
Macaulay. Then take Hallam and May's Constitutional
History; add Blackstone's Commentaries, and De Lolme
on the Constitution, because English history and English
law are peculiarly interwoven. (To give breadth to your
views, add also, here, Maine's two valuable works on
Ancient Law, and on Municipal or Village Law in the
East and West.) Now return to Queen Elizabeth.
Specimens must do. So read Shakespeare (White's, if
you can afford it; if not, any you can. Shakespeare can
be bought almost as cheap as the Bible); Spenser, and
Bacon, and Montaigne. Miss Aikin's Court and Times
of Queen Elizabeth is picturesque and comprehensive
for the general reader.

Step forward two generations. Read Clarendon's His-
tory of the Rebellion, Carlyle's Cromwell, Milton's Prose
Works, and Forster's Statesmen of the Commonwealth.
The Diaries of Evelyn and Pepys are instructive pictures
of the times of Charles II. Then read Milton's Poetry,
Bunyan's Pilgrim's Progress, and Holy War; Sir Thomas
Browne's Religio Medici and Urn-Burial, and (if you can)
Burton's Anatomy of Melancholy. Selden's Table-Talk

also belongs here; you can read *that*, or else you have
no business with this list. (For the state of things on
the Continent, read Schiller's Thirty Years' War.)

The Restoration and the Revolution of 1688 have been
dealt with already in your historical reading, prefatory
to the Elizabethan period. Omit, therefore, the war and
politics of that stirring time, and consider next the literary activity of the reign of Louis XIV. in France, and
of Queen Anne in England. Read Corneille, Racine,
and Molière; the Thoughts and Provincial Letters of
Pascal; the Letters of Madame de Sévigné; and—though
he belongs a little later—the Maxims of La Rochefou-
cauld. Read also the philosophical works of Locke, and
those of Descartes. Then, for Queen Anne's time, read
Swift, Addison, and Pope. (The writings of Bolingbroke
might be added, and a notion of Marlborough may be
obtained from Alison's Life.)

We rapidly approach the modernest times, and to-day.
After the wars of Queen Anne, the next historical epoch
is that of the wars of Frederic the Great, of whom read
Carlyle's Life. In the latter half of the century a slow,
silent victory, yet greater than Prague or Rosbach, was
won by Kant, whose Critique of Pure Reason and Metaphysics of Ethics should be read. Read also the first of
human biographies, written by one of the last of men,
Boswell's Johnson; and Burke's Speeches, and Sheridan's Comedies, and Goldsmith's Works. Continue the
philosophical strand of your cord, with Stewart, Brown,
and Reid.

Now prepare for the splitting off of the American Colonies into an independent historical career. Read the
Federalist, to show what the men meant who founded
our polity, and De Tocqueville's Democracy in America,
for a marvellous and only not prophetic exposition of
what their purpose turned out to be. (While you are

about it, shape our own history at once by reading Bancroft's mammoth preparation to begin our history, and Hildreth's dense and full annals.)

Make a backward step for France. Read De Tocqueville's Ancient Régime, to show you why the French Revolution broke out; and then Thiers and Carlyle, to show what it did. Follow with Thiers' Consulate and Empire; read Napier's Peninsular War, a wonderfully clear and vigorous narrative of the military achievements which were the real entering wedge toward Napoleon's downfall; and avoid Scott's Life and Abbot's Life of Napoleon. For German literature in these days, read Goethe (Taylor's Faust, the rest of his works as you can get them); Schiller—I mean both the Works and the Life of both.

Then take up the literary harvest of England in the first part of this century. Read Scott's Works, and Lockhart's Scott; Byron, Wordsworth, Coleridge, Keats, and Shelley; and read after the writings of each a biography of each. Read also Lamb's Writings, and those of Thomas de Quincey.

Then opens out the vast arena of the present epoch, with its innumerable writers and its numerous entirely new departments of investigation. There is a sufficient conventional excuse for not venturing to even attempt to blaze out a path through such a crowded and luxuriant forest. Yet, let the notice be ventured that the present age is notable most of all for advances in science, and what is closely related thereto: and in belles-lettres, for prose fiction. I barely name Humboldt's Cosmos, Darwin's Origin of Species and Descent of Man, Sir William Hamilton's Metaphysics and Logic, the writings of Herbert Spencer, Charles Dickens, W. M. Thackeray, and Nathaniel Hawthorne. As for all the rest, any one who has read according to this series down to this point, or half-way down to it, with fair abilities and steady, careful attention, is by that time better able to choose both departments and authors for himself than I or any other guide.

Then please to consider what a store of deep and broad and noble and beautiful thoughts, what a wide range of classes of literature, what a vast mass of facts, the knowledge of that series of books implies; and yet it is a pretty short "Course of Reading," as courses of reading go.

But I will not say I recommend it. I will say that I would dearly love to begin at the beginning of it this very day, and go straight through to the end.

Now I shall steal a little from Mr. Hale's "How to Do it." His suggestion about courses of reading is, to know, first, the Bible (I take that for granted, observe). Second, the history of your own country, pretty well; of your own State, better; of your own town best of all. Third (for Americans), "a clear knowledge of the general features of the history of England." Fourth, most of Shakespeare's plays. Beyond this, says Mr. Hale, to begin with, make up your mind what you want to read about: Mary Queen of Scots, fly-fishing, hieroglyphics, the Tenure of Office Bill, anything. Having reached this point, Mr. Hale's doctrine becomes both a *Course* of Reading and a *Method* of Reading. Take a blank book, he says, note down the chief significant words in the passage that you have read, on your chosen subject (he takes it for granted that you have read *something*); and then rummage and search for more reading about the subject itself, or about the collateral subjects named by the entries in your blank-book. If any of these are debated subjects, read on both sides. Use Poole's Index to follow your subjects into the periodicals from 1802 to 1852, where that work ends. As fast as you determine dates or other facts about your subjects, note them each under its proper word in your blank-book. Note there, also, any authorities you find named. This way of searching and recording will branch out as fast and as far as anybody will pursue it.

Some of Dr. Potter's shrewd " Cautions and Counsels" are quoted in our "Readings on Reading." Here are Mr. Emerson's three rules. They are not rules for select-ing a course of reading, but rules for not reading some kinds of books.

1. Never read any book that is not a year old.
2. Never read any but famed books.
3. Never read any books but what you like.

Now I have not one word to say against those rules; indeed, with a trifling addition, I adopt them as part of my system. This addition consists in appending to each rule the words "unless you choose."

And last of all, Mr. Horace Greeley, in the New York *Ledger*, comes and tells us what he knows about reading. First, he says, be where there are good books; though how he reconciles this with his other advice to go west and buy a farm, I do not know. But if there are none, he says, ten dollars a year will get them. Begin with Chemistry, Geology, and Botany, and devote a year to each. "Obtain the best text-book of each as a founda-tion." Read slowly and thoughtfully; if you do not master the book at the first time, read it again, and so on. If puzzled, stop and work at the place till you under-stand it. Next, give a little time to Geography and Astronomy. After Science, read History ; then Biogra-phy. Poetry and Philosophy come last.

Well—that course, also, I recommend not to pursue. If anything could be more hopeless, or more totally out of sight of the present methods of learning the physical sciences, than to read one year in books, I don't know what it is. Mr. Greeley might just as well recommend his customers to learn editing, or farming, by reading one year in a book, and stopping short at every puzzle until it is solved. It would not be very long before his constituency of readers would be every mother's son of them hanging motionless each at his puzzle, "silent, upon a peak in Darien," or just as far off from anything useful.

I shall close this "Course of Reading" discussion by one more outline of a course. It will at once be objected to, that it is not literature at all. So be it; but it has the merit of recommending reading that will not do harm, and that will do good ; and that does not require Mr. Greeley's $10 a year, though it would admit of the use of much more; and lastly, it affords a great breadth of reading that people will read, and more people, too, than can be induced to read anything else.

COURSE.

1. Subscribe for a year, paying each in advance, to a weekly paper, secular rather than religious, which gives a great and varied breadth of news. If you absolutely must have stories, take *also*, not *instead*, a weekly story paper. The two which I recommend for this purpose are, *The New York Weekly Tribune*, and . . . . Take others if you prefer.

2. Read the former of these regularly and carefully; keep up with the current of events, so as to observe the succession of causes and effects, and new discoveries and suggestions in the history that every day is bringing to pass before you. In this age of telegraphs and steam, we may know the world as well as the village.

3. When you come to anything that puzzles you, don't stop and work at it—that is, more than a little while; but go and find somebody or something that will explain

it. Whether it is the name of some public man whose previous career you want to know, or the name of a country, or of a metal, or a machine, or a party, or a philosophy, or a principle that you are not sufficiently well informed about, makes little difference. Fix deliberately on it, whatever it is, and then set to work to find out about it. Ask your father and mother. Get them to tell you about the person or thing, or to tell you where to read about it. Ask your employer; ask other people in the shop; I mean, always, so far as your acquaintance justifies you in asking. Ask the school-master or the school-mistress; ask the minister. If you find that there is a book to be read, and that you can with propriety borrow it, borrow; get it from a library if you can. And always, if there is a circulating library, or anything of that sort, belong to it. You will find, a little further on, how to make one that will do very well. If you find that there is nothing to be had about that subject, take another.

4. Having begun thus, there is no end. Before you have acquainted yourself with one thing, a hundred more will turn up. Your difficulty will be to exclude things that you want to read about. For this I recommend a moderate degree of persistence, but not too exclusive devotion to any one subject. That is, unless you come upon one that you particularly enjoy. Devote yourself to just as complete an acquaintance with that as you please. If you should even plan to master all that is known of it and then to carry human knowledge further in that direction, it is a noble and hopeful ambition. But you will be astonished to find how much has been put in books about most things.

5. For recording your knowledge, Mr. Hale's plan will do very well. Begin with a small blank-book. You are much more likely to fill first a small one and then a

large one, than a large one first.   And if you fill neither,
the small one wastes less.   I do not recommend Todd's
Index Rerum.

_____

Now comes the question, How to read ?   I refer again
to Bishop Potter's " Cautions and Counsels," for hints.
Mr. Hale says the first rules are: "Do not read too
much at a time; stop when you are tired; and, in whatever way, make some review of what you read, even as
you go along."   The handiest way to do this is, when
you have got through with any separate step in the argument or separate statement or division of the book, to
look off it and say over to yourself in careful words—not
mere indistinct thoughts, but framed sentences—the substance of that step or statement or division.   Do the
same for the chapters or larger divisions.   And do the
same with the book itself at last.   If the book belongs
to you (this is a suggestion of Mr. Hale's, and a habit of
my own, too), whenever you come to something whose
place you want to remember, note the page in pencil on
a blank leaf at the end of the book, and one or two words
to remind you what the subject is. . Choose these words
carefully.

These are plain hints; they are better than a more
complex system ; if any peculiar modes of your own suggest themselves, try them; one's own devices are often
the best for such things.

It is very often useful to read what the printers call
the " front matter;" that is, the title-page, preface, or
introduction, and table of contents.   In reading the latter take, first, the main divisions, and if you have a few
minutes to spare, and they are clear, commit them to
memory; they will make a convenient frame on which to
hang the contents of the book, and perhaps of other
books, too.   You will very likely forget them after a

time; but some neat classification or statement of thoughts will stick by you.

When a new question comes before you, read both sides of it as well as you can, so as to preserve the judge's habit of mind rather than the lawyer's. Thus, for instance, on free-trade and protection, read, on the latter side, Mr. Greeley's book, and, if you can, the works of H. C. Carey; on the former, read Bastiat, Perry, and Mill. On the woman suffrage question, read Dr. Bushnell's "Woman Suffrage" against, and J. S. Mill's "Subjection of Woman" for, and so on. This method, properly followed, gives great soundness and good sense to one's habits of mind.

A number of very good and nourishing books can be had in pocket editions, such as Bacon's Essays, Locke on the Understanding, etc. If you once get into the habit of having such a book about you, to use at odd times, you will be very likely to keep it up; it is a capital method of economizing time and thought. Sometimes a larger book can be managed by buying a copy in sheets, and carrying it about, a sheet at a time.

It is of the first importance to have as many good reference books at hand, while you are reading, as possible. If you can have but one, have Webster's Dictionary—the unabridged pictorial, if possible; and, if not, the next largest edition you can afford. They range from that imperial quarto, down to a square 16mo, at about 50 cents. The second should be an atlas, Black's, Colton's, or Mitchell's. There are others, but being sold by subscription, they are practically not to be had. For three other reference books to come next, I recommend:

1. Bartlett's Dictionary of Quotations.
2. Hole and Wheeler's Brief Biographical Dictionary; or Godwin's Cyclopedia of Biography.
3. Haydn's Dictionary of Dates; or Putnam's "World's Progress."

Use these reference books as often as you can find an occasion to; get into the habit of constantly using them. And use as many more reference books as you can afford.

The physiology of reading includes a few hints about the USE OF THE EYES, times and seasons, and other questions of a physical nature. There is no room for a treatise, hardly for a paragraph.

Do not use your eyes before breakfast until you are twenty years old. All the system is relaxed then, and any exertion is unnatural and injurious.

Do not read in a dim light, nor by a flickering light, nor by a light that shines into the eyes. The best light comes from above and behind the left shoulder.

For those who have to read much a green shade over the eyes is a great economy of sight. Gas-light is of a harsh quality, and very hot. Besides, it is better not to deal with an irresponsible monopoly when you can help it. A far better light to read and study by is the still, soft, white light of the "German Student's Lamp." This lamp can be had for either kerosene or the finer vegetable oils.

Learn to read whole words by their collective diagram or physiognomy on the paper. This is an immense relief to the eyes. One who has to read a great deal can read a good many books, not the hardest though—if printed in double columns or in a narrow page, not only by whole words, but a whole line at a time; so that the eye, instead of skipping backward and forward thirty or forty times a page, moves, deliberately, straight down it. This is an additional economy of the eyes. Look no harder at the words than is necessary. By straining with an intense stare, one can tire out one's eyes very soon over the clearest print; while careful practice of these rules will enable any one with a reasonably good pair of eyes, to read in the railroad cars all day long, without harm.   In this case, however, two other precautions are necessary : sit erect and free from the back of the seat, and do not let the arm that holds the book touch anything else.   This keeps the book at the end of a long spring, viz. : the length of the body and arm together, which reduces the jar of the cars to a minimum.

Here are three rules for reading, which Professor Whitaker, of Cambridge, gave to John Boyce, one of the translators of King James' Bible :

1. Study, chiefly, standing or walking.
2. Never study at a window.
3. Never go to bed with cold feet.

Those are sensible rules, in part. Variety of posture gives great relief, but I should say a sitting posture was best for the most part, with standing or walking for a variety.   The second rule is against drafts of cold air. The third is an excellent rule for those who do not read, as well as those who do.

Another notion which will be convenient for a great many people, is, to have two or three books going at the same time; one for hard work, perhaps, another for another kind of hard work, and a second (or a third) for amusement.   But this will not do for everybody.   Some would be in danger of devoting all their reading-time to the amusing book.   Others are not of the sort that can change readily from subject to subject, and this method might bother them more than it helped them.   It should not, therefore, be followed unless it is found to succeed well in practice.

OWNING BOOKS.

As with reading, so with owning books. Nobody can own them all.   An English nobleman once offered

more than $11,000 for one volume, and he was rich
enough to be able to_afford it. But he set out to make
a complete collection of the editions of the writings of
Martial. In spite of his wealth, and his steady pursuit,
he was thirty years in doing it. So, you may imagine—
or figure up, if you prefer arithmetic—how many hundred years it would take to collect all the works that
have been published. Hardly anybody can expect to
own more than a very few. That is all the more reason
why they should be wisely chosen. Fifty volumes of
good books is no bad library. A certain learned man
of ancient times, owned but four books. The famous
Leibnitz is said to have asserted that his library con-
tained only these nine authors : Plato, Aristotle, Archime-
des, Euclid, Plutarch, Sextus Empiricus, Pliny, Cicero,
and Seneca. There is a ludicrous remark in one of
Thackeray's novels, I believe, about some person whose
library "consisted, chiefly, of old boots." Robert
Southey's "List of a Gentleman's Necessary Library" has
four more items than Leibnitz's ; does not include a single
one of Leibnitz's ; and the old boots would make almost
as good a library, for a good many "gentlemen," as
either of them. This is Southey's list : Bible, Shakespeare, Spenser's Faerie Queene, Sidney's Arcadia, Works
of Sir Thos. Browne, Works of Rev. Cyril Jackson,
Walton's Complete Angler, Clarendon's History, Milton,
Chaucer, Jeremy Taylor, South's Sermon's, Fuller's
Church History. Nearly all those are good books, no
doubt ; but it is a fitter list for a superannuated clergy-
man than for a man engaged in the work of the world.

Private collections range all the way from the afore-
said four volumes ; or, indeed, from one book up to a
hundred thousand, or more. It is a strong scholar who
can make full practical use of as many as twenty thousand volumes. For fifty thousand there must be a sepa-

rate building, and a librarian to take care of them. Five hundred volumes is as many as could well be accommodated in the majority of American families. Fifty books is a good deal more than American families will average. Probably they are as many as would be read in half of such families. A person with a turn for literature, and who can spend a little money in it, can get great comfort and advantage from a thousand or fifteen hundred well-chosen volumes. But it is best to read most of your books—except the strictly reference books, of course—or they make you ridiculous rather than respectable.

It is impossible to go very far with a list of books of which the first shall be absolutely the best one book to own, the second the next best, and so on. After a very few items it becomes necessary to consider the preferences of the owner; and, therefore, books of very different sorts are equally good. However, let us begin. It will be very safe to procure books as follows:

1. The Bible. 2. Webster's Dictionary (the pictorial unabridged, if possible; if not, the largest edition you can afford). 3. Shakespeare.

Thus far it is reasonably plain sailing, but now our troubles begin. 4. Cruden's Concordance is perhaps as good as any; it is the best single help to Bible reading. Suppose that you have the means of borrowing a good deal of miscellaneous reading, from a public library or otherwise; here is a short list of capital reference books, which are the best books to own in such a case: Haydn's Dictionary of Dates (or Putnam's World's Progress), Bartlett's Dictionary of Quotations, Hole and Wheeler's Brief Biographies, Wheeler's Noted Names of Fiction, Walford's Men of the Time (pretty good for living foreign celebrities, but very poor for this country). That set of volumes contains, packed into a wonderfully small compass, a wonderful breadth of information, usually very correct.

If you have no access to libraries, however, you may feel unable to own so many reference books, having, instead, to own books for reading or study, rather than books for reference. It is in selecting these that no universal list can be made out. I shall, however, add three books to the four already fixed on, viz.: Bible, Webster, Shakespeare, Cruden. These are: 5. A history of the United States (Hildreth's, 6 vols., 8vo, is the best; if you cannot afford that, buy Willard's, in 1 vol., 8vo); and 6. "Smith's Student's Hume," or Lossing's History of England, for the history of England. It would be very useful to own, besides, and to know thoroughly. 7. Taylor's Manual of (ancient and modern) History. For 8, add Dana's excellent Household Book of Poetry; and for additions to your poetical department, procure the complete poetical works of one or another of the poets whose writings you find that you enjoy in Dana's specimens.

But if, instead of Poetry, you enjoy most researches and conclusions in Natural Science, get Humboldt's Cosmos, and study that, through and through.

Or, if you prefer, instead, political philosophy, get De Tocqueville's Democracy in America, and study it thoroughly.

If prose fiction is your passion, by all means get a set of the Waverley Novels, and learn to enjoy them fully. They are the best English series of novels; masterly in their kind; and, moreover, they afford a thorough and decisive training in novel-reading. The reader who has intellect enough to enjoy Scott's novels, may rely safely on his judgment in that department. A novel that he likes, he may be certain has merit; one that he dislikes, he may be sure is a poor novel.

If Mental Philosophy be your passion, it will be safest —in my opinion, it is necessary—to read two books, at least, to begin with. One should be a master of one of the later schools of metaphysical mental philosophy—Dugald Stewart will do very well; Brown is unsafe; Reid is better than either; take Mill if you prefer him, or McCosh, or Noah Porter, though this last is not nearly so strong a specimen of the religious metaphysician as McCosh, who is a very keen and clear thinker. But whichever of these you select, read, after it, either Spurzheim's Phrenology or Combe's Phrenology. You may or may not see cause to believe in their doctrine, that the head corresponds to the mind inside of it. But you will hardly care to reject their singularly clear and practical classification of the mental faculties. This can perfectly well be used in mental philosophy without the other. It is so obviously based on a congenital correspondence between the mind of man and all the rest of the universe, that very few minds that once comprehend it will ever let it go. After your two first books, read in mental philosophy exactly what you wish; but a good series to come next is the whole of Herbert Spencer, to be read, and clearly understood, and set down in brief abstracts of complete, carefully-worded sentences (not hints and half-spelled memorandums). The best general review of Philosophy is Lewes' Biographical History.

But I am sliding back into Courses and Methods of Reading. I have said enough to show how difficult it must be—how out of the question, in fact, to give one single lot of even a dozen books which are the best dozen for everybody, because, long before the dozen is completed, the preferences of the individual require to be considered. For the gratification of those, I must refer to the remainder of this little volume. I shall only say, in closing this chapter:

Own all the books you can.

Use all the books you own, and as many more as you can get.

See the hints about buying books, quoted at the end
of the "Extracts," from "An Old Bookseller." They are
very shrewd.

Book Clubs.*

In small towns, or large ones either, where there are no
public libraries, or where there are libraries which (as is
often the case) cannot satisfy the demand for books, a very
fair substitute can be found in the establishment of a Book
Club. This is a set of about twenty persons (that is the
most convenient number, and it is better to have two
clubs of twenty than one of forty), who are organized for
the purpose of obtaining good reading, somewhat as follows:

Somebody starts the club. This somebody must be
willing to do a quantity of running about and enlistment
work—a hateful job, but often necessary. Suppose it is
a lady; she had better begin—perhaps with the help of
her minister, or any well-acquainted friend—by making a
list of thirty or forty people who will, perhaps, join.
Most likely, half will refuse. If every one she asks con-
sents, she stops at twenty or twenty-two.

What does she say to her constituents? She says—but
in her own graceful and insinuating manner—in substance, these things: We want a book club. We can
get a great many new books with very little trouble and
expense. We put in four dollars apiece to begin with.
That will serve us for a year; for the next year, we can
pay another four dollars each, and add what our old books
sell for, or we can keep down to that figure and deduct
from our payments what they sell for. I will be secretary,
unless you prefer somebody else. We will meet and con-
sult what magazines to take, if any; or each may send
me a list and I will consolidate it; and, in like manner,

---

* Most of the directions under this head are shaped from a paper of the
same name, in a recent number of "Old and New."

we will decide what books to buy at once, and how much money to keep for new books as they appear; or we can have a book committee to manage these matters. Then I will write to my booksellers, ordering the books, and they will come. I will put them in order for use, and will set them going among you. Books (each magazine number counts as a book) are to be given out and to go round in the order of the residences of the members. This order might be called the Club Round; and should be so laid out that the secretary can start a book to member No. 1, who will keep it five days, according to law, and carry it to No. 2, who will do the same for No. 3, and so on, in such a manner that each shall have the shortest distance possible to go. The whole should lie in a sort of ring, so that the last can conveniently hand the book back to the secretary. Twenty members at five days apiece; it is evident that the club will be through with each book in a hundred days. It then remains with the secretary (unless some member wants it for a second reading) until the time comes for disposing of the old books, in readiness for the second year's business, or as the club may prefer.

Twenty members at four dollars each will give eighty dollars to begin with. Suppose you decide (Miss Secretary) to "club" for ten of the best monthly and quarterly magazines, American and English. This will take half your money, or thereabouts. Allow ten dollars for printing lists (of which shortly), cover-paper, etc.; and order fifteen dollars' worth of books. This will give you, as books run, perhaps ten volumes. When these books and magazines reach you, take stout brown paper and cover the books in a serviceable manner. Make pasteboard covers, as neat as time and skill permit, for the magazines; without them, they will be but a ragged regiment when they have gone the rounds. These pasteboard covers can of course be used for successive numbers. Then you paste inside of the cover of each book, a copy of the book-list, of which you have had a supply printed—say two hundred and fifty. The Putnams or others will do it for you, and send you the printed lists all ready, by mail, prepaid, for ————— for the 250 copies, if you can't get it done any nearer home. This list has the rules at the top, and below a column for the names of the members, one for dates of books received by each, and one for dates of passing the books to the next in order. It will be as follows, except that instead of five names, there will be room for twenty-two, besides a little margin at foot:

HARDREADING BOOK-CLUB LIST.

This book may be kept five days. Each member will enter date of receiving and passing. Two cents fine for each day's detention beyond the time allowed. Those wishing a second reading will enter their names at the foot of the list.

NAMES.	Received.	Passed.
Mary Arthur......	Feb. 1,187	Feb. 6,187
George Barnard	" 6,	" 11,
Mrs. C. Chauncy.....	" 11,	" 16,
Edw. Depew	" 16,	" 21,
Dr. Jas. Farnsworth .	" 21,	" 26,

2d Reading: Mary Arthur ; E. Depew.

This list, filled as above, means that Miss Arthur got the book from the Secretary on Feb. 1st, the Secretary entering that date. Miss Arthur read it and passed it to Mr. Barnard, entering Feb. 6 opposite her name. Mr. Barnard in turn enters date of receipt, and then of passing to Mrs. Chauncy, and so on ; so that when the book gets round to the Secretary, each member has written in a date, or dates. Miss Arthur is to have it for a second reading, and E. Depew after her; then it goes to the Secretary for safe keeping until further orders.

At the end of the year, sell the books and magazines by auction to the members, or to outsiders; or dispose of them as the club may direct; collect the subscription for the new year, or more, if you can; also the fines, of which you have kept a record; renew your subscriptions, and begin again. And success attend you.

Newspapers and periodicals usually print lists of new publications, but they are not to be relied upon as being complete, as they often include only such books as have been advertised in each particular paper.

There are, however, two or three bibliographical periodicals, which give full lists of new publications in the United States, and partial lists of those in Great Britain, besides advertisements, book notices, and miscellaneous literary matter of considerable service to librarians and book-readers.

The oldest of these, Childs' Publisher's Circular, is now united with Leypoldt's Literary Bulletin, and issued weekly in New York, under the title of the Weekly Trade Circular. The American Bookseller's Guide, published monthly in New York, also gives lists of publications and literary items. In addition to the above, G. P. Putnam & Sons, and many other booksellers, publish a "Monthly Bulletin of New Publications," which contains the same lists of publications, and the most important of the advertisements, and literary items.

This Bulletin can be obtained without charge, or for payment of the postage only, by writing to the publishers.

www.ingramcontent.com/pod-product-compliance
Lightning Source LLC
Chambersburg PA
CBHW030645030726
47497CB00006B/1966